Withdrawn

WONDERFUL WORLD

W9-AVI-941

ALSO BY JAVIER CALVO

Risas enlatadas (Canned Laughs)
El dios reflectante (The Reflecting God)
Los ríos perdidos de Londres (The Lost Rivers of London)

Wonderful World

A NOVEL

Javier Calvo

TRANSLATED BY MARA FAYE LETHEM

HARPER

An Imprint of HarperCollins*Publishers*
www.harpercollins.com

This book is a work of fiction. References to real people, events, establishments, organizations, or locales are intended only to provide a sense of authenticity, and are used fictitiously. All other characters, and all incidents and dialogue, are drawn from the author's imagination and are not to be construed as real.

WONDERFUL WORLD. Copyright © 2009 by Javier Calvo. English translation copyright © 2009 by Mara Faye Lethem. All rights reserved. Printed in the United States of America. No part of this book may be used or reproduced in any manner whatsoever without written permission except in the case of brief quotations embodied in critical articles and reviews. For information, address HarperCollins Publishers, 10 East 53rd Street, New York, NY 10022.

HarperCollins books may be purchased for educational, business, or sales promotional use. For information, please write: Special Markets Department, HarperCollins Publishers, 10 East 53rd Street, New York, NY 10022.

Originally published as *Un mundo maravilloso* in 2007 by Mondadori.

FIRST EDITION

Designed by Ellen Cipriano

Library of Congress Cataloging-in-Publication Data is available upon request.

ISBN: 978-0-06-155768-2

09 10 11 12 13   OV/RRD   10 9 8 7 6 5 4 3 2 1

F

ACKNOWLEDGMENTS

This novel was written by the ghost of Charles Dickens, summoned and questioned using the system of Enochian magic created by John Dee and Edward Kelley. During the process of its conception and creation, Stephen King published the following works: *The Dark Tower V: Wolves of the Calla*; *The Dark Tower VI: Song of Susannah*; *The Dark Tower VII: The Dark Tower*; *The Colorado Kid*; *Cell*, and *Lisey's Story*. May this humble book be an homage to the Most Enduring Genius of Our Times.

The author would like to give his heartfelt thanks to the true members of the Down With The Sun Society: Miguel Aguilar, Toño Angulo, Robert Juan-Cantavella, Mónica Carmona, Francisco Casavella, Eva Cuenca, Marga Durá, Isidre Estévez, Beatriz Fluxá, Rodrigo Fresán, Marc Godessart, Roger Gual, Josan Hatero, Andreu Jaume, Carola Kunkel, Claudio López Lamadrid, Mónica Martín, Gabi Martínez, Ignacio Martínez de Pisón, Nikki Murphy, Iván de la Nuez, Patricia Núñez, Lucas Quejido, Félix Sabaté, Diego Salazar, Patrick Salvador, Michael Slagle, Manel Soler, Anna Stein, Mercedes Vaquero, Manolo Vázquez. And above them all, sitting in a sunless house, Mara Faye Lethem.

This novel is about each and every one of them.

The Word of Sin is Restriction. There is no
bond that can unite the divided but love:
all else is a curse. Accursèd! Accursèd be it
to the æons! Hell.

MASTER THERION,
Liber Al vel Legis

Wear sensible shoes and always say thank you.
Especially for the things you never had.

—JHONN BALANCE

CONTENTS

PART III

"And They All Hid in the Caves and Among the Mountain Crags"

PROLOGUE: CAMBER SANDS

The sky of Camber Sands looks like those brains that live in a tank surrounded by machines. In a mad scientist's laboratory. Those brains that crackle and spark and bubble, their irregular surfaces covered with small electrical charges. Lorenzo Giraut doesn't like windows. He doesn't like being near windows. In the middle of the living room of his suite at the Hotel in the Sands at Camber Sands, Lorenzo Giraut has built some sort of small shelter using various pieces of furniture and the mattress from his bed. He is sitting on the floor of the shelter, looking at the sky on the other side of the window with a little mirror taken from the suite's bathroom.

The year is 1978. The place is Camber Sands. Not the same Camber Sands that will appear almost thirty years later in the Filial Dream about Camber Sands. In the here and now, in 1978, the Old Map Store no longer exists or doesn't yet exist or perhaps has never existed. It's the same with the Fishing Trophy Room. Dreams are like that. Filled with places that are somewhere else or at some other time or that simply aren't.

Seated with his legs crossed on the floor of the living room of the Hotel in the Sands, beneath his mattress, Lorenzo Giraut moves the little mirror until he has a good view of the Camber Sands sky. The color of the sky isn't particularly diurnal nor particularly nocturnal. It's that color that skies turn when a late-afternoon storm generates a state somewhere between day and night. The clouds filled with eddies and whirls are like a brain. There are bursts of intense blue electric sparks here and there. The sky of Camber Sands on this September night in 1978 is one of those skies you see in dramatically crucial scenes. In dramatically crucial moments that change one's life completely. Those moments that one associates with Fate. Which is only natural. Because this night in 1978, this stormy night in Camber Sands, is The Night That Ends Lorenzo Giraut's Life As He Knows It.

Someone clears their throat at the other end of the room. The American Liaison. The supposed buyer. Giraut moves his mirror, stopping when he has a good perspective on the American Liaison seated in one of the armchairs of the suite's living room. The exact term is "sprawled out." There is something particularly American in the way the American Liaison is sprawled out. With his legs completely extended and his back low in the chair and his fingers interlocked on his belly.

"I was once in a storm at sea." The American Liaison drums his enormous fingers on his enormous belly and nods to himself. "Now that was a storm. The kind that freezes your blood. The waves tossed the boat like a *goddamn toy*." He looks at Giraut and frowns. With a vaguely amused expression. "Is it *completely* necessary that you do that?"

Several feet from where Giraut is, more or less in front of the armchair where the American Liaison is sprawled out, a muted television shows images of people crying inconsolably and hugging each other in Vatican City. A phone cord comes out of the suite's telephone socket and winds along the floor before disappearing into the shelter made of furniture where Lorenzo Giraut is. The Hotel in the Sands isn't really a hotel. It is a complex of apartments that are rented out to tourists for two weeks at a time. Beside Giraut's shelter there is also a little table with wheels. Loaded with liquor bottles and smaller soft-drink bottles and an ice bucket.

"I don't like windows," says Giraut. His hand emerges from between the pieces of furniture that make up his hiding place, grabs a bottle of Macallan, and disappears again into the shelter. "And I don't like the medication they give me to make me like windows. I feel safer in here."

A clap of thunder, much stronger than any of the thunderclaps that had sounded since the storm materialized over the beach and the hotels of Camber Sands, makes everything tremble. The bottles and the ice bucket on the little table with wheels tinkle. The image on the TV blinks and the faces of the people crying in Vatican City are distorted for a second, taking on a vaguely extraterrestrial quality. In the lower part of the screen a message informs us that the images from the Vatican are being retransmitted live.

"I don't like windows," says Giraut. The pause he makes after saying this suggests that he could be taking a sip of the Macallan. "I don't like boats. I don't like open spaces." There is a shorter pause that suggests that Lorenzo Giraut could be shrugging his shoulders. "I don't like the things I don't like. And there's nothing more to say about it. To hell with the doctors and their explanations. No one's ever sent to the doctor for things *they like*. As far as I know."

A thunderclap makes everything in the suite's living room tremble again. Some sort of fine plaster dust falls from the ceiling onto Lorenzo Giraut's shelter. The American Liaison is lighting a cigar in that expert way that consists of holding the lighter near the tip while turning the cigar. On the other side of the windows, beneath the sky that looks like a brain stuck in a glass tank, the storm's wind makes the sand fly from one side to the other, triggering a constant reconfiguration of the dune landscape of the beach at Camber Sands. There are tourists running across the beach toward safety. Seen from the window of the suite of the Hotel in the Sands, their expressions and gestures could just as likely transmit carefree joie de vivre as panic over the fury of the elements. There are half a dozen police cars approaching the Hotel in the Sands along the highway that comes from Lydd-on-Sea, among the clamor of sirens. There are beach shack awnings flying above the dunes. The guy who takes care of the beach's donkeys is leading them in single file toward a place where they'll be sheltered from the fury of the elements. Lorenzo Giraut doesn't really understand why there are donkeys that give donkey rides on British beaches.

The American Liaison clears his throat again. Lorenzo Giraut's partners were supposed to have shown up to close the sale exactly three and a half hours ago. The sale in which the American Liaison is the buyer. Three hours ago the two men waiting in the suite of the Hotel in the Sands ran out of conversation topics. Forty-five minutes ago Lorenzo Giraut built his shelter in the middle of the living room and shut himself up in it with the telephone and the drink cart at arm's reach.

"Maybe their flights were canceled because of the storm," says Giraut pensively. Looking at his half-full glass of Macallan. Then he peeks his head out of his shelter's wall of furniture. He looks at the American Liaison. Lorenzo Giraut's face has a vaguely namby-pamby quality. Probably exacerbated by his droopy cheeks and his very thin, pale eyebrows. "Maybe lightning struck the airport or something like that."

The people shown on TV crying at the Vatican and hugging each other and shaking their heads incredulously are crying over the death of Pope John Paul I. For months now the television has only brought bad news. Some terrorists placed bombs in the Versailles Palace. In America, Ted Bundy is on the loose, leaving what's technically known as *a trail of blood* behind him. Martina Navratilova is the number-one tennis player in the world. The Sex Pistols are on tour despite the opposition of All the Good People of Great Britain. At the Hotel in the Sands in Camber Sands, Lorenzo Giraut is having his first inkling that tonight could be The Night That Ends Lorenzo Giraut's Life As He Knows It when he hears a sudden loud noise from where the American Liaison is sitting. Like the noise of someone that has just stood up suddenly, knocking over the armchair where they were sitting. Giraut finishes the Macallan in his glass in one sip and sticks his head out from between the barricade of chairs and chests of drawers that make up the wall of his shelter. The American Liaison is standing next to the knocked-over armchair with his smoking cigar in one hand. In a listening stance. With his head very still and slightly to one side like someone trying to hear something. Something that's not the sound of thunder or the shouting of the tourists running across the beach. The American Liaison's face looks much paler than it did a minute ago.

Lorenzo Giraut frowns and listens. There is definitely a noise approaching that is not the noise of the thunderclaps or the shouts of the tourists beneath the first large drops of rain. Giraut still hasn't realized that the new sound is the sound of police sirens. Something in the nature of the scene starts to show signs of being a dramatically crucial scene. He comes out of his shelter on all fours and serves himself a second glass of Macallan with three ice cubes.

"This can't be happening," he says, as he serves the ice with a shaky hand. "My partners would never leave me in the lurch. My partners are like my *brothers*. We've been together forever. We're the Down With The Sun Society. That's the name we gave ourselves. To give you an idea," he says.

He takes a sip from the glass. He looks at the American Liaison. The American Liaison has opened one of the sash windows of the living room of the suite and is climbing out. Onto the building's fire escape. Lorenzo Giraut shudders.

The Night That Ends Lorenzo Giraut's Life As He Knows It is undoubtedly one of those nights that can be defined as dramatically crucial. The American Liaison's face as he tries to escape through the window, lit by the lightning of Camber Sands, seems to have transformed into a grimace of panic and rage. The scene has little in common with a mad scientist's laboratory on a night of creations that defy divine will. And nonetheless, there is something in the fine plaster dust that falls from the ceiling and in the scene lit by lightning that is powerfully reminiscent of a mad scientist's laboratory. The police car sirens can now be heard perfectly from the hotel suite. Lorenzo Giraut, sixty-five years of age, the same Lorenzo Giraut that founded LORENZO GIRAUT, LTD., ten years earlier using capital of shady origin, can't go to the window. It's something that happens to him often with windows.

The same Lorenzo Giraut who became, with the help of his two partners and in just one decade, the most important antiques dealer in Spain.
The same Giraut that will restart his business after getting out of jail but
who will never be the same again. Because nothing is ever the same after
nights like this night in Camber Sands. Lorenzo Giraut knows that. He
understands everything perfectly as soon as he hears the sirens and sees
the spotlights sweeping through the inside of the hotel suite. When he
hears the shouts of the policeman ordering the American Liaison to stay
right where he is.

The Hotel in the Sands will close its doors forever in 1982 and will
be demolished six years later. In the mall that will be erected on the
same site there will be black-and-white photographs of the Hotel in the
Sands.

Lorenzo Giraut will always suspect what really happened on The
Night That Ended Lorenzo Giraut's Life As He Knew It, although he'll
never want to admit it.

"I know what this looks like," he says to himself in the living room
of the suite. Where the wind has now come in and is brutally shaking
the curtains and dragging the rain inside. Wetting his face. "But it can't
be what it looks like."

More shouts are heard, from the policemen ordering the man who is
climbing down the fire escape to stop. Someone shoots into the air. The
half dozen police cars are stopped in front of the Hotel in the Sands in
semicircular police position. With the lights flashing and the spotlights
sweeping the façade of the hotel. Which isn't exactly a hotel. Giraut
smells one underarm and then the other and shrugs his shoulders. He
runs his fingers through his long, straight hair. He adjusts the knot in
his tie. When they find him, he wants to look the way he always wanted
to look if he was found in the circumstances in which they are going
to find him tonight. Circumspect. Dignified. Seemingly unconcerned.
A police spotlight sweeps over his face. For a moment, a moment too
brief to attach much importance to, Giraut has a strange feeling. The
feeling that there is something more on the other side of the window.

Something that isn't the police or the storm. Something that floats in the air. Like a series of figures that float in the air. Searching for something. The word "Captors" comes to his mind for some reason he fails to understand.

And a moment later, it's gone.

PART I

"And, Behold, There Was a Great Earthquake"

CHAPTER 1

The Attack of the Low-Flying Airplanes

"Twenty-three days till the world release of Stephen King's new novel," says twelve-year-old Valentina Parini, lying in her hammock in the courtyard of the former ducal palace in Barcelona's Old Quarter, a building the tour guides call the Palau de la Mar Fosca, the Palace of the Stormy Sea. With a plaid blanket over her legs. She is holding up the promotional brochure for Stephen King's new novel so that Lucas Giraut can see it. "Or, to be more precise, twenty-three days and *six hours*."

Rays of late-afternoon sun fall on the balconies of the Old Quarter like the remains of a space shuttle that has disintegrated in the stratosphere. Valentina Parini, a troubled student in the seventh grade at Barcelona's Italian Academy and self-proclaimed Top European Expert on the Work of Stephen King, sways in her hammock with a pensive expression on her face. For a couple of weeks now, every time she looks at something, one of her eyes seems to stray slightly toward the edge of her visual field. Giraut takes the promotional brochure for Stephen King's new novel without getting up from his white plastic garden chair. The skyline from the edge of the yard shows one tower of the cathedral covered in scaffolding and a flock of seagulls that soar in voracious circles around some invisible prey.

Valentina Parini lives with her mother in an apartment on the first floor of the former ducal place. Lucas Giraut lives in the apartment on the second floor. The courtyard, the marble staircase and the parking area on the lower level are common space for all residents.

"My school psychologist told me I'm not allowed to read Stephen King's new novel," continues Valentina Parini. Her skinny preteen body, with its excessively long arms and legs, contrasts with her round face and tiny features that make you think of tropical tree-dwelling monkeys. Her nose is so small that the fact that it can sustain her child-sized eyeglasses, with their green plastic frames, strikes Giraut as a true gravitational feat. "Says that reading it could be very negative for me. She sent a note to my teacher and to my mom." The lips of her tiny mouth purse in a disgusted expression. "She even told my basketball coach. What a huge bitch."

Seated on his garden chair, Lucas Giraut, thirty-three years of age, pulls a cigarette out of the silver case embossed with the initials LG that he always carries in the inside pocket of his suit. His suit today is a charcoal gray Lino Rossi with red pinstripes. As he lights the cigarette he furrows his vaguely namby-pamby eyes and his pale, thin eyebrows. Valentina Parini's school psychologist is one of the most frequent topics of conversation at the afternoon meetings Valentina and Giraut hold in the backyard of the ducal palace. Valentina's clinical relationship with the school psychologist dates back to the episode known at her school as the Spanish Class Mishap.

"It's called *Wonderful World*," says Valentina. Pointing with her head at the promotional brochure for Stephen King's new novel that Giraut has in his hands. "It's the story of a man that wakes up one day and discovers that everything around him has turned perfect. The neighbors that used to hate him now give him baseball tickets. His co-workers are friendly to him. His ex-wife, too. Everything has turned perfect. The world starts functioning flawlessly. Wars end. Politicians turn *smart*. Which means something's going on." She's not trying to sound mysterious or showing any traces of preteen excitement. She's just using the natural, confident tone of someone who knows she's the Top European Expert on the Work of Stephen King. "Something alien. Something that is controlling people's minds."

"When I was your age, I wrote a novel, too." Lucas Giraut looks at the promotional brochure under the courtyard's late-afternoon light. On the cover of the pamphlet it says "WONDERFUL WORLD, BY STEPHEN KING" and "WORLDWIDE RELEASE DECEMBER 22." Giraut takes a thoughtful drag on his cigarette. "It wasn't a novel like yours, or like Stephen King's. Really, it wasn't exactly a novel. It was about Apartment Thirteen. I don't know why it's called that. In my family they've always called it that. It's a room in the floor above the place where I work. My father used to go there to hide from my mother, I think. Anyway, I was obsessed with Apartment Thirteen. I dreamed about that place night after night. In my dreams it was much bigger than it really is. It had antique lamps and rooms filled with antiques. And endless hallways." He looks up toward the Palau de la Mar Fosca. "I still have that novel in my files. I remember that it filled a lot of notebooks. That's how I spent all my time as a kid. Filling notebooks. With drawings and things I wrote. And in the notebooks I have all sorts of drawings of Apartment Thirteen. I mean, the way I imagined it then. Which is nothing like how it really is. I didn't actually get to see it until after my father died. And it turned out to be just a small, windowless room. Because of my father's illness, you remember. The problem he had with windows."

Marcia Parini's voice is heard, slightly occluded by the smoke extractor, as it comes from the window of the kitchen of the lower level of the house.

"Lucas? Is she bothering you?" she asks in a distracted tone of voice. Above the double acoustic cushion created by the smoke extractor and the spluttering of the crêpes on the grill. "Would you like a crêpe?"

Valentina Parini rolls her eyes behind her child-sized eyeglasses with green plastic frames. You could say that Lucas Giraut is the only friend that Valentina Parini has ever had. In all her twelve years.

Giraut folds the promotional brochure advertising Stephen King's new novel and returns it to her. The hammock Valentina is lying in is the same hammock that her father, Mr. Franco Parini, put up, perhaps as some sort of sick joke, the day before he left his wife Marcia and their daughter, never to return. The relationship between Mr. Franco Parini and Lucas Giraut was generally cordial. Once Mr. Parini called Giraut a "yacht club pussy" and a "fucking useless mama's boy" after Giraut leaned out onto his terrace during a conjugal dispute between the Parinis in the courtyard that included the throwing of several pieces of their domestic furnishings.

"I can't take it anymore." Valentina drops her hands in an exasperated gesture onto the plaid blanket that covered her lap. "The crêpe thing. I'm twelve years old. I don't want to have to explain again that the things I liked when I was *a little girl* aren't the same things I like now. This all sucks. My mother made friends with my homeroom teacher. The same one who says I have psychosocial problems." She makes a disgusted face that wrinkles up her tiny tree-monkey nose. "And the ophthalmologist says that I have to wear an eye patch. Only *stupid* little kids wear eye patches."

"I never wore a patch," says Lucas Giraut firmly.

The way he is sprawled out on his white plastic deck chair is slightly different from the way people usually sprawl out. His back, for example, is straight. His shoulders perfectly upright. His arms brought together in his lap with his fingers intertwined or resting carefully on the arms of the chair. The only thing that actually allows one to perceive that he's lounging is a certain barely discernible relaxation of the muscles in his face. Or, in extreme cases, the crossing of his legs at thigh height.

"Your father was a smart guy," says Valentina. "About the windows. Keeping away from windows is smart. Anyone who knows how to defend themselves knows that." She glances cautiously toward the kitchen window of the apartment on the first floor of the former ducal palace. Then she looks at Giraut. She adopts a vaguely confidential tone. "I've been perfecting a new mental attack. I call it the Attack of the Low-Flying Airplanes. It's better than the Machine Gun Attack and much better than the Hand Grenade Attack. It's the best attack I've invented yet. It's great at school, in class or when my homeroom teacher makes me do stupid stuff like go to her office or the school psychologist's office to fill out stupid multiple-choice tests. What you have to do is imagine that you're the pilot of a warplane. One of those old kinds that had a guy on top with aviator goggles that ran a machine gun. Then you imagine the people you want to eliminate. You see them from above, as if you were the guy in the airplane that runs the machine gun. And you plunge down in a nosedive." Valentina places her hands in front of her torso as if she were operating the controls of an invisible machine gun. "You see them running in every direction, but, of course, they can't escape a warplane. And you get closer and you gun them down and then you make a signal to the pilot for him to rise and then nosedive down again to wipe out all the survivors. If there are any. It's an attack that works better outside, of course. It's perfect for when there's a basketball game. When all my stupid classmates put on their basketball uniforms and are happy and I have to say that I'm sick so they'll let me sit on the bench."

Lucas Giraut raises the lapels of his Lino Rossi charcoal gray pin-stripe suit. To protect himself against the cold of the December evening. Lucas Giraut is not only fond of Lino Rossi suits. He has also developed a habit of analyzing a man's psyche and the way he perceives his place in the world, all based on the suits he wears. The name he has given that discipline in his head is Suitology. The margin of error of his suitological analyses, according to his own calculations, is little or none.

"My father was full of strange things," he says. "Like his window illness. He told me strange things all the time, and every time I asked him something he answered me in that mysterious tone of his, and then I would obsess over it. I'd get home and get in bed and I couldn't get those things out of my head." He frowned, as if something in the process of remembering was difficult for him. "Once he told me that there was a man on our block who trained vultures on his roof. That he had ten vultures in a pigeon loft and he had trained them to attack people. And once in a while the guy waited until night fell and sent one of his trained vultures to kill someone. I spent weeks obsessing over that. Every time I left the house to go to school, I walked with my back flat against the buildings, looking up at the sky."

"I signed up for the talent show at school." Valentina Parini uses her index finger to readjust her glasses on her tiny nose and looks with her tree-dwelling features at Lucas Giraut, antiques dealer, son of an antiques dealer and supposed mama's boy according to the prevailing rumors in his extended circle of friends and family. "It's something they do every year for Christmas. My school psychologist still doesn't know. And I'm planning on reading my novel. *Blood on the Basketball Court.* I'm gonna read it in front of everybody. In the school auditorium. With my basketball coach right there. With my school psychologist and my homeroom teacher and all the stupid girls in my class listening." Valentina Parini's words have what is usually referred to as A Vaguely Threatening Quality. Somehow, that quality seems to emphasize the wandering of her eye. "Maybe I'll invite my mother, too. I won't be able to read the whole thing, of course. Just some parts. The decapitation of the basketball coach. The bomb in the locker rooms. The Graduation Day Massacre."

Giraut intertwines his fingers and rests his smooth, hairless chin on the resulting double fist. About ten feet from where they are talking, on the other side of the frosted glass kitchen window of the two-story house, Marcia Parini's silhouette is flipping a crêpe in the air. Lucas Giraut's most striking physical feature is a round, largely hairless face that doesn't seem to belong to the same person as his tall, thin body with its long limbs. The brown eyes below pale brows always seem vaguely sleepy, giving his face a generally namby-pamby air.

"I made the last chapter longer." Valentina Parini adopts a tone somewhat similar to the expert acuity of a literary professional. "I added more descriptions. Of dead girls in the school yard. With their basketball jerseys riddled with bullet holes. Or burned." She pulls up the plaid blanket that's covering her legs and lap to ward off the twilight chilliness of the December evening. "Some of their heads are blown off."

From the other side of the courtyard they can hear noises from the street. Christmas carols coming from cheap municipal amplification systems. The directions guides give to the groups of tourists that cluster around the cathedral. The shouts of alarm when one of those tourists discovers that the handbag tucked under the arm of the pickpocket who's athletically running away belongs to them.

"I'm dying to see their faces," says Valentina. "At the talent show."

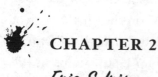

CHAPTER 2

Eric & Iris

Eric Yanel and his fiancée Iris Gonzalvo are lying on contiguous deck chairs on the enormous deck of the Palladium Hotel & Spa in Ibiza. Beneath the reasonably warm sun of Ibiza's off-season. On the hotel's private beach, made of tempered salt with a high iodine content, a group of sunbathers with permagrins watch the game of mixed volleyball that is taking place a few feet below the deck. The deck chairs where Eric Yanel and Iris Gonzalvo are lying aren't exactly arranged in parallel, but rather in slightly centrifugal angles. Perfectly symmetrical to both sides of the small aluminum table where their drinks rest. A Finlandia with cranberry juice for her and a ten-year-old Macallan with ice for him. With a partially melted ice cube floating on its golden surface, like someone doing the dead man's float under the sun.

Iris Gonzalvo sits up to take off her eye protector and watches her fiancé while leisurely stroking the golden ring that joins the cups of the upper half of her navy blue Dior bikini. Eric Yanel has a cigarette dangling from the side of his lips and is looking with a frown at a magazine open in his hands. The shadow of the umbrella with the Palladium Hotel & Spa's corporate emblem that Eric and Iris have behind them only covers the part of their bodies above the chest.

"What is this?" Eric Yanel uses the back of his hand to tap the satin-finished page of the open magazine. It's one of those glossy magazines for men. With photo essays on the breasts and buttocks of sculpted and digitally retouched women. "Who the hell is Penny DeMink? And why is there a photo of you here?"

Iris's expression is inscrutable behind the heart-shaped frames of her sunglasses. She bought those glasses after she saw them in an old movie projected onto the wall of a discothèque. A sonic amalgam of diving bodies, children's screams and the whistle blows of the hotel's social directors reach the deck from the private beach that extends below and from the hotel's complex of indoor pools. In addition to the tempered salt private beach, the Palladium Hotel & Spa in Ibiza has indoor pools on every floor, outdoor pools filled with seawater, a special aloe vera bath, saunas, Roman steam rooms, special tubs for thalassotherapy and a fangotherapy room.

"I swear I don't understand why I keep wasting my time with you," says Iris Gonzalvo. Her voice is smooth and at the same time gravelly, like the voice of someone who, due to lack of lung power, has learned to fill their tone with sharp edges. "You're not even listening to me. *I'm* Penny DeMink. It's one of those names. What are they called? And *what's important* is what it says about me. In case you haven't gotten that."

Iris Gonzalvo's body is thin. With a very flat stomach and wide shoulders. Her skin is very white in spite of the sun and has a light covering of freckles that can only be seen when you get up close. Neither of them is wearing a bathing suit, strictly speaking. Eric Yanel is wearing some jean shorts and an Armani Sport polo shirt. Iris

Gonzalvo is wearing the top of a navy blue Dior bikini and a paisley Cacharel sarong. The midday heat is that reasonably warm heat, like a caress, that's typical of the low season in Ibiza.

Eric Yanel pulls a tiny bottle out of the pocket of his shorts, one of those bottles of cocaine with the screw-on tops that come with a tiny spoon built in. He opens it, fills the tiny spoon, and raises it first to one nostril and then the other while he sniffs with a distracted expression. He reads the text of the glossy magazine for men and puts the tiny bottle back in his pocket.

"Pseudonym," he says. "But what's this? You made a dirty movie?" He shakes his head. The way he pronounces the word "dirty" betrays his French origins. "Shit. At least I've never done a dirty movie."

"It's not a dirty movie." Iris Gonzalvo takes the magazine from his lap and puts it on the little table. "It's an adult film. And of course you've never done one. You've never done *any kind* of movie. Your specialty is car commercials where no one can see you because you're *in*side the car."

Eric Yanel's long, blond, perfectly coiffed hair, which includes a somewhat larger-than-life wave over his forehead, also betrays his French origins. His habit of wearing penny loafers without socks isn't a particularly French trait, but along with his fondness for polo shirts and his long, blond, very coiffed wavy hair, helps to distinguish him as a member, or at least a descendant, of the French rural upper class.

"Of course you know why you're with me." Yanel picks up the eye protector from the little table and places it over his eyes while reclining the adjustable upper part of the deck chair. He lies back with his hands on his chest. His gesture reminds you of the position in which corpses are placed into coffins. "You're with me because if you weren't with me you wouldn't be able to be in a place like this drinking and sunbathing. Instead you'd be throwing yourself at German businessmen in convention hotels."

"Right now *I'd enjoy* throwing myself at a businessman," says Iris Gonzalvo in an even tone. "From Germany or from wherever. I'm twenty-four years old. I'm *incredibly hot*. And I'm in Ibiza. I should be fucking until I can't walk anymore."

Eric Yanel turns his head toward his fiancée and stares at her as if he could see her through the plastic eye protector. Each half of the eye protector is shaped like a mollusk shell. Beyond his fiancée's deck chair, in a spot that would be perfectly visible to Yanel were he not wearing the eye protector, a Floor Manager of the Palladium Hotel & Spa is speaking in a hushed tone to the Director of Customer Service.

"You women just don't get it." Yanel takes the tiny bottle of cocaine out of his pocket again. He unscrews the top and raises the tiny spoon first to one nostril and then the other before replacing his eye protector. "The male sex drive is much more subtle than people think. Ever since sexual liberation, women started seeing men as simple objects. That can be used at any moment. They glorify the permanent erection. But the truth is"—he makes a hand gesture that suggests resignation—"we aren't machines. It's been shown that men obtain their fullest sexual gratification through masturbation. *Scientifically* proven."

In the volleyball court on the private beach below the hotel's deck, the two mixed teams jump and shout and laugh loudly. A female player falls to the ground, gets up coated in white sand and starts brushing it off her breasts and hips amidst a chorus of naughty titters and vaguely sexual whistles.

"If *I* jerk off one more time, my clitoris is going to fall off," says Iris Gonzalvo.

Her hair is long and curly in a way that is incongruent with the decade in progress. Long and curly like the hair of some models and actresses in the eighties.

The Floor Manager and the Director of Customer Service begin to cross the smooth, sunny length of the deck toward Yanel and his fiancée. On the beach volleyball court a more tangible sexual episode is taking place. A couple of male players are laughing and chasing a female player around the court. She carries the ball nestled below her swinging breasts. The scene is strongly reminiscent of certain classic pictorial motifs having to do with the hunt of half-naked women.

"I've only been in *one* car commercial where no one could see me." Eric Yanel gazes at the off-season Ibiza sun with his eyes covered by the protector. "And I did it as a favor. That's something we actors do. Sometimes our agents ask us to do favors for their friends."

The Floor Manager and the Director of Customer Service stop in front of the deck chairs occupied by the engaged couple. The Director of Customer Service moves a step ahead of the Floor Manager, as stated in company protocol. The Director of Customer Service is very tanned and his hair is dyed blond. The only corporate emblem he is wearing on his sporty attire is his plastic ID badge pinned to the front of his shirt.

"Mr. Yanel," the Director of Customer Service addresses the face partially covered by the eye protector, "we don't have to do this out here. We can move to a more private location."

Eric Yanel takes off his eye protector calmly and delivers a perfectly proportioned smile to the Director of Customer Service. A smile that could be a perfect advertising smile except for a certain yellowish tone. He sits up and offers a hand to the Director of Customer Service. The Director of Customer Service looks at the hand as if he were having some reservations before shaking it with a neutral expression.

"Mr. Yanel. I have to ask you pay the bill that you have outstanding," he says. "You have been warned a dozen times."

"The situation is completely under control." Yanel barely alters his smile. "I spoke this morning with that man that . . ." He stops when he sees the Floor Manager from his floor. "Oh, hi. How are you, sir?" He extends his hand to the Floor Manager. The Floor Manager stares at Yanel's hand as if it were a cockroach the size of a hand. "We already spoke this morning."

"Mr. Yanel," says the Director of Customer Service. "I am sorry to inform you, but you must pay your bill."

Eric Yanel theatrically pats his pockets.

"I don't usually bring my cards down so they can sunbathe." He makes one of those pauses that are made right after a joke. Then his face takes on a serious look. "This could all backfire on you, you know that?" He frowns. "I'm talking about humiliating a client in front of his fiancée and all that. Who knows. My lawyer might find something criminal in all this."

"Sir." The Director of Customer Service looks around him furtively. "I must ask you to clear out of your room immediately and pay your bill at the reception desk."

Iris Gonzalvo lifts her heart-shaped gaze from the deck chair where she has just taken a sip of her Finlandia with cranberry juice, the glass still in her hand, and smiles at the Director of Customer Service with a dramatic smile that looks a bit patronizing.

"He can't pay the bill," she says. "Because he hasn't got any money."

A fat kid with a swimsuit printed with characters from a Japanese cartoon show takes a running start across the deck's tiled floor splattered with water. Creating a generalized tremor of swaying fat that jiggles and spills in every direction. When he reaches the edge of the pool he makes a greasy, jiggly leap and, while suspended in the air, hugs his knees so he lands in the water in the posture traditionally known as "the cannonball." Iris Gonzalvo observes, expressionless, the system of centrifugal waves where the fat kid plunged into the pool. The Floor Manager remains a step behind his superior ranking employee. In addition to the plastic ID badge pinned to his shirt front, he wears a full Floor Manager uniform made up of a blue linen bolero jacket with white pinstripes, matching pants, a white short-sleeved shirt and a corporate tie featuring the establishment's insignia.

"Of course"—the Director of Customer Service brings a hand to the tip of his nose nervously as he says this—"our company is prepared to take all types of legal action."

Eric Yanel sighs. He places the protector over his eyes and lies back in the deck chair again.

"This is typical," he says. His hand feels its way, searching for the ten-year-old Macallan on the little aluminum table. He eventually finds it and raises it to his lips. "The typical impression that people have about actors. As if we had money coming out of our asses. Like we never have any cash-flow problems. But it's not like that. It's a job that's filled with sacrifices. A job that requires patience." He points with his glass of Macallan to the two hotel employees in a vaguely accusatory gesture. "You know? Sometimes I think you have to be *very brave* to be an actor in this country."

There is a moment of silence. The fat kid that had plunged into the pool a minute before finally appears on the surface, in the midst of an upsurge of water. With his arms held high. In that radiant arms-held-high pose in which synchronized swimmers come to the surface after successfully concluding a number.

CHAPTER 3

The Fishing Trophy Room

The Fishing Trophy Room in the Giraut family house in the Ampurdan region is an enormous room located on the second floor. One wall is filled with large windows overlooking the Mediterranean, and there's a bar half hidden in some sort of nook near the door. Trophies from throughout Estefanía "Fanny" Giraut's career in sportfishing cover the walls. Stuffed, mounted fish on wooden plaques with commemorative inscriptions. Six-and-a-half-foot-long swordfish with their nose swords pointing to the other fishing trophies. Photographs of Fanny Giraut at high sea, with her vest filled with pockets and her captain's hat. Lucas Giraut doesn't exactly know why the executive meeting he is attending is being held in the Fishing Trophy Room of their house in the Ampurdan. Or, for that matter, why most of the executive meetings of the heirs to his father's company are held there. In his heart of hearts he suspects that it could be one of his mother's tactics to make him uncomfortable. Somehow his mother is convinced that she's stronger and more powerful inside this room.

Besides Lucas and his mother, a man that they all simply know as Fonseca is present at the meeting. He is Fanny Giraut's lawyer and confidant. Known in the Barcelona law world for his sycophantic loyalty to his client. Known in Barcelona by such terms as "deputy," "right hand" or even "goon" by those who feel no special sympathy for Fanny Giraut's business project. Fonseca is seated on one of the leather sofas, with a glass of Finlandia and tonic in his hand.

"This is the primary objective of this meeting." Fonseca frowns at Lucas Giraut, who is standing in front of one of the large windows. "To present you with the business plan for the coming year. Especially the plans for our International Division. Which, as you know, is now fully up and running. And that's why we've called you here. We could have just sent you the plans, you know. But that's not how we want to work with you. That's not the way your mother wants to deal with this delicate situation." He makes a tinkling sound with the ice cubes in a glass of Finlandia with tonic as he looks toward where Lucas Giraut is standing, with his back to the meeting. "I am referring, of course, to the situation that your father's death has left us in."

The Giraut family house in the Ampurdan is an art nouveau–style mansion, with three floors and forged-steel balconies, built facing a breakwater a mile away from a small fishing village. The house's name as it appears on the town registry is Villa Estefanía. In the Giraut family, though, everyone calls it the Villa. The man known simply as Fonseca is wearing a fishing vest on top of a wool turtleneck sweater and thigh-high rubber boots. On the temples of his bony face, a thick network of veins swell and deflate to the rhythm of his emotional ups and downs. Lucas Giraut is wearing a turtleneck sweater and thigh-high rubber boots, but instead of a fishing vest he has on some sort of tool belt adapted for fishing. Fanny Giraut wears a wool coat and scarf and rubber boots that only come up to her ankles. All three wear wool hats.

"The International Division," continues Fonseca. "Fifty men and women with thirteen different nationalities. With promising careers and areas of knowledge that cover the entire market." A slight note of elegy betrays his speech. A note he seems to suddenly be aware of, given that he frowns and takes a sip of his drink, a quiver of embarrassment showing in the veins of his temples. Then he shrugs his shoulders and continues. "You already know Carlos Chicote, the Director of our International Division. And you are already familiar with our restoration project for the Speyer Cathedral. That project, my boy, is the only thing right now that separates us from a position of *dominance*. From being the top European company in the field, in terms of capital and resources and client portfolio." He looks at Lucas Giraut's back with a frown. "That is why we've sent Chicote to Germany with an unlimited line of credit and with exact instructions *to have dinner* with everyone he should be having dinner with."

"We want Chicote to have dinner *more*." Fanny Giraut observes the glass of Finlandia with ice she holds in her hand with a blank expression. Seated in her favorite leather armchair. Even when she isn't showing any particular emotion, her face is a horrible mask, her lips bruised from the silicone injections and the skin tensed beyond mobility by the face-lifts. It's not a face you can bond with emotionally. Her features aren't features in the general sense of the word. "To go to the bathroom and vomit after each meal if he has to. We want him to have dinner three times a day."

Lucas Giraut is the only one who isn't seated. He's standing in front of one of the large windows that overlook the breakwater. From there he can see the window he often sat in as a boy with binoculars, watching his father during Fanny's parties. His father would stand in front of the same large window where Lucas is now, drinking a glass of Macallan and smoking a cigarette. The smaller window where Lucas positioned himself to lie in wait with his binoculars is in the part of the house known, within the family, as the North Wing or the Boy's Wing.

"But big victories require sacrifices," says Fonseca with his brow slightly furrowed. The effort of gauging his words makes the network of veins on his temples reconfigure themselves intricately, generating several localized swelling points. "Not necessarily big sacrifices. Sometimes small sacrifices are enough. Small details that can produce spectacular benefits. If we want to be first in the area of contracts, we have to divert capital. Maybe eliminate a department." He shakes his glass again, provoking a tinkling of ice cubes. "We need to get behind Chicote. Show him that, from here, we've got his back covered. Set up larger offices in Mainz and put in one of those fish tanks that take up a whole wall in his office. Germans like to see stuff like that."

"We are working *closely* with Chicote." Estefanía Giraut lifts her eyebrows to the middle of her horribly taut forehead in a self-indulgent gesture that is one of the most fearsome in her range of facial quasi-expressions. "We've frozen his salary indefinitely. We've leaked the rumor that we are very unhappy with his performance. We've given out shares in luxury yachts to all the top executives in the company except him. We've spread the rumor that we don't think he's having dinner as much as he could be having dinner. That's my way of reaching out to him." The way she takes a sip of her Finlandia with ice in no way resembles a human taking a sip. Introducing her bruised lips on the edge of the glass and carrying out some sort of rapacious suction with her appallingly taut cheeks. Just like some forest mammals suck out nests of ants. "I call it negative motivation. Much better than positive motivation, in my opinion. It's never failed me yet."

Lucas Giraut gives no sign of taking part in the conversation. The Fishing Trophy Room of the house in the Ampurdan was the place Lucas Giraut, as a child, most hated and feared in the entire world. With its six-and-a-half-foot-long sea monsters on the walls. With its sinister photographs of people holding up sea creatures. With its barely noticeable smell of unwashed tackle boxes and something else that Lucas could never quite put his finger on. Something vaguely chemical that could only be smelled in that room. In the beginning, the Fishing Trophy Room's primary function seemed to be to foster the public derision of Lorenzo Giraut. It was there that Fanny Giraut held all her cocktail parties and social events for the Ampurdan circuit. Spreading her guests out over the various leather couches and providing the evening's entertainment with anecdotes of her husband's clumsiness in the art of fishing and the ridiculous situations said clumsiness placed him in. Lorenzo Giraut always attended these social events, and would remain standing by the large window with his glass of Macallan and his cigarette, and drink in silence. While his son spied on him from his window in the North Wing. While the guests laughed behind him. From his window's parapet, Lucas could see his father's figure standing there, showing no sign of taking part in the conversation. He was never sure if his father knew that he was spying on him.

"The International Division is our future," says Fonseca. "In terms of competitiveness. And the Speyer Cathedral is our flagship. Once we have the contract, dozens more will follow. Within a year, our profits will have multiplied thirty times over. Of course, we need your signature for the restructuring." A new reconfiguration and anxious swelling of the network of veins on his temples is produced. Creating some sort of bulging membranes that beat briefly on both sides of his forehead. "Given that *technically* you are still the principal shareholder and president of the company. And technically you are above us. Of course, we would continue to rely on you. With conditions that will be very advantageous to you. You'd only have to go to a few meetings a year. We trust that you'll sign those papers, son."

"Of course he'll sign." Fanny Giraut smiles. The silicone and the tautness of her surgically smoothed skin make Fanny Giraut's smiles more like a retraction of the lips, revealing her deathly pale gums. She stares at Fonseca. "The Speyer Cathedral is ours. It's *always* been ours. See to it that everyone talks about it *all the time*. Invent meetings. Threaten people. Pay off some German journalists. Punish everyone that isn't talking about it. See to it that people talk about the cathedral as our flagship. Make sure that they use that exact phrasing. Threaten to fire Chicote tomorrow if he doesn't have dinner more. We want him to have dinner more. Until he's had dinner with so many Germans that he has nightmares of beer and sausages and sauerkraut."

"Your birthday cake is ready," says Lucas Giraut to his mother suddenly. Without turning around. Without taking his eyes off the breakwater on the other side of the large window. "With all the ingredients you asked for. Six stories high. With the message you asked for. With no mention of your age, of course. The baker assured me that it's the largest cake he's ever made. I had him put it in writing, just as you asked."

"I should have hired a professional." Fanny Giraut's surgically taut cheeks withdraw to each side. Her white gums have a texture inexplicably similar to enamel. Her bruised lips plunge into the glass once again, and emerge a moment later. "I've never seen you do anything well. And I doubt you're going to change now."

"The audiovisual material for the party is ready," continues Lucas. "The old videotapes have been transferred to digital. The photographs have been adapted for digital projection."

The most important fishing trophies in the Fishing Trophy Room, those Trophies That Justify a Fishing Life, are on the mantelpiece. Among them is a blowfish stuffed in attack mode. Attacking an invisible enemy with its spines. There is a red tuna six feet and nine inches long. The largest ever fished out of the Mediterranean. There are various gold and silver trophies. Many of them have figures of fishermen or figures of fish and other objects related to the world of fishing.

"My son never learned to fish." Fanny Giraut makes a vague gesture with her hand around the Fishing Trophy Room. "He's even clumsier than his father, and his father was the worst fisherman I've ever seen with a pole in his hands. Remember when we went out in the boat to fish tuna? Those were the few times that idiot Lorenzo ever made me laugh. The poor bastard was so scared that when they were tying up the chair's belts his face looked like he was being strapped into an electric chair. My husband was gutless." She pauses and her features come as close as they can to an evocative expression. "Not even jail gave him the guts he never had. In fact, he came out even more ridiculous and gutless. A ridiculous old man clinging to his stupid store and his ridiculous old friends. It would have been fitting if he'd dropped dead in that horrible place, amid all that junk and spiderwebs." The three-story building and its attached warehouse in uptown Barcelona that houses the commercial activities of LORENZO GIRAUT, LTD., is simply known in the Giraut family as The Store. "Getting rid of him was the best thing I ever did in my life. But it seems getting rid of a son isn't so easy."

The main discovery that Lucas Giraut made as a child while spying on his father from his window in the North Wing had to do with his father's facial expression. Which was, in essence, an expression *of terror*. Pure terror. And somehow that terror seemed to be connected to the fact that he was standing in front of the large window. Somehow the terror seemed to derive from the large window itself. Standing in front of the large window with his glass of Macallan in one hand and his cigarette in the other, Lorenzo Giraut's face was a grimace of intense, painful terror. The discovery was described in detail in Lucas's childhood notebooks.

"The band has already been hired," says Lucas Giraut. "For your birthday party."

And he arches his eyebrows as if what he has just said gives him some sort of secret gratification.

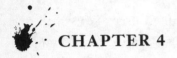

CHAPTER 4

The Beginning, Strictly Speaking, of the Story

Lucas Giraut rests his chin on the intertwined fingers of his hands and examines, his eyes slightly squinted, the image of Mr. Bocanegra, Show Business Impresario, in the monochrome monitor connected to the surveillance camera in the lobby of the building that houses LORENZO GIRAUT, LTD. Searching for familiar elements in his appearance. Elements that could awaken some childhood memory. Perhaps the coat. Over his shoulders Mr. Bocanegra is wearing a fox, or sable, or perhaps Chinese otter coat, whose cut and overall appearance is strikingly feminine. The image of a man with a strikingly feminine coat definitely seems to awaken some type of memory in the nooks and crannies of Lucas's childhood mind. The images on the monochrome monitor that watches over the lobby are a color halfway between electric blue and the gray scale. Lucas Giraut realizes that Mr. Bocanegra has looked up and is now staring into the lobby camera with an impatient look on his wide, mustachioed face.

"Send him up," Lucas says to the intern who occupies the lowest rung of LORENZO GIRAUT, LTD.'s hierarchical pyramid.

The intern goes down the stairs that lead from Lucas Giraut's office on the mezzanine to the antique store itself. Giraut looks at the monitor again, sprawled out in his office chair in that rigid way of his. The office that Lucas Giraut now occupies, and which used to be his father's, has one side that overlooks the public sales and showroom. The only furnishing element that has arrived since Lorenzo Giraut's death is the Italian Louis XV–style *cartonnier* that Lucas uses as his desk. A cream-colored *cartonnier* with ebony accents and four leather drawers above the writing surface separated by a decorative alcove, the type with compartments that can only be opened by triggering secret inner mechanisms that is technically known in the antiques world as a *magic desk*. According to most professional opinions, Giraut is the most important collector of magic desks in the country.

Bocanegra's arrival is announced by the thundering sound of his steps on the wooden stairs and a slight trembling of the floor. A moment later, he reaches the top of the stairs, wrenching an anguished creak from the floorboards. The Show Business Impresario and Reputed Best Friend of the late Lorenzo Giraut shows his teeth in a ferocious grin. Over six feet of flabby flesh with an impossibly shiny bald head crowning his wide, mustachioed face. Giraut looks Bocanegra up and down and carries out a quick suitological analysis of his beige Prada suit, with the following results: indifference; sumptuousness that becomes disdainful without ever being classy; contained violence and respectability strictly based on negative personality elements.

Bocanegra energetically extends his flaccid hand to his host. The smile on his wide, mustachioed face is cruel for some reason that's hard to discern. There's something intrinsically cruel in Bocanegra's features. Something that doesn't seem to depend on the specific configuration of said features at any given moment.

"I can't explain how *much* this means to me." Mr. Bocanegra raises a hand to his chest and wrinkles his large soft face into an expression of emotional pain. Then he makes a gesture with his large hairy mitts that includes the entire office. "*Being* here. That you called me. I don't need to say that your father was more than a brother to me. Fuck, I'd fit most of my real brothers with cement shoes and dump them in the sea. But that's another story." He frowns. "Your father was the most *significant* person in my life. I know it's strange for me to say that when most likely you don't even remember me. How old were you the last time I saw you? Four? Five? But what can you do." He gives a resigned shrug. "Your mother never liked me. Let's just say that she never wanted me to set foot in her house. Which is why you've never seen me, and why your father never told you about me. Fuck, I don't even want to think about what would have happened if she'd suspected that I worked *so closely* with your father."

Lucas makes a sign for his guest to sit down in the armchair on the other side of the Louis XV *cartonnier*. Mr. Bocanegra drops himself heavily into the armchair and leans back against the wide back with his arms extended. There is certainly something familiar about him. It's not his wide, mustachioed and slightly sweaty face, or the way he talks. It's more the way his features adjust to his different emotional states without losing a constant trace of underlying cruelty. Some sort of *background* trace. A trace that evokes large predators in ecosystems not dominated by human beings.

"My mother is a difficult woman." Giraut takes out his silver cigarette case embossed with the initials that he shares with his late father and offers his visitor a cigarette. There is a moment of silence as Bocanegra lights his cigarette with the lighter that Giraut extends to its tip before continuing. "Things tend to get complicated when she's involved."

"God bless your mother." Bocanegra takes a drag on his cigarette. His feminine coat, made of sable or Chinese otter or maybe astrakhan lamb, somehow manages to make his figure *more* threatening. Like some sort of cosmic provocation directed at no one in particular. "The truth is that I don't blame her for hating me. After all, your mother hates the entire human race. You should have seen the face I made when your father told me he was going to marry her. Why don't you just marry an electric eel, I told him."

Lucas Giraut nods.

"Mr. Bocanegra." He places both hands, palms open, on the surface of the *cartonnier*. "As you are well aware, I didn't get to know my father very well. In fact, the more I think about it, the more I get the impression that my father never made any effort to help me get to know him. Or, of course, to get to know me." He shrugs his shoulders. "The circumstances of his life and his death are a mystery to me. And my mother has made sure that it remains that way. And nevertheless,

I am pretty well versed in the professional aspects of his life. Some of his international dealings are still legendary in the antique business." He gestures toward a pile of professional magazines on top of the *cartonnier*. "And of course, since when he died he left me at the helm of his corporation, I now have access to all company documents and records. Including those documents and records which, due to their nature, have never been examined by anyone outside of my father's intimate circle. And here is where you come in."

Mr. Bocanegra seems to sprawl out even further in his chair. The way he superimposes his new position onto the original one is analogous to taking out a second mortgage on top of the one you already have. His new lounging position seems to suggest abundance in every sense of the word and a laxness bordering on defiance.

Lucas Giraut takes a file out of a drawer. He places it on the *cartonnier*'s writing surface and opens it up to the first page.

"To give just one example." Giraut examines the file's first page. Bocanegra's evident lack of any curiosity toward the file seems designed to cover up a certain degree of interest and curiosity. "Have you ever heard of the Isle of Guernsey? I confess that when I first came across that name I was a bit confused." He turns a page of the file. "Well, it turns out that the Isle of Guernsey is a British protectorate located in the English Channel. Its total surface is thirty square miles, with a population of sixty thousand people. Typical animals are the donkey and a local type of cows. Its national color is green."

Something has changed in Mr. Bocanegra's facial expression. The element of cruelty that lies beneath his features seems to have come to the surface without causing any tangible change in his facial expression. Except perhaps for a quasi-feline element of alertness. His enormous body now seems to withdraw into an alert, quasi-feline crouch.

"I'm sure you would agree," continues Giraut, "that it doesn't seem like a place where my father would go to conduct business. And, yet, the Isle of Guernsey is the headquarters of Arnold Layne Experts. A company I haven't bothered to investigate for the simple fact that it's none of my business what the people of Guernsey do. And the name isn't the only curious thing about this company. For example." He continues reading from the file he has open on the table. "The last names of the three principal shareholders are Wright, Waters and Mason. Now if one were to type those three last names into any Internet search engine, he would discover that they are the last names of the three founding members of the British rock band Pink Floyd. While 'Arnold Layne' is the title of the band's first single. Defined in musical encyclopedias as," he reads, " 'An optimistic and seminally psychedelic song about a cross-dresser that ends up in jail.' Okay"—he looks up and observes Bocanegra's facial expression—"I'm not a big fan of rock music. Although, as you already know, my father was. And, yet, the name Pink Floyd brings to my mind a series of memories. You can already imagine what kind of memories. That was the first detail that made me think. And then, of course, there's the date that Arnold Layne Experts was incorporated. The summer of 1978. Of course, it took me a little while to recall why that date was so familiar to me. I was only five years old. So"—he closes the file—"does any of this ring a bell with you?" Giraut raises his thin, pale brows over his namby-pamby eyes. "Are you, perhaps, a Pink Floyd fan?"

Bocanegra leans back and keeps smoking. His eyes squint too fleetingly to be registered as anything more than a vague sensation. In the same way that certain predators squint fleetingly while their brains take in the information necessary for their next predatory action.

"Mr. Bocanegra." Lucas Giraut puts the file back in the drawer. "I have no intention of starting to dig around in cases that are already closed and which the law has no interest in." He pauses to once again interlock his fingers in front of his face, his elbows resting on the table's surface. "However, I do have professional goals. And some of them coincide with those my father had. Did you know, for example, that while I was doing my doctorate in Dublin I visited the four St. Kieran Panels when they were on display in the Trinity College museum, and that I had the chance to study them privately for a week? And I don't know if you are aware that my father was arrested in 1978 just as he was taking steps to acquire those same four paintings on wood. I mean the same summer in which someone who was working closely with him sold him to the authorities." He pauses. "And now those paintings are coming *here*. To Barcelona. They are going to be exhibited in this city. I don't know if you're following me, Mr. Bocanegra."

Mr. Bocanegra smiles, very slightly at first. Barely a hint of teeth on an overall backdrop of facial cruelty. Then that hint widens, growing in all directions and revealing both rows of large, voracious teeth. The face of a predator baring his teeth threateningly, and then a bona fide cruel smile. Mr. Bocanegra's Genuinely Cruel Smile. Finally he lifts his eyebrows with an amused expression.

"Are you saying that you want those paintings?" He scrutinizes the round, hairless face of his host. "You called me so I would help you get them? So I would devise a plan of action and a strategy and use my experience and my international contacts?" He takes a last drag on his cigarette and crushes it in the ashtray. "After finding my number in your father's secret files or whatever? In other words, after realizing that I am the person that your father would have turned to if he wanted to do something that surpassed the normal bounds of an antique dealer's reach, et cetera and so on?"

Lucas Giraut stares for a second at the remains of the cigarette butt. Most of which seems to have disintegrated or at least no longer bears any resemblance to the typical remains of a cigarette butt.

"I can't explain it," he says. "But those paintings have a special significance for me. A special value. That's all I can say."

There is a moment of silence. The lights in Lucas Giraut's office on the mezzanine of the building that houses LORENZO GIRAUT, LTD., are distributed and calibrated in such a way that dusk prevails, all day long.

Mr. Bocanegra stands up suddenly. The way he stands up causes an emphatic lurching of various greasy areas of his face, neck and torso. The coat he is wearing over his shoulders is one of those long-haired fur coats that one associates with wealthy post-Soviet Russian women who smoke while waiting for their chauffeurs in front of some restaurant in Saint-Tropez. A second later, Giraut stands up as well. With a cautious expression.

"I never had kids," says Mr. Bocanegra, closing in on Giraut. "I'm basically a childless person. *No one* understands that pain. That hollowness inside." The face of Mr. Bocanegra, Show Business Impresario, once again adopts that expression of emotional pain that reminds one of a melodramatic silent film actor with stomach problems. Then he extends his enormous arms to both sides of Lucas Giraut's body and opens his hairy, ring-filled hands wide, and before Giraut can react he traps him in an embrace so enveloping and so strong that it makes the soles of his black Lino Rossi loafers come up off the ground. Bocanegra remains that way for a moment, embracing him in silence. Then he nods emotionally with his head. "Your father would be proud of you, boy. And if your father would be, you can bet I am, too. Don't take it the wrong way, son, but for me you're like some kind of a son. Someone incredibly *significant* in my life. And we have a lot of years to catch up on."

Lucas Giraut's face is resting on Mr. Bocanegra's right shoulder, with his chin buried into the long hair of the decidedly feminine coat. Still constrained by the embrace, his eyes meet the gaze of the intern, who is watching them from the other side of the mezzanine railing.

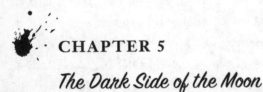

CHAPTER 5

The Dark Side of the Moon

At the very heart of the empire built up over decades by Mr. Bocanegra, Show Business Impresario, at the core of the ever-changing system of cocktail bars, nightclubs and restaurants throughout the Ampurdan that make up that empire, lies The Dark Side of the Moon, standing majestically on its corner in the Upper Ensanche. Flanked by glass commercial buildings with their uniformed doormen and looking out on the traffic of Diagonal Avenue at Vía Augusta from its glazed upper floor. Savage in its defiance of municipal ordinances. Never mentioned in the newspapers. Never the object of neighbors' complaints. Never needing advertising and always far from public opinion, as if The Dark Side of the Moon and public opinion existed in different quantum dimensions. As if they happened in parallel and never were in the same place at the same time. Nothing seems capable of displacing The Dark Side of the Moon from its dominant position in the galaxy of disreputable places in Barcelona's Upper Ensanche.

In The Dark Side of the Moon's private parking lot, Juan de la Cruz Saudade opens the back door of a rental car with tinted windows that is astonishingly similar to the rest of the rental cars with tinted windows that are already parked. Saudade has never seen anyone use the front door of The Dark Side of the Moon. Its clients always go in through the vehicle entrance in the side alley. In the parking garage, Saudade's job consists of taking the keys that the cars' occupants cavalierly deposit in his hand, then showing them the way to the elevator and parking their vehicles. As he parks the cars he tries to damage them slightly, either on the inside or on the outside, in a way that isn't immediately visible. Slight damages that will only be noticed two or three days later.

The car's occupant comes out of the door that Saudade is holding open. He squints under the milky and vaguely iridescent light given off by the garage's fluorescent tubes and then observes Juan de la Cruz Saudade with an expression bordering on horror. Saudade doesn't seem surprised by his reaction. Although technically attractive, his shapely face and tall, slim body are also windows onto a soul that is some sort of industrial oven of hostility. There is nothing remotely kind or friendly in Saudade's features. His reverberating supernova of hostility gleams around his head in exactly the same way that certain venerable old men in remote regions of Asia have an almost tangible aura of beatitude. The guy that just got out of the car takes a step back, intimidated, and his back rams into the side of the car.

"Are you gonna give me the keys or not?"

Saudade puts his hands on his hips, an inappropriate gesture for his position at the very bottom of The Dark Side of the Moon's hierarchical staff pyramid. His technically attractive face is badly shaved. The legs of a pair of powder blue and white Umbro brand sweatpants and some sneakers with worn toes stick out from beneath his corporate jacket.

The Dark Side of the Moon client drops his keys in the palm of Saudade's outstretched hand and hurries off toward the velvet-walled elevator that leads to the main level. Saudade takes a little bottle of cheap scotch from the pocket of his jacket, unscrews the top and takes a swig while thoughtfully watching the man who heads off still sneaking nervous little peeks over his shoulder. Although he is a practicing devotee of all manners of hatred, it is the hatred associated with questions of gender, race and socioeconomic status that Saudade has raised to the level of art. An art as venerable and rich in nuances as, for example, seventeenth-century Flemish pictorial portraiture.

The pounding music from the main floor of The Dark Side of the Moon travels through the walls and floor to the private parking garage. Making everybody down there feel like they are inside a living body. The light is milky and a bit iridescent. Saudade prepares to park the newly arrived car and damage it slightly in the process when another rental car with tinted windows comes in down the private parking garage's ramp. The second car stops with a screech of its tires beside the first one and its back doors open almost simultaneously. Four executive types stumble out from inside. Their business suits show the archetypal signs of executive celebration: ties loosened and pulled to one side; deep red stains on their suit fronts. Their executive hairstyles are unkempt and several locks have escaped from the tyranny of their hair gel. One of them carries an uncorked bottle of Moët et Chandon and drinks straight from the bottle.

"Hey, kid," shouts one of the executive types from the other side of the car Saudade is about to park. "What's going on? You gonna make me walk all the way over there?"

The four executives start laughing. Their laughter is that strangely shrill, not very masculine laughter that Saudade automatically associates with Piece of Shit Rich Boys laughing at someone who's lower class. It doesn't sound quite like hyenas laughing, more like someone just pretending to laugh. One of the executives slaps himself on the knee. They all wipe tears of hilarity from their cheeks. Saudade's tattooed hand, filled with thick rings, closes tightly around the small bottle of whiskey he has in his jacket pocket. His teeth gnash almost audibly in the middle of the echo-filled private parking garage. At that moment one of the executives with loosened ties and decomposing hairstyles stares at him with his eyes squinted.

"Saudade?" says the executive. "Is that you?"

One of the fluorescent tubes on the private parking garage's roof starts to blink and give off a slight mechanical hum. In that way that fluorescent tubes in parking garages blink and buzz as the prelude to a rape or a shoot-out or one of those violent acts that are usually committed in underground parking garages.

"You know this guy?" asks one of the other executives.

"Damn straight," says the first one. "Must be five or six years now. He used to do jobs for our company. Special jobs."

The four executives are silent. A silence filled of respect, cautiousness and curiosity mitigated by the fear of asking the wrong questions. Someone clears their throat. The executive carrying the open bottle of Moët et Chandon in his hand takes a swig.

"Holy shit," says the executive. "How's it going? You work here now?" he says in a shaky tone. "For Bocanegra?"

Some sort of deep tremor runs through Juan de la Cruz Saudade's tattooed arms and muscular back. The whiskey trembles inside the bottle in his pocket. Most of Saudade's tattoos are drawings or political or even paramilitary slogans associated with his favorite soccer club. The supernova of hate that surrounds his face shrinks to an iridescent, flickering white dwarf. The executive who claims to know Saudade begins to apologize in a voice choked with emotion. A couple of Bocanegra's employees who keep guard by the elevator are now watching the scene with unconcealed curiosity. Saudade's face reminds one of white dwarfs and black holes and all kinds of heavenly bodies that implode in silence and cause galactic cataclysms around them. The blinking of the ceiling's fluorescent tube creates intermittent shadows on the cement floor. One of Bocanegra's elevator operators makes a sarcastic comment. Saudade approaches the group of executives, who remain paralyzed beside their rental car, and holds out a hand with the palm facing up. The executives deposit the keys with the rental company's corporate logo on the key ring and disappear from Saudade's vicinity. After a moment the noise of the elevator is heard.

Five minutes later, Saudade has drunk what was left in the bottle of cheap whiskey, has hung up the sign that says "FULL" in front of the entrance in spite of the fact that more than half of the spots are free, and has left the parking garage through a small metal door that opens onto a back staircase for employees. The staircase ends at another identical door, a couple of floors above. Saudade uses his hand to comb his hair, exhales a mouthful of air into his cupped hand to smell his breath, and finally shrugs his shoulders and pushes the door open.

On the other side is a hallway with women in underwear and waiters in white bolero jackets and red bow ties. Saudade closes the door behind him. Two girls in underwear and stiletto heels who are sharing a cigarette stare at him with disgust. One says something to the other in a low voice and they leave.

Saudade passes through the employee area of The Dark Side of the Moon. He picks up a glass of whiskey from a drink cart pushed by a uniformed waiter and drinks it with a distracted expression. The waiter frowns. It is clear that whoever rules that enormous adult nightclub that is the universe doesn't show many signs of sympathy toward Saudade or his fate. In turn, Saudade has always devoted a large part of his physical and intellectual energy to taking his personal revenge on said ruler, either by destroying his property or venting his anger on the rest of the staff and the clients. Now he turns a corner, looks over his shoulder to make sure that no one is watching, and opens the door to one of the private rooms where the female employees take their breaks.

Inside the break room, a young woman in underwear who is lying on a sofa watching television stares at him with an irate expression.

"Not in your wildest dreams," she says. "I'm still aching from the last time. And that was more than a month ago."

Saudade closes the door softly behind him while he lowers his Umbro sweatpants. The way he is able to carry out these two operations simultaneously indicates a degree of skill that defies the laws of physics. During the next five minutes, in the heart of the empire built by Mr. Bocanegra, on a corner of the Upper Ensanche flanked by glass buildings, a symphony of shrieks, thuds and the sounds of tearing lingerie fills one of the break rooms for female personnel. Then there is silence. Saudade leaves the room cautiously. He is fixing his hair with his fingers and rearranging his clothes when a hand rests on his shoulder, a hand larger and heavier than any other hand that Saudade has ever known. A hand that defies conventional ideas about the size a human hand can reach. Saudade observes the hand and then his gaze travels up the arm, as thick as a leg, that's attached to it, and finally lands on the body and then the head of Aníbal Manta.

"Where have you been?" says Aníbal Manta. There is something incongruous in his crew cut and hoop earring. Something that doesn't quite mesh with his gigantic body or his belly that looks like a hot air balloon. Or with his custom-made Italian suit. "Bocanegra wants you in his office right now." Then he gestures with his thumb toward the stairs. "We'll talk about you leaving your work post again later."

Saudade shrugs. He follows Aníbal Manta to an elevator with velvet walls and a crystal chandelier inside and then through a hall flanked by statues. The statues, as anyone who knows Bocanegra is aware, are Bocanegra's main passion outside of work. Although that last part requires a certain speculative effort, given that no one has ever seen Bocanegra not working. It's not an easy idea to imagine either. Saudade waits with his arms in the pockets of his sweatshirt in front of the door of Bocanegra's office while Aníbal Manta announces his arrival. His gaze lands on a marble statue that represents a bearded guy with no arms wearing a sheet. Saudade shakes his head. He can understand that there are statues so old that some pieces have fallen off. What ticks him off is that there are people so stupid that they keep making new statues without arms.

The door to Mr. Bocanegra's office opens. Aníbal Manta makes a sign for Saudade to enter. Saudade stares with a half smile at the superhero comic that Manta has rolled up in his suit coat pocket, long enough to make sure he's annoyed Manta, and then finally goes into the office. More statues. More expensive rugs. More velvet on the walls. Mr. Bocanegra is seated at his mahogany desk, leaning back while one of the female employees from the nightclub files the nails on one of his hands.

Saudade sits in a leather chair with arms.

"Did I say you could sit?" Mr. Bocanegra lifts his eyebrows. His gesture makes trembling wrinkles form all over his bald pate.

Saudade gets up from the leather chair.

"I must say I'm impressed." Mr. Bocanegra nods appreciatively. He places his feet on the mahogany surface of his desk. "In the time I've had you here you've shown yourself to be, by far, the worst worker ever at The Dark Side of the Moon. And we've had some bad ones in the past." He pauses. He sighs. "Even Aníbal is capable of doing two or three things well, if one is careful not to give him tasks that surpass his intellectual capabilities. But you, Saudade." He stops and looks at Saudade, who is standing in the middle of the office without showing any special sign of paying attention. "You have shown yourself to be useful for absolutely nothing. And that impresses me."

Saudade looks out of the corner of his eye toward the part of the office where Aníbal Manta is standing, very still, as if he were trying to camouflage himself among the office's statues. Manta's stance is reminiscent of that stance soccer players take when creating a barrier for the opposing team about to make a free kick. Standing at attention with their chins high and covering their groins with their hands. Saudade doesn't know why they've called him to Bocanegra's office today, but he knows it's not because of anything he's done wrong. After all, he's not tied to a chair with that idiot Manta breaking his fingers. In his opinion, they've called him here to give him a vacation. So he can devote himself full-time to some secret, highly lucrative job of a special nature.

"I've called you here to send you on a vacation," says Bocanegra. Leaning his head to get a better view of the plunging neckline of the girl who is filing his nails. "I'm sure that everyone will be pleased to hear it. Especially the girls." He pauses. The girl who is working on his nails rolls her eyes. "I need you to devote yourself full-time to a job that's just come up. A highly lucrative job. Of course, this conversation does not leave this office. I defer to the usual threats if you talk out of turn."

Saudade clears his throat. The tip of the tongue of the girl who is filing Bocanegra's nails sticks out from between her lips in a gesture of concentration.

"You'll be working with Aníbal." Bocanegra moves the tip of his shoe on top of the mahogany desk and examines it with his eyes gathered in search of scratches or dull spots. "We will also bring in Pavel and that idiot Yanel. In other words, the whole team."

What's incongruous about Manta's appearance, about his crew cut and his hoop earring and the superhero comic book that sticks out of the pocket of his suit jacket, is the feeling that you are looking at a high school kid who's been subjected to some monstrous growth procedure through atomic radiation treatments.

Saudade looks at Bocanegra and bares his teeth in a horrible expression that, against all common sense, seems to be his way of smiling.

CHAPTER 6

Major Players

A thick blue cloud of dry ice swells and hisses around the sports car whose door Eric Yanel is struggling to open. The car's roof and doors are printed with the corporate logos of an international cigarette brand. Eric Yanel kicks the inside of the printed door. One of those patently pointless kicks people do when they are starting to lose their patience. The location of the cigarette ad shoot is a field of epic proportions, in that stereotypical way that fields are epic in television commercials. Three advertising models, in winter coats beneath which they seem to be wearing nothing at all, stand about six feet away from the sports car, waiting for orders from the director's assistant. Making those noises with their mouths that people make to show that they're cold. Standing next to the camera, with a half-eaten doughnut in his hand, one of the technicians on the shoot looks with a frown at the hissing cloud of dry ice that is moving at top speed toward the area where the crew and cars and the catering van are.

"That thing is going to gas us," he says, wiping doughnut crumbs from his mouth with the back of his hand.

"Stop the smoke machine!" shouts someone with a megaphone.

The camera mounted on a complex system of rails and cranes follows Yanel's movements as he finally gets the door open and comes out dressed in a race car driver's helmet, boots and jumpsuit. He walks up to the nose of the car and sits on it with a certain stiffness. His race car driver jumpsuit and his helmet and his boots are all covered with the corporate logos of the international cigarette brand. At the director's assistant's order, the models with the coats on let them drop simultaneously and enter the scene dressed only in tiny bikinis and high heels.

They place themselves on their marks next to Yanel, smile widely and begin caressing his shoulders while looking at the camera. Yanel takes off the helmet, shakes his blond locks in the morning wind and pulls a pack of the sponsor's brand of cigarettes out of one of the pockets of his jumpsuit. He lights a cigarette and exhales a mouthful of smoke that the wind sends treacherously back into his eyes.

"Cut!" shouts the director's assistant.

Iris Gonzalvo drums her fingers on the containing fence that surrounds the location, which the blue, sickly sweet smelling smoke from the dry ice machine is now starting to reach. She takes a drag on her cigarette and watches with a frown as someone runs through the epic-sized field toward the three models and puts their coats over their shoulders. Eric Yanel is laughing now with his perfect teeth, still seated on the nose of the car, and he offers the sponsor's brand of cigarettes to the three models. Iris Gonzalvo wears a plaid Prada coat, a head scarf knotted beneath her chin and dark glasses with enormous and strikingly rectangular frames, in that way that sunglass frames were only strikingly rectangular before 1976. She lifts her chin and moves her head and gazes with a neutral expression at the still-distant object that is approaching on the highway that skirts the epic-sized field. Headed for where the shoot is taking place.

"I thought those things were illegal."

Iris Gonzalvo points with her cigarette at the group composed of Eric Yanel, who now carries the corporate helmet jauntily beneath his arm, and the three models, whose nude legs are visible below their coats. Even though she is too far away, Iris thinks she can see the goose bumps the cold is making on the three models' skin.

"They *are* illegal," says the guy leaning on the containing fence next to Iris Gonzalvo. A middle-aged guy with long silvery hair and a leather jacket. "It's a commercial for the Asian market. They haven't banned cigarette commercials there yet. I don't think they will. Smoking is their favorite thing in Asia." The guy gazes at the women's nude legs like an atomic scientist would gaze at the reading from a particle accelerator. "Smoking and blond women. And those strange number puzzles."

Iris Gonzalvo covers her mouth with a handkerchief and looks at something beyond the cigarette commercial location. Something near the highway that skirts the stereotypical epic field. The object that a moment ago was approaching has now become a two-seater Jaguar with a folding convertible hood and personalized hubcaps.

"So you're saying that this commercial won't be shown in Spain? Ever?" she asks, her voice slightly distorted by the handkerchief that covers her nose and mouth. Most of the people on her side of the containing fence are now covering their noses and mouths to protect themselves from the blue carbonic smoke that floats over toward them. Others are waving one hand in front of their faces or simply coughing into their fists. "Or anywhere else in Europe?"

"They'd be more likely to air heroin commercials." The guy squints to see through the cloud of dry ice. "Given the new European regulations. Your boyfriend's going to be seen by Chinese folks. Koreans. That kind of people." He looks at Iris Gonzalvo out of the corner of his eye. "Because he is your boyfriend, right?"

The convertible Jaguar parks about a third of a mile from the location where the ad is being shot and after a moment a couple of vaguely human-looking individuals come out of it. Looking like they've suffered some type of hypertrophy over their entire bodies. Between the two of them, they must add up to some six hundred and fifty pounds of fat, atrophied muscle, sweaty faces and expensive Italian suits. With matching Italian loafers. One of them wears a long-haired fur coat that is clearly a woman's coat. The other locks the Jaguar's doors by pushing a button on his infrared key ring and the tune the infrared key ring emits to confirm that they are locked is the chorus to Pink Floyd's "Another Brick in the Wall, Part II."

"I hope you won't mind me asking if you have an agent." The silver-haired guy beside Iris Gonzalvo offers her a business card. "Because *I'm* an agent. I don't know if you do commercials or films. I assume you're an actress. With that face . . . And with, well, all the rest. I'm sure I've seen you in something. And I know everyone says that." He smiles beneath his silvery hair. The headband that he uses to keep his long silvery hair off his forehead and away from his face isn't a headband. It's a pair of sunglasses, a classic model from the eighties, recently rereleased as part of the aesthetic fervor for said decade. "As if I was trying to get you into bed. Do you do commercials or films?"

Mr. Bocanegra, Show Business Impresario and owner of the legendary Barcelona nightspot The Dark Side of the Moon, starts walking among the shoot's crew members, looking as if he's searching for someone. With his hands in the pockets of his markedly feminine coat. With a touch of cruelty in his squinted eyes while he scrutinizes the shoot location. His right-hand man, Aníbal Manta, doesn't have his hands in his pockets. It's not clear that they make pockets big enough to contain Aníbal Manta's hands. In the center of the shoot location, the director is looking at a small monochrome screen surrounded by a group of people eating doughnuts and watching in silence. The most common attire of the members of the shooting crew seems to consist of urban sport shoes, combat pants of various hues, and parkas. Many of them use the shooting breaks to breathe steaming mouthfuls of breath into their hands and do that thing with their feet that people do when they have to stand still in the cold. A bit like stomping on invisible grapes.

Mr. Bocanegra and his right-hand man Aníbal Manta are not wearing parkas or combat pants or any sort of urban gear. They are wearing Italian suits and loafers. They have mustaches. Aníbal Manta has a crew cut and a hoop earring that are completely incongruent with the rest of his appearance. They each weigh as much as two members of the shooting crew.

"Both," says Iris Gonzalvo. "I do commercials and films."

About six feet away, the three models with the coats laugh at Eric Yanel's comments as they drink coffee from a thermos brought to them by a girl in a parka and combat pants. The guy with the silvery hair takes some prescription glasses out of the pocket of his leather jacket, puts them on with a blink and fixes his gaze on Mr. Bocanegra and Aníbal Manta. Manta has just moved aside one of the containing fences and is now stepping to one side so Bocanegra can pass through, with a gesture that is reminiscent of a doorman in a luxury hotel or a gangster's chauffeur holding a car door open for his boss.

"You can't go through there," says the guy with the silvery hair. With a sudden frown. "Who are those guys? They look like major players."

Iris Gonzalvo watches as Eric Yanel's smiling expression turns first to shock and then to horror a second later, when he sees Mr. Bocanegra and Aníbal Manta striding toward him. The former with his hands in the pockets of his markedly feminine coat. The latter with an iron bar that he has just pulled out of some part of his Italian suit.

"I've done a couple of movies," says Iris. "Under the name Penny DeMink. They both went directly to cable."

Some of the technicians in the shooting crew gathered around the director seem to now notice the presence of the two guys with mustaches that have broken through the sealed containing fences and now seem to be talking to Eric Yanel. The trays of doughnuts from breakfast placed on camping tables are already almost empty and the only doughnuts left on them are the less popular flavors. Particularly coconut. Someone asks someone else if anyone knows those two guys with mustaches. Someone answers that they must be major players if they came out of the Jaguar parked back there. After which the crew's general attention unanimously shifts to the Jaguar.

"DeMink?" The guy with silvery hair strokes his chin without taking his eyes off of Bocanegra and Manta. "What kind of a name is that?"

Iris Gonzalvo watches with a frown as Aníbal Manta grabs the arm of one of the models with bare legs and pushes her onto the grass of the epic field. Then he smacks one of the other models on the rear end and watches with a mocking smile as she runs off in terror. The third model is already cross-country running. Iris takes off her dark glasses to better see the scene that's taking place in the middle of the cigarette ad shoot, in the middle of the already half-dispersed cloud of carbonic smoke that floats around the sports car. Now Bocanegra and Manta seem to have focused their attention onto Yanel. The guy with the silvery hair looks at Iris Gonzalvo's face now suddenly stripped of dark glasses, and his expression transforms. His cheeks get red. His neck gets red. Finally, his forehead gets red.

"Fuck," he says in a low voice. "Now I remember where I've seen you."

In the cloud of smoke semi-dispersed by the wind, Eric Yanel's race car helmet rolls in the grass. Aníbal Manta lifts his iron bar above his head in a threatening gesture. Kneeling on the grass, Yanel nods emphatically and then shakes his head emphatically and brings his hands together in front of his chest as if he were praying. With his features twisted into a grimace of terror. Aníbal Manta makes threatening, rhythmic little taps into his open palm with his iron bar. Mr. Bocanegra grabs Yanel by one ear and twists it with an expression that accentuates the intrinsically cruel elements of his physiognomy.

The guy with the long silvery hair squints his eyes in an attempt to make out the trio of vaguely visible figures through the diffuse cloud of carbonic smoke.

The scream that comes out of Eric Yanel's red, tearstained face as a response to the cruel twisting of his ear can be clearly heard at the containing fence. The guy with the long silvery hair looks at Iris Gonzalvo in alarm.

"I'm going to call the police," he says.

And he pulls a cell phone out of his leather jacket. Iris Gonzalvo takes it out of his hand before he has a chance to open it and she throws it far and high, over the containing fence.

"My boyfriend is *talking* to those guys," says Iris. And she points with her head to the place where Eric Yanel is now twisting in pain while Aníbal Manta's Italian loafer steps on his face, hard, burying it in the grass. *"Can't you see that?"*

Several figures in parkas and urban gear wipe the doughnut crumbs from their mouths and set off running toward the containing fence.

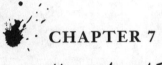

CHAPTER 7

Unnumbered Birthday

The subject of the Mexican *corrido* being sung by a mariachi with some sort of oversized twelve-string guitar seems to be Emiliano Zapata's death. Or, more specifically, the elements of injustice and emotional pain surrounding Zapata's death. Standing beside the stage, and wearing one of the intercom headsets that have been distributed among the organizational team, Lucas Giraut moves his foot distractedly to the rhythm of the Tex-Mex music that comes out of the impressive speaker system. The place is the pool deck of Barcelona's Gran Hotel La Florida. The occasion is the 2006 Unnumbered Birthday of Estefanía "Fanny" Giraut. In addition to the mariachi who plays the twelve-string guitar, the band hired for the event is made up of a lead singer equipped with an accordion, a guitar player–backup singer with a standard-sized guitar with the standard number of strings and an appropriately smaller guy that plays some kind of smaller-than-standard guitar.

"Son," says the voice of Fonseca from behind Lucas Giraut.

The pool deck of Barcelona's Gran Hotel La Florida is filled with two hundred political, institutional and business figures for the occasion of Fanny Giraut's Unnumbered Birthday. The air of the surrounding hills lends a very slight scent of pine trees that mixes with the smell of cigarettes and pool chlorine. The guests gravitate in a complex system of meta-adjacent groups around the hostess with the surgically taut face. Due to the unnumbered nature of Fanny Giraut's birthdays, her Corporate Chief of Public Relations established the tradition five years ago of distinguishing the successive birthdays by preceding the word "Birthday" with the number of the year in progress.

"Son," repeats Fonseca in the exact moment that Lucas Giraut turns to see him appear by his side with two clinking glasses.

The veins in his temples are swollen in a way that seems to indicate a medium-to-high degree of emotional stress and nervous agitation.

Fonseca puts a clinking glass filled with the evening's special cocktail into Giraut's hand. All the glasses used to serve the cocktail are inscribed with "FANNY GIRAUT: 2006 BIRTHDAY." The suit Lucas Giraut is wearing is a pearl gray Lino Rossi suit. The design of the cocktail and the glasses and the other elements of corporate imagery exclusive to the party are the responsibility of Fanny Giraut's Personal Public Relations Office.

"Son, what sort of joke is this?" Fonseca points with his drink to the four musicians wearing fancy dress Tex-Mex suits who are playing the *corrido* with the Zapatista subject matter. "Who is the *imbecile* who hired these guys? It hasn't even been three months since we buried your father."

Lucas Giraut nods as he takes a sip of cocktail with his gaze fixed on the Tex-Mex musical quartet. The musicians in the quartet smile with toothy expressions of professional optimism that are somehow particularly Mexican. The lead singer with the accordion is alluding to the fact that Emiliano Zapata's death constitutes an unforgettable event due to its negative historical repercussions for Mexican peasantry.

"Son," says Fanny Giraut's lawyer and right-hand man. "You still haven't signed the agreements for the restructuring plan. Your mother is starting to worry. She's just been made a *widow*, for the love of God." He shakes his head. "She needs a *son's* support now more than ever."

Lucas Giraut nods again and stretches out his neck to get a look at his mother, who is perfectly positioned in the center of the system of meta-adjacent groups and totally absorbed in an animated conversation with two senior officials of the Upper Franconian Ministry of Culture. As a result of her face's lack of mobility, Fanny Giraut's smile consists primarily of retracting her lips to reveal horrifically white gums. A bit farther on, at the edge of the meta-adjacent groups closest to the six-story birthday cake, the Director of the International Division of LORENZO GIRAUT, LTD., Carlos Chicote, is passing his fingertip surreptitiously over the surface of the cake. Lucas Giraut raises a hand to the earpiece of his headset and frowns with an attentive look.

"Security problem in the North Access," he says in a tone of professional efficiency. And he puts a hand on Fonseca's shoulder. "I have to go."

The members of the band are singing about the fact that Emiliano Zapata was a man with exceptional moral qualities. A man that committed himself selflessly to the cause of liberating the poor. Which is why the Indians from every town and of every stripe went to fight by his side. Lucas Giraut makes his way over to the spot where the Director of the International Division is furtively licking his fingertip and places a paternal hand on his shoulder. Chicote looks at him, his fingertip still in his mouth and an expression of primal terror in his eyes. The suitological analysis that Giraut carries out on his black Armani suit with silk tie and sixteen-karat cuff links indicates a lack of corporate self-confidence and a sycophant's anxiety to create a public image of aggressiveness and success based on self-confidence.

"Don't pay any mind to what you've heard," he says to him. "About your salary getting frozen and you being fired for poor performance. I am the president of this company. My mother and Fonseca work for me. That's how my father put it in his will, even though everyone thinks he went crazy."

Chicote tries to mitigate his expression of terror with an anguished smile. His alopecia follows that irregular and frightening asymmetrical pattern of nervous alopecia.

"I've decided to raise your salary." Giraut lowers his voice to a tone appropriate to corporate secrets. "Perhaps we could add a bonus stock option package. And maybe you could also have a yacht share." He frowns. "I don't remember exactly. Send me a report of your activities when you get a chance. To *my* secretary."

Chicote begins a labored string of sycophantic thank-yous, vows of corporate loyalty and manifestations of respect on a personal level. Giraut nods with a distracted look while he waits for him to finish. Then his eye is drawn to something located at the other end of the party.

"Security problem in the North Access," he says. He downs the contents of his glass and leaves it on a small table. "I have to go."

Lucas Giraut makes his way through the party guests. Several institutional figures drink and converse amicably in meta-adjacent groups while moving rhythmically to the music. The entire city extends with a servile air at the feet of the sumptuous pool deck. The mayor of Barcelona is doing what appears to be some sort of festive Brazilian dance to the delight of the other members of his group.

Lucas Giraut gets to the sofa where Valentina Parini is seated with a glass of Coca-Cola and he sits down beside her.

"You're not on the guest list," he says. "I know because I made the guest list."

Valentina Parini takes a sip of Coca-Cola and shrugs her shoulders. One of the lenses of her green plastic glasses is covered with a patch.

"It's because of my new punishment." Valentina rolls her eyes but you can only see one of her eyes rolling because of the patch. "My mother won't let me stay home alone. Two days ago I set the kitchen on fire. Accidentally," she adds quickly, very serious. "It wasn't an attack strategy. I just forgot the burner was on." She shrugs her shoulders. "The good thing is that there won't be any crêpes for a while. When my mother gets mad at me she stops making me crêpes."

Lucas Giraut nods and points at her eyeglasses.

"It looks good on you," he says. "The patch."

"I look retarded," says the girl. Then she points with her head toward the people standing in the party. "There's a lot of people and all that. But I know why they came. They're *afraid* of your mother."

On the stage, pushing and pulling various levers and buttons on his accordion, the lead singer of the band hired by Lucas Giraut is requesting in song that the little sparrows sing out that General Zapata was shot down in a conspicuously treacherous way. The three accompanying musicians accompany his request with professionally optimistic smiles.

"I've been testing the Low-Flying Airplanes Attack," says Lucas Giraut to Valentina Parini, who continues to sip on her glass of Coca-Cola while watching the meta-adjacent groups of party guests with her one eye. "Here, at the party. It works pretty well. I guess that's because we're so high up on a hill. Gives it that dramatic touch."

Valentina Parini stares at him and a gloomy look comes over her face.

"Everything is going wrong," she says in a tone that transmits the weary ennui of an adult more than teenage irritation. "Worse than wrong. My homeroom teacher sent another report to the principal saying that my attitude is antisocial and aggressive. And the principal called the school psychologist again. And this time the school psychologist said I have a borderline personality. I looked it up on the Internet." She makes a derisive face. "It's nothing like my personality. The thing is, my homeroom teacher called my mother again." She looks up from her Coca-Cola and at Lucas Giraut with her only visible eye. "Because now they're friends, you know. I think they go out at night looking for husbands together."

Lucas Giraut takes his headset off and puts it in the pocket of his suit jacket.

"My *mother* has a borderline personality," he says, lowering his voice a bit. "And you're nothing like her."

It looks like he is about to say something else when he's interrupted by a hand on his shoulder. He turns and stares into Fonseca's face, who in turn is looking at him with that virile severe expression of male stars from Hollywood's Golden Age. The networks of veins on his temples are belligerently swollen.

"I just spoke with the hotel manager," says Fonseca. Staring at Giraut. "He assures me there is no security problem in the North Access. In fact, there is no North Access. And I hope this doesn't have anything to do with those documents you have to sign."

Valentina Parini is staring at her nearly empty glass of Coca-Cola with an expression of concentration. Lucas Giraut takes out his silver cigarette case embossed with his initials and offers Fonseca a cigarette.

CHAPTER 8

Ummagumma 2

The plaque on the gate of the house in Pedralbes with the electrified perimeter in front of which Pavel is digging into his backpack is gilded and impeccably polished in that way that suggests the existence of someone whose specific job it is to maintain all of the gilded surfaces in the house impeccably polished. The impeccably polished gold plaque reads "UMMAGUMMA 2." Pavel takes a small aluminum hammer out of his backpack and wraps it in a rag and gives the security camera right above the plaque a couple of whacks. Several pieces of the security camera fall to the ground at his feet. The gate with the gold plaque is in the middle of a brick wall topped with an electric fence. On the brick wall to the right of the house's mailbox and right beside a sign that reads "POST NO BILLS," someone has posted a promotional poster that reads "ONLY EIGHTEEN DAYS UNTIL THE WORLD RELEASE OF STEPHEN KING'S NEW NOVEL."

The street in the neighborhood of Pedralbes where Pavel now kneels to put the hammer back in his backpack is one of those tiny Pedralbes streets where you can show up at any hour of the night and do something like break a security camera with a hammer without having to worry about anyone seeing you. The night is an improbably cold mid-December night. Pavel, however, doesn't seem to register the improbable cold. Some noteworthy elements of his appearance, besides his wearing a flannel shirt open on top of a Bob Marley and The Wailers T-shirt in spite of the cold, are the fact that he is exaggeratedly tall and exaggeratedly pale and wears his hair in dreadlocks. Not those acceptably long dreadlocks that fall in a cascade. Pavel's dreadlocks are those pointy ones still in the growing phase that someone seeing them from a distance could confuse with an Afro.

Pavel puts the aluminum hammer back in the backpack and takes out a black plastic case filled with tools and electronic equipment. A cloud of white steam materializes in front of his face each time he breathes. He uses a screwdriver from the case to unscrew the number panel whose combination opens the lock and then uses some wire cutters to cut the cord that joins the numerical lock with the house's alarm. Finally he connects an electronic device to the wire-filled inside of the lock and pushes a couple of buttons that set off a series of electronic beeps that sound like the screech of a modem. The lock on the barred door opens with a metallic click. The only sign that Pavel is feeling the effects of the cold is the fact that now and then he rubs the palms of his gloveless hands together.

A minute later Pavel crosses the yard of the three-story house with his shoulders hunched and a tranquilizer dart gun in his hand. A big dog with short hair and erect ears cuts him off. Pavel stops and stares at the dog. The dog stares at Pavel, wagging his tail amicably. With an expression of peaceful curiosity in his canine eyes. Pavel shoots him with a tranquilizer dart anyway.

Strictly speaking, one can't say that Pavel likes his line of work. Or the people he has to work with. Or much less the people that fate has chosen to be the victims of his line of work. Or the city of Barcelona. Although it's true that he didn't like Moscow, either, before he moved to Barcelona. In fact, there aren't many things that he really likes. He himself has never really understood why. As a boy, the only moments in which he can remember having experienced anything close to true satisfaction were the times he filled the old, enormous bathtub of his old, enormous post-Soviet apartment and immersed himself for hours imagining that he was a shark. Until his father or some other adult in the old collective apartment kicked the door open and forced him out of the collective bathtub by beating him with a hanger. Theoretically speaking, Pavel is a firm believer in the teachings of the Rastafarian philosophy. In the idea that the Rastafari have to work spiritually for the redemption of humanity. And yet, he almost never finds practical occasions in which to apply said theoretical concepts.

Pavel goes around the three-story house with his backpack on his shoulder until he finds what he is looking for. French windows that open onto some sort of interior sunroom on the lower floor with a glass door beside them. Pavel cuts the glass around the lock and pushes the door, which opens docilely. A pleasant wave of dry heat from the central heating system welcomes him into the house.

Pavel is exaggeratedly tall in that way in which certain people are so exaggeratedly tall and thin that they almost never manage to stand up completely straight. An essentially gawky way of being exaggeratedly tall. When indoors, Pavel is one of those people that usually have no problem touching the ceiling with an outstretched arm. Now Pavel takes a black ski mask out of his backpack with his exaggeratedly long arms and puts it on his head. He moves his neck from one side to the other to adjust the ski mask so that his mouth and eyes coincide with the openings in the mask. Then he takes an automatic pistol out of his backpack. He puts a silencer on it and checks the chamber before cocking it. He leaves his backpack on the floor and heads up the stairs. With the ski mask on and the gun held high.

Pavel now moves stealthily under the pale, vaguely orangish light that enters through the windows of the three-story house, which smells clean and like something else that it takes Pavel a moment to identify. Marijuana. The herbal and slightly acrid smell of marijuana. Pavel stops suddenly on the second-floor landing. With his heart beating in that controlled, accelerated way that hearts beat in the middle of a job in Pavel's line of work. There is a line of white light beneath a door located on one side of the landing. Only about six feet away from the place where Pavel remains stock-still. Pavel's heartbeat speeds up a bit, while remaining controlled. It doesn't seem possible that anyone has heard him from the other side of the door. Pavel crosses the landing stealthily and puts a hand on the doorknob and raises the pistol with his other hand and opens the door abruptly.

The room on the other side of the door turns out to be a very large bathroom with sky blue wall-to-wall carpeting and tiles. Pavel isn't sure if he's ever seen a sky blue carpet before. On one of the bathroom walls there is a framed poster that reads "PINK FLOYD: THE FINAL CUT." Pavel looks to one side. Seated on the toilet, looking at him with a stunned face, is a young woman. Of course, Bocanegra, that idiot, hadn't told him there was going to be a woman in the house. He hadn't even mentioned the *possibility* of there being a woman in the house. The young woman has an elastic band tied around the upper part of her elbow and a hypodermic needle stuck in the inner part of her elbow and is sitting next to a sink with a teaspoon and a lighter and a square of aluminum foil with traces of heroin on it. The only clothes she has on are a promotional T-shirt for the Costa Dorada Biosphere Park theme park and lace panties around her ankles. The young woman lifts up her arms slowly. With a shocked expression. The needle falls to the floor. Pavel immediately identifies the young woman as being of the painfully attractive type. One of those young women with painful sex appeal. Pavel puts his finger in front of the part of the ski mask where his lips are and makes the sign for "silence" in international sign language. Then he grabs her brusquely by an arm and forces her to get up off the toilet. The young woman's pubis is completely shaved except for a tiny unshaved area in the shape of a heart.

Pavel goes back downstairs, preceded by the young woman. Once on the lower floor, he indicates through gestures that she should lie on the sofa and open her legs. The young woman obeys with some sort of lazy resignation. Pavel drops his pants. He manipulates his genitals to the point of a satisfactory erection and penetrates her on the sofa. Then he leans over her. And in that moment he sees something. Something familiar in the young woman's face. Something familiar and at the same time completely improbable. Something that makes him take his penis out of the young woman suddenly and take a few steps back, spooked. He snatches off his ski mask.

"Anya?" he says. In an incredulous tone. Looking at the young woman's face with a frown beneath the tenuous orangish light. "Is that you?"

The young woman now looks at him with the same incredulous expression. With an amplified version of the same incredulous expression. Which quickly transforms into a disgusted expression.

"Pavel?" says the young woman. Sitting up with a start.

Every trace of lazy resignation or shock seems to have evaporated from her face. She lifts a trembling arm and hits him in the face with a smack that echoes throughout the entire lower floor of the three-story house bathed in orangish light. Pavel is paralyzed, the pistol still in his hand. He raises a hand to his face and looks at his bloodstained fingertips.

The moment, thinks Pavel, is one of those moments that makes him lose all his faith in any of the teachings of the Rastafarian philosophy related to spreading the Rastafarian message of spiritual redemption. One of those moments that fills him with a paralyzing contempt for the civilized Western society that surrounds him. One of those moments that intensify his displeasure toward everything that surrounds his life and makes him want to fill bathtubs to the brim and immerse himself in them. Until he is capable of satisfactorily forgetting where he is. Until the bathtub ceases to be a bathtub.

"What a *pig*!" she shrieks in Russian, her Moscow inflections painfully familiar. "What the *fuck* are you doing here?" She pauses. Her eyes cross slightly. "And what the fuck happened to your hair?"

"What am *I* doing here?" Pavel wields his pistol. "What are *you* doing here? What a *whore*. You've always been a little whore." He points toward the stairs with the barrel of his pistol. "Do you have any idea of what kind of guy's fucking you?"

"I'm no *whore*, idiot." She lifts a hand with diamonds on the ring finger and puts it in Pavel's face. A diamond ring that looks too big to be worn on any kind of finger without causing muscular injuries. "I'm *engaged*. And of course I know what kind of guy is fucking me. A *rich* man. That's the kind of guy he is."

Pavel stares at her. With an expression of intense despondency and intense lack of faith in the teaching of the Rastafarian philosophy and intense contempt for the world that surrounds him. He pulls up his pants without letting go of the pistol in his hand. He buckles his belt.

"Put down the pistol," says a voice in Spanish from behind Pavel's back. A masculine and imperious voice. A voice that feels completely at ease ordering people around. "And you can start explaining what's going on here. Because I don't have any desire to learn Russian. For example, you could start explaining why you don't have any panties on."

Pavel turns slowly and takes a look at the person who has just spoken. At first he doesn't even manage to comprehend *what* it is that he's looking at. And not exactly because of poor lighting. He's forced to look again. And what he sees does indeed seem to be a man. Although at first glance that's not entirely clear. Pavel squints to see better in the orangish half-light. The man has a very large head and a mat of white curly hair and a patch that covers one eye. And something that looks like a sheet of metal where his right temple once was. A substantial part of the right side of his face no longer seems to be where it once was. The man, by the way, is aiming a double-barrel shotgun at Pavel. Pavel throws his pistol to the floor. Now it seems an absurd, laughable and not very masculine object compared to the man's double-barrel shotgun.

"I'm a light sleeper," says the man. In a perfectly calm tone. "Unfortunately for you. And luckily for me. That's to be expected after a bomb explodes in your house while you're sleeping." He shrugs his shoulders. "Doesn't matter that it was thirty years ago."

The painfully attractive young woman dressed only in a T-shirt advertising the Biosphere Park theme park stands between the two barrels of the shotgun and Pavel's exaggeratedly tall and gawky figure.

"Don't kill him," she says in Spanish to the man that seems to be missing a substantial part of the right side of his face.

The man stares at her with a weary face.

"And would you mind telling me why I shouldn't kill him?" he says.

There is a moment of silence. Finally the young woman sighs. With a put-out expression.

"Because he's my brother," she says.

Now the man stares at Pavel curiously.

"Your brother?" he says. "I didn't know you had a brother."

Pavel's face now reflects infinite despondency and infinite contempt for the world he was born into and the role he was given to play in that world. From the front of his T-shirt, Bob Marley raises his eyes up to heaven in a look of musical ecstasy.

CHAPTER 9

A Masterpiece of Planning

Standing in front of the large window of the Upper Level of The Dark Side of the Moon, Mr. Bocanegra contemplates the hordes of shoppers that cross Diagonal Avenue with their bags from the big department stores. There is something vaguely regal, or perhaps even Shakespearean, in the act of smoking a cigar pensively in front of a large window located several stories above a commercial avenue filled with people. Or at least that's Bocanegra's impression. The self-confessed fan of his nieces and nephews and of seventies-era British rock takes a meditative pull on his cigar and observes the unmarked car parked across the street. Inside which Commissioner Farina's two lackeys are watching, as usual, with their state-of-the-art photographic equipment.

"We're in the business of *fantasy*," he says. And shakes his cigar absentmindedly in the direction of the police car. "It doesn't matter that they say we're criminals. We're just not like other people. We have fantasies. We have dreams. We haven't given up that part of our lives. That's why we steal. And once in a while we bust up a face or we shoot someone in the kneecap. There're always kneecaps that are screaming out, begging for us to shoot them, of course. Because we're people with *positive energy*. Ambition. That thing that gets lost when you work in an office and turn into a drab, colorless kind of guy." He looks, with something bordering on commiseration, at the hordes of people crossing Diagonal at intervals set by the municipal streetlight system. "Which is why I'm glad that we're getting back into action. These have been a few very lovely months of rest and all that. Some of you have had fun and others have used the time to get into trouble. Which is fine." He sighs and gazes into the large window at the indistinct reflection of the four men seated behind him. His audience for the night. The Repositories of his Wisdom. The panes of the glazed Upper Level of The Dark Side of the Moon are reflective on the outside and semi-reflective on the inside. So that someone situated where Bocanegra is now can't be seen from the outside but can see both what's going on outside and the reflection of what's going on behind his back. "Now it's back to work. The fun is over. Mr. Giraut will give you the basic details of our job. He even brought a slide projector. Mr. Giraut, by the way, is my new partner. In other words, your new boss."

Mr. Bocanegra turns around and looks at the four other inhabitants of the room. With the regal calm of someone who knows that the members of his audience have no other choice but to remain obediently seated and wait until he decides to continue speaking. The three men seated at the long table filled with small bottles of mineral water in the meeting room of the Upper Level of The Dark Side of the Moon look at him with blank faces. Aníbal Manta is seated with his giant arms crossed over his hot air balloon of a belly. With his crew cut and his incongruent hoop earring. Due to the size of his belly, his crossed arms almost touch his chin. Saudade is seated a bit farther on, apparently concentrating on getting something out from between his teeth with a finger bent into a hook. At the end of the table, Eric Yanel smokes with a desperate expression next to an ashtray brimming with cigarette butts.

Mr. Bocanegra gives Lucas Giraut a sign to turn on his slide projector. Giraut pushes a button on some sort of little switch he has in his hand, which is connected to the slide projector. The machine makes a click similar to the sound of someone cocking a pistol and the three seated men look up, startled.

On one of the white walls the image of a business property appears.

"This is Hannah Linus's gallery," says Giraut. "The most important gallerist in the country for Renaissance and Baroque art. I myself have lost some important clients to her." He presses the little switch in his hand again, causing the same vaguely ballistic sound, and on the wall the image of a young blond woman walking down a street with a cell phone at her ear appears. "Miss Linus is a woman with an impressive career. She worked at Sotheby's until some people got upset by how quickly she was getting promoted and then she left to set up her own business. Taking with her one of the world's most important group of collectors."

The three men seated at the table look at the image of the woman with feigned disinterest. Although it is hard to tell because of the cloud of cigarette smoke that surrounds his head, it seems that Eric Yanel could have a long dark bruise on one side of his face. Right below the idiosyncratically French wave of his blond hair. Standing in front of the large window in a somewhat Shakespearean stance, Bocanegra observes how one of the windows of the unmarked police car lowers and a hand throws a cigarette butt onto the sidewalk.

"In two weeks," continues Giraut, "Miss Linus will display in her Barcelona gallery a batch of objects that come from Celtic monasteries in Ireland. Nothing of great value, except for four paintings on wood from St. Kieran's church in County Limerick. Experts call them the St. Kieran Panels, and their value stems from their history and their rare subject matter. They are depictions of the Black Sun. A subject associated with the book of the Apocalypse. They are usually attributed to Brother Samhael Finnegan, nicknamed the Crazy Monk of Limerick."

Several vaguely ballistic clicks punctuate the silence of the room. Images of paintings parade across the wall, and the assembled contemplate them with expressions ranging from skepticism to uncertainty. The various images are very dark and most appear to depict scenes associated with natural disasters. Some are so dark that it's hard to see what's going on in them. In general it seems to be fires and hordes of demons invading the Earth. The sky is invariably black. The human figures in the paintings seem to always be fleeing with their arms held high and their faces shaken with fear. After a minute, Giraut stops the slide show on an image that's slightly different from the rest. It's also a dark scene filled with terrified people, but at the same time it's somehow simpler and more impressive. Its simplicity somehow makes it more disheartening. And at the same time more appealing. A mountainous landscape collapsing into hundreds of cracks and bottomless abysses. As if the entire world were experiencing an earthquake of apocalyptic dimensions.

"This is the first of the St. Kieran Panels," says Giraut. "The only one that I was able to find a slide of. The title by which it is traditionally known is a Latin phrase that means 'And, behold, there was a great earthquake.' Which is a verse from the Book of the Apocalypse. The expressiveness of the forms is stunning," he adds, pointing with his head to the human figures in the painting, most of which are falling through the cracks in the ground and going over rocky cliffs. Frozen by the magic of art in free fall toward the center of the Earth.

There is a moment of silence as they all look at the painting. Saudade turns his head to look at a part of the image that's upside down. Aníbal Manta raises a hand.

"What does it mean?" he says. Fondling his hoop earring absentmindedly. "I don't much get art. Though I do like comic books."

Lucas Giraut half turns so he can look at the slide of the painting. With a surprised expression. As if he had never thought of the question.

"I don't know exactly," he says finally. "But I guess it means that everything is going wrong."

"It's like that movie," says Saudade. He starts snapping the fingers of one hand. "I don't remember the name."

Bocanegra takes a pensive pull on his cigar while watching as an employee of the billboard rental company equipped with a harness and climbing gear hangs over one of the gigantic billboards on Diagonal Avenue. Changing the advertising message on the billboard. The new message that the employee with the harness is pasting onto the billboard of Diagonal Avenue, sector by sector, says the following: "ONLY SEVENTEEN DAYS UNTIL THE WORLDWIDE RELEASE OF STEPHEN KING'S NEW NOVEL."

"Our plan is a masterpiece of planning, of course." Bocanegra puts his hands on his hips and grabs the cigar with his teeth in a toothy grimace that momentarily intensifies the elements of cruelty in his already cruel facial expression. "As usual. As usually happens when I'm in charge. We have a three-week window of operations while the paintings are in the gallery. There will be a team of experts that will inspect them when they arrive, to reassure the buyers and all that. But no one is going to inspect them when the three weeks *are over*.

And that's where we come in." He makes a broad gesture toward the Meeting Room. Which, just like the rest of the Upper Level of The Dark Side of the Moon, is decorated with Persian rugs and fine wood and has special niches in the walls for statues. "Because the sucker who takes those paintings home and hangs them in his living room will be hanging the copies that we've had made and switched with the real paintings. Oh, they'll figure it out, sure. As soon as that sucker has them appraised or whatever. But by then we'll already have taken the real paintings out of the country, and we'll have sold them, and we'll have the money well stashed underneath our mattresses."

There is a sudden noise at the end of the long table covered with small bottles of water. Similar to the sound of someone punching the table, followed by the damp, snotty sounds of someone bursting into tears inconsolably. Bocanegra turns toward the sound. Several faces now study the origin of the sound. Eric Yanel's ashtray brimming with smashed cigarette butts is now on the carpet. Eric Yanel is sobbing with his face buried in his arms. Amid his own cloud of cigarette smoke.

"Of course," continues Bocanegra with a frown, "the plan wouldn't be a masterpiece of planning without someone able to make copies perfect enough to hang in the gallery for the necessary time without raising any suspicion. And I have to say that we have nothing to worry about in that arena. Because we have the best specialist in the field. Better than the best. We have the master. The guy who's taught everything to the current generation. The guy that's tricked half the experts at Sotheby's and Christie's. So good at what he does and so absolutely legendary that he's on Interpol's list of the hundred most wanted men. Well." He shrugs his shoulders. His gesture introduces an element of uncertainty that's unable to completely superimpose itself over the backdrop of cruelty. "We don't *exactly* have him. He isn't the kind of person who advertises in the yellow pages. We know that he lives under various false identities and moves constantly among several European capitals. Where he has people who hide him. And I can't say that he's exactly agreed to work with us. But *I can say*"—his smile seems to make his mustache come to life—"that we know where he'll be in a few days. Thanks to certain contacts that have supplied me with an address and a couple of dates on the calendar. In exchange for certain past favors. His name is Raymond Panakian. Or at least that's what the people who sometimes need his services usually call him. And you"—he points with the incandescent end of the cigar toward the three men seated at the table. One of which continues crying with his head sunk between his arms and irregular columns of smoke rising around him—"you are going to have to convince him to come work with us. That it's worth it to come and work with us because we are fabulous people who are worth working with."

Lucas Giraut still has the slide projector switch in his hand, but now it seems that the focus of his attention has moved elsewhere. Now he seems to be watching something located on the other side of the large windows. Far below the Meeting Room where the meeting is taking place. With a slight frown.

"I'm good at convincing people," says Saudade in a tone completely devoid of irony. While he examines the residue beneath one fingernail with his brow gathered. All his fingers seem to have the same uniform amount of dark residual material beneath the nails. "I always end up *completely* convincing 'em."

"There's a car out front that seems to be watching us." Lucas Giraut points with his head at Commissioner Farina's lackeys' car that is parked across the street. "They have cameras. And it looks like they're watching *us*."

"That car belongs to Commissioner Farina's lackeys," says Mr. Bocanegra. Without looking at where Lucas Giraut is pointing. "The guy that put your father in jail. And who's been on my ass since the late seventies. A real psychopath. One of those cops, you know. Loves car chases. But you have nothing to worry about." His tone is not reassuring in any kind or quasi-paternal way. It is a tone that mixes elements of quasi-paternal advice with a veiled threat. "That's all you need to know for now. In the next few days I'll give you all instructions and blueprints. Guidelines. The details of my plan. The fee is the usual one for this kind of job. In other words, a ton of money. So you can have some more fun and get yourselves in some more trouble. Except for Mr. Yanel, who has been so kind as to renounce his share in exchange for my taking lightly certain matters that he and I have pending." He expels a puff of thick smelly cigar smoke and looks at the twisting distorted images of the faces of the four members of his audience through the cigar smoke. "*Now* is the moment where you ask all the questions you need to. And I hope that they'll be relevant and intelligent questions and that none of them will be too long or complicated, because it turns out that tonight I am having dinner with my nieces and nephews. The people I love most in the world. And I don't want to show up late for my dinner with them. So go ahead." He makes a gesture slightly similar to the gesture one makes when, in a fistfight, they want to indicate to their opponent to come closer so they can give them a good slug. "Ask me your relevant and intelligent questions."

There is a moment of silence. Lucas Giraut has never heard of anyone named Commissioner Farina. Not in relation to his father or his father's arrest. The silence that has fallen over the Meeting Room allows the amalgam of female laughter and dance music to filter through from the Main Floor of The Dark Side of the Moon.

"Where's Bob Marley?" asks Aníbal Manta finally, his enormous arms crossed over the front of his suit and his eyes a bit squinted. In that way that Aníbal Manta squints his eyes and gathers his features together slightly when he is dealing with matters that challenge his ability to obtain a good perspective on what is going on around him. "Did they really *nab* him?"

Mr. Bocanegra stares at Aníbal Manta with an expression that seems to suggest that he's trying to decide if Manta's question meets the requirements he has just put forward.

"It seems," he says, "that Bob Marley has had a small streak of *bad luck*. And it's quite possible that he's going to have *another* streak of bad luck when I catch up with him. Then he may join our mission. If there's anything left of him, of course. More questions?"

Saudade raises his hand. Bocanegra's face reflects a certain degree of surprise.

"I don't mind working with Russians," says Saudade with a frown, and crosses his arms in a way that perhaps unconsciously and perhaps not imitates the way Aníbal Manta's arms are crossed. Manta is seated behind and definitely falls outside of his visual field. "Or with any kind of strange people. But I don't like working with Piece of Shit Rich Kids that don't know how to tie their own shoes. I'm talking about Mr. Rich Kid Esquire." He makes a gesture with his eyebrows raised in Lucas Giraut's direction. "I mean, I don't know who you are, Sir Mr. Rich Kid Esquire, but to tell you the truth, I get the impression that you're a shit-for-brains rich kid who has no fucking idea of how people like us do things. And that you're gonna shit your pants when the going gets rough." He looks at Aníbal Manta. Aníbal Manta looks away. "You all know what I'm talking about."

There is a long moment of silence. Bocanegra's expression seems to indicate that Saudade's question definitely does not meet with the previously established requirements of relevance and intelligence.

CHAPTER 10

Italian Academy Basketball Club

"My mother embarrasses me," says Valentina Parini, seated in a genuinely prepubescent posture on the bench of the basketball court of Barcelona's Italian Academy. She isn't seated with her back erect in the modest and elegant carriage of a postpubescent girl. Instead her legs hang down and her body leans slightly forward and she grabs the edge of the bench with her hands. "I mean when she's looking for a boyfriend to marry her. People can't tell, but I can. I can always tell." She turns to look at Lucas Giraut, who is standing with his hands in his pockets a few steps behind the basketball court bench. Dressed in a burgundy herringbone stitch Lino Rossi suit. In addition to Valentina Parini, there are three other girls sitting on the bench. Alternately paying attention to the game that is taking place on the basketball court and the conversation that Valentina is having with Lucas. "Like the other night. Sometimes she embarrasses me so much it makes me want to punch her."

Lucas Giraut nods. Marcia Parini's behavior during the last part of Fanny Giraut's Unnumbered Birthday party was pretty much the same as it always is toward the end of every Giraut family party she's ever been invited to. Rubbing rounded parts of her anatomy against the anatomy of various male guests, hanging with both arms from the neck of said guests and speaking into their ears while kissing them on the cheeks.

Giraut watches as the center from the home team, a tall plump girl, throws the ball vigorously against the opposing team's backboard. The ball bounces off the backboard and forces several players on both teams to crouch instinctively and cover their heads with their hands. The referee blows her whistle emphatically and gestures with her arms. The visiting team is a team from downtown made up of racially diverse girls with no uniforms. Some of the prepubescent and postpubescent girls from the downtown team chew gum with cruel expressions on their faces. Many of them have scabs on their knees and wear faded T-shirts of bands for teenage girls. One of the girls from the downtown team wears a faded black T-shirt of a metal band. The girls from the home team, including Valentina Parini, are impeccably dressed in uniforms with green T-shirts that read "ITALIAN ACADEMY BAS-KETBALL CLUB BARCELONA" on the front, white shorts and red socks that come all the way up to their unbruised knees.

The coach of the home team shouts something from the sidelines of the basketball court, putting her hands along both sides of her mouth and making signs to one of the players on the home team defense to sit on the bench.

"Parini," says the home team coach, who wears her hair short and seems to have something below her nose that slightly resembles a mustache. "You replace Adelfi." She looks at Lucas Giraut with clear displeasure, which doesn't seem to be based on Giraut's presence behind the players' bench but rather on the mere fact that people like Lucas Giraut exist in the same cosmos as she and her players do. "If your father doesn't mind, of course."

There is a second of silence. Some of the players from the downtown team watch the scene with their hands on their hips and spit on the floor of the basketball court.

"He's not her father," says one of the players seated on the home team bench.

"She has no father," says another of the home team players. "Her father left."

The player named Adelfi limps to the sideline of the school basketball court. She grabs the towel held out by one of her teammates and uses it to wipe her forehead and underarms. Someone mists one of her knees with a medicinal spray.

"I'm not her father," explains Giraut to the mostly hostile faces that watch him from the bench, the playing field and the portable stands located at his back. "I'm a friend of the family's. I live in the apartment upstairs," he says, and the faces just look at him with neutral expressions.

"He's not my father." Valentina Parini looks at the coach with a frown behind her green plastic glasses. "And I don't want to go out. I'm the worst player on the team. I'm the worst player on *any* team. Every time I go out everyone laughs at me. Adelfi can play better than me even if they cut off her leg." She shrugs her shoulders. "Why don't you kick me off the team?"

The players waiting on the basketball court cross their arms or put their hands on their hips and spit on the ground or bounce the ball while they roll their eyes and look at each other with bored expressions. The basketball players on the female section of the Italian Academy of Barcelona's Basketball Club are tacitly divided into two categories based on whether they have breasts or not. The players with breasts move with a discreet but firm elegance and modesty as of yet unknown to their teammates without breasts. The breasts of the basketball players with breasts move in directions related to the movement of the ball and the game in progress. They sway vertically in parallel to the ball's bouncing on the ground. They are projected forward when a player with breasts throws the ball forward and they go back in toward her thoracic cavity each time she receives a pass. When a player with breasts jumps to slam dunk, her breasts are projected gloriously up toward the heavens.

"*I would love* to kick you off the team," says the mustachioed coach. "*I dream about it.* But your school psychologist says that you're so nutso that if we kicked you off you'd lose it completely." She makes a sign with her hand to the referee, who is examining the cuticles of one hand without taking the whistle out of her mouth. "So move your rear end and get into your position."

The game resumes with Valentina Parini in the left wing position for the home team. A few steps away from where Lucas Giraut is watching the game with his hands in his pockets. Barely any of the players on the downtown team have breasts. The players on the downtown team are smaller in size and some of them are black and have Asian or Latin American features. The center for the downtown team is a tall Chinese girl with chipped teeth. The Chinese player slam dunks into the home team's basket and smiles with a look of true Asian cruelty in her chipped smile. Five minutes later a visiting player slams Valentina with her shoulder in such a way that Valentina and Valentina's glasses fly across the floor in opposite directions. Someone shouts out that someone should step on that retard's glasses. Valentina Parini walks calmly back to the bench.

"Everybody thinks you're my mother's boyfriend." Valentina sits on the end of the bench closest to Lucas Giraut. The player named Adelfi goes out onto the court again, in the midst of a small ovation from the spectators that fill the portable stands. Mostly players' parents. "And my mother is in love with you. I've been noticing. Analyzing the things she does. I don't care that they say I'm too young to understand these things. And I can see things that other people don't. Like in the books I read, for example." She takes off her glasses and examines the damage they've suffered with a focused expression that wrinkles up her tiny nose and makes her look even more like a tree-dwelling monkey. "Do you want to marry my mom? This is a serious question."

Lucas Giraut raises his eyebrows and strokes his hairless chin with two fingers. In someone else, the gesture could pass for reflective or even calculating, but in his face it only seems to transmit a certain distracted perplexity. The rest of the substitute players seated on the bench have stopped paying attention to what's happening on the court and are now openly staring at Valentina Parini and Lucas Giraut.

"She wants to marry you," says Valentina. "I've known for a long time. Remember the other night? At the end of the party? When that waiter carried her out to the street to throw up and then we stuck her in the taxi?"

Giraut searches through his memories of the trip home after the last of his mother's Unnumbered Birthday parties. The moment in the taxi when Marcia Parini began slapping frenetically on the back window with the palm of her hand. The fact that neither Valentina nor he himself were able to identify said slaps as the universal sign made by all drunks in taxis who need to get out to vomit again. The taxi driver's anger as Valentina pulled her mother out of the back door still drooling vomit and how quickly the taxi driver's anger disappeared when Lucas Giraut opened his wallet and put all the bills it had inside into his hand. And finally the walk home through the dark alleys of the

Gothic Neighborhood with their smell of urine, with Valentina and he himself carrying Marcia by the armpits, and Valentina carrying her mother's purse and high heels in her free hand. The three creating a scene that any passerby would naturally assume to be a family scene. And most likely, in the end, it did have some genuinely family element to it.

"The signs are clear." The girl puts her glasses back on and wipes off the dust that her fall has left on the sleeveless green shirt of her uniform. "She doesn't kiss you. She doesn't grab you by the neck and nibble on your earlobe. With you she doesn't act like she does with all the others. And when we're at home together she talks about you. Not all the time, but a lot." She shrugs her shoulders. "Those are the signs. So it's up to you to decide if you want to marry her."

A player in the green shirt of the Italian Academy's Basketball Club is twisting on the floor beneath the visiting team's basket with her hands on her crotch. Beside her a black player from the visiting team has her hands held high in the universal sign for innocence in sports sign language. Someone says something insulting about the defensive style of the multiracial team from downtown and a moment later the visiting player who was insulted has one of the home team players firmly locked in a neck grip. The home team player lets out a moo, her face purple and her eyes open very wide. The rest of the impeccably tricolored players watch the scene with reverential fear. The referee blows her whistle emphatically and gestures a lot with her arms.

"Sixteen days till the worldwide release of Stephen King's new novel." Valentina takes advantage of the fact that the rest of the players have shifted their focus to the multiracial struggle that is taking place beneath the visiting team's basket. "And I want my mom to let me go to the release party. In that big bookstore downtown. They leave the bookstore open until midnight and fans can go and buy a special edition. The *first* edition. But so she'll let me go I have to be good and act like I'm an idiot in front of the teachers and show up for basketball games and all that. I don't know how I'm going to stand it." She makes an impotent gesture. "This is torture. Everybody laughs at me. The teachers more than anybody. I could kill all these stupid girls, like that." She snaps her fingers. "At least these public school girls know how *to fight*."

Giraut stares with a blank face at an overweight girl who seems to have been listening to their conversation from the bench. The overweight girl looks away as quickly as she can. With a slightly offended face. The attitude of Valentina Parini's classmates toward Valentina Parini has been mainly an attitude of distrust and mockery and general lack of respect since Valentina read aloud in Spanish class an essay titled "The Prayer of Those Who Have No Father and No Mother." Which is to say, since what is known as the Spanish Class Mishap. Since then, the frequency of taunts and nicknames has increased. Along with the good-humored tortures in the school playground. And the comparisons with physically grotesque or insane film and television characters. Valentina Parini has recited The Prayer of Those Who Have No Father and No Mother on various occasions to Lucas Giraut during their meetings at dusk in the courtyard of the old ducal palace in the Gothic Neighborhood.

"Perhaps you should rethink your idea," says Giraut with a pensive expression. "I mean about reading your novel at the talent show. It could be dangerous. I think that by this point they must be watching you very closely. And don't say anything to your school psychologist about what you're writing. Or maybe tell her you're writing some other novel. One where you don't kill all your basketball teammates. One where there's no blood, or final massacre or heads bursting open or anything like that." He shrugs his shoulders. "When psychologists hear those kinds of things, you're done for."

The overweight girl is staring at them with her plump face. Shaking her head and gathering her features in an expression of intense displeasure. Some of the faces nearby turn to pay attention to the conversation taking place near the bench.

"You are horrible," she says to Valentina Parini, pointing at her with an accusatory finger. "And so is this man. And I'm going to tell the principal everything."

Valentina Parini readjusts her green plastic kid's glasses on her tiny nose with her index finger and gives the overweight girl an obscene gesture of an openly sexual nature. A gesture that any spectator would consider absolutely inappropriate to someone her age.

CHAPTER 11

Paintings of Deer

The dome of St. Peter's basilica and the vaguely extraterrestrial rooftops of the Vatican are outlined against the gray backdrop of the morning sky on the other side of the window of the hostel in the Piazza Navona where Aníbal Manta and Juan de la Cruz Saudade are staying under false names. Aníbal Manta lets his gaze wander through the room: starting at the paintings of deer that decorate the walls, then moving on to the frayed bedspreads on the two single beds and finally to the figures of Saudade and the Italian whore kneeling on the ground giving him a blow job accompanied by expert hand movements on his penis and testicles. Saudade's powder blue and white Umbro sweatpants are wrinkled around his ankles. Saudade, reflects Manta, has never been good at conversations that involve any kind of emotional communication. That's one of the reasons, perhaps the main one, why he's never liked Saudade. In the two years that he's known him, every time they have to do some job together—and their profession usually leads to long periods of forced cohabitation—every attempt that Manta has made to establish that kind of communication has been met by Saudade looking around distractedly. Or picking at his cuticles or nodding in a purely mechanical way while contemplating select parts of nearby female anatomies. Manta closes his eyes and tries to concentrate on the blow job the second Italian whore is giving him, as she kneels on the floor in front of his legs with his pants down around the ankles.

"There are some people that go around saying it's stupid to eat ice cream in the winter." Saudade has his fingers tangled in the dyed hair of his prostitute and the way her head rocks back and forth suggests that Saudade could be rhythmically pushing her head toward his crotch. "I have just one thing to say to those people—" He makes a theatrical pause. "*Fuck off.* Right now, I'd say, it's winter." He points with his chin to the vaguely extraterrestrial rooftops beyond the window. "And look at all the ice cream shops around here. Why are all those people sitting around wolfing down ice cream? Because they're total idiots? No, sir." He shakes his head with a wise expression on his face. "It's about taste. The taste is the key. In this city they make the best ice cream I've had in my fucking life and the taste is the same in the winter or the summer. As far as I know. In any case, ice cream lasts better in the winter, it doesn't start to melt before you get a chance to finish it. Ha." Saudade leans his head back and closes his eyes in that clichéd way porn actors do when they've got a woman kneeling in front of them giving them a blow job. It makes Manta a bit nervous that Saudade's penis, even when largely hidden by the prostitute's face and dyed hair, is clearly enormous. Certainly much larger than Manta's own penis. Manta's penis, even though it can't be considered small according to the standard measurements of the average adult penis, does *seem* proportionally small in relation to the size of Manta's body and the white soft sphere that is his belly. "I'm not saying that I'd rather be sitting here all day eating ice cream instead of being at home with my kid," continues Saudade, with his fingers tangled in the prostitute's hair. "But *fuck*. This is the best ice cream I've eaten in my life. That's one thing they've got in this country. In this *culture*. These sons of bitches make such good ice cream that I could stay here for a few days just for the ice cream."

The paintings that hang on the walls depict bucolic scenes in idyllic forest settings featuring herds of deer. There is something unpleasant about those paintings, thinks Manta. They all have dark red skies, skies that attempt to be dusky but are overwhelmingly unrealistic and look like some sort of postnuclear tragedy skies. The deer are out of proportion and some of them look more like dogs or other animals with deer antlers. The situation in which Manta finds himself right now, including the fact of having his pants at his ankles in a room where a prostitute is fellating Saudade's enormous, vigorous penis, gives him a familiar sensation of emotional stress. Traditionally he has never had any problem admitting that the stigma of his looks, along with his fondness for Marvel superheroes, makes up the historical basis of said sensation. A fondness that infantilizes him in the eyes of the world.

"Ice cream has *always* made me hard," says Saudade, who has begun to move his hips back and forth to the rhythm of the head movements of his prostitute. "When I was a cop, we used to go to the whorehouses on Balmes Street," he says. "Me and my partner. We used to show them our badges and act a little tough, you know. We weren't threatening or anything." He shrugs his shoulders. "We just wanted to make them a little nervous. We'd have a few drinks and we'd pick out the hottest whores. There was one, I don't remember her name. One of those Russian whores, I guess, but not the skinny kind. Kind with big tits." He raises his hands to his chest and mimes grabbing some invisible tits. "You'd sit on a great fucking sofa and they'd bring you the whore with her legs spread on a cart with wheels, like the kind they use to bring room service in hotels. With enormous scoops of ice cream on each tit. A couple different flavors with a cherry on top. And more ice cream and chocolate sauce on her pussy and ass." He sighs with a vaguely nostalgic expression as the prostitute's head movements, now freed from the hands that grabbed her hair, become quicker and more precise. "Since then I can't control myself. Every time I see an ice cream sundae, I just see it and bam!" He punches the palm of his hand, making the whore jump. "Hard as a rock."

Manta observes the brown envelope with the corporate logo of Arnold Layne Experts and the photographs strewn on the frayed bedspread. Since he has known him, Saudade has shown himself completely incapable of developing conversations that involve any type of emotional communication. Conversations like the ones that take place in most relationships of male camaraderie and professional friendship. The photographs strewn on the bedspread show a very dark man with plastic-framed glasses and a turtleneck sweater. His angular features and furtive expression in the photos, as he looks around worriedly and gets into a black car with tinted windows, make him look somewhat like a politically exiled pianist. Or perhaps an introverted chess player from the Eastern bloc. The brown corporate envelope the photographs came out of has a name written on it in capital letters in Mr. Bocanegra's unmistakably forceful handwriting: RAYMOND PANAKIAN. Manta closes his eyes again and tries to concentrate: in spite of several minutes of expert fellatio, his penis seems to have lost the desired degree of erection.

"My psychologist says I should tell you that I feel like you never listen to me," says Aníbal Manta, looking out of the corner of his eye at Saudade, joined at the waist to the swaying figure of the prostitute. "He says that I have to talk to you directly and be completely honest. That that's the only way I can solve my problems with you. He says that I have to explain how I have the feeling that you never pay attention to me and that that makes me feel bad. That I already feel bad enough because I'm big and fat and I like comic books. You're my work partner and my psychologist told me very clearly that I have to take the bull by the horns and be brave and tell you all the things you do that make me feel bad."

Manta stops when he establishes that Saudade isn't listening to him. At this point, it not only seems clear to Manta that Saudade's inability to concentrate betrays a classic case of attention deficit disorder. It also seems clearer and clearer that his colleague's sexual compulsion is a subconscious mechanism to avoid facing the here and now. Especially when that here and now involves a conversation with elements of serious emotional exchange. Now Saudade moves the prostitute's head away from his penis and indicates to her through signs that she should turn around and lean forward. The prostitute turns around with a neutral expression. She wipes her lips with the back of her hand and leans forward with her back to Saudade. Manta feels a stab of emotional stress when Saudade's enormous and vigorous penis skewers the prostitute with dyed hair from behind. With incredible ease, it seems to Manta.

"My kid has one of those things you make ice cream with," says Saudade, charging furiously with his hips against the prostitute's ass, which is soft and pale and covered in freckles. "Not one of those cheap ones where you put in some powder and mix it with water and then you freeze it with a little stick inside." He pauses and wipes the sweat off his forehead with the back of his hand before resuming the onslaught. The prostitute exudes professional sounds of sexual satisfaction. "It's one of those things that make real ice cream. The creamy kind. You can put in chocolate shavings or whatever you want. I gave it to him a couple of years ago, for his birthday I think. The kid likes ice cream." He nods, satisfied. "Like his dad."

Aníbal Manta's penis still hasn't achieved a satisfactory erection, and the prostitute kneeling in front of him finds herself forced to pause in her fellation to grab it with her hand and give it some energetic shakes. The paintings of deer infiltrate Manta's visual field obstinately. With their wrong-colored skies and their out-of-proportion deer that stare at him from the walls looking like dogs or other animals in costumes. The transition between Aníbal Manta's moments of severe emotional stress and his fits of rage, along with the control mechanisms he's had to develop in order to repress said fits, have become, over time, the main focus of his therapy sessions. The same fits that he began to experience in the school yard when he was a boy of elephantine dimensions whom the other kids called The Thing. The Thing, according to his therapist's explanations, is a superhero grotesque in appearance but endowed with solid emotional values and colossal strength who is absolutely crucial to the Fantastic Four. To the functioning of the Fantastic Four as a supergroup with balanced superpowers. Those are the elements of The Thing's identity which make his therapist consider him a superhero that embodies the difficulty and pathos and nobility of Aníbal Manta's life. Now Manta closes his eyes and tries to concentrate on those ideas of nobility and difficulty in spite of the fact that the professional noises of sexual satisfaction coming from Saudade's prostitute have turned into shrieks of pleasure that are not strictly professional. Manta's prostitute pauses, raises her head and asks him something in Italian.

"Don't worry, darling," Manta says to her, kneeling to retrieve the pants at his ankles and pull them up. The idea that The Thing has no penis beneath the blue underwear of his Fantastic Four uniform flits around his brain like a malicious little animal. "Go with those two if you want."

Saudade plows into the prostitute with dyed hair, her hands now against the wall, making all the furniture and the paintings of deer tremble. Aníbal Manta lights a cigarette.

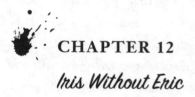

CHAPTER 12

Iris Without Eric

The set of the shoot of the second low-budget production featuring Penny DeMink is filled with those elements designed to represent opulence and sophistication that one finds on the sets of low-budget productions where no one, from the production designer to the viewer in his hotel room, seems to have ever had any experience of opulence or sophistication. Adult films that will never see the light of theaters or ever be published in DVD format. Tapes with generic titles destined to fill the late-night loops of the last television channels in airport hotels for businessmen. Films devoid of the glamour and genuine excitement of the real pornographic industry. Without real sex acts between sex goddesses and Olympic studs. Where slow motion is a way to fill time and close-ups are a way to distract attention from the lack of budget for set design.

"Get closer to her," says the director in a bored tone. In that same bored tone one uses to talk to one's mother or sister while paying attention to what's happening on TV. "And put your hand on her ass, fuck. Don't be afraid. Her ass won't bite you."

The back wall of the set is covered with a moth-eaten curtain that someone took from a bankrupted theater. It's a detail of the set that no one seems to have bothered to justify in terms of the plot. As often happens with this kind of set. There are statues that look vaguely classical depicting nude women in positions close to sexual ecstasy. There is a statue of a cherub that emits a parabolic stream of water from its tiny penis. There is a canopy bed and someone has attached what look like sequins to the gauzy curtains that hang from it. There doesn't seem to be any plot justification for the sequins. The charmingly coarse signs of opulence found in low culture. Out of the darkest sewers of the film industry. And in the middle of it all, standing beside the canopy bed, Iris Gonzalvo caresses her svelte neck with a melancholy face. Her white flesh glows beneath the lights. Like a heavenly body illuminating its own crown of rotating debris. Turning it all into mere reflections and shadows of its glow. With her Rococo-style powdered wig and her high lace-up boots and her corset that constricts and raises her breasts on which someone has painted a beauty mark with eyeliner pencil. Magnificent in spite of the infinite clumsiness of her character portrayal or maybe *precisely* because of it.

"Are you deaf?" the director asks Iris Gonzalvo. With his eyebrows raised in an incredulous expression. Then he turns to his assistant. "Is she deaf? Am I not talking loud enough? Where did we get this girl from?"

The director's assistant shrugs her shoulders and pats the pockets of her photographer's vest as if the answer to the director's questions might be in one of them. In addition to the photographer's vest, the director's assistant wears combat pants and a stopwatch hanging from a chain around her neck and a pocket protector filled with pens and one of those baseball hats with a jokey message.

"I think that she's one of the girls the boss hooked us up with." The director's assistant shrugs her shoulders. With her lips slightly pursed. "I'm not sure. They all end up looking the same to me."

Iris Gonzalvo is standing beside the canopy bed. In front of a dark-haired young woman of approximately her same age and height. They both wear powdered wigs and period makeup and are dressed in very tight corsets and lace-up thigh-high boots. They both wear thong underwear that exposes their Brazilian waxes. The only difference between their equally clumsy character portrayals seems to be chromatic.

"Let's try it again," says the director. With that expression of tried patience that consists in massaging one's eyelids with the thumb and index finger while shaking one's head slightly. Seated on his chair with a fabric back. "Let's see. What's your name again?"

"Penny," she says, with that voice of hers that is both smooth and gravelly. Filled with sharp edges that make up for her lack of lung power.

"Very good, Penny. Let's not waste any more time. The script says: 'Girl one grabs girl two sensually and kisses her and brings her over to the bed and they both sit on the bed. Cut.' You are girl one. So you have to grab girl two sensually and kiss her and all the rest. You understand?"

Iris Gonzalvo nods. She scowls almost imperceptibly. Her skin is so white that it's almost iridescent. Too bright and magnetic to be real.

The director signals to the guy in charge of the clapper board. The director's assistant calls for action. The guy in charge of the clapper board claps it and everything seems to stop. The director, along with his assistant and the cameraman and the lighting and sound technicians and the guys in charge of the spotlights and of holding up microphones in exact locations, all create some sort of a completely immobile and vaguely baroque tableau. Inside of which a second tableau comes to life, the one made up of the two young women clumsily portraying eighteenth-century ladies with thong underwear and Brazilian waxes who are about to begin an interlude of lesbian sex. The transition between the outer tableau and the inner tableau looks like those trompe l'oeil visual tricks in puzzle magazines.

Iris Gonzalvo takes a step toward her costar. She puts an arm around her waist and brings her mouth close to hers. She places her other hand on the nape of her neck and caresses the soft tangled hairs that stick out from beneath her powdered wig. She is about to kiss her when the director's shout interrupts her approach.

"What *in the hell* is wrong with you?" The director slaps his copy of the script in exasperation. "Didn't I tell you to put your hand *on her ass? On her ass!* And that's a sensual kiss? Doesn't look sensual to me. To me it looks *depressing.* Look, I'm depressed." He makes a face that's hard to decipher. "And what's wrong with your face? You don't feel well? Because that's the face I make when I have *heartburn.*"

Iris Gonzalvo turns somewhat to look at the director with a defiant face. A face so full of defiance and contempt that for a moment the director and the other members of the crew on the low-budget production stare at her in terror. Someone even goes so far as to take a terrified step back.

"I'm *acting,*" she says to the director. "Trying to live the situation as if it were real. I'm sure there are other ways that she and I can communicate besides putting a hand on her *ass.*"

The director stares at her for a moment with a perplexed face. Then he frowns. Then he stands up. His subordinates seem to move slightly away from him in that incredibly subtle way that subordinates have of giving the impression that they're moving away from their furious superiors without really budging from their spots. The director's face is literally red with rage. Especially in the upper part of his cheeks.

"*Communicating?*" he says. "And how the fuck do you plan on communicating? She only speaks Polish. We had to use fucking sign language to explain to her that she didn't have to do an *enema* before the shoot." He moves toward his assistant, who seems to have backed up a few steps more, or perhaps shrunk in size, and who is now hugging a copy of the shooting plan in such a way that any armchair fan of psychology could see is a clearly defensive gesture. "I don't care if the boss got you this job. Find me another girl the same size. And get this one out of my sight. Send her upstairs to the boss." He rolls his eyes. "I can't believe that someone can be *incapable* of acting in a movie where the only thing they have to do is show their ass."

Five minutes later, Iris Gonzalvo is dressed in a bathrobe and seated in the production company owner's office. Stroking her recently washed and still wet hair with an absent gesture. With her face clean. Taking pensive drags on a cigarette.

The owner of the production company making the low-budget film Iris was just fired from sniffs two lines of cocaine from the inner reflective glass surface of some sort of cigarette box. He lifts his face from the table and inhales sharply. He's a muscular guy with a shirt that's too small for him and waxed eyebrows. His eyebrows are waxed in that way that used to be associated with homosexuality before male cosmetic treatments became commonplace. The owner of the production company massages one wing of his nose with his fingertip.

"I don't know if I can keep giving you work," he says. With the concerned expression of someone who holds all the power. "People say that you cause problems. And honestly, I think so, too. What do you expect? That some Hollywood producer is going to see one of your films and discover your enormous talent and hire you? If you're very lucky I can get you an audition to do a porn film, but honestly . . ." He looks her up and down. A clear note of skepticism seems to have been added to the mix of concern and absolute power. "I don't think you're that hot."

Iris Gonzalvo looks up, scandalized.

"Of course I'm hot," she says. "I'm *incredibly hot*."

"Not hot enough. And you're old. You must be twenty-five years old."

"I'm nineteen."

There is a moment of tense silence. The boss's office at the production company for hotel cable movies is one of those corporate offices where everything conveys the idea of impermanence. The only furniture is a table and two chairs. The computer on top of the table is a laptop. There is no decoration of any kind. The light comes from bulbs without lamp fixtures. The walls haven't been plastered since the last occupant left, so you can still see holes and marks where the wall was drilled to hold up furniture that is no longer there. The precise term in the jargon of that specialized market that refers to the type of films prepared and filmed in the industrial space where Iris is sitting in a robe smoking is not "low-budget film." The precise term is "ultra-low-budget film." Of which ideally two or three are shot a day. To reduce costs in rental equipment.

"Listen," says the head of production. He makes a weary face designed to show that he is willing to be patient and agreeable beyond the requirements of his position. "It's fine to be ambitious, and if you feel young, that's great. That means you are on the inside. But you have to be realistic. We both know why you're here. You're here because your boyfriend hooks me up with coke and does a little job for me once in a while. Even though it's not nice to say that." He shrugs his shoulders in a self-exonerating gesture. "So okay. If I see some change in your attitude, I don't see why we can't stay in touch. In spite of the fact that your boyfriend hasn't answered my calls this week and owes me money. But you and I are another story. The only thing I ask is a small gesture on your part." He separates his thumb and index finger a little to make the universal sign of things small in size. Then he looks at his wristwatch. "I think we have one of the sets downstairs free."

There is a moment of silence.

"After all, no one's going to know," adds the head of production. "I mean it's like nothing ever happened."

Iris Gonzalvo stands up purposefully. She leans forward a bit, above the low-budget table comprised of two sawhorses and an unvarnished top, and before the boss has time to say anything she puts out her cigarette on his cheek. With a skillful wrist movement that is both energetic and vaguely circular.

The head of production's scream echoes through the entire industrial building.

CHAPTER 13

Apartment 13

The same day that Aníbal Manta and Saudade arrive in Rome, Lucas Giraut waits for closing time at the offices of LORENZO GIRAUT, LTD. He waits for all the workers to leave the building. Then he takes off the jacket of his cobalt blue Lino Rossi suit and loosens his tie and begins unscrewing one by one all the lightbulbs in his office on the mezzanine. The only lamp that he leaves on is the one right above the Italian Louis XV–style *cartonnier* that he uses as a desk. He puts the lightbulbs away in a cardboard box and puts the box in one of the not-secret drawers of the *cartonnier*. All the employees have gone and the security gates that look like bars on a medieval castle have been lowered, giving the building its ferociously protected off-hours look. The alarms are turned on. The lights are turned off except for the pilot lights connected to an independent generator and the sole lightbulb that Lucas Giraut has left on in his office. The circumstances, decides Lucas Giraut as he sticks a flashlight into his pants pocket, are propitious to begin his Filial Investigation of Apartment 13.

Lucas Giraut goes up the stairs that lead from the mezzanine to the upper floor of the headquarters of LORENZO GIRAUT, LTD. A bulge in the shape of a flashlight can be seen in his pocket. During the last twenty years barely anything has been changed in this part of the building. The doors have been repainted several dozen times. The walls have been replastered and have changed color. The technological advances in terms of alarms are visible in the increasingly weaponlike look of the alarm box models. Increasingly more *alarming*. The locks on the metal doors have been replaced by numerical code readers with tiny little red and green lights to signal, respectively, the introduction of erroneous or correct codes.

Giraut arrives at the top of the stairs and the hallway lights up automatically in response to a movement sensor. He looks up and makes a distracted gesture with his hand toward the camera that's filming his movements from the roof. The hallway of the upper floor is one of those hallways you find in industrial warehouses. With concrete walls and floor. With numbered metal doors on both sides and with bare bulbs hanging from the ceiling. The last door of the concrete hallway, around the last bend, is the door to Apartment 13. Vague images of endless hallways and rooms crossed by fleeting silhouettes come to Giraut's mind. Memories of childhood notebooks filled with sketches of movable panels that open onto secret passageways between the walls. Finally he stops in front of the door marked with the number thirteen. He introduces the numerical code and waits for the tiny green light that means that the right code has been entered.

The Filial Investigation Operation has begun.

Lucas Giraut turns on the flashlight and the beam of light runs over the inside of Apartment 13. Dust covers the floor and all the furniture. He closes the door behind him. The apartment consists of a room with a double bed stuck to the wall, a television, a built-in closet, and a couple of dressers. A door at the back of the room leads to a tiny bathroom with a shower that barely has room for one person. There are no windows. None of his father's secret places ever have any windows. Due to an undiagnosed pathology that was referred to within the family as *his window problem.* The air in the room comes from a few vents by the ceiling that are different from the rest of the building's vents and which vaguely resemble half-open mouths.

Lucas Giraut sits on the bed and runs a hand along the dusty bedspread. Sitting in this space without any natural light or windows somehow comforts him. In a certain way, he has always believed that he understood what was happening to his father. The secret inner mechanics of his difficulty with windows and daylight. What lay hidden behind his so-called window problem. The feeling of calm. That feeling of power you get from locking the world out completely.

Seated on the dusty bed, Lucas Giraut moves the flashlight beam over the room's walls and furniture. It's strange that he spent his whole childhood filling notebooks with drawings and notes about Apartment 13. Recording his recurring dreams about that apartment. Perfectly detailed dreams accompanied by all sorts of explanations and diagrams. The first phase of drawings, from his preteen years, depicted Apartment 13 as a complex system of rooms and hallways with varying layouts. According to the annotations, the apartment had no windows and the walls were covered with red velvet curtains. The annotations indicated that most of the rooms had crystal chandeliers hanging from the ceiling. And wing chairs with extensions that folded out to rest your feet on and freestanding gold ashtrays beside the arms. The large majority of butts in said ashtrays were cigar butts. There also seemed to be coatracks all around, filled with jackets and coats. Hundreds of coats, both women's and men's. Coats accompanied by hats and by canes and by other old-fashioned garments that Lucas Giraut as a child was unable to identify. Nor could he understand why there were so many coats and jackets.

After half an hour of Lucas's rummaging around, all the contents of Apartment 13's closet and drawers are carefully laid out on the dusty bedspread. Lucas Giraut has separated out to one side and classified into three groups those objects that he judges most relevant to his search:

1. A dozen cassette tapes of old British rock from the seventies. *In Search of Space* and *Space Ritual* by Hawkwind. *Tales from Topographic Oceans* by Yes, *The Dark Side of the Moon* by Pink Floyd, and *Islands* by King Crimson.

2. A postcard showing the Brighton Marine Palace and Pier with the strange domes and towers of its amusement park. Written on the back it says: "COMMEMORATIVE ACTS OF THE FIRST INTERNATIONAL CONFERENCE OF THE DOWN WITH THE SUN SOCIETY. ENGLAND (WE THINK), 1970." And another postcard, which shows a pink hot-air pig floating over an industrial sky, which says: "THE DOWN WITH THE SUN SOCIETY PROMISES TO PARTY EVERY NIGHT AND SLEEP ALL DAY FOR THE REST OF THEIR LIVES. DOWN WITH THE SUN. SIGNED: THE DOWN WITH THE SUN SOCIETY." The two postcards are written in large, loopy script surrounded by drawings of flowers, planets, and moons.

3. An obviously old black-and-white photograph showing three young men about twenty years old with long hair, various styles of facial hair, and clothing that's predominately denim, suede, and leather. The three young men have their arms around each other's shoulders in a gesture of male camaraderie.

Seated on the dusty bedspread, Lucas Giraut takes a cigarette out of his gold cigarette case embossed with his initials and lights it with a pensive expression. The young man on the left side of the photograph is his father. A barely postadolescent version of his father, with a strangely skinny and long version of his father's face with splotches on both cheeks that look like acne outbreaks. The young man in the middle of the photograph wears a leopard-print fur coat that looks strikingly feminine next to the leather and denim jackets of the other two. His face doesn't yet show any signs of balding or of a mustache, but it does show the same ineffable element of cruelty that Lucas Giraut recognizes as Mr. Bocanegra's. The young man to the right of the photograph must be the same age as the other two and also wears his hair long. His, however, is curly as opposed to Lorenzo Giraut's exaggeratedly straight hair and not-yet-balding Mr. Bocanegra's wavy hair. His face is strangely attractive despite not having a particularly harmonious set of features. Lucas turns the photograph over to examine the back. It is blank.

Lucas Giraut's first childhood drawings of Apartment 13 included marks on the apartment's shifting internal geography indicating possible sightings of people. The sightings were never clear enough for him to be sure that they weren't just optical illusions. The most conducive places for those types of sightings were the mirrors and the doorways.

Holding the back end of the flashlight between his teeth, Giraut puts the photograph into his pocket. There is something about the Filial Investigation Operation that gives him an indescribable feeling of indecisiveness. Like the feeling of sitting in front of a magic desk for the first time. Contemplating the apparently normal knobs of its drawers and its apparently normal surfaces and mentally gauging the measurements in search of ghostly spaces. He looks up and examines the walls. The paint that camouflages the plaster that camouflages the concrete. The vents that are different from the other vents in the building, more like defiant mouths. Giraut stands up on the bed and works the vent above it until it comes loose. He places it carefully on the bed and sticks his arm through the ventilation shaft. Feeling around.

With his gaze lost in the distance. In that way that people look out into the distance when they are blindly feeling around in something whose inside they can't see. Finally he pulls something out of the hole. Some kind of book. He pulls it out in a small cloud of dust and he stares at it. In that precise moment the cell phone in his pocket rings.

"Lucas?" says his mother's voice when he answers. In a tone that indicates she's in one of her Moods. A tone of voice like the crunch of a solid roof splitting beneath the weight of a hundred-year-old tree. "What the hell do you think you are doing?" Behind her rhetorical pause, Lucas Giraut can feel her crackling fury in the form of an electric tingling that raises the fine hairs on the back of his neck. "You're my *son*. What I am supposed to do with you?"

In Lucas Giraut's later childhood drawings of Apartment 13, its internal geography became even more complex. The apartment grew in size and for the first time the annotations suggested that it could have several levels, or at least one additional level, located between the ceiling of the apartment and the building's roof. That hypothetical space, based on certain differences between the measurements that Lucas had made on the outside and on the inside of the building, was dubbed the Highly Secret Level.

"Mom?" Lucas blows on the book to get the dust off and examines its black cover. He opens it and looks at the first few pages and recognizes his father's handwriting. The book consists of a succession of accounting entries, with their corresponding dates and amounts. The first dates are from the late seventies. "I'm the *president* of my father's company. I'm the primary stockholder. And that means *I* decide what the strategies are for the International Division." He blinks while still turning the pages of the accounting ledger. "Or for any other division, of course."

"Don't be stupid." Estefanía Giraut's tone of voice during her Moods is powerfully reminiscent of the sound a hundred-year-old tree makes in splitting a solid roof in half and then splitting the floor of the house's upper story, causing the entire structure to collapse. "You're going to meet with Fonseca in your office on Tuesday. And *neither of you* is coming out of that damn office until you've signed the documents for the restructuring plan."

"What about Christmas dinner?" Lucas Giraut turns the pages faster and faster. "You should let me arrange Christmas dinner, Mom. I think I can get fifty guests."

Some of the transactions recorded in the accounting ledger he holds in his hands have the initials K.C. written beside them. The initials are repeated several times on each page and appear on every one of the pages. Some of the amounts that appear beside the initials K.C. are so high that Lucas Giraut feels a touch of vertigo, as if he were looking over the edge of a very deep well and watching as little bits of rubble fall to the bottom.

"I know exactly what you're doing," says Estefanía Giraut. In a tone of voice that makes one think of pieces of broken jet fuselage cleanly splitting solid roofs. "You can't hide anything from me. And I warn you that things always turn out the way I want them to. It's never been any other way. So don't even bother trying," she says conclusively, and the loud crash he hears right before the line is cut off allows Lucas to clearly visualize his mother violently slamming down her office phone.

In his later childhood drawings of Apartment 13, the map of its shifting internal geography began to include discoveries of a different nature. By that point the map took up many pages of childhood notebooks. According to the explanations accompanying the drawings, several movable wall panels, covered by curtains and various furnishing elements, hide secret doors that open onto a secondary system of tunnels located inside the walls. The secondary tunnels, according to the conclusions recorded at the end of that second phase, were the true means of transportation between the various levels and rooms of Apartment 13. A second map superimposed on the first. In none of young Lucas Giraut's dreams, according to the annotations, was there any sighting of Lorenzo Giraut inside Apartment 13. Signs of his presence, however, were extensively catalogued in the drawings, mainly in the form of cigar butts and coats hanging on the coatracks.

In his final drawings, which were much more complex and barely intelligible, it was suggested that the tunnels of Apartment 13 could lead far beyond the physical boundaries of the corporate headquarters of LORENZO GIRAUT, LTD.

CHAPTER 14

Raymond Panakian

"You're a fat fuck and a retard," says Juan de la Cruz Saudade from the door of the corner store in downtown Rome where Aníbal Manta is flipping through Marvel superhero comics translated into Italian. Looking closely at the panels and trying to decipher the accompanying dialogue. "What kind of forty-year-old *man* reads comic books? What does your wife think about you reading comic books all day?" Saudade pauses and eats a spoonful from the cup of vanilla and strawberry ice cream in his hands, leaning on the doorjamb of the store's door and blocking the entrance with his back. "And what does she think of that potbelly so big you can't even see your own cock? Doesn't she complain when you can't find it? But I guess it doesn't matter. She's probably busy screwing the neighbors while you read comic books. She still screwing the neighbors?" He makes a taunting face while brandishing the little ice cream spoon. "What kind of a man *are you*?"

Aníbal Manta continues turning pages at top speed. The reason he's gone into the store and is trying to speed-read all the latest issues of the Marvel superhero comic book collections is his casual discovery that the Italian Marvel collections are *several months* ahead of the Spanish Marvel collections. Spider-Man, X-Men, the Fantastic Four. In Italy they're doing all the things they'll be doing in Spain *several months* from now. The idea is almost too enormous. Aníbal Manta's gaze tries to capture all the information he can in the least possible time. How did Peter Parker get a new job at a *television station*? And how is it possible that the Incredible Hulk has managed to neutralize the radiation that makes him turn green in moments of emotional stress? As hard as he tries, Aníbal Manta can't understand a single line of the Italian dialogue. The owner of the store, a tiny sour-faced Chinese woman, watches Aníbal Manta and Saudade with the same expression she'd have if she were looking at a couple of giant rats that had come into her store and started chowing down on the magazines.

"I guess I'd do the same thing." Saudade finishes his cup of vanilla and strawberry ice cream and throws the empty cup and the little spoon to the ground with a distracted expression. "If my husband was a fat retard that couldn't find his cock and spent all his time reading *comic books*."

Manta is still trying to find clues as to how Wolverine ended up in a high-security government prison when Saudade snatches the comic from his hands. Manta looks up, surprised. Saudade grabs the recent issues of all the collections on the rack of Marvel comic books and puts them all on the store counter along with a fifty-euro note. The Chinese woman picks up the bill with a look of disgust. Saudade takes the change and the comic books and leaves the store.

"What *the fuck* are you doing?" Manta feels that flush coming to his face, the one that always comes to his face moments before the desire to break someone's nose springs to his mind. "I thought we'd already discussed you treating my things with respect. And my *feelings* about my things."

Saudade heads off down the Roman street jammed with people under the midmorning summer sun. Manta manages to follow him by searching out the powder blue and white colors of Saudade's Umbro sweat suit. Occasionally bumping into groups of tourists equipped with sophisticated filming devices and provoking irritated reactions in several languages. The desire to break someone's nose begins to spring to his mind. Aníbal Manta knows perfectly well, since it is one of the main themes of his therapy, that the violence that he employs against others during his fits of rage is actually violence against himself. It's the same idea of oneself-as-one's-worst-enemy that characterizes many of Marvel's tormented superheroes, except that his personal case seems to lack all epic or admirable connotations.

Twenty minutes later, they both stop in front of the building where Raymond Panakian's apartment is located, according to the written instructions inside the brown envelope that Bocanegra gave them. Saudade examines the marble façade with its delicate restored detailing, which depicts nymphs in nightgowns and little overweight angels.

"He's a piece of shit filthy rich guy," he says, and digs some ice cream remains out of his teeth with his finger. "I love sticking it to fancy pants shit for brains rich guys."

Saudade and Manta go up the marble steps that lead to Raymond Panakian's apartment and stop in front of his door. Saudade unlocks the holster he wears hidden beneath his Umbro sweat suit. He closes his hand around the butt of the pistol and rings the bell. The Umbro sweat suit that Saudade wears is the official sweat suit of his favorite soccer club. A minute passes. Saudade and Manta look at each other. Someone is playing a classical melody on a piano in one of the neighboring apartments. Manta takes a set of picklocks out of his pocket and tries several of them in the lock before getting it open. The piano melody advances cheerfully toward an allegro loaded with arpeggios. They both enter and close the door carefully behind them.

"Mr. Fancy Pants?" asks Saudade, addressing the empty apartment. "Where are you, Mr. Filthy Rich Shit for Brains?"

"I told you what my therapist said," says Manta. "About how the things you say make me feel. And be careful. Don't make so much noise."

They both sit in facing armchairs in the living room. Saudade opens a Spider-Man comic book and begins flipping through it distractedly. A clock taller than Aníbal Manta himself fills the room with its rhythmic and vaguely soporific sound. Manta rubs his temples with his fingers and tries to remind himself of the idea that violence toward others is a mask covering violence toward oneself. He tries to remind himself about breaking the link between his emotional stress and his fits of rage and his therapist's oft-expressed conviction that he has the power and the tools to break it.

"What are all these posters?" Saudade points with his head at the wall behind Manta.

Manta turns and looks at the framed posters that cover the walls and which, in spite of being in Italian, are vaguely familiar. One of the posters seems to be a numbered list of twelve maxims.

"They're Alcoholics Anonymous posters," says Manta after a moment. "This guy used to drink everything, even mouthwash, till somebody stuck him in one of those hospitals and they turned him around."

Saudade nods with a neutral expression and returns to his reading. Half an hour passes. Manta reflects on the fact that his therapist often asks him to imagine his power to break said link as a symbolic equivalent to the superpowers of the Marvel superheroes he admires. The truth is that Manta isn't at all amused by his therapist bringing up his fondness for superhero comics. The truth is that he's unable to avoid perceiving a certain condescending and slightly mocking tone in the allusions his therapist makes to Marvel comics. Now Manta grabs a comic from the pile of superhero comics on the small table and tries to concentrate on reading. Saudade has started talking about the shame and disgust inherent in working with a fat piece of shit that reads comics.

"If you don't like soccer you can try tennis," Saudade is saying as he flips through an Incredible Hulk comic. Manta can't help but notice that as Saudade turns the pages he is horribly wrinkling and folding the cover. "I know a place my boss used to play when I was a cop. It would definitely do you good to run a little. It's obvious you have to do *something*. You can't walk around looking like that. Chicks don't like it." He closes the comic book and rolls it up to point it at Manta in a way that no comic book lover would ever roll up anything remotely resembling a comic book. "You think some chick wants to have a fat guy sweating all over her ass? Or wants to wait a half hour for some fat guy to find his cock under his beer belly? If I were you I'd sign up at a gym today. You can come to my gym if you want, but don't tell anyone that you know me. I don't want people to think that I have greasy friends like you. You'll see. Your wife'll quit screwing the neighbors when you lose forty-five pounds. There's nothing wrong with being big. The ladies like big guys, but not fat guys." He shrugs his shoulders and carelessly tosses the comic onto the other comics piled up on the small table. "I go every week for a massage. In the same place my wife goes. The chick is crazy about me. The massage chick, not my wife."

The reason why Aníbal Manta has never joined a gym, in spite of having considered the idea on several occasions when he was younger and having even gotten as far as the door of a gym, is his fear of being taunted and jeered at by all the slim and attractive gym clients. In therapeutic terms, the daily taunts and disdain seem to weigh on him much more than his potbelly. The piano in an apartment nearby is playing a melody that is powerfully reminiscent of the music in those scenes in horror films when something terrible is about to happen. Manta wipes the sweat from his forehead with a handkerchief. He would like to find some nonviolent, and therefore not therapeutically negative, way to tell Saudade to shut his fucking mouth for once and fucking all.

"Like this guy," Saudade is saying, as he points to a character in an Italian Fantastic Four issue. "Why the fuck is he blue? What a load of crap. Have you ever seen a blue guy walking down the street? And this other guy." He snorts and points at another character in a different panel. "This guy is made of *bricks*. And he's wearing underwear. Hey." He examines the panel carefully and lets out a chuckle. "This brick guy looks like you. Did you see?"

Aníbal Manta is well aware, as is anyone in his line of work, that the only really effective forms of personal attack are not heralded by any type of previous warning or maneuver that can give any sort of clue about the attacker's intentions. Which is why the sequence of events that happens next in the living room full of Alcoholics Anonymous posters in Raymond Panakian's apartment in downtown Rome is the following: 1. Aníbal Manta gets up from his armchair and leans over the small table covered with comic books; 2. Aníbal Manta punches Saudade, breaking his nose; 3. Saudade stares at Manta with that expression of perplexity typical of someone who has just had their nose broken so fast that they had no time to do anything; and 4. A stream of blood comes out of Saudade's broken nose. They are both still there, standing in front of each other, Manta stroking his knuckles and Saudade looking at his powder blue and white sweat suit soaked in blood, when the door of the apartment opens and Raymond Panakian appears in the threshold. With his glasses and his turtleneck sweater. With his angular face that looks like a chess player from the Eastern Bloc who's just fled his country to take refuge in the capitalist world.

Panakian stares at the two strangers that are respectively bleeding and stroking their hand in his living room. The two strangers stare at him. The two bags of groceries that Panakian is carrying fall to the floor. The sound of breaking eggs is heard. Manta and Saudade take out their pistols at exactly the same time and point them at him. Panakian raises his hands.

CHAPTER 15

Venus with Mirror

Hannah Linus's commercial gallery is located on an anonymous street uptown, stuck between office blocks, bank headquarters, and corporate buildings. Hannah Linus couldn't care less about the contemporary role of artists and galleries as inner-city colonists and rejuvenators. Just as she couldn't care less about any other fads and trends in the art world. In fact, she is rather proud of the profits that not ever paying attention to trends has yielded her. As she sees it, it is one of those liberating acts that have allowed her to assume control of her life and gradually become more the person that she knows she wants to be. Like when she dumped her first and only boyfriend in high school. Or when, at ten years old, she decided to renounce her parents' religion and wrote a six-page letter to the Bishop of Uppsala detailing the reasons for her decision. Offering arguments against the existence of God and declaring her disappointment with all the hours that she had wasted up to that point in her parish.

Besides her contempt for life's distractions, Hannah Linus considers thoroughness to be another of her talents. In a normal morning of work, she devotes five hours to running the gallery with an hour-long break to do her training exercises. Her glassed-in office on the upper floor of the gallery was designed to optimize productivity. It has the appropriate amount of light. The temperature remains constant. There are no sources of distraction. All the calls are screened, including those of a personal nature. Or they would be if Hannah Linus received any personal calls. But the one feature of her modus operandi that Hannah Linus would single out as essential is the fact that no one interrupts her. All of the workings of Hannah Linus's gallery are designed around the employees not disrupting her except in unavoidable situations.

Which is why that morning, when she hears someone knocking on the glass door of her glassed-in office and she looks up from her computer, she only has to see Raquel's worried face to realize that something is going to interrupt the proper functioning of things. That something is going to violate her sacred precept of not being disrupted.

Hannah Linus signals for Raquel to enter. Raquel is her assistant, whom she holds in as low a professional regard as she does the rest of her local staff. Hannah Linus considers local employees to be unreliable, lacking in initiative and prone to distraction. If it weren't for the technical difficulties inherent in the process, she wouldn't mind importing all of her employees from Sweden.

Raquel enters her office and looks at Hannah Linus, terrified. Instilling respect through fear seems to be one of the few tactics that has worked with the gallery's local staff.

"Yes?"

Hannah Linus begins to tap rhythmically with her pen on the surface of her desk. The way she looks at her assistant not only transmits her irritation at being disturbed, but also her absolute conviction that whatever reason there is behind the interruption is not a valid one. She also decides to look her up and down with a slight expression of disapproval. That's another way that Hannah has of maintaining control over her female employees: choosing employees that are less sexually attractive than she is. Hannah Linus is tall and slim and blond, while Raquel is not very attractive in that way that Hannah Linus finds Spanish women not very attractive: as if someone not terribly proficient had made them, trying to imitate a model of proper beauty. Like failed sketches of moderately pretty women. Topped off with cheap clothes.

"Sorry for the interruption." Raquel twists a curl of chestnut brown hair around her index finger as she speaks. "But there's a man downstairs. In the gallery, I mean. It's not that he's doing anything wrong, but he doesn't seem normal to me. Or to the security guard. He's a little weird, to be honest."

Hannah Linus stares at her fixedly.

"I'm not sure I understand," she says.

Raquel keeps twisting the curl around her finger. It could be a nervous gesture. In any case, Hannah Linus feels an urgent desire to smack her and tell her to stop doing it.

"Well," says the assistant. "Remember last month when that guy slipped in and sat in the middle of the gallery and said he was an artist and that his sitting there was an artistic action and I don't know what else, and in the end we had to call the police?" She shrugs her shoulders. "We're not sure what's going on with this guy. Maybe nothing. But he's a bit suspicious."

Hannah Linus sighs. She looks at her watch. Six minutes to her break. She supposes she could stop now, solve the situation, do her exercises and recoup the six minutes after closing. She takes a last disapproving glance at Raquel's body and attire, and stands up.

Juan de la Cruz Saudade is in the gallery, standing in front of an oil painting from the Bellini school. Holding up his chin on one hand and his elbow with the other. With a frown. Like one of those clichéd depictions of art gallery visitors that one finds in Sunday magazine comic strips. He even wears glasses hanging from a little chain around his neck.

Hannah Linus meets Raquel and the security guard at the foot of the stairs. She looks first at her assistant, then at the guard and finally at Saudade.

"So?" She crosses her arms in an irritable gesture. "What's the problem? I don't see anything strange. He's not doing *anything*."

"That's the problem," says the guard. "He's been like that for almost thirty-five minutes. In front of the *same painting*. In the same position. I swear he hasn't moved a muscle." The guard shakes his head. "I think that he's some other moron like the one last month. He's waiting for us to call the police so he can be in the newspaper."

Hannah Linus has never been afraid of complicated or uncomfortable situations. Even in her student years in Sweden one could see her strength of character reflected in other people's faces. In their respectful and uncertain expressions. And in the vaguely stammering way that people addressed her. Those reactions never made her uncomfortable. Although they meant she was condemned to exclusion from the circles of friendship and camaraderie she saw around her. But that was the price to pay for being who she was, she said to herself. For getting the best grades. For being the perfect daughter and the employee of the month, every month. And it was in complicated situations where others withdrew that she could take a proud step forward and shine in all her magnificence. Hannah Linus from Uppsala. The absolute queen of the World of Hannah Linus.

Now she uncrosses her arms and walks across the gallery. Under the gaze of the paintings that make up the exhibition of sixteenth-century oil paintings. Some of the court members and peasants and mythological figures that populate the oil paintings seem to look at her with terrified expressions as she crosses her own gallery with a frown.

"Good morning," she says to Juan de la Cruz Saudade when she reaches his side. "Have you consulted our price list?"

Saudade stares at her with an amused look of surprise. For a moment they both remain that way, looking at each other, he looking slightly down and she looking slightly up due their differences in height. Saudade is wearing a black suit on top of a salmon Prada for Men shirt and has his hair slicked back along his perfect skull. Hannah Linus feels some sort of very soft tingle in her abdomen.

"Lovely," says Saudade. Then he takes off the eyeglasses hung on a little chain and sticks one of the arms between his lips in a flirty pensive gesture. His lips are large and fleshy and flanked by two perfectly symmetrical lines that constitute Saudade's most sexually attractive facial element according to a significant majority of his past lovers. "I mean this, of course." He points to the painting with the arm of his glasses. He smiles. "It's incomparable. Ahem, fascinating," he says after a brief hesitation.

Hannah Linus looks at the painting. It's a Venus in front of a mirror from the Bellini school. Frankly a minor piece, even in a two-bit exhibition such as this one. Chosen as a filler and duly situated beside the door to give the impression that the walls are filled without attracting too much attention. The Venus is looking at herself in the mirror with a bored face, beside an open window that shows a rural landscape as dictated by the conventions of the period. Her pale, cellulitic body is naked except for the gauzy, unnaturally twisted sheet that covers her sexual parts.

"How can I explain it?" Saudade squints. "The chick is in her birthday suit and it's obvious she's a hottie." He shrugs his shoulders. "Or must have been in her day. And yet, that's not the important thing. It's not like when you see a naked chick in a porn movie. I don't know if you get me. This is like something more . . ." He takes an ever so slight pause to give emphasis to the word, *"artistic."*

Hannah Linus stares at Saudade. For a second it seems as if she is going to say something. Then her gaze shifts toward the extreme opposite end of the room, where Raquel and the security guard are watching her with quizzical expressions. Then she looks at Saudade again.

"Is this your gallery?" says Saudade. Looking at the painting again. With the same half smile. "That's great. I like art a lot. I could spend hours looking at pictures and all that."

Hannah Linus seems confused. The man seems to be in no way terrified by her presence, nor by the tone of voice with which she questioned him. A tone that she has been perfecting over the years. He shows none of the terrified uncertainty that she usually inspires in people. The man gazes at the painting and when he looks at her he does so with some sort of superiority. Of amused self-confidence. With an expression so openly insulting that Hannah Linus can't help but feel intrigued. And then there's the man's face, and his body. The man is so tall and slender and sexually attractive that it's hard not to look at him. Even with his suit and his glasses and his impeccable veneer of civilization, the man provokes in her mind sharp images of brutality and violent sex and powerful genitals. Hannah Linus wipes a drop of sweat from her forehead. She looks at her assistant again and then looks at Saudade.

"Are you interested in buying this Venus?" she says.

Saudade looks at her as if he doesn't understand.

"I mean the painting," she says.

Saudade frowns a bit. Hannah Linus can see the tip of his tongue playing with the tip of the arm of his glasses. Hannah Linus's mind fills with strange images.

"I don't know," Saudade finally says. "These are good paintings, but in general I like the paintings that are in more out-of-the-way places better. In discreet places where no one can see them."

Hannah Linus nods.

"I think I have what you want."

Twenty minutes later, Hannah Linus is crawling on the floor of the gallery's storeroom, picking up articles of her clothes one by one. All the light in the storeroom comes from some energy-efficient fluorescent tubes that give the space a sad and vaguely dangerous look. Like in a movie set in a spaceship where a nonhuman intruder decimates the crew one by one. After searching the entire room, she finds what's left of her panties behind a radiator. She holds them up and stares at them with a vaguely melancholy face. The largest piece could still be identified as panties by someone with good investigative skills. Then she wrinkles her nose like someone who has just noticed an odor someplace it shouldn't be.

"You can't smoke in here," she says to Saudade, who is lying contentedly on top of a pile of cardboard and bubble wrap. "Smoke destroys paintings. And you're going to set off the alarms."

Saudade lets the ash from his cigarette fall into his cupped palm and takes another long drag with that powerfully insulting half smile that seems to be his default expression. The natural arrangement of his features. His posture as he lies on the cardboard pile gives Hannah Linus the strange sensation that his penis is watching her. Saudade's penis, as she sees it now, is like a curled-up animal resting after the sexual act while still keeping an eye on her. Hannah Linus often gets that same feeling from the penises of men she has just had sex with. She can't say it's a feeling she particularly likes. Saudade's penis isn't exactly the same color as the rest of his body. Saudade's skin is a toasted color reminiscent of dark bread and fishermen under the sun, while his penis is a sickly color that makes one think of skinless animals slithering out of their shell.

Hannah Linus begins to dress. Turning her back to Saudade. Her naked body provides the perfect complement to her dressed body. Not a gram of fat. Muscular without becoming masculine. With strong legs and a thin waist and breasts belligerently projected aloft. It's the essentially pointy nature of her breasts and their upward orientation that give them their ballistic air. An atavistic piece of weaponry.

"That was stupid," she says, putting on the skirt of her business suit. "A very unfortunate episode. I'd appreciate you leaving through the fire exit and never coming back to this gallery. I don't want my employees losing respect for me. If you want to buy a painting, do it by telephone." She stretches out her arms to close her bra hooks behind her back. Then she shrugs her shoulders. "Although frankly, perhaps you should spend your money on something else."

His silence makes her turn her head toward the place where he's lying on his cardboard bed. There is something strange about his cardboard bed. Something not so much ridiculous or grotesque as genuinely disturbing. Something that makes her think of naked saints and martyrological images. Saudade's penis stretches idly and stands to look at her face-to-face. Hannah Linus halts in the middle of putting on her blouse. In some part of the storeroom the click of an automatic device is heard. Hannah Linus surprises herself by taking a couple of hesitant steps toward Saudade. His penis watches her, amused. She kneels down slowly. Above her head a fine rain falls from the fire alarm's sprinkler system.

WONDERFUL WORLD

~~~~~~~~

By Stephen King

CHAPTER 17

Chuck Kimball opened the door to the kitchen, stuck his head out cautiously and finally went into the backyard. He closed the door behind him and went across the yard toward the shed, trying to act naturally.

Underneath his Red Sox cap he wore a double layer of asbestos. He had folded the layers of asbestos from the blinds and the false ceiling and now, as he walked through the yard trying to keep his nerves from betraying him, a part of the inner lining of his cap stuck out through the back. He was lucky that They didn't always see so well. But the asbestos couldn't protect him forever.

He made it to the door of the shed. He tried not to look over his shoulder as he put the key into the lock and unbolted the door. He opened the screen door covered in asbestos and then removed the steel bar that blocked the inside lock. The assholes could smell his fear, he told himself. And just as he reminded himself he regretted having thought it, because a shiver ran down his back, from his neck to his tailbone.

Once he was inside the shed, he took a look around him. Everything was just as he had left it a few hours earlier, he told himself as a way to keep calm. The computer was carefully unplugged and covered with strips of asbestos, just like the radio station. After what happened the week before, he was perfectly aware that They could somehow get into computers and make them work even though they weren't connected to the Internet or even plugged in. They probably already had control of the entire network, just like the television channels and all the rest.

He walked up to the calendar and tore off the January 10 page. It had been exactly six days and ten hours since his last, terrifying phone call with his son. How much time did he have left? The minivan was almost ready to make the trip south. The entire top had been lined with a layer of asbestos and then upholstered. The false bottom beneath the seats was almost finished and included a compartment for provisions, a tank for potable water and a hiding place for weapons and ammunition. The satellite positioning system, even though it would probably be useful given the circumstances, had been taken out due to the risks it involved.

He checked his watch. Two hours until nightfall. It would be best to leave once it got dark. A few final touches and everything would be ready. On the outside, the car looked like a regular family minivan. With the Red Sox' mascot hanging above the glove compartment and swinging its bat in its hands. The back of the minivan was still missing a little paint where it had hit Clarissa's car.

He had planned to make the trip without stops of any kind. That could be a problem, since he had had another sleepless night working on getting the car ready. And that morning he had barely been able to get to sleep as he hugged his shotgun tightly under the twisted sheets. He still had several tablets of Adderall and a whole box of Ritalin from his raid on the pharmacy but, at the rate he was going, the Dexedrine wasn't going to last him more than a couple of

days. It was funny that, in spite of everything, his
gradual relapse into the worst habits of his Black
Year was now the least of his problems.

He opened the door of the minivan and sat in the
driver's seat. He lit a cigarette, and as he exhaled
a cloud of smoke with his eyes half closed he took
the stereo equipment out of the glove compartment.
He cut the cables with wire cutters and then, using a
bowie knife, he began to take out the part that was
built into the dashboard. Even though he had no intention of turning it on throughout the whole trip,
the radio was too big of a risk.

He hadn't thought of an explanation to give the
police if they stopped him on the highway. That was
another one of the trip's dangers. The very idea of
talking to the police was terrifying, since Chuck
wasn't entirely sure whether They could read his
mind or not. The way They acted seemed to suggest
that all of their minds were interconnected, but
there was no way of knowing if They also had access
to the thoughts of those who were apparently immune,
like him.

He threw the remains of the car stereo into the
barrel and sprinkled them with gasoline. He was about
to toss his cigarette butt in, too, when a noise
stopped him short. At first he couldn't identify it.
It was an intermittent, insistent buzzing. Hard to
pinpoint because of the asbestos lining on the shed
that acted as soundproofing. Suddenly he froze. What
else could that be except the doorbell? The bell to
his house! For a moment that seemed to stretch into
an eternity, he remained still in front of the barrel
with the cigarette butt in his hand. He couldn't move
at all. Meanwhile, the bell kept ringing with terrifying insistence. He had no idea how long it had
been ringing when he finally approached the window of
the shed with trembling legs.

He moved the curtain aside just three-quarters of
an inch and looked out, his brow furrowed, at the
slight, chubby woman illuminated by his porch light.
It was Mrs. Kopinski. She had a plate in one hand

covered with some sort of tea towel and her other hand was ringing the bell again and again.

Her face was the most terrifying part.

A completely blank face. That just looked straight ahead without blinking. Like all of Their faces when They don't realize anyone is watching them. Faces that make you think of unplugged machines.

Chuck lifted up one of the shed's back windows very carefully so as not to make any noise. He thanked God he had oiled all the windows less than three months earlier, when he returned to his empty house after they released him from the clinic. He had decided to use those kinds of domestic tasks as an exercise to improve his discipline. He went out through the window and hopped over the fence into the Carringtons' yard. Less than two weeks earlier, before all the animals in the neighborhood disappeared, he wouldn't have been able to do that without his neighbors' two retrievers attacking him.

He crawled along the fence, taking care not to be seen from the porch, although he knew that the porch light was now right between him and Mrs. Kopinski—or whatever was now occupying Mrs. Kopinski's body. Then he set off running through the trees and a minute later appeared walking along the sidewalk. His face was covered in sweat and he had two dark, round stains under his arms, besides which his heart was beating like mad from the tension and the Dexedrine, but he trusted that the layer of asbestos in his cap would protect him as much as possible.

"Mrs. Kopinski!" he said in the most cheerful tone he could muster when his steps became audible from the porch and Mrs. Kopinski turned with an alert look on her face. "What brings you here at this time of the day?"

He was even ashamed himself of how artificial that had sounded. Mrs. Kopinski, however, merely traced one of those smiles. Those impossibly enthusiastic and cheerful smiles that now surrounded him every time he went out. Yet, whatever was going on was something different. He tried to gauge how long it

had taken him to get out of the shed, go around the
Carringtons' property and show up on the corner. Mrs.
Kopinski—that thing that looked devilishly like Mrs.
Kopinski—had had her finger on his doorbell for at
least fifteen minutes. This wasn't one of Their routine visits. Something was going on. Maybe something
in his behavior had tipped them off. Chuck didn't
manage to hold back a shiver.

"I brought you a nice piece of Mrs. Kopinski's
own meat loaf, Charles," said that thing in front of
his door, with the same impossibly cheerful smile.
"That's why I've come. Mr. Kopinski didn't finish his
and I have to watch my weight." She let out a sinister cackle. "And I thought of you, son. Lately you
look skinny. And we don't want skinny folks in the
neighborhood." Her expression suddenly changed. Still
smiling, something in her gaze turned threatening.
"We don't want scruffy folks in the neighborhood."

In some place in the back of his mind, Chuck
couldn't help noticing the irony in that. Before
things began to change and everyone around him started
acting like characters in a Frank Capra movie, Mrs.
Kopinski had always gone out of her way to make her
dislike for his family, and for him in particular,
quite clear. Whether by telling off Ollie, with that
crowing voice of hers, every time he went out into
the backyard to play basketball, or by muttering
under her breath and shaking her head crabbily when
she passed him or Teri in the mall, the old harpy
made her feelings for the whole family quite clear.
And it goes without saying that she would have cut
off both her arms before bringing him a leftover
piece of meat loaf.

Chuck went up the porch steps, wiped the sweat
from his forehead with his sleeve and took the plate
with the piece of meat loaf that the woman held out
to him.

"You shouldn't have," said Chuck in an uncon-
vincing tone, growing more and more alarmed by the
presence on his porch. Out of the corner of his eye
he thought he saw Mr. Kopinski waving from one of

the windows of the house across the street. "But I do appreciate it, of course."

There was a moment of tense silence, much more tense if one stopped to think what might be going on. Chuck cleared his throat and opened the screen door.

"Well, I guess it's getting late," he said.

Mrs. Kopinski didn't move. Chuck tried to decide what he could do. He didn't have any weapons on him because he knew that They had ways of knowing such things. And as if that weren't enough, the way that smiling old woman was looking at him now gave him the impression that she knew perfectly everything that was going through his head.

"Would you like to come in and have a cup of tea?" he said, aware that his tone was sounding desperate. He had the vague sensation of being watched from behind every curtain on the street.

Mrs. Kopinski responded to the invitation by widening her smile even further.

The lights inside the house were turned off, which didn't keep the old woman from stopping for a moment in front of the door to the living room to take a good look around in the half-light before entering the kitchen. Chuck felt himself becoming gripped by fear. He knew very well what the woman was looking at. Almost all the living room furniture had been taken down to the basement to leave room for the enormous table where he had been putting together his models of famous buildings. A whole week's work of hiding his thoughts. Something started to change in Mrs. Kopinski's expression. Her features seemed to harden. Was it possible that some of Them had already sounded the alarm after discovering that the models had been stolen from the store? Chuck remembered what the women in the basement had told him about keeping his mind blank when They were nearby. As he filled the kettle and put it on the stove, he went through the multiplication tables in his mind.

The kettle seemed to take forever to start whistling. Chuck was already finishing the nine times table and was about to start again when he noticed Mrs. Kopinski's reflection in the kitchen window. She was standing in front of the garbage can, with that blank expression again. What was she looking at? Chuck turned around. And then he saw it. Mrs. Kopinski was looking at the empty model boxes piled up in the kitchen garbage. And then he understood. It was too late to continue pretending. They had found him out.

Without letting the conscious idea of what he was about to do stay in his mind, Chuck smacked Mrs. Kopinski in the head with the kettle. The woman staggered. He hit her one, two more times, until the woman backed up a couple of tottering steps and finally collapsed on the counter, her face full with blood and some kind of horrible dent in her forehead.

An intense pain in his temples left him instantly stunned. They had been watching. They had been listening. The collective mind was tuned in at that precise moment to the kitchen in Chuck's house. And he could feel it in his head. Like a furious scream.

There was no time to lose. He left the house running and entered the shed through the still open window. Through the corner of his eye he could see people coming out of their houses. He got into the minivan and turned the ignition key. He stepped hard on the accelerator and charged at the large wooden door, which broke open with a tremendous crunch. The minivan made it to the street in the midst of a rain of splintered wood.

As he drove down the street, he had time to see something. Something that was flying over the rooftops of the neighborhood. Something too low and too slow to be a light aircraft. He stepped hard on the accelerator, pushing it all the way to the floor, and turned down Main toward the outskirts of town.

PART II

*"And the Sun Turned as
Black as Sackcloth"*

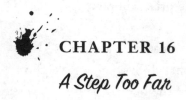

CHAPTER 16

A Step Too Far

Pavel looks at himself in the mirror—which is too low and too small—above the sink in his jail cell, which was designed for four prisoners and is currently occupied by eight. He's definitely satisfied with the texture of his dreadlocks, but not with the length. His dreadlocks are now as long as Bob Marley's were in 1973, when he recorded "I Shot the Sheriff" and appeared smoking a gigantic spliff on the cover of *Catch a Fire*. Which is to say, dreads that still defy gravity and extend lionlike in all directions, so that someone seeing him from afar could come away with the impression that his dreads were actually an Afro. The kind of dreads that Pavel wants are the ones that cascade down his back and can only be partially contained by a wool hat, like the dreads Bob Marley began sporting toward the end of the seventies, in the *Exodus* period. Pavel is infuriated by how slowly dreadlocks grow. He has a very precise idea of the personal image he wants to have, within the Rastafarian aesthetic, and he doesn't want his stupid scalp ruining that image.

"This mirror is for midgets," he says in Russian, screwing up his face and looking at it in the mirror. "And for pinheads. And it's broken."

Besides Pavel, the cell holds six Ecuadorians with bandannas on their heads and a guy from Minsk who's locked up for lighting a restaurant owner's bathroom on fire, with the restaurant owner inside. The way to fit eight prisoners into a cell originally designed for four reflects an ingenious institutional strategy that consists of placing foldout beds in every nonessential area of the cell. The guy from Minsk sticks his head out from his bunk, where he's reading a pornographic novel in Russian from the collection of Russian pornographic novels that circulate in the prison library, and takes a quick look at Pavel.

"I'm not surprised they left you here to rot," the guy from Minsk says to Pavel. With his Belarusian accent that always makes Pavel think of farmers with sun-toasted faces. "You're the biggest pain in the ass I've ever seen in my life. This is *fucking jail*, not a five-star hotel. I wish I was like those guys and didn't understand Russian." He points with his pornographic novel to the group of Ecuadorians with bandannas on their heads, who are seated at a folding table on the other side of the cell and betting rolled-up bills on cards. "It's obvious you've never been in a Russian jail. I'm going to ask them to put me in solitary."

Pavel looks in the mirror at the rest of his appearance, his Wailers T-shirt and his black sweatpants, and deems them satisfactory. What would please Pavel most right now would be to give the guy from Minsk two smacks. It's difficult for Pavel to reconcile the teachings of Rastafarian philosophy with people like the guy from Minsk. He knows that a real Rastafari lives for the people and with the people in universal love. He knows that Rastafari have to work biblically, universally and spiritually for the redemption of humankind. And yet, every time he meets up with some representative of humankind, all the universal concepts fall apart. Someone knocks on the door of the cell from outside and the main elements inside rearrange themselves as fast as possible. The Ecuadorians with the bandannas hide their rolled-up bills and their cards in several types of pockets, drawers and hiding places around the cell. The guy from Minsk sticks his Russian pornographic novel under the mattress of his bunk and puts his hands behind his head in the universal body language representing the act of "resting" from all activity. Pavel turns and watches as the door opens.

There are two guards at the door. The one who's just opened the door looks first toward the group of Ecuadorians with bandannas. Now that there are no cards or rolled-up bills in sight, the Ecuadorians are just seated at the table with their hands on top of it. Or standing with their hands in their pockets. Not looking anywhere in particular. Showing profuse signs of inactivity with their body language. The way the Ecuadorians are spread out around the cell gives the impression that they are posing for one of those group photographs of Hollywood celebrities. Or one of those group photos of pop bands. The guard looks the other way, toward the Russian-speaking side of the cell.

"Congratulations, Bob Marley," he says to Pavel. "Your cop boyfriend's here to see you." He swings the bunch of keys he has in his hand with a distracted expression. "It's amazing how cops love you."

"I don't think he's that handsome." The other guard looks at Pavel with a calculating expression. "I don't know why the police love him so much."

On hearing this, the Ecuadorians' body language transforms into gestures of penitentiary contempt. One of the Ecuadorians spits on the floor of the cell. Pavel lets himself be handcuffed, goes out into the corridor escorted by the guards and takes a last look at his bunk with an almost nostalgic expression.

"Don't come back," says the guy from Minsk as he takes his Russian pornographic novel back out from under the mattress. "Please."

The group composed of Pavel and the two guards travels through a muddled succession of hallways, stairways and rooms. Pavel can't make out any trace of cruelty or sadistic pleasure in the guards' faces, or any other traditionally penitentiary or police attitude that he's familiar with. In the visiting room, Commissioner Farina is at a table on which sit a thermos of coffee, a pile of plastic cups one inside the other, half a dozen croissants and various paper napkins. Beside the napkins are a group of the kind of folders that are used to transport police files. Commissioner

Farina is flipping through a magazine about cars as Pavel sits at the other side of the table and waits for a guard to take off his handcuffs.

Pavel glances around. Several inmates at the other tables of the visitors' room look at him with expressions of penitentiary contempt. Pavel sighs. Commissioner Farina looks up from his automotive magazine as if he had just realized Pavel was in front of him and nods with admiration.

"Those hair things of yours have grown a lot," he says, closing the magazine and leaving it on the table. Commissioner Farina has one of those chubby-cheeked faces and that very dense, black hair that are common in male adults from Barcelona. "The last time I saw you they were so short you looked like one of those puppets on TV." He furrows his brow and turns to the lackey standing behind his chair. "What do they call those puppets?"

"Puppets?" The lackey frowns. "I think I know the ones you mean."

"Doesn't matter." The commissioner rolls up the magazine and starts hitting the edge of the table rhythmically with the rolled-up magazine, as if he were playing a simplified version of a drum kit. "The important thing here is that we're very happy to see you. We haven't seen you in *months*. Come by the station once in a while. You're neglecting us." He makes some sort of sad face. "We're so happy to see you that we wanted to bring you a present. Some Bob Marley CDs or something like that." He turns toward the police lackey again, still playing his simplified drum kit. "Did we bring him his Bob Marley CDs?"

The lackey seems to be staring at the legs of the wife of one of the prison inmates that are looking at Pavel with contempt.

"CDs?" says the lackey without taking his eyes off the woman. "I think we forgot them."

"We forgot them." Commissioner Farina shakes his head the way people shake their head when they want to emphasize that something's a real shame but, in the end, that's how life is. "But let's see. We must have something to give you. What do we have around here that we could give you?"

He kneels down and gets something from under the table. He places it on top of the table. It is a plastic tray with Pavel's street clothes, along with his watch, his wallet, his keys and his pack of cigarettes.

There is a moment of silence. Commissioner Farina and his lackey smugly contemplate Pavel's terrified expression.

"No," says Pavel finally. After looking at the plastic tray with his belongings for a long moment. His terror seems almost *moral* in nature. As if in the tray there were a check for a million dollars in exchange for his letting Farina fuck his sister.

"No *what*?" asks Commissioner Farina. Leaning a bit over the table as if he was having trouble hearing what Pavel was saying.

"No," repeats Pavel. "No way. I don't want to leave."

"You don't want *to leave*?" Commissioner Farina points with his head around the visitors' room. "This is jail, son. *Everyone* wants to leave."

Pavel finds Commissioner Farina a perfect example of the kind of humankind that makes the vast majority of his universal Rastafarian concepts fall apart. A perfect example of the things that he doesn't like about the so-called civilized Western world. When he sees signs of Western decadence of Farina's stature, Pavel starts to feel tired and depressed and in a bad mood that seems to screw him into the chair he's sitting in, there in the middle of the visitors' room. That seems to multiply the force of gravity.

"We want you to leave." Commissioner Farina opens the thermos and fills a couple of little plastic cups with steaming coffee. "You're going to waste here. I've always thought that you had a lot of potential." The commissioner waits for his lackey to respond with a sycophantic little laugh. "A kid like you. So elegant. So *tall*."

Commissioner Farina takes half a dozen little plastic cups from the pile and spreads them out on one side of the table. Then he takes the croissants and spreads them out on the other side. He takes the thermos and places it at a point equidistant from the group of little cups and the group of croissants.

"Imagine that all these things on the table are your friends." He points to the group of little plastic cups. "Those are Leon's gang. Russians like you. Lifelong friends. And you've got that little one that's had an operation on his vocal cords. What's his name?"

"Something Duck," the lackey prompts.

"These ones over here are Bocanegra's gang." Commissioner Farina now points to the group of croissants. "More recent friends, but good friends just the same. You've got your old friends and your new friends, too. That's life. And what else do we have?" He points to the thermos. "Turns out you also have a *sister*. A dancer, says the file. I see there's an artistic streak in the family."

"One day I went to the bar where she works," says the lackey. Looking out of the corner of his eye at the legs of the woman who is now standing as she ends her visit. "I like those Russian babes."

Commissioner Farina shakes his head.

"He's kidding," he says. "We wouldn't do something as *disgusting* as lay your sister. But let's just say your sister has paid your bail. Your sister hasn't actually paid your bail. I doubt the poor girl knows how to pay someone's bail. That is, if she had the money. And if she even remembered you exist. But just between us." He leans over the table to say something in a confidential tone. "We forgive you. *Arrivederci*." He makes a gesture with his hand as if he were waving good-bye. "And don't you forget to visit us every once in a while." He smiles with his chubby-cheeked face. "And don't change your cell phone number."

In Pavel's opinion, the civilized Western world is a giant ocean of shit where everyone ends up drowning, sooner or later. Pavel doesn't really know if the rest of the world is an enormous ocean of shit or not. The only thing he's sure of right now, at that table filled with croissants and little coffee cups, is the basically shitty composition of the civilized Western world in which he currently finds himself. With no little islands in view to grab on to. He also has no doubt that right now he seems to find himself in the middle of the largest concentration of shit he has ever seen in his life.

"This not possible." Pavel rubs his temples. "It is not good you, not good me. Why would you want them shoot me right here?" He points to the back of his neck. "You profit nothing. You put me out there, okay, you already know who's waiting for me. I went *a step too far*. Well, I made a mistake." He slaps both palms simultaneously on his knees in an exasperated gesture. "Let me stay here. I confess everything. I spend twenty years here. The food is bad, that's okay. What you want me confess to? I'm dangerous criminal. Carjacking. Jewelry stores. Whatever you want. I did it all."

Commissioner Farina stares at him for a moment. Then he gives him a chubby-cheeked smile.

"That was funny, wasn't it?" he says. "You're a funny guy."

"Bob Marley's a funny guy," corroborates the lackey. "And they say Russians don't have any sense of humor."

Ten minutes later, dressed in his street clothes and with a look of absolute desperation on his face, Pavel leaves through the disappointingly small metallic back door for inmates who've completed their sentences. The traffic on the highway is light but continuous. Pavel walks as fast as he can under the blazing midday sun, feeling annoyingly conspicuous in his black clothes, to a phone booth in front of the gas station attached to the prison complex. When he enters the booth, he stares at the numbers on the phone with a perplexed face. When he really thinks about it, any number he could dial means vast risks to his personal safety. He spends a couple of minutes slamming the receiver against the phone's casing with a rage that is not Rastafarian in the least. Until the receiver is nothing more than a twisted broken piece of plastic in his hand. Then he wipes his hands on his pants and decides that this would probably be the most appropriate moment to pick up where he left off with his old life plans, ones having to do with one-way tickets to legendary islands in the Caribbean.

CHAPTER 17

Fonseca

Lucas Giraut's office on the mezzanine of LORENZO GIRAUT, LTD., is dark except for the circle of vanilla-colored light that the only lamp projects on the rosewood surface of his Louis XV *cartonnier*. The darkness hides the fact that there have been recent changes to the furnishings in the unilluminated areas. Although there is something ineffable in the office's atmosphere that produces the sensation that changes have in fact been made. The lighting, in any case, is clearly inappropriate for the business meeting now taking place in the office between Lucas Giraut and his mother's lawyer. Clearly inappropriate for any type of meeting. The rigid, hard-looking armchair where Fonseca is seated also seems clearly inappropriate. Especially for someone Fonseca's age.

Lucas Giraut is sitting at his desk. Drawing something with his fountain pen beneath the lamp's insufficient light. One of those distracted doodles people make while having a conversation. Fonseca leans over the *cartonnier* and makes a vaguely threatening gesture with an extraordinarily light and firm hand that resembles the extremities of certain birds.

"You need to sign these documents *as much as we do*," he says. "Probably more. That's what I am trying to make you see. And you have to believe me. Without the restructuring plan you're left alone. And in a delicate position. How do you plan on running this company? You have no experience. You know nothing about business. You can't do anything with what you have, son. You have the majority of the stock shares, but your mother has the rest. The money. The houses. The boats. And you can't even do anything with those shares. Put your feet on the floor, son.

We're doing this because we appreciate you. Step aside and let the adults take care of adult matters." He leans his body back again and reclines against the rigid armchair. As if to show that the bottom line of his speech had already been delivered. Then he softens his tone. "Listen. Your mother wants you to know that she appreciates your effort to stand up to her. Contrary to what you may think, your mother knows how to appreciate these kinds of things, things that another kind of person could find irritating. Your mother is a person that appreciates insolence. Like your attempts to sabotage the International Division. Like raising Chicote's salary and giving him all those stock shares. Or generally doing everything that upsets your mother and is bad for our international campaign. What the hell." He shrugs his shoulders. "Who understands you better than your own mother?"

"My mother has *never* understood me." Lucas Giraut runs a hand through his straight blond hair and admires the drawing that he is making under the lamp's insufficient light. "She doesn't even know me," he continues. "The only reason she speaks to me is because my father named me primary stockholder. Before that she hadn't called me in six years. And she'll stop talking to me when she manages to get me out of the way. I know that she makes fun of me all the time. And that she doesn't care about what I want. She never has. It's like when I was a kid. She never did anything to make me feel good. She always gave me birthday presents I didn't like. It was almost as if she gave them to me *because* she knew I wouldn't like them. They were usually fishing-related." The drawing Lucas Giraut is scribbling with his fountain pen on the top page of a block of notes depicts a vaguely human and vaguely female figure whose most striking element is a very flat oval face that transmits no emotion whatsoever. "Fishing rods. Fishing vests. Hats. Things like that."

"For the love of *God*." Fonseca rolls his eyes. In the margin of the beam of light, his hands seem extraordinarily strong and firm in spite of the lightness of his limbs. Giraut thinks he has seen the same phenomenon in certain birds. "What the hell does *that* have to do with it? And what are you trying to pull by making me sit here in the dark? And in this chair? I'm *sixty-five years old*. Do you think any of this is going to do you any good?"

"I was a kid," says Giraut. "I don't think my mother understood what that means."

The suitological analysis of Fonseca's gray Armani suit offers the following results: corporate discretion, a firmness impervious to obstacles and an absolute acceptance of his place in history. Just as Lucas Giraut has a chance to prove once again, still doodling on the top page of his note block, Fonseca is completely immune to any suitological criticism. He is also immune to all the different Attack Strategies thought up by Lucas Giraut and Valentina Parini in the courtyard of their house. With his face reduced to a network of gnarled tendons and treelike veins. With whole parts of his face sunken in, giving the impression that his face is nothing more than a layer of skin and nerves and tendons stretched over a bird's skull. Seated in a rigid chair that is absolutely inappropriate for any type of interpersonal business meeting, Fonseca is the second most immune person to any type of mental attack strategy that Lucas Giraut knows.

"Listen to me, son." Fonseca keeps his face out of the lamp's conical beam of light. "We don't have much time. Your mother is not going to let me leave this office without you signing those papers. You know how she is. I figured you would have realized it by this point, but now I'm going to tell you even more clearly. It is not in your best interests to get in her way. Even though you're her son. So let's quit dancing around the subject. Tell me what it is that you want. If it's reasonable, you'll get it. And this"—he lifts a skinny but powerful finger—"*is not* a negotiation. It's a gift. A small gift to show you our goodwill."

Lucas Giraut slowly tears out the page he's been drawing on and balls it up, without looking at his mother's lawyer. He throws it in the wastebasket.

The question of Lucas Giraut's childhood birthdays takes up dozens of pages in the secret childhood notebooks that constitute his subjective chronicle of those years. Year after year, Lorenzo Giraut systematically forgot his son's birthday, in spite of the many, not very subtle hints in the form of anonymous notes and red circles in engagement books that Lucas left during the days leading up to his birthday. Often Lucas Giraut wondered if there could have been something true in those systematic and perfectly predictable oversights. In his father's slightly amused expression and in the cheerful melodies he whistled when he got up on the mornings of his childhood birthdays. As he stared at him from the other side of the breakfast table.

"I need to know what happened the night they arrested my father." Giraut concentrates his gaze on the next blank page of his block of notes with a look of concentration. "I mean the night at Camber Sands. In the summer of 1978. I need to know the details. Someone held the cargo in the port that my father was going to sell and someone called the police. I've been reviewing my father's accounting ledgers and his desk diaries, as well. That night there should have been someone else in the hotel room. Some sort of business partner. Someone who didn't show up. And who called the police." He starts to trace the contours of a new drawing. With a frown. With the tip of his tongue sticking out artistically from between his lips. Finally he lifts his gaze for an instant in Fonseca's direction. "I need to know if my father was betrayed. And if so, I need to know who it was."

"Son." Fonseca looks at him with theatrical fatigue. "Your father was a strange man. Who did strange things, like turn off all the lights and cover the windows with newspaper pages. Or like leaving you the majority of the company stock in his will. Which could only be a joke. A strange joke. Which is why I'm here today. To tell you that your mother is willing to forget everything. To forgive things other people wouldn't forgive, and perhaps to give you a job more suited to your talents. Perhaps in some other part of the world. Let's be honest: you were never exactly the son your parents expected. I think that in many senses the word *disappointment* could be used." He pauses. Giraut doesn't, not even for a second, see Fonseca make any sign of being uncomfortable in his hard, rigid chair. "And as far as what happened to your father"—he shrugs his shoulders—"who could know about that at this late date? Your father was a disturbed man. Who associated with undesirables. And it doesn't seem prison helped him at all. When he got out, I don't think it could be said that he was himself."

According to the hypotheses laid out in Lucas Giraut's childhood notebooks, Lorenzo Giraut's systematic and inexplicable forgetting of his only son's birthday was somehow related to other inexplicable elements of his paternal behavior. Like the fact that he never directly answered his son's questions. Like the fact that he invented strange explanations for everything. Like the fact that he lived and died without letting his son know basically anything about who his father was.

"I know about the Down With The Sun Society," says Lucas Giraut. He now seems to be prolifically drawing a group of three figures with their arms around each other's shoulders in a gesture of male camaraderie. All three have long hair. "I've been investigating. I know there were three of them. I know they were friends. And I know that they were together in what they were doing." He pauses and wipes a lock of straight blond hair off his forehead to admire his drawing. One of the three long-haired guys in the drawing wears a coat whose shape seems to suggest that it is a woman's coat. "I need to know their names. Who they were and what they were doing. That's the price."

Fonseca leans back and the network of shadows on his face darkens until they fuse almost completely with the darkness.

"There's a reason why no one ever spoke to you about those people," he says. His distance from the light making him inscrutable. "Why your mother kept you far from certain things. Your father had gotten involved with dangerous people."

"What did the Down With The Sun Society do?" Lucas Giraut puts the finishing touches on the long, slightly tangled hairdos of the figures in his drawing. "How was it involved in what happened in Camber Sands? Were they the ones who betrayed my father? Is that what happened?"

Fonseca looks fixedly at Lucas, for a long moment, his facial cavities and treelike elements beating in the darkness. Then he sighs. He leans slightly forward to pick up his briefcase from some area in the dark at the foot of his chair and opens it on his lap. He takes out a bulky file and puts it on the table. Then he takes his own fountain pen out of his suit pocket and leaves it on top of the file. He taps the paper a few times with the tip of his finger. The scene seems to be frozen in that moment. The two men stare at each other across the table. The treelike beating of veins in Fonseca's temples can only be intuited. Lucas Giraut's hands have stopped drawing and seem to be resting in an alert state on the *cartonnier*'s surface. It is difficult not to think of duelists watching each other with their pistols held high at each end of a frozen field. It's difficult not to think of opponents in an action film in one of those scenes where the action freezes and the camera turns dizzyingly around the two men. It is difficult not to think about inexpressive chess players from the Eastern bloc. Finally Lucas Giraut lifts his eyebrows. He lifts his chin.

To his surprise, Fonseca lowers his gaze.

"They are named Koldo Cruz and Bocanegra," he says. And he uncaps his fountain pen. "Lorenzo's childhood friends. They were two-bit thieves. Your father was the brain of the operation. Until they got tired of splitting the money with him." He opens the file to the first page. "Sign on every page. Here on the bottom. On the dotted line."

Lucas Giraut's hand opens one of the drawers of his *cartonnier* and puts away his notepad and then the fountain pen he was drawing with. Then he pushes a button on the intercom on his desk and waits to hear his secretary's voice.

"We're finished," says Lucas Giraut to the secretary. Without taking his eyes off of Fonseca. "Please escort Mr. Fonseca out."

The silence is only interrupted by the barely audible click of the intercom button on Lucas Giraut's desk when he removes his finger. The darkness that surrounds the two men in the office is like a feeling of uneasiness on the edge of your visual field. Sort of like a headache. Fonseca's face starts to transform. The branches of arteries on his temples change color and texture and swell up noticeably. The swelling extends rapidly through the rest of the blood vessels on his face. Like the expansive wave of an explosion. Like a porcelain funereal mask that has remained intact for millennia at the bottom of a tomb but splits with cracks when it comes into contact with the outside air.

CHAPTER 18

Donald Duck

Tied to a chair in a greasy-smelling corner of the warehouse commonly known as LEON'S GARAGE, THE GREASY GARAGE or MR. LEON'S EMPIRE OF GREASE, Pavel confirms that the last vestiges of his Rastafarian desire to come together with all his fellow human beings in universal love are vanishing. He is tied to the chair in the classic posture of prisoners about to be subjected to an interrogation with torture. With his arms immobilized behind his back and his ankles tied together.

Immediately in front of Pavel is Leon. The owner of LEON'S GARAGE. Sitting backward on a chair. With his forearms resting on the back of the chair and his legs extended on both sides. Which is to say in the classic position of someone about to use torture as an interrogation technique. Leon runs a gigantic hand through his greasy hair and exhales a mouthful of Russian black tobacco smoke toward Pavel's bruised face.

Pavel focuses on kicking a rat that is sniffing his foot. The depression and fatigue and bad mood that contact with his fellow human beings usually produces in him now manifests itself as an increase in the pull of gravity on the muscles that hold up his head. A decidedly un-Rastafarian weariness. A sinking feeling of the overall decline of the Western world that surrounds him. Of corruption in the very marrow of the world around him. All of it decidedly anti-Rastafarian.

"I know what you're thinking," says Leon in Russian. With a high-pitched voice that doesn't match his gigantic arms and bald, vaguely bullet-shaped head. "You're thinking: How could this guy be so *elegant*? It's not because I flaunt my money or anything like that. I'm one of those people who believe that true elegance is worn here, *on the inside*." He brings a hand to his chest. He's wearing a paisley shirt and a mustard-colored suit jacket, which even though they aren't too small on him produce an almost painful feeling of smallness. "It's a simple question of dignity. Like this tie, for example." He picks up his tie with two fingers. It is red and has a repeating gold saxophone pattern. "This lovely tie was a gift from my daughter. And that's why I'm wearing it. I'm passionate about family. And, after all, how do you want me to dress?" He shrugs his shoulders. "You want me to dress like Donald Duck?"

In Pavel's opinion, an overwhelming majority of the population of the modern Western world are complete idiots. We might be talking about seventy percent. The absolute preponderance of complete idiots is not only an obstacle for the evolution of the human species and the realization of ideals such as Rastafarian universal love. These idiots also make life much more difficult on a day-to-day basis. You can leave your house one morning to buy cigarettes, for example, and never come back as a result of a run-in with some complete idiot.

"Oh, did I just mention Donald Duck?" Leon, the complete idiot, furrows his brow. "Now why would I do that? Well, I wouldn't worry if I were you. I don't see any outlets around here. Although wait." He rests his chin on the back of the chair he's sitting backward in and looks around at the walls covered with grease and calendars and Russian posters. "Isn't that an outlet over there?" He makes a surprised gesture with his enormous palms. "Who knows. Maybe Donald Duck is around here somewhere."

Several rats, as greasy as everything else in LEON'S GARAGE, scrabble around at the edges of Pavel's visual field. Pavel can't see them well because of the swelling in his right eye and the dreadlocks falling in front of his left eye. In fact, the only thing he can see clearly from his chair is Leon's square, unibrowed face. Beyond Leon, past the groups of rats that scrabble around and which Pavel can only see as quick little stains on the floor, he glimpses another figure. Someone too corpulent to be Donald Duck. And too far from the lightbulb that hangs from the ceiling of LEON'S GARAGE for Pavel to see his face. The only thing that Pavel can make out about him are his shoes and his pants. Shoes and pants that Pavel can only identify as Really Expensive.

"I like your style," continues Leon. There is something intrinsically greasy about Leon's appearance. Something that has nothing to do with his greasy hair, or even with the extremely greasy condition of LEON'S GARAGE. A certain component of his persona that gives the impression that he would continue to be greasy even right after a hot bath. "I like that black man's hairstyle that you've got. And that guy on your T-shirt, who is he?" He squints his eyes. "It's hard to see with so much blood. Oh, Bob Marley. Of course." He shrugs. "Bob Marley's not bad. He's got rhythm and all that. But of course, all blacks do."

Pavel squints and tries to see something more of the man with the Really Expensive shoes and pants in spite of the swelling in his eye and the dreadlocks that hang in front of his face. He makes a mental list of the things that he would like to do to Leon if he weren't tied to a chair in the classic position of prisoners about to be tortured. The list includes, among other things, the rectal insertion of various objects whose morphology makes their insertion into a human rectum very difficult.

"Do you know the joke about the black kid who says, 'Mommy, I'm white'?" Leon stamps out his cigarette with his shoe and goes back to fixing his greasy hair with the fingers on one hand. "It's too much. The black kid goes to the kitchen, where his mother is making dinner, and puts his hands in the flour. Then he rubs his hands on his face and says, 'Look, Mom, I'm white.' And his mother up and slaps him. Then the boy goes into the living room and says to his father, 'Look, Dad, I'm white.' The father punches him. And the kid says, 'I haven't even been white for five minutes and I already can't stand these damn niggers!' " He lets out a laugh. "It's too much."

The unknown man with the Really Expensive shoes and pants clears his throat to draw attention to the fact that Donald Duck has just appeared on the scene. He's just come in and now seems to be looking for an outlet along the walls near the door. In one hand he carries an extension cord and in the other a drill. Donald Duck's famous drill. His overall appearance, with a sweater full of holes and a filthy Barcelona Football Club cap, seems to indicate he got trapped in an office building as it was being demolished and was forced to survive for days on end among the ruins without changing his clothes. He also seems to be strangely small. Not small like a child, but small like a large child. Around his neck he wears some sort of metallic surgical collar with a battery-operated voice synthesizer, like the type that people who have had an operation on their vocal cords wear.

"Is this for real?" says Pavel.

Donald Duck starts talking with his voice synthesizer, the basically unintelligible buzzing tone of which does indeed sound like Donald Duck's voice. He kneels next to the wall outlet and starts to extend the extension cord until he reaches the place where Pavel is sitting. Finally he connects the drill, tests it and lets out a synthesized sentence whose modulation could very well suggest an angry inflection.

"What the fuck is he saying?" says Pavel.

"He says," explains Leon, "that he's had a shitty day. One of those shitty days that make you want to drill into things that move and gush blood."

Donald Duck chatters on with his voice synthesizer.

"He says that drilling works like a painkiller," translates Leon. "*Better* than a painkiller."

Donald Duck chatters on with his voice synthesizer and puts both hands in front of his belly in a broad gesture that suggests that he is holding a very large ball against his belly.

"He says," translates Leon, "that his wife doesn't wanna fuck. It's one of those superstitions Russian women have when they're knocked up. Something to do with the fact that if you let your husband fuck you while you're knocked up the kid will grow little horns or something. And it's been a couple of months already. Russian women are usually superstitious," he adds in a wise tone. "That's one of the disadvantages of Russian women. Who for the most part have a lot of advantages. Obviously."

The imminence of the interrogation with torture doesn't manage to dispel Pavel's sensation of decidedly un-Rastafarian weariness. In some part of his mind circulate images of secluded beaches and jungle settings. Images of him floating faceup on crystal-clear waters under a sky much bigger than any sky he's ever been under before. Letting the late-afternoon tropical sun warm him. Letting the pleasant feeling of warmth and humidity bathe his skin. Soaking his clothes and filtering through his pants. Someone clears their throat. Pavel opens his eyes and blows to get the dreadlocks out of his face.

"I never thought you'd be one of the ones that piss themselves, Pavel." Leon gestures with his head toward the wet spot that is beginning to spread from Pavel's fly down his right pant leg.

Donald Duck chatters on with his voice synthesizer and places a small drill bit onto his electric drill.

"Donald Duck says he never imagined you'd be a pisser," translates Leon. "That you're the last person in the world he thought he'd see piss himself."

Donald Duck chatters on with his voice synthesizer for people who have had their vocal cords operated on and opens up his box of drill bits organized by size on the floor, in front of Pavel's tied-up feet.

"He says he doesn't have to tell you that the pissers are the scum of the earth," translates Leon. "That even little kids know that."

Pavel wrinkles his face into a disgusted expression as Donald Duck finishes fitting the bit into Donald Duck's Electric Drill, kneels in front of his crotch and turns it on. In the back of Pavel's mind an idea begins to emerge, an idea that isn't in the least reassuring. The electrical sound comes closer and closer to his soaked right leg. Until the tip of the drill makes the fabric of his pant leg tremble.

"Wait a minute," he says, speaking up over the whir. He can feel Donald Duck's breath on his damp crotch. "Tell this moron to stop that thing."

The sound of the drill stops. Pavel can feel the bill of Donald Duck's hat touching just below his belt buckle.

The guy that's too far from the light to be visible clears his throat again and takes a step forward. His torso and face materialize above his Really Expensive pants and shoes. Pavel looks at him with his eyes squinted. Beneath a mop of white hair the vaguely reflective surface of a metal plate appears, where the right part of the guy's forehead should be, and beneath that a black fabric patch covering his right eye. Pavel frowns. It's the same guy. The one from the house. The one that's screwing his sister. Pavel feels a new wave of weariness and negative feelings toward the world in general. Whatever mess Bocanegra has gotten him mixed up in this time, it doesn't exactly look like he's going to be able to get out of it with every part of his body intact.

"I love that you're asking me to wait a minute." Leon lights another cigarette with a match and shakes the match out with more force than necessary. The size of his arms seems to indicate a muscular strength that is potentially dangerous in most everyday situations. "Because I'm dying to hear what you have to tell me. Now in my life I've seen people up to their necks in shit, but you take *fucking* first prize. First of all, I find out you broke into a house. And not just any house. My boss's house. Second, you let yourself get caught by the cops. And third, I find out that you are having a coffee with the cops and they slap you on the back and let you go free." He exhales a new mouthful of Russian black tobacco toward Pavel's bruised face. "So I have *three* good reasons to leave you here with Donald Duck and come back tomorrow to scrape up what's left of you."

Pavel realizes that while he was paying attention to Leon's words, a rat has started chewing on the tip of his shoe. Other rats observe from a prudential distance.

"I need to go to the bathroom," says Pavel, shaking his shoe. "I swear I won't try to escape."

Donald Duck is adjusting the bit on Donald Duck's Drill as he chatters on with his voice synthesizer that brings to mind cartoon characters. The guy with the metal plate in his forehead and the patch on his eye remains just outside the reach of the lightbulb's light, in such a way that his head goes in and out of the darkness creating a vaguely flickering effect. Leon holds his cigarette between his index finger and his thumb and blows the smoke out with his eyes half closed.

"And yet," he says with a pensive face, "my boss tells me it's not a good idea to leave you here with Donald Duck and come back tomorrow to scrape up what's left of you. In fact, he tells me that it makes no sense to interrogate you or let Donald Duck get any information out of you because in fact *we already know* who the idiot is that paid you to break into his house. In fact, and he's got a point, we don't have anything to ask you. What he tells me is that we should untie you and let you go, but that we shouldn't let you get *too* far. Like when you go fishing. Like when you're fishing and you let out the line, *but not too much.*"

Pavel tries to imagine the implications of the fact that the guy with the metal plate and the eye patch is Leon's boss while at the same time trying to kick the rats away.

"Don't kill me," he says finally. "Think of my sister and my poor sick mother."

Leon smiles a wide smile with a smattering of gold.

"If you don't shut up," he says, "I swear we're gonna leave you here with Donald Duck. I'm serious."

Donald Duck holds up his drill sadly. And takes a poignant look at Pavel's knees.

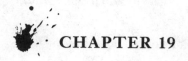

CHAPTER 19

The Most Exciting Adventure

Shortly after the sun sets over the fairground glow of Christmas lights, Lucas Giraut gets out of a taxi on the anonymous block of banks and office buildings where Hannah Linus has her gallery. He leans forward a bit to help Marcia Parini out of the cab. She's wearing a backless sequined evening gown. With a matching bag. All by Givenchy. The Lino Rossi suit that Giraut has chosen for the opening is the brandy herringbone and he's added the festive detail of a white rose in the buttonhole. A girl with a green Lycra minidress and in-line skates skates over to Giraut. She stops in front of him with an expert turn of her legs and skates and hands him a promotional brochure. Giraut looks at it: on the brochure there is the same smiling koala as on the young woman's green Lycra dress. "BIOSPHERE PARK," says the brochure. Or perhaps it's the smiling koala that's saying it. "THE ENVIRONMENT IS THE MOST EXCITING ADVENTURE."

Lucas Giraut looks up, but the young woman in the green Lycra dress is already skating away down the street.

"Damn it to hell," says Marcia Parini. Looking with a frown at the group of people gathering in front of the gallery doors. "Don't tell me that bitch has the same bag as me."

The scene on the sidewalk in front of the gallery doors is a slightly better-attended and slightly more exciting version of all the openings the important antiques dealers in Barcelona hold. With the same thirty-odd guests. With the same journalists feigning somewhat snide indifference. With the same cluster of surly waiters. The only thing that makes this opening exciting and special, filled with nervous laughter and conversations in furtive tones and clandestine cell phone calls, is that Hannah Linus is at its center. That vortex of envy and illicit admiration and hatred and desire. That gravitational center of the world of Barcelona antiques dealers.

Lucas Giraut and Marcia Parini walk arm in arm along the sidewalk. They enter the group of guests and journalists and surly waiters that mill around the entrance to the gallery. Which has become a forest of waving hands and chins lifted in recognition and drinks that move in silent toasts. Antiques dealers from Barcelona and employees of antiques dealers and specialized journalists. All spread out to create a collective scene that is vaguely reminiscent of the Renaissance pictorial representations of Classical schools. Bathed in the multicolored fairground glow of the Christmas decorations. Lucas Giraut's gaze finds Hannah Linus's above the forest of heads.

"Giraut," says Hannah Linus when they finally meet up in the opening's gravitational center. Hannah Linus's face is iridescent beneath the colored lightbulbs of the Christmas decorations. They kiss each other on both cheeks while gazing off into the distance. "I was beginning to worry you wouldn't show. I'm really sorry about stealing all those pieces from you." She shrugs her shoulders. Her face doesn't convey any sign of regret. Or of sarcasm. It is a perfectly neutral face. "But I'm sure you're going to love the exhibition."

Giraut nods with a weak smile. Looking above the heads. The exhibition is comprised of about fifty religious paintings, wooden sculptures and liturgical objects. The small pieces are in long glass cases that run along the gallery's backbone. The way the glass cases are lit from within projects their light upward onto the visitors' faces. Giving them a diabolical appearance.

"And this is Mrs. Giraut?" ventures Hannah Linus. "Or perhaps the *future* Mrs. Giraut?"

Marcia Parini seems to crouch down and become rigid under the openly disapproving look that Hannah Linus gives her dress and her figure. The same way certain animals crouch down and become rigid when they find themselves cornered by a larger animal.

"We're not engaged," she says. In a chilly tone. Then she crosses her arms in a gesture that seems to transmit both anger and modesty. "We're actually neighbors. I live below Lucas."

Hannah Linus nods, her brow furrowed in a gesture of interest. The gesture is correctly calculated to be experienced by Marcia as a slap across the face. Then she shrugs her shoulders.

"I'll leave you two *alone*," she says. "And don't forget to try the venison sashimi with pear. They cost me six euros each." And she heads off. Not without first taking a perfectly deliberate last glance at Marcia's purse. The same purse that hangs on the shoulder of the wife of one of the other antiques dealers.

Lucas Giraut frowns. He is vaguely aware that Marcia Parini is muttering something under her breath. The waiters and waitresses move with the skill of professionals through the meta-adjacent groups of guests. Carrying round trays filled with cups of Moët et Chandon. Filled with piles of carefully molded venison sashimi with pear. The same round trays of undefinable color that every catering service in the world seems to use. The same round trays that appear in every graphic depiction of waiters around the world. Lucas Giraut can't manage to make out exactly what it is that Marcia is muttering. Or maybe he's having trouble concentrating on what she's saying. His attention now seems to be tracing a wide circle around the room. As if he were searching for something.

"She has hickeys on her neck," Marcia Parini is saying. In a voice low enough that only Lucas Giraut can hear. As she takes a sip on the glass of Moët et Chandon that she's plucked from a tray. "At *her own opening*. And the Moët isn't cold enough."

Lucas Giraut doesn't show any sign of listening to what she's saying. It's becoming more and more clear that he's looking for something as he gazes around the room. His gaze wanders among the meta-adjacent groups of guests. Among the surly waiters and among the minor figures in local politics who roam around looking for respect. Finally his gaze lands on one of the photographers.

It is, as far as Lucas Giraut can see, the largest photographer he has ever seen. In fact, it's one of the largest *human beings* he's seen in his life. There is something in his mass that suggests supernatural transformations of comic book superheroes due to chemical or radio-active leaks. It's not one of those cases of gigantism that causes an exaggerated lengthening of the bones. He is holding a professional camera with an adjustable telephoto lens in front of his chest and his size makes it seem like a toy. One of those plastic kid's toys in the shape of a camera. There is also something strange about the way he holds the camera, with those hands as big as small mammals. A certain uncomfortableness. Or better put, a certain inadequateness. As if a bird was trying to smoke and hold the cigarette with his wings. The enormous photographer holds the camera uncomfortably and with his brow furrowed and takes photographs of the paintings and the various corners of the gallery. Placing the camera in the right position and then pushing the button with his giant finger and a concentrated ex-pression that suggests his hands aren't up to the task. Lucas Giraut stretches his neck to see above the guests' heads. His first impression was right. The photographer is Aníbal Manta.

"Six euros?" Marcia Parini is saying. With a frown. Chewing on a venison sashimi hors d'oeuvre with her face wrinkled in disgust. "For *this*?"

Aníbal Manta raises one hand and makes a gesture toward the other end of the room. Some sort of signal. Ambiguous enough so that no one would recognize it if they weren't waiting for it. Lucas Giraut looks in the direction of Manta's signal. It only takes him a second to recognize the surly-faced waiter in uniform that receives the signal on the other side of the room. His characteristic wave of blond hair has been plastered down with gel and stuck to his skull. His unhappy expression has been replaced by a professionally surly face. But there's no doubt about it. It's Eric Yanel. With a tray professionally raised in the air so people can take glasses of Moët et Chandon.

"She has it set up well," Marcia is saying. She has finished her first two venison sashimi hors d'oeuvres and now reaches out a hand to grab the third with her slightly greasy fingertips. "I won't deny that." She shrugs her shoulders. "The gallery isn't bad. But your place is much bigger."

Lucas Giraut continues looking around the gallery. Finally he looks up and his eyes find a staircase leading to a locked upper floor. In the landing halfway up the stairs a group of guests has gathered. Or better put, the party's inner circle. The people closest to Hannah Linus.

The first thing that Giraut sees is the hand that's grabbing Hannah Linus's butt. As she chats with a couple of guests from her inner circle. Giraut's gaze follows the strong arm that grabs her butt until he reaches the shoulder and then the face. The face is looking at him with a snide smile. As he grabs Hannah Linus's butt in a way that Lucas Giraut finds inappropriate to the circumstances. Saudade's face looks at him with a snide smile and makes an obscene gesture with his tongue and then articulates in silence something Lucas Giraut could swear included the words "Mr. Fancy Pants, Esquire." A small shiver runs up Giraut's spine.

"You aren't listening to me, are you?" says the voice of Marcia Parini. "You haven't heard a word I've said since we came in."

Giraut looks at her.

"I'm not very good at parties," he mumbles. He looks at his hand and discovers he's holding a glass of Moët et Chandon that Marcia must have put there some minutes before. He takes a sip. "But I think I'll be better once we see the paintings I told you about. The St. Kieran Panels." He pauses as if he didn't quite know what to say next. "I think that will perk me up."

Marcia stares at his face and her expression slowly transforms into one of amusement. One of those amused expressions that many women use when contemplating signs of male eccentricity. Just like they're looking at a small, stupid, harmless animal.

"Of course," she says finally. "I'm sure those paintings are really great."

Lucas Giraut takes Marcia Parini's hand. Together they head away from the sculpted wooden crucifixes and the polychrome virgins. Leaving behind the crucifixes inlaid with jewels. Leaving behind the tunics and cloaks with swastikas and other Celtic signs assimilated by Irish Christianity. Leaving behind the rooms filled with paintings and large sculptures taken from dimly lit apses. Leaving behind the last meta-adjacent groups. Leaving behind Aníbal Manta's gigantic body, which is pressing the button on his camera with an uncomfortable expression. And as they leave behind all these things, the spatial layout of the things in the gallery seems to reconfigure in a more profound way. The party no longer seems to be organized around a system of meta-adjacent groups surrounding an inner circle. Now Lucas Giraut and Marcia Parini can see the entrance to the room where the St. Kieran Panels are hung. Covered by a curtain so that no outside light enters. As tradition dictates, the four paintings are hung in a room where the light has been lowered to a minimum. Giraut reaches the entrance and stops cold.

Marcia Parini stops behind him. They both stare at the entrance curtain for a moment. Somehow it is easy to understand Giraut's gesture as one of reverence and respect toward the tremendously rare and sublime art objects.

Things are not like they used to be. At least from Lucas Giraut's perspective. The entire gallery seems to now be organized around a black, pulsating center: the room closed off with a curtain. Which somehow gives the impression that it *shines* from within. That the curtains aren't there to keep outside light from getting in but rather to keep something more powerful from getting out. Something like the black light of a radiant, pulsating black lamp. Something that, if one opens the curtain, will bathe the entire gallery with its radioactive glow and will blind everyone and make all those present fall to their knees and cover their eyes.

Marcia Parini takes Lucas Giraut by the hand. Giraut sighs deeply. And opens the curtain.

CHAPTER 20

The Winter of Our Discontent

"I don't know many people that would paint their office walls this color," says the redheaded lawyer who is sitting in an armchair covered with towels in Lucas Giraut's office on the mezzanine of the headquarters of LORENZO GIRAUT, LTD. All of the office furnishings are covered by sheets and towels of different sizes and colors. The redheaded lawyer gestures with his head toward a wall that has recently been painted black. The way he makes his comment suggests an element of sarcasm mixed with something else. Something similar to a veiled threat. "But I've been given to understand that there is a *vein of eccentricity* in your family. Something having to do with your father and the way he decorated places, and with the fact that he didn't like *windows*." The redheaded lawyer smiles in a way that suggests an expression of mild pain. "Correct me if I'm wrong."

The Louis XV *cartonnier* in Lucas Giraut's office is covered with a sheet. The shelves have been taken down from the walls. The way in which everything is covered with sheets and towels suggests a house being renovated.

Lucas Giraut is on his knees next to the latest addition to his collection of magic desks, with his stethoscope in his ears. A mahogany Victorian magic desk, circa 1860, with nine drawers, a frieze of vegetable and animal decorations and a green leather writing surface inlaid into the top. The end of Giraut's stethoscope without ear tips hangs over the front of his shirt like some sort of cybernetic elephant trunk. Giraut leans over one side of the Victorian desk and finishes applying a label with nonabrasive glue to its green leather surface. The label reads: REF. 3522. MAHOGANY VICTORIAN DESK 9

DRAWERS. VEG./ANIMAL FRIEZE, BRONZE KNOBS, 183 X
107 X 80 CM, PRIVATE COLLECTION OF LUCAS GIRAUT.
Then he smooths the sticker onto the surface of the desk with his fingertips. The new Victorian desk has a large main drawer in the front,
two small drawers on either side of the main one and three graduated
drawers on either side of the twin pedestals. To anyone trained in
deciphering magic desks, the distance of about two inches between
the upper edge of the main drawer and the leather-covered top is an
obvious indication of the location of the secret drawer. Giraut knocks
his knuckles along the top of the desk as he applies the stethoscope to
the animal-vegetable frieze two inches up and furrows his brow with a
vaguely medical expression.

"My mother's lawyer is named Fonseca," Lucas Giraut tells the redheaded lawyer as he applies the stethoscope to different points on the
magic desk's animal-vegetable frieze. "He's been my family's lawyer for
thirty years. So I find it hard to believe that you represent my mother.
My mother has never trusted anyone besides Mr. Fonseca."

The redheaded lawyer places his briefcase on his knees and opens
its silver clasps with his fingertips.

"My participation in this case is the result of a personal friendship
with Mr. Fonseca," he says, taking a dossier out of the briefcase open on
his knees. "The reasons that have brought me here today as Estefanía
Giraut's representative are detailed in this dossier. I have also been asked
to represent the injured party due to my legal specialty." He takes several
documents out of the dossier and he places them one by one on top of
the *cartonnier*'s sheet-covered surface. "This one here is a *subpoena*. The
details are inside and et cetera. *This one* is a summons for you to visit a
forensic psychologist. Of course, you have the right to ask for the opinion
of any other psychologist that you choose. For the record."

The redheaded lawyer seems to be one of those redheads whose
skin and hair give him a perpetually sickly appearance. His facial epi-
dermis has that rosy and perpetually irritated appearance, as if it had
just been scalded with boiling water. His hands have pigmentation

spots and his wrists are covered with a sickly-looking layer of fine hair. The redheaded lawyer did not take off his coat when he came into Lucas Giraut's office. Which makes any sort of suitological analysis on Giraut's part difficult.

"I have mostly come to convey a message, one of concern," says the redheaded lawyer, with one of those smiles of his that looks like an expression of mild facial pain. "Concern about certain behaviors that remind one of that *vein of eccentricity in the family*. Behavior that is incompatible with the presidency of a company in the process of international expansion. I represent people who love you, Mr. Giraut. People who *love you personally*. People who are now worried." He gestures toward the ceiling of the patriarchal office under renovation, which has also been painted black. The lamps have been taken down from the ceiling and are in a corner. Covered with sheets. Creating a lighting situation clearly insufficient for any type of meeting. "I am referring to your attitude toward furniture, Mr. Giraut. Toward furniture and curtains and windows. Something that has already caused your family a great deal of pain in the past. Imagine how concerned the people who love you are when they see these things *starting to happen again*. The black walls and the darkness and the opaque curtains and the furniture moved to the middle of the room."

"Help me." Lucas Giraut frowns and pushes on a vegetable motif in the frontal frieze of the Victorian desk. "Put your hand here. And push," he says. "I've been waiting for some time for my mother to try to divest me of my stock holdings. So I'm not surprised that she's questioning my mental health."

The redheaded lawyer sighs and gets up from the towel-covered armchair. He kneels down beside Giraut. The basic difference between the Louis XV *cartonnier* and the Victorian mahogany desk has to do with the degree of complexity of the mechanisms that unlock the openings to their respective secret compartments. It's what the experts call N-Grade of a magic desk. In technical jargon, the mahogany desk circa 1860 is a Grade 5 magic desk. That means it takes five steps to open its secret compartment. The particular opening of the Victorian magic desk requires a series of operations with the bronze knobs of the different drawers and with the animal-vegetable motifs on the frontal frieze as well. The specific mechanics of the Victorian desk are the following:

1. First of all, you have to press two different animal-vegetable motifs on the frontal animal-vegetable-themed frieze, namely, an oak leaf and the inner part of a bird's wing that exactly replicates, in reverse, the leaf's structure according to the classic trompe l'oeil technique. The two animal-vegetable motifs must be pressed *simultaneously*.

2. This simultaneous pressing unblocks the turning mechanism at the base of one of the knobs on the desk's left pedestal. Said knob can be turned to four different positions, each separated by a 90-degree angle of rotation. The knob must be turned five times, which is to say it must be moved 450 degrees, clockwise.

3. Then, and with the first knob turned, a second knob becomes unblocked on the right pedestal. This second knob must be turned 270 degrees, which is to say it must be placed in the third position, always *counter*clockwise.

4. This third step unblocks a third knob on the left pedestal, but *only for a five-second interval*. During those five seconds the third knob must be turned five more positions, but this time alternating clockwise movements with counterclockwise ones. Therefore, obviously, the third knob will end up having moved 90 degrees clockwise respective to its initial position.

5. The fifth step, and undoubtedly the most complex, requires the triggering of a fourth knob that has been unblocked by the third, which must be turned three times counterclockwise but keeping in mind that each turn must be carried out at *precise intervals of ten and a half seconds*, not including the time it takes to make the turn, so the three successive

turns must be done at seconds 11, 22 and 33 of the triggering sequence. Any error in this sequence blocks the entire
mechanism. The correct triggering raises the green leather
cover on the top and reveals the two-inch-deep secret compartment. Due to the complexity of this fifth step, a stethoscope is just about essential in order to hear the primitive
clockwork timers inside the piece of furniture.

Lucas Giraut is pressing on one of the animal-vegetable motifs
of the desk's frieze with a frown when the silhouette of LORENZO
GIRAUT, LTD.'s intern appears on the frosted glass door and knocks.
Giraut maintains the pressure on the frieze's ornamental motif and
extends his other arm as far as he can to push the button that opens
the door. The click of the door opening sounds at the same moment
as the click of the desk's inner gears when the two ornamental motifs
of the frieze give way. The intern enters with two cups of coffee and a
little pitcher of milk on a tray and looks at the two men squatting on
the office floor with her brow furrowed.

"Of course," says the redheaded lawyer, still pressing his hand on
one of the animal-vegetable motifs of the frieze, "I feel obliged to take
note of the state of this office and of everything I'm seeing here. For
legal record."

The intern leaves the tray with coffee and milk on top of one of the
furniture surfaces covered with towels and leaves without saying anything. Now Giraut begins to turn the desk's knobs, his face gathered in
concentration as he listens to the inner gears with the stethoscope.

"I represent people who are extremely concerned about *inappropriate relationships.*" The way the redheaded lawyer is squatting, with
his arms extended and his hands resting on various points of the
desk, makes you think of childhood games involving placing your
hands and feet on different colored spots on a plastic rug. "Relationships that are somewhat disquieting. Like that girl, for example. You
know what girl I mean. A twelve-year-old girl. Imagine the possible

repercussions if some impertinent journalist decided to make public the fact that you have done certain inappropriate things with a *twelve-year-old* girl. In the event that we went to court on this." One of Giraut's arms is intertwined with the redheaded lawyer's extended arm. "Which is something, I insist, that *no one* wants."

Lucas Giraut has his shirtsleeves rolled up above his elbows. The jacket of his slate gray Lino Rossi suit is hung over the back of one of the sheet-covered office chairs. The coat the redheaded lawyer who claims to represent Fanny Giraut is wearing doesn't reveal enough of his suit to allow for a suitological analysis. Giraut is now triggering the third knob in the sequence of knobs that open the secret compartment of his new collector's item.

"We are only looking to put you somewhere safe," says the redheaded lawyer. "Somewhere where you can't harm yourself. Or anyone else, of course."

The leather-covered top of the Victorian magic desk circa 1860 lifts up, revealing the secret compartment. The redheaded lawyer takes a sip of his coffee.

"I want curtains." Lucas Giraut stands up and wipes the sweat from his forehead with a meticulously folded handkerchief. "If you stay for a few minutes you can help me choose curtains."

In some part of the office a towel-covered telephone rings.

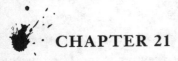

CHAPTER 21

The Day of the Publisher's Advance Excerpt

Valentina Parini readjusts her butt on the toilet lid where she is sitting with her legs crossed and her brow furrowed as she tries to concentrate on her reading. And it's not exactly easy. It's dark inside the stall and one of her eyes is covered by the stupid patch they make her wear, and someone is knocking insistently on the stall door.

"Parini!" shouts the prepubescent voice again from the other side of the bathroom stall door. "Come out already! I know you're in there! This time you're really in for it!" There is a moment of silence, perhaps to give Valentina Parini the chance to answer. Or perhaps the voice outside is considering how far it can go with its threats. "They're saying the principal's going to make the janitor come bust the door down with an ax!"

Valentina Parini readjusts her green glasses on her nose that's barely big enough to hold them up and sighs. She came down to the first-floor bathrooms at school a little more than half an hour ago, and she knew they would come looking for her. But she didn't imagine that everything was going to happen so quickly. Things must *really* be bad out there, she tells herself. She goes down to the bathrooms to read every time she gets a chance to slip away, often during basketball practice. Sometimes she can spend two hours locked in a stall before someone comes looking for her. But this time, it's obvious something's different. She's been hearing shouting and commotion in the hallway outside for a while now. On a couple of occasions she's heard her name mentioned in a frantic tone. And finally someone came looking for her. It's Adelfi, the retard. And all this has to happen just on the day that she got the Publisher's Advance Excerpt in the mail. With the first four chapters of Stephen King's new novel.

"Pariniiii!" screams the voice from the other side of the door. Drawing out the last vowel with exasperation.

When Adelfi, the retard, came into the bathroom about ten minutes ago, her voice already sounded pretty agitated. After insisting for a while, Adelfi had started to sound frustrated and finally worn out. Maybe she'd get tired of bugging her soon and go back to wherever she came from.

The Publisher's Advance Excerpt arrived at Valentina Parini's house that morning, in a brown envelope with the publishing house's logo on it. She had taken it out of the mailbox using a long serrated bread knife. It took her almost five minutes to get it out of the mailbox because her hands were trembling with excitement. Then she had only had time to tear open the envelope and admire the barely fifty-page booklet before her mother came down the stairs. Forcing her to hide the Excerpt and the bread knife in her school backpack as fast as she could, before adopting an innocent smile that her mother had looked at suspiciously before deactivating the car doors' locks with the remote control on her key ring.

The four chapters, which she is now almost done reading in a bathroom stall on the first floor of the Italian Academy of Barcelona, have not disappointed her at all. The story, or at least what the excerpt allowed her to guess at, is reminiscent of *The Stand*, but with touches of *Tommyknockers* and even *Dreamcatcher*. The main character, named Chuck Kimball, is a journalist in Portland, Maine, the author's hometown. Like so many of Stephen King's heroes, he's middle-aged, divorced and has a son. He is also in recovery after a drug and alcohol crisis. One day Kimball arrives at work at the news desk of his local paper and discovers that everyone has started to change. His coworkers and even his boss, whom he's given the nickname "Cosmic Bitch," are suddenly friendly and filled with team spirit and comradeship. Kimball doesn't know what to do. The same thing happens in the bar he goes to after work, where he is about to relapse and have a drink, and later with his neighbors. No one seems alarmed by the transformation. The truth starts to come out the next morning, when Kimball discovers that his best friend at the newspaper, Gary Revkin, has disappeared. Everyone on the newspaper staff works as a team to hide his disappearance. They even get mad when he asks about it. Finally Kimball finds Revkin dead inside a garbage Dumpster. His colleagues on the paper seem to have killed him in some sort of collective ritual. There are insinuations of mind control and a race of psychic beings that are like angels.

A door slamming is heard from outside. Valentina Parini furrows her brow and listens. For a moment she thinks that Adelfi the retard might have left, but she soon hears the sound of more steps and several prepubescent voices talking.

"Did you find her?" says one of the voices.

"She's hiding in there," says Adelfi.

Valentina Parini feels the sudden attention of several stares, almost like a physical force that pushes the door inward and tries to destroy her.

"Hey, freak!" shouts the first voice. "You don't have to hide! It's all over! This time they say they're finally gonna put you in the loony bin!"

"There you can hang out with other freaks like you," says Adelfi. And she laughs one of those typically teenage laughs. One of those laughs that aren't about happiness or hilarity, but are simply invocations of group complicity. "You'll finally have *friends*."

Valentina Parini snorts, irritated.

"I'm not hiding!" she shouts.

The insinuations by her school psychologist that Valentina hides in the school bathroom always manage to infuriate her. Valentina isn't afraid of anyone at school, and she has nothing to hide from. It's just that the bathroom stalls are the only place she can lock herself in from the inside and not have to see anyone. Making them considerably more pleasant than any other place at school.

More laughter devoid of happiness is heard. More invocations of group complicity that make you think of gregarious carrion eaters in the hyena family. Then an abrupt door slam and a deep silence. Too deep to mean anything but the arrival of an adult to the bathroom.

"*Signora direttora!*" shouts Adelfi the retard with renewed enthusiasm. "The freak is in here! I mean Parini! And *I'm* the one who found her!"

The soft, dry echo of a slap resounds throughout the entire bathroom.

Ten minutes later, Valentina Parini is in her homeroom teacher's office, sitting in a chair for adults that makes the tips of her feet hang an inch off the floor. The school psychologist is staring at her with one of her classic severe expressions she saves for those moments when Valentina has committed a serious offense or has exhibited behavior that goes against the spirit of their therapy. To one side of where Valentina is sitting, her homeroom teacher is passing tissues to Marcia Parini and stroking her back comfortingly. Marcia Parini is crying uncontrollably. On a couple of occasions during the last few minutes she's suffered hyperventilation fits, which the psychologist had to help her get through using controlled breathing exercises.

Valentina frowns behind her green frames, the way you frown when you've just realized that something is going wrong. How did her mother get to school so quickly? It occurs to her that maybe it really has been *more* than a half hour since she left class to go read in the bathroom. Now that she thinks about it, she is vaguely aware of having read the four chapters of the Publisher's Advance Excerpt more than once. Maybe a few times in a row. Sometimes that happens to her. She has misleading perceptions of time. Especially when she's locked in peaceful, pleasant places like the bathroom.

"Valentina," says the school psychologist. Still staring at her, like she's trying to hypnotize her or something like that. "Do you understand why you're here? Do you understand why we had to call *your mother*?"

Valentina hates the slow, deliberate way the woman says it. As if Valentina had problems understanding the language she was speaking. Then she gestures with her head to two objects on top of the homeroom teacher's desk. They are the manuscript of *Blood on the Basketball Court* and the bread knife she used that very morning to get her package out of the mailbox at home. Both from her school backpack.

"Those are my things," she says. "They're *private property*. They shouldn't be there. If you give them back, I'm willing to forget all about this," she says, remembering the phrase from some movie she saw recently.

Marcia Parini pauses in her sobbing. For a moment it seems that the pause is some sort of reaction to what her daughter just said. However, a second later it becomes clear that she was just taking in air to cry even harder. From the place where Marcia is sitting comes a torrent of hiccups, sobs and something similar to mooing. Valentina notices that her mother's wearing jeans and a T-shirt. Which means that she left the house in a terrible rush. Marcia Parini is not a person who under normal circumstances would be seen in public dressed in jeans and a T-shirt. Actually, thinks Valentina, her mother is a person who would probably rather die than be seen by certain people in jeans and a T-shirt.

"This is all my fault," Marcia Parini manages to say between sobs.

Then she lets out a hiccup and says something that sounds like "thithewit." The homeroom teacher continues stroking her back and hair comfortingly, passing her clean tissues from a box that can't have many tissues left in it and every once in a while shooting Valentina murderous glances.

Valentina thinks. She hates to admit it, but maybe Adelfi the retard was right. This time she's gotten into a mess that she can't see her way out of.

"Valentina." The school psychologist bathes all those present in a gigantic wave of professional consternation. Her face is gathered in an expression of worry that reminds Valentina of her own face when she really has to go to the bathroom and her mother is in the middle of one of her long makeup sessions. "I suppose you're aware that with these two things there's enough to call the police." She gestures with her head toward the two objects on the table.

To Valentina's right, her mother threatens to choke between hiccups. Her face is turning a vaguely bluish color. At some point a piece of tissue has gotten stuck to one side of her nose.

"What you've written here," the psychologist continues, "is—is too horrible to paraphrase. It would be horrible if an adult had written it, much less a twelve-year-old girl. Do you really want to do these things to your classmates? And to your basketball coach? Or to me, or to your homeroom teacher?" The string of questions hangs in the air of the school office. Like some sort of foul-smelling gas that no one wants to breathe in. Valentina is aware that three pairs of adult eyes are now watching her expectantly. Even her mother is looking at her above the semi-disintegrated pieces of a tissue. "I can't believe that these atrocities came out of your head. Has someone been giving you ideas, Valentina?" She makes a final theatrical pause. "Has someone told you those things or told you to write them?"

Valentina crosses her arms in the chair that's too big and makes the tips of her feet hang an inch off the ground. The walls of her homeroom teacher's office at the Italian Academy of Barcelona are covered with symbols of national identity. A tricolor flag with a golden flagpole that ends in some sort of a spear point. A framed portrait of Silvio Berlusconi in a place of honor on the wall, right behind her homeroom teacher's desk. Photographs of stupid places in Italy like the Roman Colosseum and Florence's Ponte Vecchio and that place where supposedly they had chariot races but now all that's left is a big hole. Valentina hates Italians. She thinks they're the stupidest people in the world. Ever since her father went back to Italy, Valentina has often gotten into bed and covered her head with a pillow and spent hours imagining natural disasters that destroy Italy and decimate its population. Giant waves sweeping through narrow streets filled with motorcycles. A river of lava coming down the stupid Scala di Spagna.

"It's not your fault," her homeroom teacher is saying to Marcia Parini. In a comforting tone. "It's not anyone's fault. We do what we can to instill respect and human values in our children. Here, too, in ethics class. Valentina is sick." She shakes her head sadly. "And we all have to help her."

"You admit that you wrote this?"

The school psychologist brandishes the manuscript pages the way district attorneys in the movies brandish incriminating evidence. The way she rolled them up and now is shaking them in front of her face makes some of the pages come loose from the manuscript.

"It's not finished," says Valentina in an apologetic tone.

"And what do you have to say about the knife?" whimpers Marcia

Parini. Her face has become a stiff mask in a color close to burgundy. The swelling brought on by her crying has made it impossible for her to open her eyes more than half an inch. Valentina has trouble believing she can really see through those tiny slits. Now that the box of tissues is empty a shiny glow of snot begins to condense under her nostrils. "Were you planning on *using* it? On someone at school?"

The three adult women stare at the girl. The sudden silence causes the normal school noises to come floating in through the windows. The screams of the girls in the school yard. The squeal of sneakers on the basketball court. The engines of passing cars. Even the far-off hum of the guard's television, two floors below. For some reason, the fact that life continues its normal course on the other side of the closed office doors astonishes Valentina. For a moment, it seems that nothing that is happening to her is real. That she's not in her homeroom teacher's office, and if she closes her eyes everything will disappear. And she'll be back in her bed, beneath the blankets, or maybe locked in a bathroom stall at school.

"I joined Stephen King's Spanish Fan Club," says Valentina finally. Avoiding the three women's eyes. "They're all idiots. I only did it so they would send me the Publisher's Advance Excerpt. . . ."

Marcia Parini's reaction is surprisingly quick and dead-on, considering her crisis state complete with sobbing and partial hyperventilation. Her arm flies out and grabs her daughter's closest ear. Valentina doesn't have time to duck. The homeroom teacher doesn't have time to stop her. On the other side of the desk, the school psychologist in charge of Valentina's case is too far away to stop her.

With her face transformed into a toothy mask of rage, Marcia twists her daughter's ear furiously. Making her green eyeglasses fall to the floor. Valentina lets out a scream that reverberates throughout the entire school.

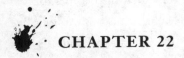

CHAPTER 22

The Universe According to Hannah Linus

Seen from the high window of the hotel where Juan de la Cruz Saudade and Hannah Linus are staying, the storm looks like a living thing. Some sort of living turbulence that advances along the streets, blinded by rage and crashing into buildings. Seven floors below, the street has become a quick, shallow river that drags tons of twisted Christmas decorations and garbage bags. The entire world has turned a dark gray color except for the infinitesimal moments when lightning strikes. In those moments it turns a bluish white color. The few pedestrians that venture onto the street don't so much carry their umbrellas as they get dragged *by* them.

Juan de la Cruz Saudade is standing on the king-size bed of his hotel suite. Naked and posing in a way that makes you think of bodybuilders posing for bodybuilding magazines. Looking at his perfectly muscular and abundantly tattooed reflection in the room's full-length standing mirror. There is genuine admiration in his face as he looks at himself. There's admiration and there's something more. A blend of sexual desire and that hypnotic fascination with which we watch traffic accidents from car windows or pornographic films broadcast in the middle of the night. Bolts of lightning illuminate his perfect system of muscles and tattoos. The way the storm's electrical flashes illuminate his postures suggests camera flashes. Hanging between his legs, his penis also appears to be posing for a battery of invisible photographers. Partially erect and with something similar to a lazy smile on the glans.

"What the fuck are you doing?" Hannah Linus stretches on the other side of the king-size bed. "What's wrong with you? Are you ten years old?"

The position in which Hannah Linus is lying facedown on the other side of the bed suggests very recent and very frenetic sexual activity. Her blond hair, which is normally organized into two very straight symmetrical braids at either side of the nape of her neck, is now a sticky tangle of damp locks. A coital flush still covers entire areas of her body.

"A moment ago you weren't thinking I was ten years old." Saudade makes that gesture characteristic of bodybuilders, flexing an arm held high with his gaze fixed on the bulging bicep. "When you asked me to do that thing again. That thing that broke the table."

Hannah Linus rolls her eyes. She feels around for the pack of cigarettes on the night table. She takes one out and lights it with squinted eyes.

"I'm not tired," says Saudade. Distractedly watching a figure with an umbrella being dragged by the fierce wind, seven floors below, on the other side of the window. "You don't have to feel bad about that. A lot of women get embarrassed. I mean, when they can't take any more. When they can't keep up with my pace. But there's no need to be embarrassed." He shrugs his shoulders. "I understand."

Hannah Linus takes a drag on her cigarette. The waves of postcoital tedium that overtake her now are almost overwhelming. In fact, sometimes the feelings of impatience and disgust provoked by being in the same space as a man with whom she has just had sex, or even just having to talk to him, are almost unbearable for her. She's not one of those women that need the approval or companionship of the male gender, nor does her self-esteem depend on arousing the male sexual appetite. She has no elements of dependence in her personality and she certainly feels no curiosity for the partially pleasant sensations similar to degradation that can be found in sex with socially or intellectually inferior men. In point of fact, Hannah Linus feels no conscious curiosity about anyone. She considers herself her favorite person and the model on which to gauge other's failings. The way other people fail to be like her is like the way flies hit the windowpane again and again. Hannah Linus yawns. That seems to be the essence of The Universe According to Hannah Linus: several million employees, taxi drivers and lovers that a Scandinavian divinity with turgid breasts and Hannah Linus's features has placed on the Earth for her to use and enjoy. Saudade isn't so different from the rest of the people, she says to herself with a sigh. Just stupider.

"We could call a whore," Saudade is saying. Provoking rhythmic contractions of his abdominal musculature in front of the mirror and proudly contemplating how his muscles contract and expand. "That way you wouldn't get so tired. It's easier if there's two of you."

"Call a whore if you want." Hannah Linus stands up and stubs out the cigarette in the disposable ashtray on the night table. She checks the time on her cell phone. "You can stay with her. I have things to do."

Saudade watches out of the corner of his eye as Hannah Linus walks with lazy steps toward the bathroom of the hotel suite. The suite bathroom is reached through a mirrored door located in the middle of an entire wall of mirrors. From the height of the bed where Saudade is, and through the doorjamb of the half-open door, a massage table and a platform with three steps leading to the Jacuzzi can be seen. Then he looks in the opposite direction. Toward the slightly elevated living room where a thirty-six-inch plasma screen is showing a loop of adult films. And toward the trail of clothes that leads from the suite's vestibule to the remains of the broken table in the living room. And there, in the middle of the stream of clothes, his gaze finds what he was looking for: Hannah Linus's bag. A vaguely wrinkled black leather Chanel bag with gold rings. The same bag that Hannah Linus keeps with her at all times and where she keeps the magnetic security codes of all the buildings she is responsible for. And then something surprising happens.

A flash of lightning illuminates the suite bedroom and Juan de la Cruz Saudade's face for a fraction of a second. And during that infinitesimal fraction, Saudade's face reflected in the pane of the high window is not at all the face that had been talking and having sex with

Hannah Linus up until that point. It is a mask of pure hatred. An open iron door to an industrial oven of hostility. Without any of those elements of basic kindness or sociability that we associate with being human. A hatred that has elements associated with gender and socio-economic status but that transcends them broadly, to cover everything that moves and breathes on the Earth. A hatred that rarely is seen outside of certain sculptures and ritual masks from prehistoric civilizations. Then the lightning ends. The vision only lasted that random fraction of a second. Saudade's face recomposes itself.

"All chicks like to fuck other chicks," he says. "It's a *proven fact*. So you don't have to get embarrassed. And you don't need to act tough. About the whore. All women get jealous. That's another proven fact."

Saudade listens. Hannah Linus's voice comes from the bathroom, muffled by the shower door. He thinks he can vaguely make out the words "ass" and "idiot." Then he hears the sound of plumbing for a second and finally the regular, comforting murmur of the shower's water falling into the stall.

Saudade jumps off the bed as soon as the shower comes on. His naked, muscular movements seem to have lethal precision. He crosses the suite to the living room and picks up Hannah Linus's bag. He takes out her wallet, which by this point is familiar to him, examines the cards inside and finally chooses one. A gold card with Hannah Linus's corporate logo, which Saudade has seen her use on various occasions to open the gallery building's security devices. He heads toward the little table beside one of the living room windows and opens the curtain. He looks down for the only figure on the entire street who is not being dragged along with an umbrella by the wind. After all, the figure seems too big for a simple storm to be able to budge him from his place in the middle of the sidewalk. Aníbal Manta looks up toward the curtain of the seventh floor of the hotel that has just opened and nods in silence beneath the rain. Saudade raises his thumb toward the enormous, steadfast figure on the sidewalk and closes the curtain again.

"Tell me something," says the voice of Hannah Linus from the shower stall. Mixed with the sound of the water. "You're married, right?"

Saudade directs his attention to the telephone on the small table. He turns it over and leaves it upside down on the varnished wood surface. Like an animal on its back. Then he opens one of the drawers of the small table and takes out a screwdriver no bigger than a toothpick. He uses it to take out the four screws that hold the body of the telephone to the base. The speed and skill with which he does it suggest previous training monitored by someone with a stopwatch. The inside filled with cords and electronic devices is now visible.

"Married, me?" says Saudade. With his face gathered in a concentrated expression. "Men like me don't get married, sweetheart. It would be a waste. I come and go, you know." He wipes a drop of sweat from his forehead with a tattooed wrist. "I have a duty to my work."

Saudade examines the inside of the telephone until he finds a piece of plastic attached to the base with recent soldering. The piece has a long, deep slot on one side and a plate with circuit and cords on the other. A red pilot light stares at him from the telephone's guts. Saudade runs the magnetic strip of Hannah Linus's card through the slot, several times, until the pilot light turns green. A click is heard inside the recently soldered piece.

"I think you *are* married," says the voice of Hannah Linus from the shower. "I've seen how you look around you every time you come in or out of the gallery. Or the hotel. You married men have the same secretive air." She pauses. "It's in everything you do. You're like a criminal committing a crime."

Saudade dials a telephone number on the numeric panel of the telephone with its guts spilled out. After a couple of seconds, the magnetic card reader installed inside the body of the telephone begins to retransmit the card's information. With a shrill, irregular buzz. Saudade closes his eyes and wipes another drop of sweat from his forehead. The retransmission lasts exactly fifty-two seconds. Hannah Linus's postcoital showers last on average two and a half minutes according to what

Saudade has had the chance to witness. The transmitter's buzzing is like a very sped-up version of the noise made by Teletypes and Morse code transmitters in old movies. The sound of the shower doesn't have those momentary interruptions of people who turn off the faucets to save water while they soap up. On the other side of the curtains, seven floors below, a group of kids look at Aníbal Manta admiringly and point at him with their fingers and make hyperbolic comments about his body size.

"I don't care," says Hannah Linus from the shower. Her tone of voice is that loud voice people use when they are showering to talk to people outside of the shower. A loud voice that's not quite a shout but close. "That's fine with me. I almost always get involved with married men. More comfortable for me. I don't like to have guys following me around all the time."

The buzzing of the transmitter ends. Saudade starts to put the screws back in place.

The sound of the shower stops. From where he is, Saudade manages to see a hand stick out from inside the shower door and feel around for a towel.

Saudade puts the magnetic card back in Hannah Linus's wallet and the wallet back in Hannah Linus's bag.

Hannah Linus comes out of the shower drying herself off with a towel. She ties the towel around her body the way women do. Which is to say above her breasts. Leaving her knees and part of her thighs in view. She finally enters the bedroom. Braiding her hair with her head leaned to one side and a distracted expression. She stares at Saudade with a slight look of disgust.

Saudade is lying on the bed. He gathers his face in a smile that Hannah Linus finds repulsive and moves aside the sheets to show her his penis, again completely erect. A giant clap of thunder makes the glass panes of the high windows and the suite's furnishings shudder. It occurs to Hannah Linus that coexistence in the same physical space with men she has just had sex with is getting harder every day. Almost like a sensation of physical repulsion. Must have to do with getting older. Although she can't remember ever having slept with anyone as moronic as this guy before.

"I'll give you two hundred euros if you get out of here right now," says Hannah Linus when the thunderclap's vibration dies down. Still braiding her hair. With her head still leaned to one side. "Three hundred. I just want you to get out. The money's in my bag."

Saudade doesn't seem particularly surprised. He shrugs his shoulders, the smile still on his face. About ten feet from where he is lying, and reflected in the bedroom's full-length mirror, the thirty-six-inch plasma television continues to broadcast a muted loop of adult films.

CHAPTER 23

Universal Sign Language for Food

Aníbal Manta looks up from his X-Men comic book and studies Raymond Panakian's figure from a distance. Panakian is sitting on his wicker chair in front of the painting he's already been working on for four days. Aníbal Manta's stomach is growling. He's in a bad mood and his stomach is growling and he doesn't have the faintest idea how someone can spend four whole days working on the same painting. And it's not like the painting is any great shakes either, in his opinion. He claps his comic book shut. He stretches his arms in his chair and lets out a long and noisy yawn while his stomach continues growling. The chair he's sitting in isn't a wicker chair. It's one of those metal fold-up chairs that after an hour cause intense pain in the middle of his butt. He looks at his watch. The warehouse of LORENZO GIRAUT, LTD., is completely silent in the midafternoon. There is a compact disc of Jamaican music in Bob Marley's stereo system, which belonged to Bob Marley before he disappeared, but putting it on is completely out of the question because it skips and the music turns into a series of bursts of labored and irritating hiccups.

Manta stands up. His degree of boredom and uneasiness is dangerously close to that degree of boredom and uneasiness that makes people do inexplicable things. The temptation to go over to where Panakian is working and kick out a leg of his chair and knock it to the floor, for example, is a temptation that Manta finds inexplicably difficult to resist.

And it doesn't seem that things are going to change until the very day of the job in the gallery. Every morning at nine sharp Raymond Panakian sits on his wicker chair with his little pots of paint and his palette and his blue work coveralls like the blue coveralls people wear to work in car repair shops or in industrial plants, people who work nonstop until eleven at night. Beneath the light of a small lamp that emits a strange blue shine. Yanel comes to watch him in the mornings and Manta usually arrives at three to relieve him. Six or seven hours watching a guy sitting in a wicker chair copy a little painting from an illustration he has stuck to one side with thumbtacks. There's no cure for that level of boredom. No supply of comic books can alleviate it. The X-Men one he has in his hand, for example, he's already read six times. For the first time in his life, Manta has the feeling that the X-Men comic books from the classic period could be something other than half an hour of fascinated contemplation and unrivaled aesthetic experience.

Panakian doesn't turn to look at him or make any movement that seems to acknowledge that Manta has stood up. His blue work coveralls with paint splotches over his turtleneck sweater make him look like a worker from another era, one in which human faith in socialist utopias hasn't yet waned. Manta doesn't have any idea what damn language the guy speaks.

Manta walks around the warehouse three times and smokes a cigarette. What he'd really like to do is head over to the supermarket two blocks away and buy some food to eat during the rest of his endless shift. The end of the workday in the warehouse isn't marked by any hour in particular or any visible progress in the work. The workday simply ends when Panakian gets up from the wicker chair and washes out his brushes and walks over to the exit and waits there. If that weren't enough, the security conditions in the warehouse don't allow Manta to leave him alone for even a minute. Not even to go to the supermarket. Every time he goes to the bathroom in the upper floor of the warehouse, Manta has instructions to handcuff Panakian's wrist to a pipe.

After pacing the warehouse three times, Manta throws his cigarette butt to the floor, stands right behind Panakian and looks over his shoulder at the half-painted picture. With his brow furrowed.

Aníbal Manta has his reservations about the second St. Kieran panel, which is the one Panakian is copying now. In narrative terms it could be a continuation of the one he was copying last week, the one with the guys falling through cracks in the ground. Or not. After all, Manta is a seasoned comic book reader. The second painting has very small figures in the lower part, but mostly seems to be a representation of the canopy of heaven. A black sun in the middle of a black sky. The sun is a simple black sphere surrounded by a crown of dying flames. Overall it's quite strange. The sky isn't black like the black sky in nocturnal pictorial representations. It is a much more absolute black. Without stars. Without night clouds and without any nuances of any kind. It is a black that seems to absorb one's gaze in a fateful way. A black that's more like no sky at all. On the Earth below, there are columns of smoke and fire. The little figures seem to be fleeing. Not in any specific direction, but in every direction. If you look closely, you can see terrified expressions on their little faces.

"Fuck it," says Manta after a minute of contemplation. His stomach lets out an enthusiastic growl. "I could give two shits."

Panakian doesn't look up from his work when he hears Manta cursing. Manta grabs him by the shoulder and shakes him. Panakian stares at him with his glasses that look like they should be on a pianist or a political refugee chess player. Like those glasses devoid of any traces of style that the state gave out free to the citizens of socialist countries.

"Let's go find some grub." Manta brings together all the fingertips of one hand and points to his mouth several times with the joined fingertips. Then he rubs his belly. Then he points at Panakian. That should be enough, he thinks. It's possible that he's incapable of saying, "You're an asshole and when we finish this job I'm going to beat you so hard your own mother won't even recognize you" using just his hands, but if there's one thing Manta is an expert in it's the Universal Sign Language for food. "Both of us. Come on. You're coming with me. And no funny stuff. At the first sign of anything funny, I bring you back here and break your leg. As far as I know, you don't need two legs to paint that eyesore."

Manta pushes Panakian out of the warehouse and locks its metal shutter and stares at Panakian in the middle of the parking lot. He opens his jacket to show Panakian a pistol and waits for Panakian to nod. Then he pushes him to the sidewalk.

The fresh winter air on the street fills Manta with optimism and a generic will to live. Next to him, Panakian shivers and his teeth chatter. They walk a couple of blocks and go into one of those supermarkets bathed in a fluorescent glow from above that makes you think of the light paradise must be bathed in. Manta grabs a plastic basket and pushes Panakian through the aisle that leads to the canned goods section.

"Take a good look, asshole." Manta sticks two bags of crinkle-cut potato chips with monosodium glutamate into his shopping basket. "The wonders of capitalism. I bet you don't have places like this in the piece of shit country you come from."

Manta pulls on Panakian's arm and pushes him through the aisles of the different sections of the supermarket bathed in heavenly light. For a moment, and without really knowing why, the idea comes into his head that the supermarket light from above is the opposite of the black of the painting's black sky. Next to the crinkle-cut chips he puts six cans of beer into his basket, and a package of boiled ham slices, bread with six kinds of seeds, blue cheese, green olives stuffed with anchovies, a family-size bottle of Coca-Cola, Oreo cookies, a bag of freshly made muffins and, after some hesitation, a precooked roast chicken wrapped in some sort of very taut plastic second skin. The plastic basket threatens to overflow. In the canned goods section, Manta turns and looks at Panakian with an expression of theatrical adoration and a can of cockles in his hand.

"Look at this, loser." He brings the can of cockles less than two inches from Panakian's face. "Cockles. The best invention in the history of mankind. I take my hat off to the fucking genius who thought up taking these guys out of the sea and sticking them in a can."

Panakian looks at the can of cockles and then looks at Manta. Manta gives him another push toward an even better-lit section of the store, where an employee dressed in white is serving cuts of meat and imported cheeses. Manta gets in line and points to a spot on the floor for Panakian to stay there.

"You stay still, right here," he says. "Where I can see you."

Standing in the line for the deli section, with his overflowing basket in one hand and the other hand in his pocket, Manta decides that in the end there's no reason why this has to be a bad day. He has a couple of comics left in the warehouse to reread and, besides, one of them is an issue from a limited-edition series that Marvel devoted to Wolverine. Manta's favorite superhero of all time. Sometimes, when he reads comics in bed while his wife is chatting with one of the neighbor ladies or borrowing a cup of sugar or watching TV in the upstairs neighbor's apartment, Manta imagines that he has an unbreakable skeleton and a miraculous capacity to cure his own wounds through mutant tissue regeneration. Not to mention the retractable and completely unbreakable claws. Claws that sink into Saudade's stomach, or into the stomach of any of the male neighbors in the building. Now he sighs in the supermarket line. The image is so beautiful it often dazzles him.

The line advances quickly until the tiny old woman in front of Manta gets to the head of it. The old woman speaks very softly and her wrinkled finger trembles so much when she points to the products on display that the employee has to stick half of his body out above the counter. Manta starts to get impatient. In his opinion, the glut of senior citizens is one of contemporary society's biggest problems. To the point of jeopardizing the system of social benefits for taxpayers. He doesn't even want to imagine what it must be like to pay taxes. The old woman shakes her head every time the employee shows her a different hunk of meat and looks around her with a disoriented expression. It seems to Manta that she is crying a little bit. The people behind Manta in the line seem to have spontaneously divided themselves into those who feel sorry for the old woman and those who find her irritating. After a minute of confused glances and indecisive pointing with her wrinkled finger, Manta puts the basket down on the floor and punches the counter.

"Goddamn it, ma'am." He lowers his head to speak very close to the old woman's face. The old woman looks at him in terror. "Don't you have an Ecuadorian to do your fucking shopping? And what about the rest of us? We don't have all night, you know?" He turns toward the employee dressed in corporate white and points at him with an enormous threatening finger. "You, give her a fucking steak and send her on her way, goddamn it."

There is a moment of silence. The trembling of the old woman's finger has spread to her entire arm and a good part of her mouth. Manta straightens up with his hands on his hips and looks at the place where Panakian is. Or better put, where Panakian is not. Because Panakian is not in the exact place where Manta told him he had to wait until he finished shopping. In fact, Panakian does not appear to be in the Deli Section. Manta starts running down the closest aisle. His speed and the poor visibility at the supermarket aisle intersections cause him to crash into several customers. Three intersections later, Manta makes out the distant figure of Panakian running toward the exit with a bottle of whiskey under his arm.

"Motherfucker," says Manta, and starts running toward the exit.

Once he's out in the street, Manta stops on the sidewalk. There is no trace of Panakian in either direction. Panakian's running out on him awakens staggering waves of emotional stress in Manta. That feeling of stress has definitely been Manta's cross to bear, his whole life. Like when he puts up with Saudade's digs. Like when he put up with the teasing at school, how people laughed at him and called him The Thing. The same emotional stress that, according to his psychologist, has kept him from achieving satisfactory levels of personal growth and has held him back, trapped in a painful crossroads of anxiety and violence. In the words of his therapist.

Manta takes the pistol from the holster beneath his jacket, cocks it and starts aiming in every direction. Screams are heard on the street. Some passersby walking along the facing sidewalk throw themselves to the ground.

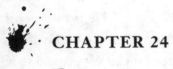

CHAPTER 24

Tics

It gives Hannah Linus a particularly comforting feeling when the gallery offices empty out. In general she has always felt comforted by any kind of empty corporate spaces. They give her a feeling of power, sweet and calm, mixed with a certain very subtly tragic atmosphere. And that's why she's now eating alone in her office in the deserted office area, while the gallery office staff is out, like every day, on their lunch break. With her shoes tossed any which way beneath her desk and her feet up on top. Listening to music in her portable MP3 player and chewing the strictly vegetarian salad from the plastic container she holds in her hands.

None of that stupid chitchat from her local employees, she says to herself as she chews. Letting her gaze wander in that way that anyone eating by themselves, anywhere in the world, lets their gaze wander. Not sitting uncomfortably at a table in a cafeteria that smells of grease, surrounded by the smoke of half a dozen cigarettes. No putting up with the way her female employees laugh absurdly at her male employees' jokes. To hell with all of them, thinks Hannah Linus as she stabs a cherry tomato with her fork and brings it to her mouth.

The cherry tomato remains suspended a couple of inches from her open mouth. It remains suspended in the middle of its trajectory from its plastic container to Hannah Linus's mouth because of something that she has just seen. Something that's approaching the reinforced glass door of her office with furious strides. Through the deserted office area. A young woman wearing jeans and a sweatshirt that's a knockoff of a well-known sports brand. Hannah Linus pulls out first one earbud and then the other and stares with her brow furrowed as the woman furiously enters her office and bolts the door from inside. The woman's ponytail is an obviously erroneous stylistic choice, considering the structural features of her face.

The two women stare at each other in silence. The most characteristic facial feature of the furious woman that has just come in is a nervous tic that makes her wrinkle her forehead compulsively at regular intervals. As if approximately every half second she was surprised at something.

"First of all," says Hannah, moving the container of salad to one side and placing the plastic fork next to it. "I don't know who you think you are coming into my office unannounced. And second of all, I *demand* you unbolt that door." She examines the woman from head to toe. "Are you the cleaning lady? This office was already cleaned this morning."

The woman holds Hannah Linus's gaze. Hannah discovers that it is difficult to concentrate on what she wants to say, because of the woman's nervous tic, which makes her appear constantly surprised about everything.

"You're Anna, right?" says the woman with the sportswear and the nervous facial tic finally.

"Hannah," answers Hannah. "Hannah Linus."

"Go to hell," says the woman.

"What?" Hannah seems perplexed.

"I said go to hell." The woman remains leaning on the bolted reinforced glass door, staring into Hannah's face with a furious expression that her tics contradict approximately every half second with random infiltrations of surprise. "Nobody tells me how to talk. Much less some bitch from England."

"I'm Swedish . . . ," Hannah starts to say, but she stops when she sees the woman with the tics take her back off of the door and start walking toward her desk. Her gaze rests for a fraction of a second on the intercom on her desk that can put her in touch, through a simple sequence of button pushing, with the gallery's security guard. She is beginning to suspect she could be in a potentially dangerous situation. "Hold on. How did you get in here?"

The woman stops on the other side of the desk and sends deceptive facial messages of surprise while her mouth twists in an expression of disgust. She leans her body over the desk and rests her palms on its surface. Her rhythmically convulsive facial features could be found attractive by someone attracted to features that convey permanent dissatisfaction mixed with potentially explosive fury. The locks of hair that escape from her ponytail and fall over her face give her a certain air of matricidal heroine in a Greek tragedy.

"I'm Saudade's wife," says the woman.

Hannah Linus lifts a hand to her mouth and begins to chew on a cuticle while inside her the feeling that she could indeed be in a potentially dangerous situation grows. The door that connects the gallery with the office area is not locked, and the woman must have gotten in when the guard was distracted. Her hand tries to surreptitiously approach the intercom on her desk, but before she has a chance to reach it the woman grabs the device with both hands and pulls on it with all her strength, trying to rip it from its network of different colored wires. She doesn't manage it on the first try, or the second, and the woman continues wrestling with the intercom in her hands. Pulling furiously and fruitlessly on the network of wires. Hannah Linus looks past the woman. Past the office's reinforced glass wall. Toward the security guard who has just become aware of the situation that is going on and is now running through the empty gallery toward the reinforced glass door.

"I don't deny this is a delicate situation." Hannah Linus looks at the security guard. He has just arrived at the door and is now struggling with the door handle, not yet realizing that it's bolted from inside. "This is all very unpleasant."

The woman with the nervous tic opens her eyes very wide in a gesture that paradoxically does not emphasize the elements of compulsive surprise already present on her facial landscape.

"You're a whore," she says. "If you ever see my husband again I'll kill you."

She pauses and seems to realize that she's still holding up Hannah Linus's desk intercom. She looks at it for a moment as if someone had just put it in her hand as an annoying joke and she places it back on the desk.

Hannah closes her eyes and raises her hands the way people raise their hands when asking for a moment to think. The security guard's struggle with the door is now clearly audible as the glass door beats against its metal support structure, causing a weak vibration of the other glass walls. The woman continues to lean slightly over the desk and observes Hannah Linus with an expression in which surprise seems to have completely disappeared in favor of rage. A rage that's present in all of her features as small seismic tremors.

"I'm not going to see your husband again." Hannah makes small pacifying movements with her hands. "I swear. Step back a bit. This is making me quite nervous."

The security guard has stopped struggling with the door and is now talking on his walkie-talkie while making a series of hand gestures in Hannah's direction through the glass door of her office. The security guard's gestures seem to be both asking her to wait a few seconds and assuring her that everything is going to be resolved in a satisfactory fashion. The woman in sportswear with the nervous tic and not very flattering styling that was probably created without the help of a professional stylist takes a step back. Her mouth still gathered in an irritated expression.

"I'll kill you." The woman backs up slowly toward the door and stops to point at Hannah with her index finger and thumb extended upward. With that universal threat usually known as the Finger Pistol. "You understand?"

Hannah Linus rolls her executive chair a couple of inches back and picks up a pen from her desk. She holds the pen by the end opposite the point and makes a series of taps on the desk with the cap end. It is a gesture that she has been perfecting over hundreds of executive meetings. Meant to both attract the attention of whomever she is talking to as well as dramatically underscore her words.

"Talk to your husband." Hannah Linus looks at the woman with some sort of renewed confidence. In the background of her visual field, her administrative assistant, Raquel, is running a bunch of keys over to the place where the security guard is waiting. The security guard is now looking at Hannah Linus with a reassuring smile whose main message seems to be that the situation of imminent danger to Hannah Linus's personal safety is already in the process of being defused. "This type of situation *can* be solved. Contrary to what they say."

What happens next takes Hannah Linus by surprise. Probably because she was already anticipating an uncomplicated conclusion. So that she is unable to interpret the movement of her adversary. Nor does she manage to get out of the way when the woman comes around the desk and attacks her. Causing the chair and its occupant to fall over onto the carpeted floor. The two women are rolling around on the ground with several locks of Hannah Linus's hair tightly grasped in the other woman's hands when Raquel finally manages to open the glass door. With the fourth key that she tries in the lock.

CHAPTER 25

A Momentary Lapse of Reason

"On one hand you've got Gilmour." Mr. Bocanegra takes a drag on his enormous cigar and looks through the windshield of his two-seater convertible Jaguar, stopping at the stoplight on the corner of Pelayo and Ramblas. "Gilmour is, basically, a numbskull. And on the other hand there's Waters. The guy who wrote *Dark Side of the Moon. The Wall. Wish You Were Here.* I mean, he's a genius. With one of those strange minds. His music is strange, I won't deny that. Waters is the guy that Gilmour kicked out of the group."

This afternoon it is not Mr. Bocanegra at the wheel of his brand-new convertible Jaguar, which now turns the corner of Pelayo and Ramblas and heads down the Ramblas. It is Aníbal Manta that's driving. With his wrist resting on the open window and his enormous hand hanging outside the vehicle. And with two pieces of cotton stuffed into the nostrils of his nose, which was broken last night by Mr. Bocanegra. After he confirmed that Raymond Panakian had escaped the headquarters of LORENZO GIRAUT, LTD. A nose that in its present state no longer looks like a nose. It isn't very clear what exactly it looks like now, but it definitely bears some resemblance to a swollen, irregular meteorite that crossed the stratosphere and crashed violently into the middle of Aníbal Manta's face.

"It's as if Watson fired Sherlock Holmes," continues Bocanegra. Drumming with his fingers on the glove compartment to the beat of the Pink Floyd compact disc that's playing on the Jaguar's compact disc player. "As if that Indian that went around with the Lone Ranger one day just up and handed the Lone Ranger a pink slip and started trying to do everything the Lone Ranger did. Which would be absurd." He shows his teeth in a cruel smile. "Because the Lone Ranger can only do what he does *because he is* the Lone Ranger."

The Ramblas are as congested as they are every evening. The center walkway is mostly filled with groups of British citizens singing and drinking beer from enormous plastic cups that they then throw at each other or simply let drop to the ground between heaves. The image makes one think of hordes of native British Islanders before the arrival of the Romans. There are also groups of drunk girls that stagger up the main lane of the Ramblas and seem to be celebrating something undefined. Hugging each other. Raising swaying arms to halt taxis and struggling to remain vertical.

"It's as if one day you show up at my office and you kick me out of my own business," says Bocanegra with a frown. He can't imagine what so many drunk girls could be celebrating. Except perhaps International Drunk Girl Day. He shrugs his shoulders. "It's as if you come to my business and throw me out and from that moment on you sit at my desk and you smoke my cigars and you decide that *you* are going to run *my* business. Not caring that I *invented* my business. Or that I am the best at what I do, or that in the end it's the only thing I'm good at. Because you are a numbskull and a loser and I am the guy that invented what I do. Well, that's what happened in Pink Floyd. When Gilmour the numbskull kicked out Waters the genius." Bocanegra leans forward to turn up the volume on the compact disc player. The CD that's on is *A Momentary Lapse of Reason* by Pink Floyd. The song that's playing is "Learning to Fly."

The British people that fill the main walkway of the Ramblas have very short hair and sportswear and carry lit cigarettes and very large plastic cups filled with beer. Their necks are that intense red color that rural Americans' necks supposedly are. The main brands of their sportswear are Burberry and Nike. Many of them wear soccer jerseys of British teams. Some of them are naked from the waist up, in spite of the fact that the giant thermometer at Puerta del Ángel has dipped below the area where there are numbers to represent the temperature. A couple of them are wearing full-body rabbit costumes of the kind that seem to have become popular that winter in Barcelona. Costumes sold in souvenir stores for tourists, filling the streets with giant rabbits.

"The history of Pink Floyd is like life." Bocanegra takes a pensive drag on his cigar. "Or perhaps one should say that life is like the history of Pink Floyd. First there was Barrett. The origin of it all. The original genius, if you will. But nobody remembers. How the hell could they remember? The only people who saw Barrett perform with Pink Floyd were a few Englishmen so stoned they can't remember what they saw. That was in the sixties, of course. Then came Waters. And that was the worst of all. Because it turns out that there are people who remember Waters. We remember him. And now we have to bear the fact of remembering Waters and remembering his genius and his music. And all we have is *that memory of better times*. And Gilmour the numbskull. Playing songs that don't belong to him and ruining everything with his lack of genius. You understand?" As the Jaguar gets to the end of the Ramblas, the landscape changes. The tiny street entrances on either side are filled with shady-looking people. With that stereotypical gesturing that people use when carrying out illegal transactions. Looking around furtively. Making transactions below waist level and looking over their shoulders with serious expressions. There are also guys vomiting with the palms of their hands resting on the façades of buildings and their heads hanging between their arms.

"It's a *symbolic* thing. It's like the ages of man or something like that. Barrett and then Waters and then Gilmour. It's like life. It's like remembering old friends that aren't around and not being able to do anything to make them come back. Maybe you'll understand when you get to be my age."

The Jaguar gets to the end of the Ramblas and turns onto the circle with the monument to Christopher Columbus in the middle, and takes the coastal road that's moderately filled with traffic at this hour of the early evening. The thrashing that Mr. Bocanegra gave Aníbal Manta last night wasn't limited to breaking his nose with a head butt. When Manta fell to his knees, Bocanegra grabbed the baseball bat held out by a terrified Saudade and beat him on the chest, back, and arms with it. While Saudade and Eric Yanel and Lucas Giraut watched in terror. Bocanegra found it particularly pleasurable to beat up Aníbal Manta in front of Lucas Giraut. Due to the warmly paternal feelings he has toward his old friend's young son. A clearly paternal pride came over him as he heard Manta's ribs crack under the bat. Something similar to that warm feeling you get showing your son how to bait a hook or cast a line over the waves. While Aníbal Manta trembled on the ground, shrunk into a fetal position and protecting his head with his hands, Mr. Bocanegra looked at Giraut with a warm smile. Bocanegra had to repress an ineffable desire to give him the bloodstained bat, tousle his hair affectionately and encourage him to finish the job.

The coastal road becomes more and more empty as they leave behind the city and the airport. Soon the highway begins to flow placidly through an astonishingly uniform landscape of coastal housing developments and roadside bars. With withered palm trees flanking the road. Many of the roadside bars have multicolored blinking neon signs whose bulbs form exuberant female outlines.

Bocanegra takes out his portable organizer equipped with a satellite global positioning device and introduces the exact location of the roadside bar where his contact has indicated he can find Raymond Panakian. That's one of the big advantages of being Mr. Bocanegra: the fact that no one can hide from him. Thanks to his ubiquitous and always alert network of contacts, spread out everywhere. Or at least within the area of influence of his empire of cocktail bars, nightclubs, discothèques and restaurants. That empire with The Dark Side of the Moon at its center, which is like a living creature lying in wait for its prey. Always awake. Always sniffing around in search of those things that Mr. Bocanegra wants to find. And always willing to make a little call to Mr. Bocanegra's cell phone to let him know, merely as a little insignificant favor, where a certain individual, of certain renown in the underworld, that Bocanegra has lost just a few hours earlier, can be found. Something that is always appreciated. And something that Aníbal Manta in particular should appreciate. Because, after all, said phone call has just saved his skin.

"We're almost there," says Mr. Bocanegra, still drumming his fingers to the beat of the Pink Floyd compact disc. And giving copious signs of being in a good mood. "Keep going past two more blocks of apartments, then three roadside bars, take a left exit and look for a neon sign in the shape of a girl with devil's horns," he says, tracing the directions that appear on the screen of his global positioning system with his finger. "The place is called Judas."

Five minutes later, Aníbal Manta parks the Jaguar in the client parking lot of the roadside bar named Judas. From where, less than an hour ago, came the casual call to Mr. Bocanegra saying that the individual commonly known as Raymond Panakian was having glass after glass of Macallan at the hostess bar and sticking wrinkled fifty-euro bills into the dancers' panties. The building that houses Judas is a block of cement similar to a warehouse, with a neon sign on the roof and surrounded by withered palm trees. With no windows. With an exaggeratedly well-lit main entrance that's protected by a couple of security guards with headphone intercoms.

"We have to do this discreetly," says Mr. Bocanegra when Aníbal Manta turns off the engine and takes out the ignition key, making David Gilmour's voice suddenly stop. "These people are our *friends.* We don't want to make a scene. I know the owner of this bar. He's a good man. His business is based on discretion. Just like ours. And we wouldn't like anyone making a ruckus in one of our places. Right?"

Aníbal Manta nods. He gives the Jaguar's keys to the parking valet and gets out of the car, followed by his boss. The two security guards at the door step aside to let them through with barely the slightest shudder of the muscles behind their identical sunglasses, betraying the fact that they've recognized the two men. Once inside the bar, Bocanegra and Manta wait a second for their eyes to adjust to the reddish half-light. An old single from the English band Iron Maiden plays on the sound system. Aníbal Manta feels a warm wave of recognition. When he was a troubled teenager traumatized by the stigma of his physical appearance, Manta used to listen to Iron Maiden tapes. In his opinion it's obvious that Iron Maiden were much better than Dio. Better than Saxon. Even better than Megadeth.

The bar employee who approaches them with an obsequious smile is dressed in stiletto heels and sequined panties. She also has something like sequins, maybe glitter, sprinkled over her face and torso.

"My name is Anaïs," the employee says to them. "I'm here to ensure you have an unforgettable evening."

"His name is Mr. Bocanegra." Aníbal Manta points to Bocanegra with his thumb. His plugged-up nostrils turn his voice into some sort of rich, buzzing boom. "We came to look for a friend of ours. If everyone minds their own business, I don't think anybody will end up getting hurt."

Anaïs's obsequious smile melts like a bar of soap that's fallen into a vat of steaming sulfuric acid and is replaced by an expression of immense terror. She nods several times and moves away from the two men as quickly as her stiletto heels allow her. Her speed gives her bare breasts an exaggerated rhythmic vertical sway. Some of the clients that have been watching the scene surreptitiously also begin distancing maneuvers. Some of which are so subtle as to hardly be noticed, and others so hasty that they leave behind unfinished cocktails and scantily clad companions.

Raymond Panakian is sitting on a stool at the hostess bar with his back curved, dressed in the same blue, paint-stained coveralls he was wearing when he escaped the night before. His facial expression suggests that he's been sitting on that same stool for a long time and has drunk several dozen glasses of Macallan. Under the bar's strobe lights, the paint smatterings on his face and hair make him look like a lazily trancelike model from some seminal work of the psychedelic film genre. At one point he extends his arm in an almost nostalgic gesture to touch the genitals of the striptease dancer dancing in front of him. Something that looks like a string of saliva falls from the corner of his mouth.

Aníbal Manta and Mr. Bocanegra sit on the stools beside Raymond Panakian. One on each side. The striptease dancer dancing in front of him begins to distance herself subtly. Still dancing.

"Under normal circumstances," says Bocanegra to Panakian's bowed and vaguely drooling head, "I would be the one to take care of you. As a question of hierarchy, of course. I'd be the one that'd make you understand that it's not right to leave a job with no notice, et cetera. And without finishing the job, obviously. It is one of my duties as supreme chief. To give those who are doing something they shouldn't a few good tugs on the ear and then smile and pat them on the back and tell them not to worry about it after all. That we're all friends here and that we've never held a grudge. And yet, given the present circumstances"—Bocanegra points with his head to Aníbal Manta, sitting on the stool on the other side of Panakian—"I think that my friend Aníbal is interested in being the one who has that little chat with you *personally*. And I'm going to let him have that." His lips trace an enormous cruel smile. "That is if you don't mind, of course."

Panakian turns his head slowly to look at Manta. Aníbal Manta nods his head and says something that's unintelligible because his nostrils are clogged with dried blood and broken cartilage and cotton balls. The only words that can be understood are "recognize" and "mother."

Raymond Panakian's next movement is completely unexpected from a man of his age and complexion, especially a man who seems to have drunk so many dozens of glasses of Macallan. As if he had some sort of spring in his lower body, or perhaps a jet engine. Panakian shoots forward and up toward the spot where the dancer had been just a minute earlier. It's probably one of those physical feats born of absolute desperation and fear for one's life. Which can only be pulled off when the seized-up, desperate mind forgets for a second that the body is incapable of it. And it almost works. Raymond Panakian is about to successfully jump from his bar stool to the stage. Except for the fact that just as he is hanging in midair, Aníbal Manta manages to grab him by the ankle. Causing Panakian's floating body to jerk and fall facedown on the edge of the stage. Breaking most of his teeth against it.

"Grrfssslll," says Panakian from the floor. Spitting out pieces of teeth and protecting his head with his hands.

"I don't understand," says Mr. Bocanegra with a frown. He raises a hand to his ear in that universal gesture meant to show someone that they haven't spoken loudly or clearly enough. "What do you think he said?"

"I don't know," says Aníbal Manta. "Must be one of those weird languages."

Mr. Bocanegra picks up a pool cue from a rack beside one of the pool tables. By that point, the vast majority of people in the establishment have already left or are taking cover behind some piece of furniture, watching with fascinated horror. Bocanegra grabs the pool cue by both ends and breaks it in half over his knee. Then he tosses the larger piece to Aníbal Manta. Manta catches it airborne.

What happens next is quick, efficient and not pretty. Manta grabs Raymond Panakian by the scruff of the neck and lifts him to shoulder height. He pushes him against the edge of the stage in such a way that Panakian's body is conveniently folded in half with his rear end slightly projected outward. In one swift tug he pulls down his pants and his underwear.

"Be careful with the hands," says Mr. Bocanegra.

Aníbal Manta looks at his hands quizzically.

"No, you idiot, with his hands."

Manta lets out a grunt of acquiescence. Then he looks at Panaki-an's pale, scrawny backside. With the splintered piece of pool cue in his hand. With the same facial expression that Olympic archers have before releasing an arrow. Or bowlers before sending the ball down the lane. The spectators groan and make horrified faces and shake their heads. Aníbal Manta smiles beneath his broken nose.

CHAPTER 26

The Lost River Within

Eric Yanel stretches out his neck periscopically to see above the heads of the party guests, who are nothing like any idea Yanel has ever had about what party guests should be. In spite of the fact that it's perfectly clear that a party is being celebrated in the uptown nightclub. There are uniformed waiters strolling with trays of filled glasses, which are being replaced with empty glasses at a dizzying rate. Everyone is animatedly drinking and smoking and talking. But Yanel can't seem to reconcile the *guests* with his idea of a party. Many of them are fat. Others are old, and some are both things at once. No one is wearing really expensive clothes and most of those present have no discernible hairstyle. A veritable ocean of spare tires, beer bellies, fat ankles, swaying double chins and nonexistent waists as far as the eye can see. Many of the guests look as if they've never set foot in a gym in their lives.

After a moment, Yanel locates Iris Gonzalvo at a distant point of the party. Talking to a guy with a wide face and metal-rimmed glasses. The most striking aesthetic element of the guy talking to Iris seems to be an ass much larger than any ass Yanel has ever seen on a man. An ass that would even be too big on a woman. Big and fat. It used to be that Iris would never have been seen in public talking to a man with an ass like that. Yanel feels vaguely alarmed. With his drink in his hand, and trying not to touch anyone more than strictly necessary, he makes his way through the mass of unlikely party guests that separates him from his fiancée.

"I don't think you should feel bad," the guy with the unbelievably fat ass is saying to Iris when Eric stops in front of them with his drink in his hand. "For having put out your cigarette in that man's face. Of course it is annoying that he's suing you and all that. Especially when you say you're going through a difficult moment financially." He shrugs his shoulders. Now that he can see it up close, Yanel speculates that the guy's face is actually wider than it is long. "But you definitely were expressing what you were feeling. Solving a complex communi- cative situation. It was brave to do what you did. And, more impor- tantly, you were completely sincere."

Iris Gonzalvo turns partway toward Eric Yanel and looks at him with a slight frown. Yanel doesn't detect anything in her gaze that resembles sympathy. Which causes him certain confusion: Was there ever anything positive in the way his fiancée looked at him, or is he feeling nostalgia for something that only ever existed in his imagina- tion? The truth is he can't remember.

"Eric," she says to him, "This is Álex Jardí. He writes books. Those things people read. I was telling him about my problems, about you never being able to get it up anymore. And how no one wants to give you work anymore and we have no money and no one has called us in months." She takes a sip on her drink without taking her eyes off of Yanel. Then she gestures with the half-empty cup to the guy with the unbelievably fat ass. "Álex published a best seller a few years ago. One of those books that help people find themselves and live happier lives. Called *The Lost Rivers of London*."

"They're four independent stories," explains Álex Jardí. "But in- terconnected. I consider it a sort of manual. To finding your own inner lost river. That's what I call that person we all have inside of us. The person we want to be. We all have one inside but we have to learn to let it out. To metamorphose."

Yanel looks at the guy with the fat ass. His face is wide in a way that makes you think of cartoon characters that have been hit by a falling piano, making them more horizontal than vertical.

"I don't understand anything," says Yanel. "I don't understand what these people are." He points with his head toward the people around him. His facial expression makes one think of Muslim clerics at a summer foam party. Of Oxford graduates in the middle of a slum. Of Japanese people in any social event outside of Japan. "I also don't understand why we're here when we could be in some normal party. Who's throwing this party? I don't know anyone."

"You don't know anyone because this is a *literary* party," Iris tells him. "The people here are writers, editors and journalists. Which is to say not the kind of party that you're used to. There are no naked whores carrying around trays filled with lines of cocaine. And you're probably gonna have a hard time finding someone to suck you off in the bathroom." She makes a vague gesture with the hand that holds her drink, toward Yanel's crotch. "Although it must not be very fun for you anyway. Considering you can't get it up anymore."

Eric Yanel rubs the wings of his nose with a circular movement of his index finger and thumb, which is one of his traditional nervous gestures. One of Eric Yanel's Classic Nervous Gestures. One of those gestures that people who know him automatically associate with his idiosyncratic gesticular repertoire. The wings of Eric Yanel's nose seem to be always red. As the result of some kind of localized skin irritation. Eric Yanel's other Classic Nervous Gestures are (a) sniffling loudly and often while wrinkling up his entire face, and (b) abruptly tossing his head back to reconfigure his coiffed blond hair, the way hair models on television shampoo commercials toss their heads back to shake their long locks and the way regular people shake their long hair in parody of the shampoo ads. In Yanel's case, however, there doesn't seem to be any attempt at parody. Parody seems, in general, to be foreign to his expressive repertoire.

"Everything works fine when I masturbate." Yanel looks at Iris with a frown. "I've told you many times. So it's not strictly true that I can't get it up. It's not the same thing that I can't get it up *with someone else* as if I can't *ever* get it up." He pauses. Several of the guests located in groups meta-adjacent to where Yanel is talking to Iris are looking at him out of the corners of their eyes. "I could give you a thousand excuses. That's obvious. But I'd rather not. That's something that I think you should appreciate. As my fiancée and all."

"Iris told me that she wants to become a famous actress," says Álex Jardí. His ass is excessive, according to every known canon, yet its enormous size seems to give him a certain quality that's hard to explain. A certain moral solidity. Or a certain extraordinarily solid anchoring to the ground. "She also told me that you might try to thwart her success. Due to envy brought on by your own failure as an actor."

Yanel makes a pained face and leans forward to massage his knee with his hands.

"Who *is* this guy?" he says. With his waist doubled forward and still stroking his knee. "And why are we here? I've never read a book, I don't think. Maybe when I was a kid." He looks up at Iris Gonzalvo, who is now looking at him with her arms crossed and an impatient expression. "And what do you mean by all that? And why are you talking to me in that tone of voice?"

At this point it is difficult not to suspect that some of the members of the groups meta-adjacent to the group composed of Eric, Iris and the man named Álex Jardí have subtly moved closer in order to eavesdrop on the conversation. Some vectors and degrees of head leaning seem to corroborate this suspicion.

"I mean," says Iris, "that I'm tired of deodorant ads where you can only see your armpit. What makes you think I want to marry someone who's in commercials where you can only see his armpit?

Same goes for ads where my fiancé is running the marathon with two thousand other people. Not to mention the car commercials." Now all the expressive elements of her face and body seem to be focused on transmitting fatigued repugnance: the crossed arms; the rolled eyes; the head slightly cocked to one side. "We are here because I've decided to start meeting interesting people. For the first time in my life. And I can't believe you're going to start that number with your knee. Do you *really* think it's going to work again?"

Eric Yanel leaves his drink on a passing waiter's tray and squats on the floor. With a look of intense pain. Grabbing his knee with that expression, like he'd just eaten something rotten, that athletes have as they grab their knees or other recently injured body parts.

"It's one of his tricks," says Iris Gonzalvo to the man with the fattest ass Eric Yanel has seen in his life. "The knee thing. He does it to get pity. In situations like this. Shit." She snorts in irritation. "I can't believe I used to fall for it."

Now Eric Yanel is sitting on the floor. Hugging his leg, with an expression of intense pain on his face. Several of the party guests approach him and ask if he's okay. Yanel looks up from his knee and at where Iris Gonzalvo was just a moment before. And where she is no longer.

Yanel leaps up. He extends out his neck periscopically and searches the room with his gaze. Several guests continue to approach him with glasses of water, putting their hands on his arm and asking him if he needs anything. Solicitous men with bellies hanging like basketballs. Women with horribly cellulitic thighs. Bloated calves. Yanel pushes them away and finally manages to see Iris's svelte figure and long dark hair in the distance. In the section of the party closest to the exit. She seems to be getting her fur coat and her tall, furry Moscow-inspired hat from the coat check. She waits with a neutral expression for an employee to help her put her coat on and then leaves the nightclub with majestic strides. Yanel's face is as shaken as if someone had hit him over the head with a mallet.

"Something similar happened to me once," says the guy with the fat ass and the comically wide face. While Yanel looks toward the exit, his face shaken. "I mean those erection problems you have. When it happened, my wife and I used all kinds of sex toys. Even vibrating objects and electronic thingamajigs. And once in a while, I didn't mind paying some guy to fill in on certain conjugal duties," said the guy with the fat ass. His expression transmits a strange enthusiasm. An enthusiasm reminiscent of Oriental holy men. At the happy end of their chain of reincarnations. "We also enjoyed public places, or unlikely settings."

Eric Yanel begins to shiver. At the center of a circle of glasses of water and solicitous offers of medical help. His lower jaw seems to be out of joint and trembling at the same time. In spite of what he said a few minutes ago, it's not entirely true that he has no problem getting satisfactory erections in private. He has actually begun to have problems with the very idea of an erection. The erection as the central distinctive element of the male condition. Yanel has been feeling an unpleasant pressure on his male psyche for months now. He doesn't like to think about his penis and when he does, it's with certain anxiety. He avoids looking at his penis when he showers. Which has been creating a sort of blind spot in his showers. A blind spot located at the height of his crotch. To draw his attention away from it, Yanel has put a portable compact disc player in the bathroom and he sings along to commercial pop songs from the eighties while he showers. Eric Yanel's favorite pop singer is Madonna. Particularly her records from the eighties. The rest of the time, Yanel attributes his general lack of interest in phallic sex to his fiancée's phallic obsession, and the stress that obsession generates in him. On a couple of recent occasions he has paid prostitutes to have them masturbate in front of him, or to let him lick their anuses or vaginas.

After a moment of paralysis, Yanel blinks. In that surprised way people who've just come out of a trance blink. He stammers out something unintelligible about his knee and starts to limp as fast as he can through the guests.

Yanel reaches Iris at the corner of the Pedralbes street where Iris is standing in front of a traffic light, her arms crossed over her chest and her body leaned slightly forward and to one side the way people do when waiting for a taxi. Eric Yanel approaches her limping flamboyantly. It is one of those bright winter nights when the scattered stars and the positioning lights of planes in the sky generate metaphors of the Implacability of Cosmic Loneliness and the Possibility of Life Being Shortened by Cancer. Iris's fur coat and her tall, furry hat, in the urban landscape of wrought-iron garden gates and early-twentieth-century mansions, bestow the scene with the unmistakable quality of a romantic theater piece. Yanel left his jacket in the coat check.

"I'm ready to give it another try," says Yanel. His panting creates misty little clouds of steam in the frozen air. "I mean fucking. Not that I really want to. I've already explained how bad the pressure and everything make me feel. But I can try. Really."

There is a moment of silence. Iris's silhouette is genuinely romantic, with her arms crossed over her fur coat. Yanel is standing before her, turned to one side, with his back curved forward and one hand on his knee. A bit like a Russian soldier in a romantic play, wounded and leaned elegantly toward one of those Russian ladies.

"You can try." Iris takes some sort of powder compact out of the pocket of her coat. She picks up a little bit of cocaine from inside of it with a key and sticks it into her nostril. Then she sniffs. "But not with me. I'm leaving you. Good-bye. We're not engaged anymore." She lifts her eyebrows. "We're not even boyfriend and girlfriend anymore."

"I swear things are going to change." Yanel takes a wallet out of his pants pocket and starts rifling around inside it. "For real this time. I mean, not like the last time I told you things were going to change. You hear me? This time things are *definitely* going to change. My career is really going to take off. This time *for real*. I met someone. One of those eccentric millionaires. His name is Giraut." He finally finds what he was looking for in his wallet. A business card. He pulls it out with trembling fingers and gives it to Iris. "He lives in a gigantic mansion. I've been there lots of times. A patron of the arts. A good friend of mine. He's going to produce a movie for me. As the star. Scriptwriter. Director. Whatever I want. You can be in it, too, of course."

The vaguely orangish glow of the streetlights on the wrought-iron garden gates and early-twentieth-century mansions and Iris's Moscow-inspired silhouette intensify the atmosphere of a Russian romantic theater set. Like those orangish spotlights they project right onto the actors in romantic plays set on winter streets with streetlights painted onto the backdrop. Iris examines the card with an impatient expression.

"It doesn't say anything here about him being a film producer," she says. "It says here: Lucas Giraut. Antiques Dealer. By Appointment Only."

"You don't understand these things." Yanel looks desperately at an empty taxi that approaches the stoplight where they are standing. "This guy is an intellectual. His family made a fortune off antiques. Oriental art. Old paintings of eclipses and stuff like that."

Iris gestures to the taxi with her hand. The taxi slows down and finally stops in front of her.

"You can't leave me." Yanel tries to take a cigarette out of a pack but his hand is shaky and several cigarettes fall onto the sidewalk. "I gave you everything you have. You owe me your career." He pauses. "If you leave me I could *kill you*," he adds in a dubious tone.

Eric Yanel watches as the taxi drives off with Iris inside, showing him her middle finger through the window. Then he starts to head off down the street, dragging his leg.

CHAPTER 27

The Day of the World Launch of Stephen King's New Novel

The Day of the World Launch of Stephen King's New Novel is coming to an end. The rays of late-afternoon sun fall through the balconies of the Gothic Quarter like the incandescent ashes of a silent fire. The chromatic range of the late-afternoon sun on the roofs also suggests that something is burning in some part of the sky.

Valentina Parini is sitting with her legs crossed on her bed in her bedroom on the first floor of the Palau de la Mar Fosca. Experiencing a feeling of imminent danger. The Christmas sounds filtering through the wall and closed windows of the former palace not only fail to dispel the feeling of danger but seem to increase it. A few hours ago Valentina Parini discovered that she can only mitigate the feeling of danger by sitting with her legs crossed at the head of her bed and rocking backward rhythmically so that the back of her head hits the wall.

"Tina?" calls her mother from the bathroom where she is blow-drying her hair during the preparatory phase of her Friday-night Husband Hunting Expedition. "Will you come here for a minute?"

In front of her bed, in a niche of the wall that Marcia Parini thinks looks too much like an altar, is the broken alarm clock that Valentina Parini was carrying in her hand the last time she saw her father. The last day she ever saw her father. When she went out into the street looking for him so he could fix the broken alarm clock and she found him putting his last packed-up belongings into the trunk of his car. And she stayed there, with the broken alarm clock in her hand, planted in the doorway of the former ducal palace, while her father just said good-bye with a nervous smile, got into the car as fast as he could and drove off, never to return. The day when things really started to go bad in Valentina Parini's life. Not to say that they were good before.

"Valentina?" Her mother's voice sounds somewhat opaque and at the same time somewhat shrill from inside the blow-dryer's aerial sound cushion. "Remember what we talked about, about having your head in the clouds."

The feeling of danger that Valentina Parini is experiencing tonight, which forces her for some reason to rock back and forth and hit the back of her head against the wall, began at some point this morning. At first she didn't pay it much attention. At first it wasn't much more than some kind of pins and needles. Like the feeling you might be being watched. It got worse at lunchtime and during her afternoon classes, until her hands were too rigid to hold a spoon or a pen. Later, at home, the feeling became incredibly urgent. Like someone aiming at your head with a loaded weapon.

Valentina checks the time on the clock on her desk: it's eight thirty. The back of her head, which she's been hitting against the wall for quite a while, hurts. To be precise, it seems that the *combination* of the rhythmic motion and the pain is what helps to mitigate the feeling of danger. Now she leaps up from the bed and walks through the hallway holding her breath and clenching her fists tightly. Like those people in horror movies who walk through the hallway of an abandoned house seconds before someone bursts into the darkness of the hallway with a butcher's knife. From the doorway of the bathroom she sees her mother drying her hair in her mother's traditional hair-drying posture: leaning forward, sticking her butt out and moving her head alternately to dry the respective hair that hangs from one side of her head and the other. Valentina bites a knuckle with a pensive expression and observes her mother's ass. She's always found her mother's ass strange and unpleasant. Absurdly soft and flaccid. Tonight, however, she finds the sight of Marcia Parini's ass almost unbearable, and it conjures up all sorts of mental images of marine mammals. Once Valentina saw something on TV about marine mammals and ever since then she's been haunted by those images of greasy beings with mottled gray skin and horrifying warts.

Valentina goes into the bathroom with her face wrinkled in disgust. She kneels in front of the toilet and vomits a couple of streams of something liquid and bitter. Marcia Parini lifts up her head and looks at her daughter while still drying her hair.

"Did you stuff yourself with chocolate again?" she says. With the same simultaneously opaque and shrill voice that she uses to make herself heard over the blow-dryer. "It serves you right. Didn't I tell you to defrost yesterday's leftover lasagna?"

Valentina lifts the palm of one hand to indicate that she's okay and for a moment she has to repress the desire to hit her head against the edge of the toilet.

"You're going to be alone for a little while tonight." Marcia Parini turns off the hair dryer and puts a tight dress on over her underwear. "If your grandmother calls, tell her I went to a Book Club meeting. You can watch TV, but just regular TV. No satellite stuff." She looks in the mirror and adjusts the straps of the tight dress with her fingers. "And leave the lights on in the living room and stairway, the last time I almost broke my neck."

Valentina proceeds to rinse out her mouth as her mother leaves the bathroom. Then she hears the clickety-clack of the high heels her mother wears when she goes out husband hunting and, a minute later, the noise of the door to the street closing.

Valentina Parini leans her head slightly and squints her eyes and concentrates on trying to hear Lucas Giraut's footsteps in the apartment upstairs. Sometimes she follows his itineraries through the house: from the sofa to the fridge, from the kitchen to the television, from the bed to the bath. When she's home alone with her mother, it comforts her to know that Lucas is in the apartment upstairs. Doing his usual routines, seated in front of the computer or simply reading his professional magazines about antiques. Tonight no footsteps are heard, or any other noise that would indicate that

Lucas Giraut is in his apartment on the upper floor of the former ducal palace. In Valentina's opinion, Lucas Giraut isn't stupid like other people. In the moments when Valentina Parini isn't wishing with all her heart that her mother wasn't her mother, she wouldn't mind if Lucas married her.

At eleven thirty on the Night of the World Launch of Stephen King's New Novel, Valentina puts on her parka and goes out. She crosses the Plaza Sant Jaume with its stupid institutional crèche made entirely of recyclable materials and takes Ferran Street. At this time on a Friday night, the streets of the Gothic Quarter are filled with groups of drunk British and Irish tourists singing British and Irish songs and vomiting on the sidewalks. Although she walks with her head bowed and her hands in the pockets of the parka, several British and Irish tourists start following her, saying things in English and even trying to touch her. A couple of teenage Arab petty thieves try to corner her against a wall, but she stares at them and something in the way she stares at them makes them back up, terrified. When she finally gets to the Ramblas, the contrast makes them seem like a much more pleasant place. With their hordes of tourist families and sleepy policemen.

The entrance to the franchise store in the Plaza Catalunya where the Launch Party for Stephen King's New Novel is taking place has been decorated for the occasion with a gigantic promotional banner that has the title of Stephen King's new novel, WONDERFUL WORLD, above a stereotypically idyllic image of an American suburb. Valentina Parini goes up the escalator wringing her hands. The feeling of danger that she's been feeling all day seems to have solidified and concentrated around this moment and place. The moment she's been waiting for for weeks, but which for some reason seems to have transformed into a vortex of danger. Some of the customers of the franchise store move aside to let her pass.

When she gets to the floor where the bookstore is, she finds hundreds of Stephen King fans lined up in front of the counter where the first copies will soon be available for sale. The fans on line are mostly wearing promotional T-shirts and caps for different Stephen King novels and films, and heavy metal bands. One of the fans is wearing a full-body bunny costume, the kind they sell at the souvenir shops. Some of them look at Valentina with terrified expressions and move aside as she comes through. She advances with erratic steps to the end of the line.

A couple of minutes pass. A pair of salesgirls wearing the store's two-tone corporate vest hand out promotional T-shirts for WON-DERFUL WORLD to the fans on line. With the same bucolic suburban scene and the same inscription, WONDERFUL WORLD, that adorns all the display stands and banderoles. When she gets to Valentina's spot in line, the employee looks at her with a concerned smile and offers her a large T-shirt.

"I only have sizes L and XL left," the salesgirl starts to say, but she stops short when she sees Valentina's face. Who is now gnawing on the inside of her cheeks to mitigate the feeling of danger. "Okay, kid," she adds in a slightly annoyed tone, "you don't have to get like that."

One of the fans in the line is dressed as a zombie. He has white makeup on and his hair is covered in some sort of green gel and he has a fake scar on his neck that seems to be trying to indicate that he recently had his throat slit. Another of the fans on line has the frighteningly outdated hairstyle and pointy fake ears that characterize those born on the planet Vulcan. Some of the fans chat in low voices, as if they were in some sort of religious setting, and make jokes that can only be understood by Stephen King fans. Photographers, and even a couple of local television cameras, mill around the line taking photos of the fans. In her spot at the end of the line, Valentina Parini can feel her heart rate speeding up and she starts to see strange kaleidoscopic figures in the margins of her visual field. A minute later someone cuts a ribbon like the ones at the openings of official buildings and a burst of applause is heard accompanied by camera flashes. The line begins to advance as the first shoppers acquire their copies of *Wonderful World*.

The first buyer holds his copy up over his head like people do when they've just won a sports trophy.

"Excuse me," the person behind Valentina Parini in line says to her. "The line is moving."

Valentina Parini has once again begun to rock back and forth. The number of fans that look at her strangely and distance themselves has increased in the last few minutes. After a moment, Valentina leaves her place in the line. The Christmas noises seem to come from everywhere and nowhere. The canned corporate carols. Valentina walks toward the desk where smiling employees with two-tone vests are ringing up sales. She takes a copy from the desk and hugs it against her chest.

"Hey," says a fan who's buying his copy right then. "Where are you going? Get back in line."

Valentina Parini snatches the book out of his hands and then tries to do the same thing to another fan near her, but the second fan holds on tightly to his copy and pushes Valentina.

"Excuse me," says one of the employees to Valentina. "You have to wait in line. You can't do that."

Valentina looks at the fan that pushed her with a face filled with hate. One of the employees puts a hand on Valentina's shoulder, and she turns and pushes him so hard against the desk covered with Stephen King's new novel that he falls onto the table. Knocking down all the piles of copies. Shouts are heard.

"Get out," screams Valentina. As the walls of the bookstore begin to spin around her. Or maybe she's the one who's spinning. "*I'm* the only one who can solve this. Leave me *alone*."

Most of the Stephen King fans have opted for moving away from Valentina, who seems to be about to lose her balance. A security guard approaches the scene with his walkie-talkie in his hand. Pushing aside a giant rabbit that is actually a person in a full-body rabbit costume. Valentina kneels on the ground, still hugging the book against her chest. Someone approaches her and she hits them in the crotch with her copy of *Wonderful World*. The employees in charge of selling Stephen King's new novel are explaining what's going on to the security guard, who looks at Valentina with a frown. Some of the press photographers are taking photographs of the girl kneeling on the ground. Someone asks if all this is part of the launch of Stephen King's new novel.

"Fuck," says the Stephen King fan who has the outmoded hairdo and the ears of a Vulcan. "A *real* nutcase."

On her knees on the ground, hugging her book, Valentina Parini bares her teeth threateningly. And in that precise moment, as the clocks in the Plaza Catalunya mark twelve on the dot, the lights in the store begin to flicker. A moment later they go out. The book section where the launch of Stephen King's new book is taking place is completely in the dark. Someone screams. After a moment, most of the Stephen King fans gathered there start shouting in terror.

CHAPTER 28

Eclipse

Eric Yanel observes the upper part of the anonymous building uptown that houses the Hannah Linus Gallery with an anguished expression. Planted in the middle of the sidewalk, in front of the building's fire escape. He is wearing tall rubber boots and a protective jumpsuit, the kind people wear when working with toxic materials. On his jumpsuit there's a silk-screened schematic drawing of a lightning bolt cutting an insect in half and the words "ARNOLD LAYNE, WOOD PARASITE SOLUTIONS." Behind him is Aníbal Manta, disguised in an identical, but much bigger, jumpsuit. The biggest protective jumpsuit Yanel has ever seen in his life. They're both wearing backpacks and have gas masks hanging from their necks. They're both standing on the sidewalk, looking up at the first-floor fire exit, which is directly connected to the offices of Hannah Linus's gallery. A few minutes before midnight on the Night of the World Launch of Stephen King's New Novel, and the street is deserted. The building is dark. The gallery occupies the first three floors, and the rest of the building is all offices. A company that promotes Barcelonian cuisine in the Far East. A company that subcontracts telephone customer care companies for the sale of telephone services. And the offices of a board game distributor on the top floor. The entire building is empty. Each corporate space is protected by its own alarm system. And the winter moon floats lazily over them all.

"Have you looked in a mirror lately?" Aníbal Manta says finally. He looks at his colleague disapprovingly. "What's the point of us dressing like this if you're gonna show up with that face?" He shakes his head. "Why don't you just wear a sign that says 'I'm a criminal'?"

Eric Yanel doesn't look as if he's shaved in many days. The skin on his face has that crusty look of someone who's barely gotten out of bed for days. His traditional long blond wave of hair has turned into something closer to a twisted Mohawk. Rigid and greasy at the same time. His nose and eyes are red, like he's been crying. Now he sighs. He looks over his shoulder at Manta, who gives him a sign to wait. A pedestrian has just turned the corner and is now approaching along the sidewalk. Carrying a couple of department-store bags filled with Christmas gifts and walking with his head bowed, absorbed in the little clouds of steam of his own breath. Manta waits for him to get far enough away and lifts a thumb toward his partner in crime.

"Now," he says. "And make sure your hands don't shake. I'm not in the mood to have you fall on me."

Yanel grabs the lower end of the building's fire escape ladder. He climbs up to the first landing and drops onto the steel structure. Aníbal Manta crosses the street with that paradoxical gracefulness of his that makes you think of superheroes genetically altered by radiation. Yanel picks up the backpack his partner tosses to him and then releases the ladder. The entire steel structure trembles and clatters and threatens to collapse under Aníbal Manta's weight.

Yanel unfolds his case of small, shiny instruments in front of the fire exit. He chooses from the selection of rods and tiny tools that look like miniature dental equipment and spends a minute or two working on the lock. In spite of the cold, a drop of sweat slides down his cheek and falls onto the frost-covered steel of the fire escape. Followed by another. The infinitesimal little noises that his actions produce inside the lock are transformed into an electronic signal and monitored by a little digital device that Manta has stuck to the surface of the door next to the lock. Yanel moves his rods with his gaze fixed on the little device's screen and finally a click is heard, loud enough to cause Manta to let out a satisfied grunt. They both gather up all their vaguely dental equipment as fast as they can and push the door open. Yanel sniffs and Aníbal Manta realizes that what he had thought were drops of sweat were actually tears. Yanel dries his cheeks and takes a deep breath. Like a tormented actress regaining her composure just before going onstage to act in a comedy.

Inside the building, they both place bands with special nonreflective flashlights onto their heads. They have a dark hallway in front of them. From the building's blueprints they know that the hallway ends at the back exit of the gallery's office complex. And that is where they stop. In front of the door's security panel with its magnetic card reader. In front of the office's alarm system box that hangs above the door. Everything seems to converge at that door for an instant. An instant of cosmic respect. Of reverential fear. Aníbal Manta farts in the silence of the hallway.

Yanel runs the copy of Hannah Linus's magnetic card through the reader. A little green light turns on. Beneath the vaguely bluish glow of Yanel and Manta's nonreflective flashlights, Hannah Linus's complex of offices is somewhat like an underwater world. The switched-off computers are banks of coral. The photos of family members, stuffed toys, and other artifacts designed to humanize the desks are the remains of shipwrecks. The broom closets are dangerous underwater caves. On the other side of the office complex lies the door to the gallery. The real Treasure Cave. Yanel opens it with the copy of the card.

The two intruders remain in the threshold for a moment. The gust of air-conditioning that comes in from the gallery brings with it a scent of old things. A scent of wood and earth and something that could be the aroma of moth-eaten fabric stored at the back of a closet. They both look at their watches. Two minutes to midnight. Their operation has so far taken four and a half minutes.

The Night of the World Launch of Stephen King's New Novel is extremely cold and triggers that feeling of distress you get in the seconds before a great disaster. Aníbal Manta and Eric Yanel noticed it in the car on the way to the Hannah Linus Gallery. Hannah Linus herself is noticing it right now, in the form of a sexual session with Saudade that is less satisfying and exhausting than usual and much less filled with moments of evil, self-degrading pleasure. Marcia Parini notices it as a vague fear that something terrible will happen in the discothèque where she is having drinks with a potential sexual partner. Raymond Panakian notices it in the middle of his delirium tremens shakes. Everyone notices it, although just during a few seconds of confusion. Objects are more defined than normal. The fine hair on your skin stands on end when touched, with the exacerbated sensitivity of a high fever. The same empty gallery that on any ordinary night would be placid suggests imminent catastrophe. Like those things that hunt children in their dark bedrooms. Those nameless, shapeless things.

Aníbal Manta and Eric Yanel leave their backpacks on the floor and take out the zippered bags designed to transport fragile works of art. They are silver bags that from the outside are strangely similar to the bags used to transport refrigerated foodstuffs. Each one of their movements inside the gallery has been scrupulously rehearsed and calculated. To save time and enhance the operation's internal efficiency. They take the four St. Kieran Panels off the wall and leave them on

the floor next to their backpacks and zippered bags. The distance between the edges of each painting's base and the hooks that hold it to
the wall have been replicated to the millimeter. Everything is going
well, in spite of the vague, general sensation that everything is going
badly. Then something happens. The two intruders look at each other.
At first it's just a slight trembling of the outlines of things. It takes
them a moment to realize that it's the light flickering. Or, better put,
the lights. The pilot light of the gallery's security circuit. The glow
of the streetlights that enters through the gallery's skylight. Even the
light from the flashlights attached to their heads. Everything blinks
for a second. And then goes out.

Aníbal Manta and Eric Yanel remain in the dark for a moment.
Listening to the noise of their own breathing. Even though they're at
least three feet away from each other, the darkness is so complete that
they can't make out each other's movements. The world seems to have
just disappeared.

"What's going on?" says Yanel.

"It's a blackout," says Manta.

Neither of them mentions the fact that their battery-powered
flashlights have also gone out. They deliberately don't mention it.

"Let's wait." Manta lifts a finger even though he knows Yanel can't
see him. "And let's not lose our cool."

They both remain in their places. After a moment an erratic noise
is heard, coming from where Manta thinks Yanel is. Some sort of soft,
damp cough that slowly turns into a choked, hoarse weeping. Aníbal
Manta takes the band off of his head and taps the flashlight with his
finger. He brings it to his ear with a frown. Perhaps unconsciously imitating the classic gesture of bringing a wind-up watch that's stopped
working to one's ear. A second later, as he's placing the elastic band
around his head again, the lights come back on with a flicker. The
pilots of the security circuit and the flashlights and all the rest. The
blackout, if that's what it was, lasted less than half a minute.

Manta holds his breath. He waits a second. Two. Three. But

nothing happens. The return of the electricity didn't set off the alarms. He doesn't hear the symphony of sirens, bells and howls that usually fills the streets when the electricity comes back on after a power outage. Everything is just as it was before. As if the blackout had never happened.

Manta takes a look around. Then he kicks Yanel, who is sitting on the floor with his back against the wall and whimpering with his face sunk into his hands. Yanel lifts his damp face and looks around with a frown. Four minutes later they have hung the copies of the paintings and put the originals into their backpacks and are back on the street. Walking away from the gallery with nimble, but not hurried, steps. Just as the centuries-old tradition stipulates that criminals should flee crime scenes. Precisely calibrating the speed of their flight.

Eric Yanel stops in the middle of the street. With a frown. With his meticulously waved and conditioned hairdo transformed into a twisted grotesque Mohawk. Like one of those comedic characters that get caught in bad weather and whose hair freezes into impossible crystalline forms. He makes a half turn and stares at the gallery building at the end of the street.

Manta looks at him quizzically.

"That thing that happened in the gallery," says Yanel, "wasn't normal, was it? That wasn't a normal blackout."

Manta shrugs his shoulders.

"Who cares?" he says. "We have the paintings. And if you get your ass in gear, everything will work out fine."

Yanel starts walking behind Manta, who has resumed his departure with his own brand of paradoxical gracefulness. Which stems from the seeming impossibility of anyone his size achieving any sort of gracefulness. Now the two men turn a corner and a tall office building with a parking area at back appears before them. The few pedestrians that walk after midnight through the neighborhood of bank headquarters and corporate buildings walk alone and stare intently at the ground in their path.

"I've seen that before," says Yanel, jogging a bit to keep up with Manta. The speed makes his wave of blond hair undergo a new rhythmic, vertical waving. "The exact same thing. I didn't know before what it reminded me of, but I just remembered. And you should remember, too. I bet you've seen it in your comic books."

Aníbal Manta goes into the building's parking lot and walks between the parked cars toward the van at the back of the lot with the corporate logo of "ARNOLD LAYNE, WOOD PARASITE SOLUTIONS" printed on one side. With the lightning bolt splitting the insect in half. Manta walks toward the frost-covered window of the van's cab. He lifts up one of his colossal arms and makes a series of taps with his knuckles on the window, causing several pieces of frost to fall to the parking lot's asphalt floor. No reply comes from inside the van.

"I remember it from movies about aliens." Yanel uses his index finger to push the nonprescription glasses that are part of his disguise back on his nose. "When the spaceship passes by. You know. And everything stops working for a moment."

Manta cleans the windowpane with his hand and looks inside. There is no one in the van's cab. His face transmits several degrees of shock and anger. Then he walks with furious strides toward the back doors of the van, followed by Yanel. He pulls open the back doors, which for a moment give the impression they're about to go flying. Manta and Yanel stare into the back of the van.

Saudade seems to have found a way to partially remove the "ARNOLD LAYNE, WOOD PARASITE SOLUTIONS" jumpsuit in such a way that the whole thing lies empty and wrinkled around his ankles. The naked young woman on her knees in front of his open legs has goose bumps. Saudade looks up and stares at Manta and Yanel. The young woman looks over her shoulder with Saudade's penis still in her mouth and stares at Manta and Yanel with a not-very-friendly expression. A little cloud of steam comes out of her mouth.

"This is how you keep a lookout?" says Manta. Blushing.

Saudade shrugs his shoulders.

"I thought I could start celebrating the job," he says. "I knew you guys were gonna do everything right."

Manta closes his fist so tightly that his knuckles turn blue and then break out in a slight layer of flush as a result of the sequence of bursting capillaries. Everyone present can clearly hear the wave of metacarpal bones cracking. Manta would love to do something extremely violent to Saudade's face. Something that would leave the entire inside of the van dripping with blood and would make Saudade's whore flee buck-naked through the wintry parking lot, shrieking feminine little shrieks and covering her mouth with her hands. But he can't move. He is held back by the same emotional stress due to feelings of inadequacy and physical grotesqueness that has always left him paralyzed in situations like this one. A shame too deeply buried to be grabbed by the ear and pulled out into the open for once and for all. Saudade's penis seems to be looking at him with a mocking, defiant expression. Enormous and perfectly erect. As if Saudade were mocking him and defying him to break out of his paralysis with the image of that perfect penis.

"Shouldn't we get out of here?" Yanel says in that moment.

Manta snaps out of his ruminations with a blink. Saudade is lighting a cigarette.

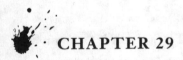

CHAPTER 29

Children and the Heart

Lucas Giraut opens the gate to the private parking lot of the offices of LORENZO GIRAUT, LTD., with his remote control, so that the van that reads "ARNOLD LAYNE, WOOD PARASITE SOLU-TIONS" can enter. The van is driven by Aníbal Manta, who parks it in the spot right next to Mr. Bocanegra's convertible Jaguar. The winter moon bathes the parking lot in a silvery light that makes you think of frolicking fairies. Among the things illuminated by the silvery light are Lucas Giraut and Mr. Bocanegra, standing motionless in the middle of the frozen cement floor, the latter sheathed in a long-haired fur coat that no one would hesitate in classifying as completely feminine. According to the news, this night that is drawing to a close will be the coldest of the year. Giraut and Mr. Bocanegra watch as the back doors of the van open. Eric Yanel and Saudade come from inside, each carrying a couple of special zippered bags for the transportation of fragile works of art.

Mr. Bocanegra starts clapping. In spite of the obstacle posed by the open bottle of Moët et Chandon he has in one hand.

"Bravo," he says. His voice slightly nasal because of the cigar he holds in his teeth. "I can't say I'm proud. Who could be proud of morons like you. Not even your mothers. But I'm pleased." He nods emphatically. He takes a sip on the bottle of Moët et Chandon. "You've made old Bocanegra happy."

Five minutes later, they are all gathered in the warehouse of LORENZO GIRAUT, LTD., which Mr. Bocanegra has had decorated with a multicolored assortment of garlands and Christmas ornaments. With reflecting plastic balls and strings of multicolored lights that blink in mysteriously rhythmic patterns. Even the windows have been decorated with a special spray that imitates, with limited success, the texture of snow. There are a couple of those portable refrigerators that are like futuristic baskets filled with bottles of Moët et Chandon. There are folding tables on one side of the warehouse with hors d'oeuvres and cakes cut into triangular pieces. Everything is ready for the celebration to begin as soon as the last step is completed.

Raymond Panakian walks through the group of men, leaning on a pair of crutches. Lucas Giraut can't help but think that Panakian no longer really looks like himself. His socialist factory worker coveralls are the same, no doubt about that. Giraut has learned to recognize the odor of unwashed clothes and unwashed male body that emanates from the garment. The swelling still hasn't gone down enough on Panakian's face, however, for the new him to look like the old one. His shredded, swollen lips are sunken in where there used to be teeth. His jaw and mustache area seem to have turned a black color that makes you think of rotten steaks.

"Our friend Mr. Panakian has decided to change his appearance," says Mr. Bocanegra in an explanatory tone. "You can never be too careful in his line of work."

A derisive grunt rises up from the area of the warehouse where Bocanegra's minions are. Out of the corner of his eye, Giraut sees movements among the three men that could be nudges. Slaps on the knee. Now that he is closer, Lucas Giraut can see that Panakian's work coveralls have paint stains in every imaginable color and texture. Something about the stains suggests that they have been produced over several different decades. An archeological record of paint stains. The strings of blinking, multicolored Christmas lights project onto the coveralls producing once again that impression that Panakian is a dazed actor from the era of psychedelic cinema.

Panakian leans his crutches against the wall and puts on some latex gloves. He opens a briefcase and takes out an instrument similar to the adjustable lens of a professional camera. Lucas Giraut follows his movements attentively, as he sips on his bottle of Moët et Chandon and pretends he's not paying attention. Even Bocanegra's minions are paying attention. More or less. Each of them according to their possibilities.

Finally Raymond Panakian places the instrument that looks like a camera lens up to his eye and leans forward to examine the St. Kieran Panels. Which have been extracted from their special carrying bags and placed on individual easels. The entire process takes a couple of minutes. Finally Raymond Panakian stands up straight, making pained gestures and expressions that seem to be focused on his lower back. He puts the instrument away in his briefcase. He closes it and turns toward Bocanegra. He nods his head.

A clamor of clinking bottles and shouts of joy fills the warehouse of LORENZO GIRAUT, LTD. A couple of streamers fly through the air. Saudade is emptying a bottle of Moët et Chandon Grand Reserve over his head. After a moment, Bocanegra lifts a hand, asking for silence. And, of course, there is silence.

"This is a happy moment," says Mr. Bocanegra. With that deliberate slowness he reserves for moments in which he has a captive audience. An audience that can't avoid being the recipients of his wisdom. "Happy for all of you because you are going to have money to keep having fun and getting yourselves in trouble, although this time the money is going to last you longer than usual. This time you can build yourselves a swimming pool and fill it with money, if you feel like it." He pauses to receive the cheers that obediently arrive from his minions. Saudade has finished emptying the Grand Reserve over his head and he now gleefully throws the empty bottle against the wall. The bottle bursts with a noise similar to a groan. "And yet, it is also a particularly happy day for me. Not only because it is our most lucrative job to date. A job that will let us all buy luxury homes and pools to store the money in. But because I did this job with Lucas Giraut. The only son of my best friend ever. And someone who I consider my own son. Someone almost of my blood. Much more than just a nephew," he says, and raises the half-drunk bottle of Moët et Chandon in a toast. There is a burst of slightly less enthusiastic applause from the minions. The clapping dies down after a moment. "And that is why, since today is a really special day for everyone, I've decided to make an announcement." New pause. Someone shuffles their feet nervously. Aníbal Manta tries to put on a sycophantically intrigued face. "It is something I have been planning for months. A project for the rest of my life. To fill me up here inside." He raises a fist to his heart. "A reason to live. I've already found the land. And I've got the work permit. Now all I have to do is build it with the money from the sale of these little paintings. Which already have a buyer. Thanks to my contacts and to Mr. Giraut's privileged brain. And that's what I want to show you all today. On this very special day."

Mr. Bocanegra makes a half turn and grabs something that's leaning against a wall. It is some sort of thick paper rolled into a cylinder. He puts it on a table and unrolls it. The others come closer to have a look. The paper shows some sort of rural villa. With gardens. With enormous windows that look out on a rural landscape. And with statues. Dozens of statues everywhere. In the garden. In the greenhouse. At the entrance for cars. All of it in the middle of a landscape with all the idyllic elements rural landscapes are meant to have. Herds of cows. Wild horses frolicking. Barns shaped like giant mushrooms. Lucas Giraut draws his face closer to examine the page in detail. It isn't a photograph. It is one of those computer-generated landscapes. A simulation.

And on top of it all, dominating the image of the house and the statues and the computer-simulated rural landscape, written in enormous, optimistic letters, it reads:

THE ARNOLD LAYNE CHILDREN'S CENTER AND FOUNDATION

Everyone present looks at the sheet of paper for a moment. Someone clears his throat.

"It's . . . nice," says Aníbal Manta cautiously.

"But, *what is it*?" says Saudade, who has somehow managed to get himself another bottle of Moët et Chandon on his way to the table and is now looking at the sheet of paper as he takes sips on the bottle.

"*All my life* I've wanted something like this," says Mr. Bocanegra. His cruel features give way to those slightly trembling and slightly moist elements that indicate an Emotionally Intense Moment is approaching. His enormous bald head trembles. His mustache trembles. The long luxurious fur of his unmistakably feminine coat trembles a tiny bit, too. "All my life. There is nothing my heart loves more than children. Like an uncle. The truth is I feel like an uncle to every child. My heart has enough room. Because I don't have any children of my own. And I'm getting old. It's the loneliness of a childless man." He takes a deep, melancholy drag on his cigar. "That's why I decided to set this up. A home. For children without parents. Or for the ones that have shitty parents who beat them. You know. I'll run it myself. I'll be like an uncle to each one of those kids. Once it's built, of course." He claps his enormous hands one time. One of those claps that serve as a signal to return from a fantasy back to the surrounding reality. "Meanwhile, you all should know that everything you're doing, all our work, will help give a home to all those poor little kids."

There is a moment of solemn silence. In some part of the warehouse a commotion is heard, like furniture being violently moved around.

"My father beat us," says Aníbal Manta with a pensive face. "But it never occurred to me to think about that stuff about loneliness."

The sound of furniture being moved violently is followed by an abrupt, muffled din. Like something heavy falling from a certain height. Mr. Bocanegra frowns.

"What's over there?"

He points with a big, hairy, ring-filled finger in the direction the noises are coming from. It is one of the unused wings of the warehouse, connected to the main part by a metal door that is now ajar.

Lucas Giraut shrugs his shoulders.

"It's a storage room," he says. "For tools. Old furniture. Things like that."

Noises continue to come from the door, now weaker. Like muffled echoes.

"Has anyone seen Yanel?" says Aníbal Manta.

Everyone looks around. In the warehouse lit by little multicolored blinking Christmas lights there are only five men. Saudade is polishing off his third bottle. Raymond Panakian seems to be talking to himself in whatever language it is he speaks while he fills his mouth with pieces of cake. But there is no trace of Eric Yanel. He seems to have disappeared in a moment of distraction.

Mr. Bocanegra starts to walk toward the half-open metal door. Followed closely by Lucas Giraut and Aníbal Manta.

The storage room on the other side of the door is dark and smells damp and like it hasn't been opened for months. The spiderwebs that hang from the ceiling get tangled in their hair and faces, forcing them to walk through the room swatting. Eric Yanel is hanging from the ceiling, too, from the lamp fixture in the middle. With the belt from his pants around his neck. With his face blue and kicking the air frenetically the way people do when they're choking. It's never very clear if the kicking means the person has changed their mind right in the middle of hanging themselves or if they are just experiencing the intrinsic emotional pain of the hanging. At his feet there are several dozen objects and pieces of furniture knocked over by the kicking.

The three men look at each other for a moment.

"But what the fuck is this?" says Mr. Bocanegra.

"I think he's committing suicide." Aníbal Manta scratches his head pensively.

Yanel looks at them with his face blue and his eyes bulging. Still kicking.

"There'll be no suicide," says Mr. Bocanegra in a firm tone. "And much less on such a happy night. Tomorrow is *Christmas Eve*, for fuck's sake. And *you*"—he points at Yanel with his cigar—"still owe me money. So don't even think about trying to get over."

Mr. Bocanegra leaves the room with an indignant air. Aníbal Manta sighs and carefully tries to get closer to Yanel. Trying to avoid his frenetic kicking.

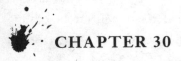

CHAPTER 30

Stuck in the Armpit of Love

Christmas in Barcelona looks like a story by Stephen King. Not exactly because of the combination of Christmas lights, streetlamps lit up in the early evening, shop windows and corporate signs. A combination that's yellow and doesn't cast a single shadow. Not because of the institutional carols that hundreds of public-address speakers simultaneously emit. Not because of the hordes of people crossing Diagonal and other avenues, loaded down with bags from the big department stores either. It's their faces. The happy faces you see on people. The way the children laugh and run through the streets, and their parents' tired but happy faces. Like in those Stephen King novels where entire towns are controlled by a Central Intelligence. Those novels where one of the main characters, who's immune to the central control, runs through the streets shouting and crashing into hordes of happy-faced pedestrians. And suddenly, as soon as the sun sets behind the hills, the people begin to disappear. The streets are deserted in mere minutes. Like in those novels by Stephen King about mind control where night falls and wild dogs take over the city.

Iris Gonzalvo drives her brick red Alfa Romeo through the deserted blocks of the Upper Ensanche. With her wrist leaning on the upper curve of the steering wheel, and the car's interior flooded with an analgesic blend of music at top volume and cigarette smoke. She reaches into the purse on the adjoining seat and pulls out her key chain equipped with some sort of miniature remote control that opens the door to the garage. Without ever looking in the direction of the purse or the key chain, her gaze fixed on the deserted street in front of the Alfa Romeo. When she gets to the corner where her parking garage and her apartment are she makes an abrupt turn, causing a lingering family of holiday shoppers to scatter in every direction, shouting and dropping their bags full of gifts.

Once she's parked, Iris turns off the music and grabs the Blockbuster bag that's on the backseat. She goes up the stairs awash in yellow light that leads to her apartment and puts the high-security key into the lock. The kind of Stephen King novels that the staircase leading from the garage to the apartment is reminiscent of are those zombie novels where there's a couple of zombies lying in wait in a parking lot staircase. When Iris enters the apartment, there's a commercial on TV for a channel in which several famous people are toasting with cava. The way they're staring at the camera makes them look like they're being controlled by some Central Intelligence. With enormous smiles. And dubious expressions of clichéd enthusiasm.

Iris drops the Blockbuster bag and takes a look around her. With a frown. She opens the bedroom door and looks behind the sofa. She looks into the room with the exercise equipment and opens the bath curtain to see what's in the tub. Finally she opens the door to the walk-in closet and finds Eric Yanel sleeping inside the laundry basket. In his underwear and hugging a bottle of Macallan. She closes the door to the walk-in closet again. The television is playing a cava commercial that shows a boy dressed in old-fashioned clothes carrying a gigantic bottle of cava under his arm and looking at the camera with a malicious smile. Iris makes herself a Finlandia with tonic and places it on a tray next to eight very long and perfectly straight lines of cocaine. Then she takes out a DVD box of the eighth season of *Friends* from the Blockbuster bag and puts the first disc into the DVD player. She sits on the sofa with the tray on her lap and pushes the PLAY button on the remote.

Mr. Bocanegra, Show Business Impresario, is lounging in his chair with a napkin tied around his neck. Seated at a table in the restaurant where the Bocanegra family celebrates Christmas Eve every year. He is surrounded by his complex system of brothers, sisters, brothers-in-law, sisters-in-law and the expectant looks of half a dozen nieces and nephews, their eyes lit up with greed. A greed that Bocanegra has already been feeding for a couple of hours with the smiling transfer of plentiful one-hundred- and two-hundred-euro bills into the trembling hands of his nieces and nephews. Some of them are so anxious with greed that they have barely touched their desserts.

"Isn't it time to open presents?" Bocanegra wipes the sauce from his mustache with a corner of his napkin.

A roar of wild joy emanates from the throats of the half dozen children who are now running toward the Christmas tree under which a restaurant employee in uniform has placed all the Bocanegra family gifts. The employee in uniform moves away instinctively.

"You haven't spent a ton on presents for the kids again, have you?" one of Bocanegra's brothers asks Bocanegra, who is smiling beneath his mustache with quasi-parental pride.

Around the Christmas tree, Bocanegra's nieces and nephews are kicking aside all the gifts that aren't wrapped in the distinctive red and green paper that Mr. Bocanegra has his Christmas gifts wrapped in each year. Some of the adults seated at the table exchange uncomfortable looks. Mr. Bocanegra's nieces and nephews rapidly identify their gifts and tear off the red and green paper and shout with enthusiasm when they confirm that the professional sports equipment and portable technology that they have received this year are the most expensive models on the international market. There are more uncomfortable looks exchanged among the adults seated at the table. One of the nieces, kneeling beside the tree, cries with happiness as she hugs something that looks like a robot in the shape of a dog that has just come out of a box with Japanese writing on it. Another nephew screams with joy and pretends to play an electric guitar that he has just taken out of its case. At a sensible distance away from the group of children, the employee wearing the uniform of the exclusive uptown restaurant observes the scene with an element of horror in his smile.

Aníbal Manta is lying in his double bed with several large pillows behind his enormous back. With his reading glasses on. Carefully examining an Italian issue of the X-Men and consulting at regular intervals the Spanish-Italian/Italian-Spanish dictionary he bought a couple of days earlier in a downtown bookstore. His wife appears in the doorway of the bedroom with a bathrobe over her nightgown and a blender in her hand, one of those ones that look like miniature spaceships.

"I'm going over to the neighbors' house to return their blender," says his wife. "I'm taking the keys in case I stay to chat and end up coming back late." She smiles with a vaguely obsequious expression. "Just so you know."

Manta looks at the alarm clock on the bedside table. It's ten past eleven. Manta sighs.

"I won't wait up, then," he says in a soft voice.

"Good idea," says his wife, who is already on her way to the door. "Don't wait up." A couple of seconds later the sound of the door closing is heard.

Since he started reading the Italian X-Men comic that same afternoon after lunch, Manta has managed to decipher four and a half pages. Which, considering the comic has thirty-two pages, seems to indicate that his reading is going to take him at least the rest of the week. The deciphering process is hindered by the fact that Manta, who has suffered from severe dyslexia since childhood, has trouble finding the words in the dictionary. He is often forced to pause and try to remember the damn alphabetical order by counting on his fingers the way they taught him in the special school. On a few occasions his therapist has seemed willing to admit the idea that his dyslexia could be a result of the traumas he experienced during his childhood because of his excessive size and his schoolmates' taunting.

He has only one panel left on page five when the doorbell rings, twice, two long and incredibly high-pitched rings in the silence of the apartment. Manta takes off his reading glasses and stands up stealthily. He looks at the alarm clock. It's already past midnight. He walks barefoot toward the hall closet and takes out a three-foot-long iron bar with his initials written in permanent marker on one side. He tiptoes toward the door while two more nervous rings buzz.

"Whoever you are," says Manta through his teeth, trying to see into the door's peephole, "you're gonna get it."

Manta unlocks the lock and opens the door with the iron bar ready in his other hand. It takes him a second to recognize the messed-up individual who is standing on the other side of the door. His face is familiar. In spite of the dried blood and bruises. And the hair that falls in bloody dangling bits. The hair is definitely familiar. Manta frowns. The individual brings together two crudely bandaged hands in front of his bloodstained sweater in the universal sign for begging.

"You gots to help me," says Pavel, his pleading hands together at his chest. "I'm in *really* serious trouble," he says, but he has to stop talking to lift his arms and protect his head from the iron bar coming toward him. "*Wait.*"

Manta chases Pavel on the landing, hitting him on the arms and back.

The eighth season of *Friends* is a terribly complex amalgam of implied psycho-emotional references, relationships tainted by traces of lust and the complex forms of reproduction associated with heterodox sexualities. Iris Gonzalvo leans forward to snort a line of cocaine and uses the FAST FORWARD button on her remote to skip the parts that are less relevant to her grasp of the show's psycho-emotional drama. At the end of the seventh season, Monica and Chandler had finally managed to consecrate their love at the altar. After the fleeting intrigue triggered by Chandler's disappearance the night before the wedding. While still far from consolidating his relationship with Rachel, Ross had finally managed to establish a fairly satisfactory rapport with his son, Ben, whose mother, Carol, had divorced Ross in one of the early seasons after discovering that she was a lesbian. In a last unexpected twist, Phoebe and Rachel find out that one of the show's female characters is pregnant. Iris thinks she hears knocking on the door of the walk-in closet coming from inside, but she can't be sure because there are firecrackers going off in the street. The eighth season, as is customary in *Friends*, begins right where the previous one left off. In this case, minutes after Monica and Chandler's wedding. In which the best man was Joey dressed in a World War I uniform for an upcoming role. As the first few episodes play out, the cliffhangers from the previous season are resolved. Rachel turns out to be the one who's pregnant and

Ross, after maintaining the suspense for a while, admits that he is the father. Yet not even the child they are about to have can bring them together. Instead they both continue going out with other people and Ross hooks up with a girl named Mona that Iris doesn't like at all. As the season progresses and the lines of cocaine disappear from the tray, things get complicated because stupid old Joey falls in love with Rachel. Iris isn't sure if she likes this new plot twist. *Friends* provokes complex networks of identification and repulsion in Iris. Of the three female leads, she doesn't think she has much in common with Monica, although she finds her the best-looking by far and the one she would sleep with if she were to have a lesbian relationship within the world of the show. Rachel is pretty stuck up and not very cute, although Iris admits that they share certain traits, while Phoebe is clearly just too histrionic. She has fucked the three male leads many times in her imagination, together and separately, although Joey is the one that she finds most sexually attractive and he would be her favorite if only he wasn't such a pinhead. In general, Iris considers herself a compendium of the virtues of the three female leads, without any of their snotty, stuck-up nonsense. It's true that the girls in *Friends* seem to live better than her, but that's because Iris hasn't yet achieved Fame and Success in Life. After half a dozen episodes, she doesn't hear firecrackers in the street anymore. The lines of cocaine have vanished and been re-placed. The Finlandia with tonic on the tray is the fourth Finlandia with tonic. Iris isn't sure if she likes that Joey is going out with Rachel. The whole point of *Friends* is that Rachel ends up married to Ross. Iris has no doubt that she's going to achieve Fame and Success in Life very shortly. In fact, she's completely sure that the coming year will be the year she achieves Fame and Success in Life. Iris doesn't know exactly how she knows these things, but she knows she knows them, and that's good enough for her. Iris isn't like other people, thinks Iris. The eighth season of *Friends* is known for the appearance of a good handful of Hol-lywood stars as supporting characters in the series. Brad Pitt appears in the eighth season of *Friends*. So do Alec Baldwin and Sean Penn, both as guys Phoebe is dating, something Iris finds pretty unrealistic. It is completely silent now on the streets of Barcelona as Iris continues using the PLAY and FAST FORWARD buttons to watch her favorite show. A sound similar to a moo comes out of the walk-in closet where Eric Yanel seems to be unconscious inside the laundry basket.

Juan de la Cruz Saudade frowns as he examines the covers of a dozen DVDs from his lavish porn collection, lying in the bed of the bedroom he shares with his wife. He always ends up in the same dilemma when choosing a porn movie: big asses or little asses. The decision becomes even more complex given the size of his collection and its extraordinary range. The tits have to be big, that is the second most important rule. The pubic area has to be shaved. That is the first and most sacred of the rules. The absence of a shaved pubis is reason enough not to fuck his wife, currently absent from their household. Saudade sighs. Often the ass question mires him in a state of indecision that threatens to hinder the very process of porn watching. The visual and tactile sensations aroused by a small ass are radically different from those produced by a big ass. And yet, it can't be flatly said that one category is intrinsically better than the other. The pros and cons of both types of asses are fighting a fierce battle in his mind when he hears a series of timid little knocks on the bolted door of the bedroom.

"Daddy?" says the voice of his eight-year-old son. From the other side of the bolted door. "Can you open up for a second, please?"

Saudade clicks his tongue. He gathers up all the DVDs spread out on the bed and sticks them underneath the comforter. He sits on the bed, lights the stub of the joint he has in the ashtray on the bedside table and takes two drags as his son's knocking continues. He opens the window and waves his arms to get rid of the smoke like certain teenagers do after secretly smoking joints in the bathrooms of their parents' houses. Finally he opens the door and looks at his son with a defiant face. His son looks at him with a frown. Dressed in footsie pajamas that are too small for him and visibly squeeze his neck and shoulder area.

"What?" asks Saudade.

"Why is the window open when it's so cold out?" asks the boy with a frown. "And what is that bulge under the covers?"

Saudade puts his hands on his hips.

"Do you mind going back to your room?" he says. "It's Christmas Eve, for the love of God."

Cristian Saudade, eight years old, only child of the civil marriage between Juan de la Cruz and Matilde Saudade, lowers his eyes. The multicolored patterns on his too-small footsie pajamas depict the four main characters in *Los Lunis*, a kids' show on TV that's like a poor man's Muppets. His father remains motionless at the door to his room wearing only briefs and a promotional T-shirt of a heavy metal group that peaked in the eighties.

"When is Mom getting out of jail?" asks the boy.

Saudade rubs his temples with his index finger and thumb.

"Mom is not in jail," he says. "How many times do I have to tell you? She's at her mother's house. Do you understand? Fuck."

"Dad," says the boy in an impatient tone. "Mom *called* the other day and said she was in jail."

Saudade sighs. He opens up the drawer on his bedside table and begins to search through the papers inside. After a moment he pulls out a wrinkled piece of paper and smooths it with his hand.

"Here." He gives the paper to his son with a hostile expression. "Your mother's coming back on Tuesday. Are you happy? Eat what's left in the fridge and when it's gone, call your aunt and tell her you have to spend a couple of days with her 'cause we're having some work done on the house. You understand?"

Cristian Saudade, eight years old, goes off down the hall dragging his feet. Saudade bolts the door. Then he closes the window and puts a movie with big asses into the DVD player. Then he lies down on the bed and uses the remote to skip the transitional scenes that precede the first anal sex scenes. Anal sex scenes are, in Saudade's opinion, the main element of a good porn film. Oral sex scenes are also very important because they show an actress's technique. But there's no denying that the anal sex scenes are what give pornography true meaning. He usually fast-forwards the vaginal sex scenes with the remote or just skips them with the Skip Chapter function on his DVD player. Once he's found the most adequate scene, he lights his joint with a lighter advertising his favorite soccer club and takes a couple of hits before putting it back in the ashtray. Then he sticks his hand into his briefs and proceeds to carry out the controlled stroking that makes up the main phase of the mental-physiological operation he's nicknamed "recharging the batteries."

Stretched out on the sofa in her living room with the DVD player's remote in her hand, Iris Gonzalvo alternately pushes the PLAY and FAST FORWARD buttons to select those fragments of her favorite show that release emotional responses of identification, desire and repulsion in her. It's possible that the sun has already come up. It's hard to tell because she closed the blinds hours ago so she could concentrate on what was happening on the TV. She isn't hungry or sleepy but that doesn't mean anything when you take into account that by now she's finished off the reserves of cocaine she had in the kitchen. She moves the sofa cushions to make herself more comfortable, closes her eyes, and imagines how things will be when she achieves Fame and Success in Life. She imagines the magazine interviews and the photo sessions and the dates with famous men in restaurants. The kinds of things, she thinks, that make life worth living.

Marcia Parini is crying beside the bed at the prestigious psychiatric center for children where her daughter Valentina is sleeping with white plastic straps around her wrists and ankles and a drip delivering sedatives into a vein of her arm. She cries and dries her tears with a wrinkled handkerchief and once in a while holds her daughter's inert hand. A nurse with a bruise on her face and her arm in a sling comes in to check the reading on the ECG machine. Marcia looks up at the nurse with a troubled face.

"Oh, for God's sake," says Marcia to the bruised nurse. "You have to give me your medical bill." She shakes her head sadly. "I never imagined the poor little thing was so strong."

The nurse smiles weakly.

"We're insured against patient attacks," she says. "It's one of the downsides of the job." She pauses and looks at Valentina with her eyes gathered together. "Does her father know she's here?"

Marcia dries her tears with her wrinkled handkerchief.

"Her father's in Uruguay," she says. "Anyway, Tina doesn't get along with him."

The nurse nods. There is a moment of silence punctuated by the barely audible beep of the ECG machine.

"We have a coffee machine on this floor," says the nurse kindly. "If you want we can go have some breakfast together. After all, it is Christmas, isn't it?"

Marcia Parini smiles and nods as she blows her nose into her wrinkled handkerchief. Marcia and the nurse leave the room.

In her bed in the children's hospital, surrounded by machines and white furnishings, Valentina Parini opens her eyes suddenly. Her pupils dilate and begin the trembling, rough dance of sleep's rapid eye movement phase.

CHAPTER 31

The Down With The Sun Dream

Lucas Giraut lifts his head, trying to get his bearings on the deserted, wind-swept avenue that Tottenham Court Road seems to have become. Not a neon sign as far as the eye can see. No rivers of shoppers with their plastic bags from department stores and no giant West End theater marquees. Lucas Giraut takes refuge in a doorway and lifts an arm to protect his face from the gale winds. There may be someone nailed to the Astoria's door. Lucas doesn't want to get closer to check. The wind drags dried leaves and tattered newspapers. Lucas catches one in flight. He reads the date: August 7, 1972. He starts to count on his fingers. With a frown. It's really amazing how many pieces of newspaper are flying along Tottenham Court Road.

Three blocks farther up, he arrives at the pub he has to go to following the internal logic of the Filial Down With The Sun Dream. It isn't hard to find: above the pub, tied to the roof of the building and floating in the night sky, is an immense hot air balloon in the shape of a pig. With pig ears and a pig tail. And with an inscription on the side in those cloudlike letters that were popular in the early seventies. It reads: "WELCOME TO THE DOWN WITH THE SUN DREAM." Giraut shakes off the pieces of newspaper stuck to his back and shoulders and pushes the pub door open.

Inside the pub it's warm and full of people, and yet no one is speaking. Everyone is silent. The faces that stare at Lucas Giraut when he enters are terrified faces.

"In the back room, darling," says a blonde on the other side of the bar who looks terrified and wears a T-shirt advertising the Filial Down With The Sun Dream.

Lucas Giraut thanks her for the information with a half smile and continues walking among the crowd of fearful faces.

"In the back room, buddy," says a guy smoking a pipe.

Lucas Giraut enters the back room and looks at the three official members of the Down With The Sun Society. They're cheerfully occupying a round table filled with empty pint glasses, on which a shockingly young and not yet bald Bocanegra has just put down four full pints of beer. Lucas looks at Bocanegra. Then he looks at Koldo Cruz. Then he looks at his father. Finally he looks at the fourth figure seated at the table. The fourth figure has no face. His entire body is wrapped in bandages like those Egyptian mummies in old horror movies that come back to life. The bandages are stained with blood in various spots. On the wrists and the ribs and the forehead. Neither its height nor the configuration of its limbs is particularly human. There are two yellow lights where there should be eyes, which can be faintly seen through the bandages.

"David Gilmour's over the hill," Bocanegra is saying as he puts the beers on the table and sits between Cruz and Lucas's father. "I don't think the band will last another year. I mean, let's be serious. Roger Waters is Pink Floyd. They're synonymous." He pauses. He looks in the direction that his fellow members of the Down With The Sun Society are looking and notices Lucas, standing in front of the table. "Ah, Lucas! You're late. We should have toasted to our invisible house twenty minutes ago."

Lucas Giraut sits on the paisley sofa where the club members are seated and takes the pint of beer that someone offers him. The five figures around the table bring their pints together and all take swigs before putting them back down on the table's wooden surface. Lucas looks around him. The three members of the Down With The Sun Society have long, tangled hair and denim jackets over paisley shirts. There are eight necklaces among the three of them. Seated beside him on the paisley sofa, Koldo Cruz holds a joint between his index finger and thumb and is looking at it with a lethargic smile. Without a metal plate on his right temple. Without a patch covering his right eye. With glitter sprinkled over his face. None of the three members of the club seem older than twenty-five.

"The invisible house is what paid for this trip," explains Lorenzo Giraut. Looking at his son with a kind smile. Lorenzo Giraut's arm is resting on the shoulders of the inhumanly tall figure covered in bloody bandages the way young men lean on their girlfriends' shoulders. "Which isn't really an invisible house. It's just a house that doesn't exist. We sold a house that doesn't exist. That is how the Down With The Sun Society was born. We sold an invisible house and took a vacation to London with the money."

Lucas recognizes something of his own vaguely namby-pamby seriousness in the way his father talks. That sort of namby-pamby seriousness that often causes people to get easily distracted and stop listening. Lucas changes position on the sofa with a pensive face and his feet splash in an enormous puddle that he could swear wasn't there a moment ago. He examines the floor planks near their table. Obviously there must be a pipe broken somewhere in the bar, because water is coming from somewhere and flooding the room. Koldo Cruz has taken a bag of marijuana out of one of the inside pockets of his denim jacket and is rolling another joint with the same lethargic face. Bocanegra leans in toward Lucas to whisper in his ear.

"Don't even ask." He points with his pint of beer to the figure covered in bloody bandages. "We don't talk about that at this table."

"Is that why everyone's so quiet?" Lucas Giraut looks at Bocanegra, who has abruptly moved away and now seems to be acting like he hadn't said anything, his eyes fixed on the legs of some terrified-looking girls at the next table. "Is that why it looks like everyone is afraid? Because of this . . . ? Because of the one with the bandages?"

"Listen." Lorenzo Giraut stops kissing the bloody cheek of the bandaged figure and looks at his son with a namby-pamby serious expression. "You're here for a reason. This is the night it all began. And not only for obvious reasons. This is the real beginning of the story. If you want to understand it, pay attention. What happens between us three tonight is the real beginning of everything."

"It's like that story about the butterfly that flutters its wings in China," says Koldo Cruz. With a lethargic expression. His long hair is curly while Bocanegra's is wavy and Giraut's is straight and blond.

Lucas Giraut can't help noticing that his father and the bandaged figure of inhuman proportions are seated at an interpersonal distance normally reserved for people who are physically intimate. The bandaged figure's hand, Lucas notices with a slightly disgusted expression, is quite close to his father's crotch. Koldo Cruz finishes lighting his joint and begins to perform some sort of undulating, vaguely snakelike dance with his arms and neck to the beat of the song playing on the wooden speakers by the bar. Bocanegra and Giraut move their heads rhythmically in acknowledgment of the song. The guy singing through the wooden speakers sings that when the moon eclipses the sun one can't technically speak of a dark side of the moon since, technically speaking, both sides are dark.

"That doesn't make sense," says Lucas Giraut finally. Looking at his father and the other figures around the table. "That's not how dreams work. Dreams are made of memories. But I was never here. I wasn't even born. I've never seen this man." He points to Koldo Cruz. "And no one's ever told me any of this. So how could I remember it?"

Bocanegra stares at Lorenzo Giraut with a theatrical expression of shock. The cruel smile that Lucas knows so well in the real-life Bocanegra is already there in the face of the Bocanegra in the dream. In an embryonic stage, if you will.

"Oh, shit," says Bocanegra. "Who has the Temporal Paradox Survival Manual? Because I forgot mine." He pats down his pockets mockingly.

Everyone at the table starts to laugh, except for Lucas Giraut. The figure wrapped in bloody bandages doesn't laugh, either. It just looks at Lucas out of the corner of his eye. With those points of yellow light.

"Listen." Lorenzo Giraut once again takes on his namby-pamby serious tone. "We don't have much time. Not to mention the water level." He points to the floor. Where the level of the water waterlogging the floorboards has now risen an inch or so and forces the pub regulars to walk on tiptoe and lift up the hems of their long skirts. "Your mission is to discover what happened between us. You have until eleven approximately." He quickly checks his wristwatch and then looks at his son with a kind expression. "IDT, of course."

"IDT?" Lucas furrows his brow.

"Internal Dream Time," says Bocanegra. He empties his pint in one gulp and bangs noisily against the table's wooden surface with the base of the empty glass. "Anyway, around here everything closes at eleven."

The pub's back room has been clearing out and now the only other people left are a little man with a corduroy suit reading a British newspaper and two sinister-looking guys with leather jackets and bowl cuts. They all have their pants rolled up. Lucas takes a sip of his beer and tries to determine what it is about this scene of the Down With The Sun Dream that seems so powerfully familiar. Bocanegra lifts a leather bag off the flooded floor and places it on the table. It is a bottle green Puma sports bag. He unzips the bag and gestures to Lucas, inviting him to look inside.

"This is our new business project," says Bocanegra.

Lucas extends his neck to see what's inside the bag. Inside the bag there's a pile of female body parts. An arm filled with bracelets and a perfectly manicured hand. A torso with small, slightly wrinkled breasts. A foot here and knee there. Bocanegra rummages around inside the bag until he finds what he's looking for and holds it up for Lucas to see: it's the face of Estefanía "Fanny" Giraut, with lips bruised by silicone injections and skin pulled horribly taut from behind the ears. With a nose so surgically reconstructed that it no longer looks like a nose. Just a strange cartilaginous protuberance. Something that makes one think of vestigial tails and appendages with teeth. Fanny Giraut's face looks irritated as Bocanegra, grabbing it by the ears without the slightest consideration, sticks it back in the bag.

"We think we can get almost a million for this. It was Lorenzo's idea. Getting into the antiques business. He thought of it after visiting that museum with the mummies here in London. We set up a bogus company. To send out fake invoices. On a little British island with a special tax regimen."

"The island is a center of telluric energies." Koldo Cruz brings his joint to his glitter-covered face. His long curly hair falls onto his sparkly face and red eyes. "The druids have always known it. That's why our plans can't fail."

Lucas Giraut pulls his feet up out of the water and puts them on the sofa. The water that keeps coming must be about eight inches above floor level by now, forcing everyone to get up on chairs. The waiters have their pants rolled up to the knees and are having trouble moving through the water, holding their trays filled with pints of beer precariously and sometimes dropping them when a wave hits them from the side or from behind. Of course, thinks Giraut. That is exactly what's familiar to him about the scene. When he was a boy, in his childhood bedroom in the North Wing of the Giraut family house in the Ampurdan, he had a recurring dream in which the Mediterranean rose, flooding the beach and reaching the house in a question of minutes. Covering the first floor and then the second, where the Fishing Trophy Room is. In his dream, Lucas would watch the water level rise until the furniture and the lamps and the paintings on the walls started floating. Finally the house flooded completely, the water reaching the ceiling. The fish overran the hallways and the rooms. The only thing that little Lucas could do in the face of the rising water was go farther up the house's marble staircase. First he got trapped in the attic and then, when the water flooded that part, too, he pushed open the trap door and went out onto the roof. Where the same landscape always awaited him. The Ampurdan coast had disappeared. The sea covered everything. The rocky hills of the northern coast had become little dwindling islands. There was no trace of terra firma. Minutes later, Lucas was floating in the water, grabbing a plank of wood or some other remains of the flood.

Someone shouts in the front of the pub. The two guys with bowl cuts in the back room have gotten up on one of the tables and are trying to climb the curtains. The little man with the corduroy suit clicks his tongue and tries to move between the tables, but he's dragged by a wave. On the table occupied by the Down With The Sun Society, Lorenzo Giraut, Koldo Cruz and Bocanegra are consulting a messy pile of maps and blueprints. With a conspiratorial air. The way they are consulting the maps and whispering to each other is not so much genuinely conspiratorial. It's more like the way someone whispers theatrically, giggling and rubbing their hands together, when they want to make abundantly clear to any spectator that they're conspiring. Giraut looks at his Lino Rossi suit with a devastated expression as the water rises above the level of the sofa and the tables. He finally decides to dive in and head to the stairs that lead to the upper floor. Toward which the rest of the pub's regulars are already swimming.

As Giraut swims under the murky water, he passes fish and aimlessly floating pieces of furniture. The figure wrapped in bloody bandages is the only figure that remains in its chair as if nothing was going on. Now it seems to be reading a Stephen King novel. With some sort of dark mist of blood oozing from its bandaged wounds beneath the water. Lucas Giraut looks around him, searching for his father. Lucas Giraut's cheeks are puffed out like the cheeks of people swimming underwater in movies and cartoons. With a small trail of tiny bubbles rising from his mouth. After a minute he appears on the surface.

"Hey!" he shouts to Bocanegra, who is connecting cables to a T-shaped detonator. "Has anyone seen my father?"

The detonator Bocanegra is connecting the cables to is one of those T-shaped detonators that have to be pushed down with both hands. Like those detonators that Wile E. Coyote always uses to try to finish off the Road Runner. The cables Bocanegra is connecting to the detonator are different colors. There is no trace of Lorenzo Giraut anywhere.

"I haven't seen Sir Intellectualoid." Bocanegra speaks in a nasty tone. While still working on the detonator. "What makes you think I've seen Mister Tightass Bookworm? Mister I'm More Important Than Everybody Else Because I've Read A Lot Of Books And My Ass Is Shaped Like A Library Chair?"

Lucas Giraut's gaze follows the different-colored cables that come out of the detonator and go up one wall and continue along the ceiling to the far end of the room. And which then go down the opposite side until they reach the spot where Koldo Cruz is standing on top of the bar. Clinging to a large bottle rack to keep from being dragged down by the waves. The cables connected to the detonator end in a string of dynamite sticks that someone has tied around Cruz's waist with strips of black adhesive tape. The sticks of dynamite have the peace sign drawn on them.

"Mr. Cruz!" shouts Giraut, splashing around in the water. "Be careful . . . !" he starts to say.

But a tremendous explosion blows Koldo Cruz to bits. The entire wall collapses onto the spot where Koldo Cruz was just a second before. Creating a cloud of smoke. Creating a tsunami that instantly sweeps away Giraut and everything around Giraut.

WONDERFUL WORLD

~~~~~~~~~~

By Stephen King

CHAPTER 42

Chuck Kimball woke up on his third day in Boston beneath a layer of cardboard boxes and lice-infested blankets in an alley without streetlights or lights of any kind. It was obvious that the cardboard boxes and blankets had belonged to someone else at some point, to one of the many bums and drunks that used to fill the streets of the historic Beacon Hill neighborhood. They had disappeared, too. A couple of bottles of cheap wine in brown paper bags marked that corner of the alley as the former property of one of those modern nomads. Chuck stretched and looked around him, slightly alarmed. The street at the end of the alley seemed calm. Since he had taken apart his wristwatch, his notion of time had almost completely disappeared. He slept for intervals of several minutes at a time, always waking up with a start and drifting back into nervous lethargy. His cravings for Dexedrine seemed to have completely disappeared.

After peeing in a corner, Chuck studied himself in a piece of broken mirror. There was no doubt his appearance would give him away if he dared to go out onto a busy street. Judging by the light, the sun should be coming up in less than an hour. His stomach sent him one of its irritated messages. A hungry grumbling mixed with a warning that diarrhea, and the danger of dehydration, could arrive at any moment.

First crawling and then dragging himself along the ground, Chuck got to the end of the alley and peeked out. He was about fifty yards from the corner, between Beacon and Dartmouth. The landscape was strangely familiar and at the same time ineffably disturbing. With its old gas streetlights and cobblestoned streets and the rolling rows of elegant redbrick houses. There wasn't a soul out at that hour. Not a car. Not a bird. The desolation that had been following him for the last few weeks seemed to have taken on a decidedly different component.

Where were the groups of people chatting in front of the stores? The happy-looking pedestrians walking to their workplaces or exiting the T stations in an orderly fashion? In that moment he understood what was newly disturbing. It was the silence. First the animals had disappeared and now the people. When they began their transmissions, little more than a month ago, the populated areas had kept up the semblance of normality. Everyone had maintained that irritating farce of routines and jobs and family life. Something in the atmosphere of that deserted corner told him that things had changed. That they were entering a new phase of the colonization.

Chuck started walking along Beacon Street. At first he walked with hurried steps, plastered to the gates of buildings and to the redbrick walls. Looking over his shoulder for signs of Captors in the sky. They seemed to be hiding, too. There was no smoke coming from the chimneys of the houses, in spite of the cold. No movement could be seen at the window curtains. Chuck shivered and slowed his pace. There was a supermarket cart abandoned in the middle of the street. With bags inside. Something that They would undoubtedly never do.

He approached the cart, still studying the sky,

and examined the bags' contents. He was so hungry
that, for a few moments, he forgot to keep his guard
up and monitor his surroundings. He found several bags
of snacks, which he tore open and devoured like an
animal. Bringing fistfuls of potato chips to his mouth
and swallowing them without chewing. He drank sips of
soda until he could feel the stimulating rush of sugar
in his veins. He ate a piece of ham and took several
bites of a still bleeding steak. And then he saw it.
While he was still pulling on the piece of meat with
his teeth, streams of blood sliding down his chin.

There They were. They were all there. He didn't
need to see anything more than the black cloud to
understand that. The black cloud that floated over
the giant golden dome of the State House, at the
peak of Beacon Hill, above the trees and avenues of
Boston Common. It was blacker and denser than any
cloud Chuck had seen before. There must have been
dozens of Them flying in circles over the dome, maybe
hundreds. Up until then Chuck had seen some of the
Captors flying low above rooftops or floating in groups
of three or four above their centers of control. It
was their way of communicating, that he was sure
of. Of creating focal points of transmission with
whatever it was that They were transmitting. Places
where their waves were concentrated and therefore
dangerous places that not even someone immune like
him could go near without running certain risks.

Chuck dropped the piece of raw meat and spit out
the pieces he still had in his mouth. He set off
running down the deserted street without taking his
eyes off the black cloud of Captors. Like every time
he saw Them, there was something that attracted his
gaze fatefully. Something impossible to define, which
was surely the explanation of why some cultures in
the past had confused them with angels. That's if
the Captors weren't the basis of human belief in
angels to begin with. Now, due to the concentration
of all those dozens of specimens, Chuck felt that
mesmerizing effect stronger than ever. Each Captor
must have been between ten and fifteen feet long

from the top of their snakelike heads to the tip of their tails, although with their wings completely unfolded They could sometimes double that figure. They flew in circles over their control centers like some sort of established dance, with concentric turn after concentric turn that Chuck suspected must have something to do with those vortexes that Saunders had told him about. Creating vaguely conical black clouds, like tornado funnels.

Judging by the concentration of Captors over the gold dome, Boston's State House must be the main control center in the city, if not the state. Chuck advanced slowly. Now it seemed that he could hear them, too. Some sort of deep, constant buzzing that either came from the beating of their wings or from some kind of frequency that They used to communicate among themselves.

The fact that he had never heard them before didn't surprise him in the slightest. As the colonization grew day by day, the signs had been multiplying. The night he saw them for the first time soaring over the highway he had had that powerful sensation that he had noticed their presence before. Of course, that had to do with the mechanisms They used in order to not be seen. Chuck suspected that their previous invisibility must have been due to something like collective hypnosis. Something that made people not notice them in spite of the fact that They were right in front of them and could be easily seen.

He was now about three blocks from Beacon Hill and the wrought-iron gates that separated the street from the park's landscaped grounds. He decided to stop there. He got behind a tree trunk and extended his neck as far as he could to see what was on the other side of the fence.

His heart skipped a beat.

There were people there. A lot of people. At first glance, Chuck calculated that there must have been at least a thousand. Beneath the elevated redbrick portico and the Corinthian columns of the State House. Most of the people there were lined up to get

into the building. It was the way they were lined up
that terrified Chuck. Even though he'd seen similar
things dozens of times in recent weeks he still
hadn't gotten used to them. They were in a perfectly
orderly line. In total silence. No arguments, no nervous leg movements and no impatient glances at their
watches. Just standing motionless in the line, each
one staring at the nape of the neck in front of them.
The line snaked from the State House entrance, going
down through the garden to the wrought-iron gates.

Another several dozen people seemed to be keeping
watch around the line and the entrance doors. Observing
the surroundings, some of them with binoculars.

Now Chuck was paralyzed. His legs wanted to run
far away from there without waiting to see any more,
but his brain told him he shouldn't move. That he
had miraculously managed to get that close without
being seen, but now any movement could give him away.
He was right out in the open, in the middle of the
street, three blocks from where those things were
scoping out the surroundings with binoculars and
maybe a third of a mile from the dome darkened by the
shadow of that black cloud of Captors.

And lastly, a part of his mind was telling him
that he might have reached the end of his journey.
His fate. That it was likely that Ollie was there.
Among all those people. His son could be just one
more of the masses, controlled by the vortex in that
communication center, but there was also the possibility that he was like him. One of the immune. A
survivor.

Now Chuck rummaged through his pocket and grabbed
the pistol with a trembling hand. Probably a totally
useless instrument in that situation, but comforting
in spite of it all. A vestige of the old civilization.

That was when it happened. Chuck didn't need to
turn around to know that the cold pressure on the
nape of his neck was the barrel of a gun and that
the metallic sound that echoed down the empty street
was the sound of a pistol being cocked.

"If you were one of Them I wouldn't have been able to get this close to you without you reading my thoughts," said a low voice right behind his head. The guy that had just rested his gun on the nape of Chuck's neck had to be very close to his head, maybe just an inch away. Chuck could feel his hot breath on the back of his neck. "And if you were one of us, I'd know you. So, who the hell are you?" said the voice. "And more importantly, how did you manage to get here?"

The pressure of the gun's barrel was removed from his neck. Chuck raised his arms and turned around very slowly. The guy that was aiming at him with an automatic weapon must have been twenty-five years old at most. He was dressed in a sweatshirt and jeans worn out at the knees. His expression conveyed deep concern mixed with curiosity. It had been many days since Chuck had seen a face like that. A real face with a real expression. Since he had left Saunders to his fate in the basement of his house. Chuck couldn't control his reaction. He started crying like a baby. Before the other man could do anything, Chuck wrapped his arms around him in a trembling hug. He had found another real human being. In the middle of that deserted street.

He was hugging him, his head resting on his shoulder, when the young man spoke in a tone of genuine shock.

"Mr. Kimball?" said the young man. "Is that you?"

Chuck moved away abruptly. He stared at the young man's face, examining his features. A lump formed in his throat. He knew those features, though it must have been several months since he'd seen them. It was as if the young man's face had aged ten years in that time. Wrinkles had appeared on his forehead and worry lines around his eyes, but there was no doubt. It was Paul Clark. His son's basketball coach.

"Paul?" said Chuck. He couldn't believe his eyes.

They both looked at each other for an instant without knowing what to say.

"Congratulations," said Paul Clark finally. "You've found the Boston Resistance."

PART III

"And They All Hid in the
Caves and Among the
Mountain Crags"

CHAPTER 32

Take Me to Your Leader

Lucas Giraut is sitting in the study of his apartment in the former ducal palace, working on his Louis XV *cartonnier* that, up until a few days ago, was in his office on the mezzanine of LORENZO GIRAUT, LTD. There is no natural light. All the light in the study comes from an art nouveau lamp on a coffee table near the desk. On top of the desk, open like an anesthetized animal with its legs splayed in a veterinarian's office, is a copy of *The Lost Rivers of London* by Álex Jardí, into which Giraut is transplanting pages of Stephen King's new novel. Carefully extracting the original signatures and replacing them with others meticulously trimmed to the right size. All with the help of his kit for restoring and repairing books. A motley collection of bradawls, rods with serrated ends and small, sharp, surgical-looking blades. On top of the *cartonnier* there are also nonabrasive glue and nonabrasive cleaning products.

Giraut has just pasted the central signature of *Wonderful World* into *The Lost Rivers*, the signature that contains the central block of chapters thirty to thirty-six, when his doorbell rings.

He looks up from his work and frowns into the darkness that surrounds his worktable. For a split second, his mind tells him that it's Valentina. Making one of her Friday afternoon visits. Then he remembers what happened the week before. On a normal Friday after-

noon this is the time Valentina Parini would come looking for him to
go down to the courtyard. There he'd sit in a chair while she took the
hammock and together they would succumb to the pleasures of conversation. Usually about something related to Stephen King's books
or movies. Like Victorian gentlemen conversing phlegmatically beneath the trellis of a colonial villa. With the sound of cannons firing
in the background.

The doorbell rings again. Giraut sighs and takes off the latex gloves
he's been wearing to work on the transplant of signatures. He doesn't
recognize the figure that appears on the other side of his apartment
door. It's a tall, slender woman who's much more sexually attractive
than any woman he's ever had dealings with before.

"Are you Mr. Lucas Giraut?" The woman at the door looks through
her dark glasses at the ochre-colored Lino Rossi dressing gown Giraut
is wearing over his clothes. With no decipherable expression on her
face. "The *antiques dealer*?"

There is something genuinely strange about the woman at the
door. It's not her evening gown with a shawl over her shoulders, or
her high-heeled shoes with straps up to the knee, or her dark glasses
inappropriate to the late-afternoon light, or the decidedly outmoded
scarf she wears tied around her head. Although Giraut's suitological
analysis is mainly applied to men's suits, the woman's brand names
and indicators of social distinction are conspicuous. Prada. Miyake.
Dolce & Gabbana. What is strange about the woman's appearance,
however, is the fact that both her haughty posture and her attire
seem completely detached from reality. They seem more like the
haughty posture and attire of certain tragic, tall actresses of the
American studio system of the forties and fifties. Her acceptance
of the body she was born with brings to mind images of loneliness
in ivory towers and hotel night tables filled with bottles of barbiturates.

"I'm looking for Mr. Lucas Giraut." The woman rummages in her
leather purse that has a gaudy Roy Lichtenstein print on it, and pulls

out one of Lucas Giraut's business cards. Giraut takes the card and stares at it as if it contained some clue to the woman's identity or the reasons behind her late-afternoon appearance. "It's very important. His neighbor downstairs let me in." The woman zips up her purse. "May I come in?"

Lucas Giraut and the woman with the aesthetic predisposition to ingest barbiturates both remain seated for a moment on leather sofas in the living room of Giraut's apartment. In silence. With facial expressions that dance around the concept of the smile. Now that it's closer, Giraut can see that the Lichtenstein image on his strange visitor's purse depicts a sensual woman saying, "TAKE ME TO YOUR LEADER." Giraut clears his throat with a fist in front of his mouth. The tall, haughty woman has her legs crossed at her knees and is smoking a British brand of cigarette with her fingers extended. Her leg is slender and very white and has a braided crown of thorns tattooed on the ankle.

"This doesn't look like a mansion to me," the woman says finally. Her voice is deep, the way tall women's voices usually are. "It's a nice house with good furniture, but that's it. Are you rich?"

Giraut considers the question. His hands are casually intertwined and holding up his chin.

"I am the primary shareholder and president of a multinational company." He shrugs his shoulders. "My family is rich, so I guess I am, too. And you are . . . ?"

The woman seems to be thinking for a second. As if she wasn't entirely sure who she was. She takes a drag on the British cigarette.

"My name is Penny DeMink," she says.

"Miss DeMink." Giraut frowns. "Can you remind me of when we've met? Is it somehow related to my business, perhaps? Did I sell you something? Or are you looking to buy?"

The woman seated on the sofa is definitely the most attractive woman that Lucas Giraut has ever had any dealings with in his entire life. The crux of her sexual appeal isn't in her almost perfect adherence to the prevailing canons of physical beauty in the fashion, film or television worlds. Nor in her long, slender legs crossed at knee height, which now occupy the absolute center of Giraut's visual field. Nor is it related to external signs of self-assurance or absolute sexual confidence. But rather, her appeal could be chalked up to a certain general inscrutability. To the fact that the color of her eyes and her hair is a complete mystery, or how it's impossible to know what she's looking at behind her dark glasses. Her expression, her clothes, her general attitude—none of it seems to correspond to anything known or familiar or real. The resulting visual sensation is like television static. Like something fleeting, or like the profound ontological instability of things that are too perfect.

"Haven't you ever had the feeling that you've been robbed of something *vital*?" The woman releases a little cloud of smoke from between two rows of apparently perfect teeth. "I mean something really important. Something that they took from you when you were a child. Something that makes the difference between a good life and a shitty life. They stole something from me." She nods. "I can't say exactly when. Maybe when I was too little to realize. And since then everything has been shitty. I mean everything has gone really badly. I'm sure you've noticed that I'm an exceptionally attractive woman."

Even though her eyes are invisible behind her dark glasses, Lucas Giraut has a certain inexplicable feeling that the woman's pupils have moved vertically toward her own body. "I've always wanted to be an actress. And I'm not only good-looking. I'm talented, too. I'm intelligent. I can play dramatic parts and that kind of thing. I dance, too. So I ask myself: Why do I have this shitty life when I've got everything anyone could want in life? Well, it's because I'm missing something essential. Something that was taken from me. Maybe before I was born. I think you can be *born* missing something they've taken from you. You know what I mean. And in my case, what they took from me has something to do with a guy named Eric Yanel. I think you know him. It's not that he's the one who robbed me, or that he has what they took from me. But I'm convinced that he has something to do with all this. That's why I ended my personal relationship with Mr. Yanel. And my professional relationship with him." She makes a pause during which she stubs out the butt of her cigarette emphatically in the ash-tray shaped like the Roman Colosseum on the coffee table. "I don't know if Mr. Yanel has spoken to you about me. Maybe he has. Maybe using another name, I don't know. He told me that you produce films. And that perhaps you had a part for me." She pauses. "Do you think you could bring me a drink?"

Giraut considers the possibility of going down to the first-floor apartment, for a wider selection of drinks than he has in his. After a moment he comes back from his office with an unopened bottle of Macallan and two highball glasses with tinkling ice cubes. He makes some remark about the fact that he doesn't usually receive guests in his apartment, as an explanation of his lack of alcoholic options, and serves the whiskey with his gaze fixed on the woman's crossed knees. As hard as he tries to focus on one part of the woman's anatomy or clothing, he keeps having the same sensation of ontological fleeting-ness. The same sensation of having something in front of him that's too good to be real.

"Miss DeMink." Giraut forces himself to move his gaze from her knee to a neutral spot in the living room. "I assure you that I do not produce films of any kind. The person you mentioned is not on my client list, nor among my professional associates," he says very slowly, as if gauging the scope and implications of his words. "It's possible that I could have some idea of who the person you mentioned is. But per-haps I should warn you that it is not in your best interests to continue on that course. The person you mention could be associated with dan-gerous people. People involved in shady dealings."

Iris Gonzalvo, alias Penny DeMink, alias Penny Longlegs in her early films, takes a sip on her glass of whiskey. The way she sips her whiskey is extremely skillful, harkening back to outdated ideas of femininity. It gives the impression that she's only just wet her lips but causes the liquor level to descend considerably. Barely leaning her head back at all. Without gathering her features together or wrinkling her mouth. Without any visible changes to her facial musculature.

"Mr. Giraut." The woman puts her glass on the table without any unpleasant noise of glass hitting against glass. "Consider this a gift. The fact that I came to your house. Something very lucky. I think you want to sleep with me. You don't have to apologize. What I want to make clear is that there's nothing you can find in Eric that you can't find in me. In a better version, I mean." The woman's face, while still inscrutable behind her dark glasses and scarf, is now facing Giraut. He is trying to avoid staring at his visitor. "I won't disappoint you. That is the message I want to convey to you above all. In regard to any agreement you might have with him. It's in your best interests to stick with me. I can do everything he can, and much more. So *I'm* what you need."

The woman lights a cigarette with the gold lighter that Giraut holds out to her face, protecting the flame with the palm of his hand. For the second it takes to light the cigarette Giraut thinks he can make out a slight wrinkle on her brow. Their bodies are now much closer than they have been since the woman arrived. The tattoo of a crown of interlaced thorns that the woman has around her ankle is actually a classic ornamental motif that Giraut is very familiar with. Found on many moldings, and in decorative stenciling on furniture and interiors from several periods. The woman exhales smoke and looks at Giraut with her eyebrows raised questioningly. That's when the doorbell rings again.

Giraut stands up, pushing his hands against his knees. On the other side of the door he finds the slightly worried face of Marcia Parini. With one of those hesitant smiles she often uses to try to hide her worry. Marcia raises her hand to one side of her head and tucks her hair behind her ear with her fingers. One of Marcia Parini's characteristic gestures, which evoke in the spectator some kind of helpless charm. Helpless charm, by the way, seems to be Marcia Parini's main type of charm.

"I think we should go out tonight," says Marcia Parini. She looks at Giraut's dressing gown and then looks over Giraut's shoulder at the living room where Penny DeMink has just lit a second English cigarette. "You and I. Have dinner in a nice restaurant. My psychologist told me I should go out more. Especially now that Valentina isn't at home. That I have to be honest with myself and spend time with people that I really like." She extends her neck to get a better look at the woman seated in the living room and places a hand on Giraut's chest to push him softly out of her sight line. "People that make me feel loved."

Giraut nods. Fondling the lapel of his dressing gown thoughtfully. Squinting his eyes in a vague defense against the light coming in from the palace's staircase.

"Someone's here right now," he says. "An unexpected visit."

Marcia Parini smiles hesitantly and grabs the sleeve of Giraut's dressing gown in a helplessly charming gesture. In that completely helpless way children grab adults' sleeves when strolling through zoos or other places filled with potentially terrifying experiences. She takes a couple of steps into the apartment's entryway until she has a clearer image of the woman sitting on Lucas Giraut's leather sofa, smoking. Of her incredibly long, slender legs and her perfect body, according to all the canons of physical beauty.

"I don't mind you bringing women home," she says finally. Without letting go of the sleeve of his dressing gown. "You have the right to do what you want with your life."

Lucas Giraut doesn't say anything. There is a moment of silence while Penny DeMink uncrosses her legs and leans forward slightly to have a look through her sunglasses at what's going on in the entryway. Her face is wrapped in a vaporous little cloud of cigarette smoke. Marcia Parini's silence has become a solid, enveloping entity. Like one of those shapeless monsters in old horror movies set in the Arctic.

CHAPTER 33

The Prayer of Those Who Have No Father and No Mother

The renowned children's psychiatric center where Valentina Parini has been hospitalized indefinitely is located on one of those blocks in uptown Barcelona that seem to have been built according to a strictly centripetal logic. With its back to everything that isn't located within the block. Surrounded by walls and closed off to the city's traffic. One of those centripetal blocks of uptown Barcelona that have private inner parking garages and barriers of perennial trees and security guards in little huts that keep watch over the entrance to the psychiatric complex.

Lucas Giraut is sitting in the middle of a row of armless institutional seats in the reception area of the renowned children's psychiatric center. Dressed in an ash-colored linen houndstooth Lino Rossi suit. In front of him there is a family composed of a mother with dark circles under her eyes and a shockingly obese boy dressed in a school uniform that looks like it's about to burst at several points. The shockingly obese boy is chewing on a rubber object that looks very much like those rubber objects that dog owners buy for their dogs to chew on. Lucas Giraut has an anthropomorphic-looking package on his knees, wrapped in the gift wrap of a popular comic book store downtown. The Admissions desk of the children's psychiatric center is protected by a reinforced-glass partition decorated with Christmas garlands and shiny balls. With those shiny balls people hang on Christmas trees and with bunches of mistletoe. The shockingly obese boy is furiously chewing his unidentified rubber object when knocks are heard from inside the partition. The nurse in charge of the Admissions desk signals for Giraut to come closer.

"Are you a relative of Valentina Parini?" asks the nurse when Giraut gets to the desk.

Her voice sounds vaguely robotic and inflectionless through the small microphone/speaker that's set into the glass partition.

"I'm a friend." Lucas Giraut examines the mistletoe branches hanging from the partition. They are plastic branches with plastic berries meant to look like mistletoe. "A friend of *the family*."

The nurse looks at the package.

"Is that a gift for the inmate?" She signals for Giraut to place the package in some sort of trap door in the partition, designed for transferring objects from one side to the other. "I must remind you that we have strict rules here."

The nurse sticks her arms into the trap door, takes the package and starts to remove the wrapping paper. Now some sort of guttural growls are heard behind Giraut's back. From the place where the shockingly obese boy is sitting. The nurse finishes unwrapping the gift and is staring at the figure, about a foot and a half high, inside. It's a clown wearing white face paint and exaggeratedly large shoes, the kind clowns traditionally wear. The white face has a psychotic smile filled with fangs. A rolled-up electrical cord extends from one of his exaggeratedly large shoes.

"It's one of those lamps to leave on when you go to sleep," says Giraut. "It's Pennywise the Clown. From the novel *It* by Stephen King."

"We don't allow the inmates to have electrical devices." The nurse stands up and carries the figure of Pennywise the Clown to a coat check filled with coats and bags. "You can pick it up on your way out. They sell flowers in the kiosk at the end of the hall."

"Valentina hates flowers," says Giraut.

Five minutes later, Giraut is sitting on a folding chair with a bouquet of flowers in his hand. In front of the folding chair where Valentina Parini is sitting. For some reason, Giraut had imagined his visit with Valentina would take place in a sunroom with views of a flower garden. One of those sunrooms where meetings with psychiatric patients and their loved ones take place in Hollywood movies. In the midst of a vaguely melancholy atmosphere. Watching as patients stroll through the garden on their caregivers' arms. Instead, Giraut and Valentina's meeting takes place in the first-floor bathroom of the girls' wing. In the common area between the toilet stalls and the long sink with a horizontal mirror that covers the wall in front of the stalls. Leaning against the back wall, a day nurse serves as chaperone for the meeting.

"Are you sure you wouldn't be more comfortable in another chair?" Giraut fondles his bouquet of flowers absently.

Valentina's eyes are red and her face is swollen, like that of an adult who has just gotten up after a night of little sleep. She isn't wearing her green plastic glasses with one lens covered. Without her glasses and with her eyes swollen, her face takes on an unexpectedly grown-up look.

"I tried that thing where you don't swallow the pills and put them under the mattress," says Valentina in a low voice. "But they caught me and now they give me shots that make me sleep all night." She shrugs her shoulders. "I don't care. Their drugs don't work. They don't make me drool or spend all day looking at the wall or anything like that." She looks around her. "Although sometimes I do it, when I know that they're watching me. This is the only place on the whole floor without cameras. The only safe place to talk."

Lucas Giraut can't think of any reason why Valentina isn't wearing her green plastic glasses with one lens covered. Nor can he explain exactly why Valentina's face has suddenly taken on some indefinite element that is more appropriate to adults.

"Those are the same flowers my mother brought me." Valentina points to the flowers with her chin. "Those are the same flowers *everybody* brought me."

Giraut shrugs his shoulders and throws the bouquet of flowers into the metal wastebasket next to the sink with the horizontal mirror. Marcia Parini has also received citations from the same redheaded, sickly-looking lawyer to testify in the preliminary hearings of the trial that Estefanía "Fanny" Giraut's lawyers have begun. The parties involved in the trial, in mutual agreement, are also considering the possibility of calling Valentina Parini to be present in said hearings. In the case that the doctors decide that it wouldn't be harmful to Valentina's treatment. The nurse chaperone stares at the bouquet inside the metal wastebasket. According to Giraut's lawyer, it is likely that Fanny Giraut's lawyer will try to discredit Marcia Parini as a mother unfit for custody of her daughter. It is also possible that they will bring up, as an aggravating factor in the case, a supposed romantic relationship between Marcia and Lucas Giraut.

"When they caught me hiding my pills they took away Stephen King's New Novel." Valentina lowers her voice and moves closer to Lucas to speak to him in a confidential tone. "I have to get it back. My mother brought me another copy on the sly but they caught her, too. I need you to find a way to bring it to me. They have cameras everywhere. And microphones. It's almost impossible to hide stuff."

Lucas Giraut looks out of the corner of his eye at the nurse chaperone seated at the back of the bathroom. She looks back at him with a neutral gaze and nods her head almost imperceptibly. The nurse chaperone doesn't look like the nurses in psychiatric centers that Lucas Giraut has seen in movies. She isn't stout or frowning and she looks like she'd rather be somewhere else. She's younger than Giraut and has svelte legs and the badly dyed hair and excessive makeup that one usually associates with women from working-class suburbs.

"I know how to get it in," says Giraut. "But I don't know when I can come visit you again. My mother is trying to kick me out of the company."

Valentina makes a gesture with her hand that is powerfully reminiscent of that gesture with which adults dismiss obviously irrelevant questions. Questions that are insignificant given the gravity of the circumstances. Valentina signals for Giraut to bring his ear close to her mouth. He does.

"I've discovered how they do it," says Valentina in a whisper. "How they make everything work. Or make it *seem* like everything is working. They divide the population into five groups. Each group with their special instructions. There are the Repairers. Like the people that work here. The doctors and all that. There are the Developers. The scientists and the engineers and the people that work building machines and preparing their arrival. There are the Hunters. The ones who hunt people like us. They don't have to go around dressed as policemen or anything like that. It could be a little old lady that lives on your street and has known you all your life. Then there are the Providers, who make sure that they have food and all that. And the Priests. Who are the ones that talk to them and get their messages and create the transmissions for the population." She pauses and moves a little bit away from Giraut's ear. "Those are the most dangerous."

Giraut leans back against the chair. With his shoulders very straight and his arms crossed over his lap. He studies Valentina's soft face and straight hair over vaguely dull eyes. The nurse chaperone with too much makeup and svelte legs clears her throat.

"If you make her nervous I'm going to have to take her away." The nurse uncrosses her legs that were crossed at knee height and immediately crosses them the opposite way. In a clearly nervous gesture. "You've been warned."

"The most dangerous?" Giraut asks Valentina with a frown, in the exact moment that the door to the floor's communal bathroom opens and a second nurse enters, leading a sleepy little girl about seven years old by the hand. "Does this all have to do with the book by Stephen King?" He looks out of the corner of his eye at the nurse and the sleepy girl that have just come in. "Is that why you need a copy of the book?"

The girl with the sleepy face walks holding on to the second nurse's hand and seems to have some kind of psychomotor problem that gets in the way of her walking in a straight line. As she passes by Giraut's side she stares at him with glassy eyes. The nurse patiently guides her toward one of the toilet stalls. Giraut thinks he can see a bit of saliva on her chin.

"I'm talking about the Captors, of course." Valentina grabs Giraut's arm. She stares at him with slightly squinted eyes. Like the eyes of someone who has a bit of a headache or who spends too much time looking at a computer screen. "It's them that did all this. I can't *say* that they're the ones who put me here. There are a lot of things I can't say. The cameras and the microphones aren't the only problem. They have a lot of ways to find out what we are saying here. Right now they're hiding. They fly over the city, but they're invisible. They're waiting for everything to be under control. *Then* they'll show themselves." She looks at the nurse chaperone with something like malice. "At first they look like angels. Or that's what they say."

The nurse clears her throat once again. She looks ill at ease.

"Sir," she says.

"I'm not hearing voices!" Valentina raises her voice. "Who's hearing voices?"

The second nurse is gently pushing the sleepy-faced girl into the stall. The girl stopped walking when she got to the stall and is now grabbing the door frame with both hands. Letting out a soft noise similar to the mooing of a calf.

"It doesn't matter that you can't see them yet." Valentina turns toward Giraut again with her brow slightly furrowed. Giraut notices a smell of urine. "The signs are there. Everywhere. Look at *Barcelona*. Didn't you ever ask yourself why nothing ever happens in Barcelona? People just shop, cook and go to work. They sleep and watch TV. Doesn't that seem suspicious to you? I mean, normally things happen. And everybody seems so happy . . ." She brings a tense hand to her inner thigh. "But they just *seem* that way. Because they're not them anymore."

The nurse chaperone stands up in alarm. From the stall comes a sound of intestinal exertion that is somewhat reminiscent of the noises that opponents in martial arts movies make in the moments before attacking.

"Please." Valentina looks intently at Giraut. "You have to make sure that at least one of us is still around. In case they erase my memories."

A couple of nights ago, Lucas Giraut visited Marcia Parini's apartment with two deluxe set menus from the Thai/Japanese restaurant on their street and a copy of the movie *Carrie* in DVD. For some reason he didn't think it was a good idea to bring a bottle of wine. A seriously sedated Marcia Parini opened the door and then, after making some unintelligible comment, tried to kiss Giraut on the lips. Giraut turned his face so that the kiss landed on his cheek. Later Marcia and Giraut were sitting very close to one another on the sofa in the living room of the Parini house watching the movie. The same sofa where they both usually sat with Valentina to watch a movie almost every Sunday. Usually horror movies related to Stephen King's literary and film works. Remastered editions in DVD of *Cujo* and *The Dead Zone* and *Misery* and *Children of the Corn*. While watching *Carrie*, Marcia spent a good long while nibbling on Giraut's earlobe before falling asleep with her head resting on his shoulder. For some reason the main character in *Carrie* makes Giraut think of Valentina. For some reason he can't explain.

"Sir." The nurse comes toward them with a worried face. "The girl has peed on herself, sir."

Valentina moves even closer to Giraut and grabs him by the arms. She brings her lips close to his ear again.

"This is the Prayer of Those Who Have No Father and No Mother," she says. "Listen carefully and memorize it. If you want you can write it down."

"Sir," repeats the nurse. "I'll remind you we are a center with very strict rules."

"We are the people who have no father and no mother," says Valentina. "The world began with us. And we are better than the rest. Because we are stuck in the armpit of love. And the things that smell bad are the things that make us strong. We started the world. Because no one is our father and no one is our mother."

The sounds of vaguely Asian intestinal exertion coming from the stall continue, muffled by the door. It is one of those doors that don't reach the floor or the upper part of the frame. The nurse is talking to someone on some sort of an institutional walkie-talkie.

"Get me the book," says Valentina. "The prayer works better when you repeat it several times."

The nurse takes Valentina out of the bathroom. Valentina says good-bye with a strange hand gesture before leaving. Giraut is left alone in the bathroom of the children's psychiatric center. With the two folding chairs and the bouquet of flowers in the wastebasket. The sound of intestinal exertion coming from the stall has changed into something similar to a gurgle of satisfaction.

CHAPTER 34

A Waste of Time in an Expensive Suit

Lucas Giraut would like his lawyer to stop looking lasciviously at the legs of the Legal Mediator sent by the District Court. Legs that are slender and tanned like the legs of many professional women. The Legal Mediator is sitting with her legs crossed at knee height in a position that causes her skirt to rise above her knee and reveal a triangular section of thigh through the back slit. The way the lawyer is looking lasciviously at the Legal Mediator's legs is: leaning his body way back and sprawling in his chair, with his legs very wide open, and his head tilted so he can see the Mediator's legs to one side of the meeting table. Chewing a pen with an expression that's rife with over-tones of sexual predation. The Mediator is young and wears glasses and her hair is short. Lucas Giraut's lawyer is Arab or maybe from the Indian subcontinent and wears a very short beard, the way Peter Gabriel did in the eighties, which accentuates the lascivious elements of his expression. His expression is lascivious in that spontaneous, effortless way that the faces of many Arab men, or men from the Indian subcontinent, are.

The rest of the people seated at the meeting table of the conference room at the legal firm are: Lucas Giraut, Fonseca, and the sickly-looking redheaded lawyer who visited the mezzanine of LORENZO GIRAUT, LTD., a week ago with the subpoena. Of all of them, only Fonseca has taken off his suit jacket and is leaning his elbows on the table. Both Fonseca and Giraut are seated beside their legal representatives in a way that accentuates the divisions between the two camps at the meeting table. With the Mediator seated at one end of the table, lateral to both groups.

"The terms of the agreement that Mr. Fonseca is offering are what we call an *amicable solution*," the Mediator explains with hand gestures and a facial expression that somehow are structurally conciliatory. With a slight maternal/condescending overtone in the details and emphasis of her gestures. "Which of course would end the legal action. And cancel the legal and medical measures set in motion by Mr. Giraut's family. And these terms, to sum up, are specifically four. First of all, that Mr. Lucas Giraut renounce, voluntarily and in writing before a notary, two percent of his stock in LORENZO GIRAUT, LTD., with which he would go from being the holder of fifty-one percent of said stock to holding forty-nine percent, with which he would continue to be the individual shareholder with the largest percentage of the company's stock. The plaintiff wants it to be noted that the defendant will continue to be the primary shareholder. Second, in exchange for said renunciation the shareholders' committee will guarantee Mr. Lucas Giraut the position of Director of Archives and Catalogues at

LORENZO GIRAUT, LTD., with important economic compensations independent of his condition as nonprincipal shareholder. Third, the plaintiff would also agree to finance the psychiatric or psychological treatment most suitable for Mr. Lucas Giraut during however long it is necessary. Guaranteeing Mr. Giraut's continued employment and salary for the duration of said treatment. And fourth, in exchange for the renunciation specified in the first point of the offer, the plaintiff represented at this table by Mr. Fonseca and his legal representative agree to withdraw the lawsuit that has been filed and close all legal actions associated with these proceedings. And now, please." She looks around her with a conciliatory smile that makes her nose wrinkle beneath her glasses. "This is the moment to ask questions if any one of those points has not been completely made clear."

Although he wouldn't swear to it, Lucas Giraut has the distinct impression that his lawyer is now touching his crotch in an improper way. While looking at the Legal Mediator's legs. It's a crotch-touching that's ambiguous enough that it's unclear if it's inappropriate or not. It could perfectly well be an automatic response to some sort of small discomfort. Like, for example, a slight itch or a poor placement of the contents of one's briefs. The Arab or Hindustani lawyer, by the way, is not Lucas Giraut's regular lawyer. He is a regular professional colleague of Mr. Bocanegra, who recommended him to Giraut to help with his problems with the family business. The slight clacking heard in the room is coming from the Arab/Hindustani lawyer's little, unconscious nibbling on the pen in his mouth. The Legal Mediator looks at the meeting's attendees one by one without her smile losing even a hint of composure. She finally leans forward to listen to something the redheaded lawyer is saying into her ear with a frown while making small explanatory gestures with his hands. The Legal Mediator nods several times and uncrosses her legs.

"My client has something to say," says the redheaded lawyer without looking at anyone in attendance. "Something important in terms of what is being discussed here. My client would like to state that we are looking into the possibility of having the defendant's representation deemed unfit. And I would like to personally introduce the idea that we are dealing with someone who is a *disgrace* to my profession. A regular partner to organized crime and someone who has been involved in several cases of judicial corruption and coercion of juries. We have brought some of the documentation that incriminates him." He takes a shockingly fat dossier of documents out of his briefcase and puts it on the table. Giraut can't help noticing that his fingers and the back of his hand have pigmentation stains and that the whiter parts look painfully irritated. They even have that texture of flesh that's been scalded with boiling water. "Including indictment certificates and photographic documentation. Mr. Giraut." He looks at Giraut. "I assume you realize how damaging this professional association is to you. In terms of how your case is going to be received in a courtroom. I don't need to tell you that this could go further. That things *do* get leaked to the press."

Giraut interlocks his fingers and rests his chin on the resulting interwoven fists. According to the observations he has been making over the years, Estefanía "Fanny" Giraut considers her only son a mentally weak individual, completely incapable of doing anything worthwhile with his life. With serious problems of introversion close to autism that make him live in an inner world of childish fantasies partially inherited from his father. With a total lack of the mental mechanisms necessary to carry out the natural socialization process that everyone carries out during their prepubescence. As a result of which he has never had what is commonly known as a Circle of Friends. Those male friends that one goes out for drinks with, or plays golf with, and those female friends that could potentially become girlfriends and/or wives. Someone who hasn't gone through those necessary natural phases that are known as the Ages of Man, among which are sexual awakening and the entrance into adult life. A mediocre student. A person who lacks initiative. A thirty-three-year-old total virgin. A misfit, in other words. A failure, because of his congenital deficiency, and definitively ruined by a father who was also defective and a criminal repeat offender. On one occasion, Fanny Giraut made a comment alluding to the fact that Lucas Giraut lacked the sufficient degree of masculinity for carrying out a typical act of coitus with a woman. It is true that Lucas Giraut is a virgin in many more senses than he would be willing to admit publicly.

"Son," says Fonseca to Giraut, in that serious tone that Fonseca usually adopts when he assumes some sort of quasi-parental role. "You still have time to stop this all. Let's call it a misunderstanding. We are people who love you." Giraut can't perceive any kind of nervous beating in the treelike network of blood vessels on Fonseca's temples. "No one wants anything to happen that could change the fact that we are people who love you."

The Arab or Hindustani lawyer removes the pen from between his teeth and his smile, surrounded by his short little beard, grows even closer to the lecherous, evil expression of a villain. Of one of those Arab villains in those American movies centered around the conflict between American freedom and the Arab lack of respect for all that is sacred.

"My client wants to express his absolute indifference to the plaintiff's offer," he says in a high-pitched voice with a slight Near Eastern accent. "My client would like to make clear that the offer seems to be clear proof of the plaintiff's true intentions. My client is the principal shareholder of LUCAS GIRAUT, LTD. There is no indication of inappropriate relationships. Et cetera. My client wants to make clear that he finds this all to be a waste of time." He clears his throat. A lock of black curly body hair sticks out of the upper edge of the collar of his shirt. "Regarding the accusations on my person, everything that has been said here *in front of witnesses* could be the basis of taking legal action. I am a citizen who has never been formally accused of any crime. Now my client and I would like to take our leave. See you at the trial. None of what was said here is going to be overlooked."

Once Estefanía Giraut called her son A Waste of Time in an Expensive Suit. On other occasions she has referred to him as: Drooling

Runt, More Useless Than Sandals in the Arctic, Born Loser, International King of Failure 2003, The First Step Toward the Extinction of the Species, Pile of Genetic Remains and Complete and Utter Idiot. In one of Lucas Giraut's childhood notebooks from fifth grade, Giraut describes in detail how his mother is run over by a cattle train and killed. Including a diagram of the distances at which they found the different pieces of her corpse. For several months, and until the child psychologists sounded the alarm, Giraut was telling anyone who would listen the story of the cattle train and his mother's death.

"Are you threatening me?" Fonseca sends a defiant eyebrow gesture to the non-Caucasian lawyer. A certain palpitating vascular movement is apparent at his temples. "Be more *specific*. Is Bocanegra going to send his heavies after me? Are they going to shoot me in the knee?"

Lucas Giraut's lawyer has already gathered up his papers from the table and put them away in his briefcase. He has already stood up and is about to leave the meeting room of the plaintiff's law firm. The Legal Mediator lifts her palms in a placating gesture and also stands up. She repeats several times the idea that nothing of what has been said during the ongoing meeting figures in any legal document of any kind. She appeals to the professionalism of those present and she pulls her skirt down, which had inched up as a result of her sitting with her legs crossed. Her facial expression and body language are slightly more tense and slightly less self-assured versions of her conciliatory and quasi-maternal expression and body language. Still seated at the table, Lucas Giraut surreptitiously seeks out the gaze of the sickly-looking redheaded lawyer. From the door, the possibly Semitic or Persian lawyer indicates that the time to leave the room has come. In the pink-eyelashed gaze of the plaintiff's representative, Giraut thinks he has found a mix of professional greed and killer instinct that he finds somehow essentially legal but, at the same time, impossible to disassociate from the basic fact of being redheaded.

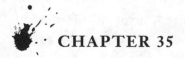

CHAPTER 35

Hannah Linus: Reprise

Hannah Linus's body movements loosen up until they meld with the waves' aquatic vibration. The water is warm as it can only be after an entire day beneath the subtropical sun. None of the waves are strong enough to disturb her feeling of inner peace. Hannah Linus focuses on the idea that she has finally found a place where no one can bother her in any way. No one can interrupt her idyll with herself in this sub-tropical island where the sand is white and fine and the sea is always calm. With no jellyfish or sharks or aquatic animals. She lifts an arm and repositions her green plastic eye protector. With no work obliga-tions. Without having to talk to anyone, although that was a personal option she had chosen out of the many on the promotional brochure. The sensation is vaguely sexual. She couldn't exactly say why she finds the sensation sexual, but in general terms Hannah Linus has never been very good at describing her sexual feelings or communicating to other people her sexual impulses. Without even mentioning the fact that those impulses clearly make her uneasy, conceptually.

Hannah Linus is opening her mouth in a tension-releasing yawn and moving an arm to hold her eye protector when her head hits some-thing soft and flabby. Something that judging by the tactile sensation could very well be a butt. Hannah Linus frowns and raises a hand in apology. Her eye protector floats off across the thermal saltwater pool toward the edge lined with relaxing candles. Hannah Linus can't imagine who the idiot is who lined the pool with little candles. She curses in Swedish and makes her way through the floating bodies and the erect bodies of the aquatic therapists toward her eye protector.

Besides Hannah Linus, there are half a dozen clients of the Spa-

Center floating in lethargic poses in the pool's salt water. Hannah Linus makes her way with difficulty through the salt water, following the green stain that the artificial waves carry farther and farther off. Through the fog that floats over the heated pool she thinks she can see someone signaling to her from the entrance to the dressing area. According to the Spa-Center's promotional brochure, salt water heated to the exact temperature of thirty-eight degrees Celsius supports most of the body's weight. The vertebrae and muscles relax more easily and the spine is freed from the force of earth's gravity. The complete holistic treatment lasts sixty minutes. And the heated salt water produces an optimum energy-conducting effect. Hannah Linus couldn't care less about what the Spa-Center's aquatic therapy promotional brochure says. Nor is she particularly interested in the emancipation of her muscular and skeletal systems. What she really wants is a place where everyone leaves her alone and where she can shut her eyes and imagine that she has rented an island paradise to get away from it all.

Around her, the aquatic therapists are leading the lethargic floating bodies through the pool with gentle motions and intermittent immersions. Hannah Linus finally traps the green stain that is her eye protector. A few steps away from her, framed by the candle's little flames, a Japanese master of Reiki therapy is laying his hands on a patient to transmit his flow of vital energy.

"Miss," says someone from a corner of the pool. Hannah Linus squints her eyes to see through the fog. It is a young man with the official swimsuit of the Spa-Center chain, pointing with one finger to his diving watch. "Miss. I think your sixty minutes ended two minutes ago."

Hannah Linus gathers her things from the locker and dries her hair vigorously with a towel. Then she knots the towel below her underarms and starts to walk toward the dressing rooms with her sports bag hanging from her shoulder. She is walking between the bubbling hydromassage pools when a shaved head with swimming goggles emerges suddenly from the bubbling surface of one of the pools. Causing some sort of heated wave that splatters the floor and walls. Hannah Linus stares with a frightened face at the guy now coming out of the hydromassage pool, leaning effortlessly on his muscular tattooed arms. The guy takes off his swimming goggles and looks at her with a wide smile. Hannah Linus is paralyzed with horror, her towel splattered with water and her sports bag hanging from her shoulder.

"You," she manages to finally mutter. "What are you doing here?"

"Me?" Saudade points to his chest with his eyebrows widely arched. "Are you a client of this place, too?"

Hannah Linus sets off running through the hallway that leads to the dressing rooms, grabbing the upper edge of her towel with one hand and the strap of the sports bag with the other. Halfway there she slips and crashes into a middle-aged woman, who falls stiff as a board into one of the hydrotherapy pools. Hannah Linus doesn't turn to hear the complaining voices. Nor does she stop to avoid a cart of towels whose handler stares at her with a mix of hate and prudence. Saudade reaches her a few steps from the door to the women's dressing room. He grabs her by the arm and turns her toward his smiling face. Hannah Linus sticks a hand into her sports bag. She takes out a travel-size spray can and points it in Saudade's face.

"You can't imagine what this does," she says through clenched teeth. "You can't imagine what it can do to *your eyes*."

Saudade looks at the spray with a frown.

"Ecological hairspray," he says. "You're gonna blind me with that?"

Hannah Linus looks down and reads the label on the spray can. She puts it back in her sports bag and takes out the personal self-defense spray that she bought a month ago, after she was attacked in her own office at the gallery. Saudade sighs.

"How dare you follow me," she says. In a voice that is both low and tense. "Your wife put me in the *hospital*. You could have called to see how I was."

"I came *now* to see how you are." Saudade shrugs his shoulders. He looks Hannah Linus over with a vertical visual sweep. The kind of look usually associated with the first phases of a sexual advance. "And it looks like you're fine. Although it's hard to tell, with that towel on."

A couple of people with the official swimsuits of the Spa-Center chain are attending to the middle-aged woman who was violently knocked into the hydromassage pool. Other clients of the spa franchise have gathered around the scene of the fall to check on the victim's state. Hannah Linus begins to experience that whole chain of sexual feelings that simultaneously produces a certain feeling of conceptual uneasiness. Saudade sticks a hand beneath the towel she has knotted below her underarms. Hannah Linus realizes that she has been holding up the personal self-defense spray for a minute, with the nozzle orifice not exactly pointing in Saudade's direction. Nor is she entirely sure that she's broken all the security seals necessary to be able to trigger it. The tension she is feeling isn't exactly the tension you feel when your personal safety is in danger. It's a tension of contrasting elements. It looks like they are finally taking the woman out of the hydromassage pool. Her face is very red and her swimming cap has shifted on the crown of her head in such a way that it now looks sort of like the Smurfs' flaccid, fallen hats.

Hannah Linus is experiencing a certain difficulty concentrating. Saudade is saying something about the fact of having an important professional career and a son at a difficult age. He is saying that his career and his son take up a lot of his time and barely leave him opportunities for socializing. Or for visiting people in the hospital.

"I'm going to call security," she interrupts. Looking with something like curiosity at the hand he's placed beneath her towel, which is now playing with the elastic edge of her one-piece bathing suit. "And when I leave here I'm going to ask for a *restraining order*. For you and your crazy wife."

"I had to pay the whole month's fee just for them to let me in," says Saudade, with some sort of martyrological face. "If that doesn't show you I love you, I don't know what I have to do."

The sexual feelings that Hannah Linus is now having manifest themselves in the form of small shivers and strange sensations that are like slight temperature changes and tingling in her middle section. Something located in the lower part of her spinal column. One of the reasons that Hannah Linus isn't good at communicating her sexual impulses, and experiences a feeling of conceptual uneasiness toward them, is the fact that her sexual responses usually seem to be mixed with ideas of submission and self-degradation in a violent context. With images of struggle and twisted arms. Of violent penetrations in underground parking lots. Hannah Linus has no idea why the dominant culture links violent penetrations with underground parking lots. The facilities of the Spa-Center Diagonal franchise are impregnated with a characteristic odor. A mix of dampness and bath salts and incense. The odor doesn't contribute to the sexual sensation but it does accentuate the strangeness of the situation. The knot that holds up Hannah Linus's towel below her underarms comes undone with a sigh and falls to the ground. The towel lies wrinkled at her feet. Imparting a certain atmosphere of classical mythology to the scene. The unveiling of the classic defenseless female. Her exposure to the forcefulness of the classical phallus. Leda and the Swan. The Rape of the Sabine Women. Hannah Linus sticks her hand beneath Saudade's swimsuit and grabs his penis. A group of Spa-Center clients, who are passing by at that moment, whistle and clap.

After a taxi ride and an hour of violent sex, Hannah Linus is lying in the bed in her apartment beside Saudade's sweaty tattooed body. Overcome by postcoital sloth. The layout of their horizontal bodies on the king-size bed of Hannah Linus's apartment is the following: He is faceup, with his hands interlocked beneath the nape of his neck. With his legs extended and his feet slightly sticking out over the bottom end of the bed. Whistling some optimistic postcoital song. She is at a semi-fetal angle, with her body curled and facing away from Saudade's, massaging her temples with the fingers of one hand. Victim to that wave of postcoital pessimism, and waiting for the Minimum Acceptable Time to pass so she can kick her sexual partner out of her bed and her apartment. The colossal tedium of having to share the moments after orgasm. The uncontrollable urges of freedom. Saudade springs from the bed, still whistling, and leaves the bedroom. Hannah Linus takes advantage of the moment alone to put on her underwear and a skirt.

"Don't make plans for this summer," says Saudade. The distance and the specific degree of echo to his voice indicate to Hannah Linus that he has entered the kitchen. That he's probably holding the door of the refrigerator open and examining its contents. "I'm gonna take you to Thailand. To one of those hotels on the beach that have absolutely everything. Where they do everything for you. You know what I mean. You're gonna love it." Hannah Linus thinks she can hear the noise of pantry doors opening and closing. "Even though you're not into chicks. The chicks there touch you in a way that makes you forget about everything. Forget about those snooty places you go to. With the little bubbles and all that. There are no massages here like the ones they give you there, darling."

Hannah Linus notices a strange smell. She sits up with her vaguely sore limbs and puts on a shirt. Saudade's voice now sounds slightly occluded and distant, as if he were eating something and had moved to the living room. Hannah Linus puts on a shoe and limps out of the bedroom with the other shoe in her hand. Saudade is seated on the sofa with the television remote control in one hand and a lit cigarette in the other. He looks at Hannah Linus with a smile.

"I'll pay for everything, of course," he says. "I'm gonna be loaded. Very soon."

Hannah Linus throws her shoe with all her might toward Saudade's smiling head. He has no problem avoiding the projectile with a lateral head movement. Still maintaining his optimistic expression. The heel of the shoe leaves a nick in the wall's plaster in the shape of a heel of a shoe.

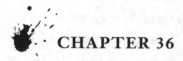

CHAPTER 36

Mutagenic Explosions

A ten-foot-long Venezuelan crocodile hangs, suspended from a half dozen cables, from the ceiling of the main room of the Atomic restaurant in Barcelona's Ensanche. Above and to the right of the slightly lateral table where Iris Gonzalvo and Lucas Giraut are seated. At dinner hour. In the main room, which is packed on a Monday dinner hour. The restaurant's walls are decorated with framed reproductions of photographs related to nuclear radiation and genetic mutations. In the entryway, right above the reservation desk where an employee dressed in an aseptic-looking red kimono checked Iris and Giraut's reservation, an enormous black-and-white photograph shows a human silhouette stamped into a wall in Hiroshima by radiation. It's similar to a shadow in negative. The effects of instantaneous disintegration. The employees with aseptic red kimonos come and go through the various sections of the restaurant, looking like characters in one of those science-fiction films where humankind has evolved to the point where human emotions have been systematically eradicated.

"Miss Gonzalvo," Lucas Giraut starts to say.

"Iris," she interrupts.

"Miss Iris." Lucas Giraut contemplates the contents of his plate with a vaguely devastated expression. Something that appears to be a bone-colored cube surrounded by a garland of herbs, with no apparent relationship to its designation on the menu. "What I'm trying to say is that I'm willing to help you. In the terms that you yourself suggested. It is true that there is an opening. I've been looking into it. Mr. Yanel has not only stopped showing up for work meetings. He doesn't answer his cell phone, either. One could say he's disappeared without a trace. And that has made the people he works with a bit nervous, naturally. And I want it to be clear that I'm not saying that you have anything to do with what's happened." Giraut looks at his companion's plate. The soup on Iris Gonzalvo's plate is the same color as the employees' uniforms. In it float shavings of something unidentifiable. He clears his throat. "In spite of the fact that you showed up at my house practically the same day as the disappearance occurred. In any case, I can help you to get that job. It doesn't have anything to do with a film. I've already told you about Mr. Bocanegra. And the sort of work he does. Bocanegra is the man Mr. Yanel worked for. And my partner in the project we're in the middle of now. I could create a spot for you. However, there is something I want to ask you for. Something that you could do for me. That is, if it's okay with you."

Lucas Giraut buries his spoon into the bone-colored cube. The texture of which looks like the texture of flan or of a soft pudding. The suit he is wearing that night is a tobacco-colored suit with dark pinstripes. From Lino Rossi's new line.

"You want me to fuck you," says Iris.

She tries a spoonful of aseptic red-colored soup. In that blank way that one takes medicine or tastes something tasteless.

"Listen." Lucas Giraut makes an annoyed face. Or his version of an annoyed face. A simple fleeting nuance of worry mixed with an element of impatience. "I'm not explaining myself well here. I know this is going to sound ridiculous to you. Like the typical story pulled from a movie or some novel, some thriller. It's still hard for me to come to terms with sometimes, I assure you. But Mr. Bocanegra has *a gang*. Like a gang of gangsters. That steal very valuable paintings and all that. And then there's another gang. The boss of that other gang is named Koldo Cruz. Most of its members are Russian, from what I understand. And I think that these two gangs are at war. Wait." He lifts a hand to keep Iris Gonzalvo's reaction in check. She has begun to have the trace of a vaguely mocking smile. "I know that this all seems silly. But I have a theory. My theory is that in the beginning there was only one gang. A long time ago. Thirty years. They called themselves the Down With The Sun Society. And there were three of them, that's the most important part. There was Mr. Bocanegra and Koldo Cruz, and my father, too. Who was something like the brains of the gang. And then something happened, I don't know exactly how, but it must have been something terrible. Someone betrayed my father. He went to jail. He was never the same again. You could say I never knew him. You have to understand. This is very important for me. I'm talking about *my father*."

Iris Gonzalvo blinks. Her soup-eating style consists of bringing the spoon to her mouth with the precise amount of soup and introducing it into her mouth with only a slight separation of her lips and with nothing even remotely resembling a slurp or that unpleasant pursing of the mouth that some people do when eating soup. Without that gaze off into the distance or into oblivion that some people have when eating that makes one think of people's animal origins.

"Miss Iris." Giraut lowers his voice. "I want *to take revenge* on the people that betrayed my father. I have some idea who they were. That is my project. And I'd like for you to help me. If you don't mind, of course."

There is silence at the table where Iris Gonzalvo and Lucas Giraut are seated. Allowing the background noise of the restaurant to invade the space between them. That sarcastically sophisticated murmur of expensive restaurants. On the wall closest to them there are photographs of guinea pigs and laboratory animals before and after having been inoculated with artificially mutated organisms in an attempt to find new vaccines. On the walls there are panels explaining the contents of each photo. Right behind the hanging crocodile, in the direction his three-foot-long tail is pointing, there is a series of framed photographs, in black and white, of blind animals from the area surrounding Chernobyl's nuclear power station. At first glance, one wouldn't notice anything mutant or special in the anatomy of the crocodile that hangs from the ceiling. Nor would one see anything that explains why so many people would want to dine in a restaurant with such decoration. In any case, it seems clear that the Atomic's strategy of surrounding diners with unpleasant or potentially nauseating images is the key to its success. A success echoed in reviews around the world. On many television channels. With pixels covering the photographs' contents. The last word in Barcelonian design. With imitations already up and running in Tokyo and Chelsea. Iris Gonzalvo finally leaves her spoon by the side of her plate and shrugs her shoulders.

"I have no idea what you're talking about," she says. "But I understand the part about your father. Fathers are important. Mine was a tall, very handsome man. And I was his favorite daughter. Because I was the prettiest and all that. I guess it's because of my father that I am the way I am. And because of him that I'm here right now. I mean that I do everything I do because of men. *For* men. If it weren't for men, I wouldn't be an actress. But I am what I am. And I guess men are the audience for what I am." She makes a gesture that could indicate helplessness. Iris's gesticulation isn't exactly a question of nuances. It's more defined by what's missing. Like the silhouettes created by atomic explosions. "And I guess it's all my father's fault. And that I wanted him to like me all the time and that kind of thing."

One of the waitresses, with the restaurant's trademark blank expression, asks for permission to remove their plates and bring their second courses. Both Giraut and Iris have chosen something called The Manhattan Project, according to the embossed menu in the shape of a nuclear mushroom. Among its ingredients is something called Projectile Squid Sashimi.

"Miss Iris," says Lucas Giraut, once the waitress has gone.

"Lucas." She interrupts him again. Now that she's not wearing sunglasses, her eyes are large and green and have those kinds of large, thick lids that give the impression that her eyes are never fully open. "I think it would be better if you just left out the 'miss.' It will make things easier if we're going to end up fucking."

Lucas blinks.

"That isn't what I'm trying to suggest," he says. "You are mistaken as to my intentions. I'm not doing this so I can sleep with you."

Iris takes out a pack of English tobacco from her purse and places a cigarette between her lips. She waits for Giraut to take out a lighter and light it for her, protecting the flame with the palms of his bony hands. Then she exhales a mouthful of smoke.

"You're a good guy," she says. "A bit odd, maybe. But that's to be expected, considering you're an antiques dealer and all that. You aren't like all the other men I've met, that's for sure. You still haven't tried to fuck me. You haven't offered me drugs or tried to impress me. And I don't think you're into guys. I'm good at seeing that kind of thing. I don't know why I like you. It must be intuition," she says. She pauses while one of the waitresses places their second courses on the table. The raw squid in the dish known as The Manhattan Project really are shaped like torpedoes or projectiles about to be launched from a plane. "I think we can work together. I'm not saying that you're doing what you're doing just so you can fuck me. That's clear for the moment. My romantic relationship with Eric has been a pretty negative experience. That doesn't mean I'm doing things out of spite or to try to make him feel bad." She pauses. There is nothing in her attitude that suggests she has any intention of eating her second course. "Although I have to admit that I chose this place so we would be seen together. A lot of Eric's friends come here."

Lucas Giraut looks around him. Since they arrived at the Atomic restaurant, which is full at dinner hour, he's had the feeling that the other customers have been watching Iris Gonzalvo. Although they've only known each other for a few days, he has already realized that this seems to happen everywhere she goes. Like a vortex. Like some sort of magnetic force field that moves along with her.

Causing reactions at neighboring tables and in practically everyone that crosses her path. The most shocking photographs at Atomic aren't in the main room. They are in the wide, well-lit hallway that leads to the bathrooms. A series of photographs showing different types of burns and wounds on victims of nuclear explosions. The location of said photographs is a question that isn't explained by any of the restaurant reviews that Giraut has read. Now he notices a man who is staring at Iris Gonzalvo. The man takes a pair of glasses out of his pocket and puts them on so he can see her better. He blinks several times and furrows his brow. The man is dressed entirely in white. His white suit has scallop trim and frills embroidered into the lapels and the sleeves that give the suit a certain Mexican air without actually making you think of Mexico at all. His face is unrealistically tan.

"I don't know who that woman that came to your apartment the other day was," says Iris Gonzalvo. "But she wasn't your girlfriend. I can always tell these things. An ex-girlfriend, maybe."

The tall man dressed in white has stood up and is now walking toward their table without taking his eyes off the low-cut back of Iris's dress. Iris follows Giraut's gaze as the tall man dressed in white stops beside their table and crosses his arms.

"Santi." Iris looks at the man with a cold smile. "What a wonderful surprise. Let me introduce you to my friend Lucas Giraut. This is Santi Denís."

"Terrific." The face of the guy with the white suit is one of those artificially tanned faces where the entire complex system of facial wrinkles has transformed into a moving network of white lines. The effect is reminiscent of how spiderwebs are depicted in comic books. "As far as I'm concerned you can screw the king of Spain if you want. I was expecting a slightly more remorseful attitude after you lied to the security guards at my party and snuck into my bedroom. But that's not what I wanted to talk to you about. In fact, the less I talk to you the better. Your asshole boyfriend owes me a lot of money. I haven't had his face broken yet only because I can't find him. But you." He uncrosses his arms and sticks a big tan finger into Iris's bare shoulder. "You *do* know where he is. And I'm not going to make a scene here. As much as I'd love to give you a good beating. But give him a message for me. He has twenty-four hours to give me my money."

According to the restaurant review of Atomic that appeared in one of Barcelona's biggest newspapers, the place "descends to the kingdom of the atavistic as it confronts food and death. There is nothing in this place that doesn't bring you back to death's primal impulse and the fear that it arouses, from the employees' surgical garb to the hanging crocodile and the allusions to unnatural births and deaths. The masterpiece is undoubtedly the images of muta-genic explosions in the hallway leading to the bathrooms, where the nutritional act/mutated birth finds its parallel in the elimination/ death by disintegration." Iris Gonzalvo exhales a final mouthful of cigarette smoke and stubs out the butt in the saucer that holds the table's candle. She looks at Lucas Giraut with a slightly tense half smile and shrugs her shoulders.

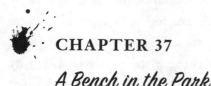

CHAPTER 37

A Bench in the Park

The park on the outskirts of Barcelona where Matilde Saudade and her son Cristian have agreed to meet with their husband and father, respectively, is one of those parks on the outskirts of Barcelona with a cement floor and rusty metal constructivist sculptures. The only places in the park where the color gray doesn't prevail are those places where the wastebaskets are overflowing with fast-food wrappers, soft-drink cans and pornographic magazines. An irritated-looking pigeon alights on the ground in front of the bench where the three members that comprise the Saudade family unit are seated, and pecks at the grime on the cement floor. Looking to either side with an irritated expression. The three members of the Saudade family unit have been sitting for five minutes in silence on a metal bench in the park that gives its name to their neighborhood. Juan de la Cruz Saudade takes a pack of Fortuna cigarettes from the pocket of his powder blue and white sweatshirt and puts one between his lips. The new year has brought with it a cold snap that the press is calling Siberian. Siberian cold snaps are inexplicable, but relatively normal, occurrences in Barcelona's climate. Matilde Saudade extends a hand in a silent request for a cigarette but her husband has already put the pack back in his pocket.

"I talked to my mother and my sisters." Matilde Saudade sighs, sitting on the bench in a vaguely childlike position, swaying her legs, grabbing the edge of the bench with her hands and looking at her feet. "They say I have to give you another chance. *The last* chance. Honestly, I don't understand why I have to give you another chance. I don't see any difference between this time and the ones before. Or why I have to let you come home."

Matilde Saudade's most characteristic facial trait is a nervous tic that makes her compulsively wrinkle her forehead at regular intervals, as if she were surprised about something approximately every half second. The tic also makes everything she says sound slightly hesitant. As if she herself didn't believe the words that were coming out of her mouth. Matilde Saudade is wearing white stretch jeans and high-tops and a sweatshirt of a well-known sports brand that is actually an imitation of that brand's sweatshirts. Saudade's sweat suit is the official Umbro sweat suit of his favorite soccer club. The way the three members of the family are seated is the following: (a) Matilde Saudade on the right side of the bench, grabbing its edge with her hands and not looking directly at her husband or her son;

(b) Cristian Saudade in the middle, covering his ears with his hands; and (c) Juan de la Cruz Saudade on the left side of the bench. Not so much seated as lounging with his legs open very widely and his head resting on the part of the back of the bench where most people rest their backs, smoking with large puffs and exhaling the smoke in his son and wife's general direction.

"Come home?" Saudade frowns. "But *you're* the one who left home. Taking my son with you, by the way. Must be one of those illegal things." He searches for the words. "Abandoning the home or something like that. I think it's *seriously* illegal. And I have a right to see my son, don't I?"

"And I have a right to break that bitch's face." Matilde looks up and wrinkles her forehead spastically. "And the bitch up and reports me for breaking her face. Her *bitch-ass* face."

The irritated-looking pigeon that landed in front of them is now moving its head from one side to the other to look alternately at Saudade and his wife. With an element of irritation in its gaze that seems to contain elements of repressed rage. Eight-year-old Cristian Saudade is still sitting in the same position: covering his ears with his hands and with his eyes tightly shut. Saudade exhales smoke from his cigarette and makes an annoyed face.

"Here we go again," he says. "We've talked about this a thousand times. About your imagining things. Didn't I have my friend Aníbal call you and swear there was no one but you?" He pauses and adopts the tone of emphatic indignation that he always adopts when he suddenly thinks of a point in his favor in the middle of an argument. "Aren't you *ashamed* to make up all this shit in front of our son? These kinds of things get stuck in kids' heads. They can turn into *fags*."

Juan de la Cruz Saudade and Matilde Saudade both look at their son Cristian, who is sitting between them with his eyes closed and his hands over his ears. Matilde pats him on the shoulder.

"Why don't you go play?" Matilde says when he takes his hands off of his ears. "And leave me and your father alone for a little while?"

Eight-year-old Cristian Saudade stares at his mother impatiently.

"How can I go play?" he says. "I don't know *anyone* in this park. What am I gonna play?"

Matilde Saudade shrugs her shoulders as her son covers his ears with his hands again. Juan de la Cruz Saudade is smoking with that satisfied expression of someone convinced he's winning an argument.

"If it's all in my imagination," says Matilde, "then who's that English bitch whose face I broke?" She pauses and a proud tone creeps into her voice. "They had to put four stitches in her head."

Juan de la Cruz Saudade throws his cigarette butt to the ground beneath the pigeon's gaze filled with repressed rage. He shrugs his shoulders.

"She's not English," he says. "And it's normal that you have to vent your anger on somebody once in a while." His tone of voice has taken on that vaguely condescending tinge of someone forced to concede a minor dialectic point to their opponent. "It's not easy being a woman. Especially when your period is about to come. It's not me who says so. It's the doctors."

A group of teenagers of Latin American descent occupy a metal bench located right in front of the metal bench where the Saudade family is seated. They place a large portable sound system on the ground and then someone pushes the PLAY button on the compact disc player. A hip-hop song at full blast invades the park's relative silence. The pigeon that was watching the Saudades flies off with a furious expression toward another area of the park, one that is free of urban subcultures. The teenagers begin to move to the music's vaguely jungle rhythm and to improvise rhyming lines of rap while a couple of them are rolling hash joints. They are all wearing enormous pants and some sort of handkerchiefs knotted around their heads that are morphologically similar to giant condoms.

"My brother says he's going to break your face," says Matilde Saudade, raising her voice to be heard over the hip-hop music. "If he sees you on the street."

Juan de la Cruz Saudade stares at his wife with a perplexed expression.

"*Your brother* is gonna break my face?" he says, as if his wife's statement involved some sort of enigma. "Mine? But he works in a restaurant. How tall is your brother? And when has he ever broken anyone's face?"

"He works in a pizzeria." His wife wrinkles her forehead in three consecutive expressions of surprise. "And he doesn't work in the pizzeria. He delivers the pizzas on a motorcycle. I mean he's strong. And at least my brother worries about me. He worries about what happens to me and all that."

The Latin American teenagers continue rehearsing dance steps that make them seem, alternately, like robots, marionettes and people with central nervous system disorders. The vaguely rhyming sentences that they rap in time to the music are peppered with the words "respect," "brother" and "city."

"I worry about you," says Saudade, lighting another cigarette. "I'm worried right now."

Cristian Saudade takes his hands off of his ears.

"Grandma says that if she has to put up with our shit one more day," he says, "she's going to be the one to pack her bags and get as far away as possible." He pauses and looks with a thoughtful expression at the group of teenagers that are moving like people with central nervous system disorders. "She says that she knew that all this was going to happen when my father hooked up with that chick on your wedding day."

"That chick," corrects Matilde, "is *your* aunt."

The teenagers are now passing the joints among themselves and taking nervous drags on them while they nod to the rhythm of the music and raise their thumbs to indicate urban subcultural satisfaction.

"She also told me that if I want pizza," continues Cristian, "I should ask my mother or my pig of a father for money and go buy some pizza. But nobody ever gives me money."

Saudade looks at his wife with a triumphant expression.

"You see?" he says, now almost shouting to make himself heard over the music from the portable sound system. "The kid wants to come home. You're wrecking a home with these things you imagine." He looks at his son and puts a patriarchal hand on his shoulder. "You want your mother to let you come home, right?"

Eight-year-old Cristian Saudade looks alternately at his father and at his mother.

"No," he says. "I don't know."

The joints seem to have stimulated the dancing skills of the group of Latin American teenagers, some of whom have put on gloves and have started to rehearse break-dance movements on the ground. The others clap rhythmically and some imitate the sound of rhythm boxes with their mouths. A couple of them now look out of the corner of their eyes at the strange family group seated on the bench in front of them with a child in the middle who is covering his ears with his hands. Juan de la Cruz Saudade puts out his cigarette and spits on the ground between the legs of his powder blue and white sweatpants. One of the Latin American teenagers shyly approaches and offers the Saudades the joint he's smoking. The gesture seems rich in connotations of subcultural sociability and universal chemical brotherhood. Saudade stares at him with an incredulous expression.

"You want me to break your legs, *asshole*?" he shouts at the teenager who is offering him the joint. "Take that *shit* away from *my son*!"

Half a minute later the group of teenagers, with their jungle dances and their portable sound system, have disappeared without leaving a trace beyond a vague rhythmic pulsating of the park's cement. A couple of irritated-looking pigeons alight on the area surrounding the Saudades' bench. Flapping their wings irritably and shooting hateful looks.

"I'll give you one last chance." Matilde scratches her head nervously. "You can come home, but with certain conditions. You have to follow some rules. First of all, no seeing that bitch. Second, no other bitches neither." She thinks for a moment. As if she had forgotten the rest of the rules and was searching for them in her memory. "And that's it. Two rules."

Cristian Saudade turns his head slowly toward his father, without taking his hands off his ears, and watches him in silence. Matilde looks at her husband with rhythmic gestures of surprise in her face. With something similar to expectation. With her hands in the side pockets of her knockoff sweatshirt. The situation is generally one of family expectation. With two pairs of eyes observing the patriarch of the family unit. One of those moments that seem crucial to the future evolution of the bloodline. Saudade pulls his back up against the back of the bench. He lifts his feet and clears his throat in acknowledgment of the special relevance of the present family moment.

"Baby," his tone is simultaneously contrite and obsequious, the standard universal tone of Husbands Returning to the Fold, "I know I did terrible things a long time ago. But it's those guys I work with, you know. Aníbal and Bob Marley and the rest. Bob Marley is that Russian I told you about. I think they're a bad influence on me." He pauses and looks at his wife, who is rolling her eyes *while at the same time* convulsively wrinkling her forehead. "They're always trying to make me be like them. You know what I mean. I'm almost positive they've put stuff in my drinks plenty of times. Ecstasy and shit like that."

Matilde Saudade hugs herself against the cold. The new year has just started and at a few minutes to noon the park seems to be empty except for the Saudades. Matilde Saudade makes a gesture with her hand toward the pack of Fortunas that her husband has in the pocket of his sweatshirt. Saudade snorts impatiently and offers his wife a cigarette.

CHAPTER 38

Darts

"Are you completely sure we've never met this girl before?" Mr. Bo-canegra takes a pensive drag on his cigar. Pursing his mouth and mustache in the shape of descending curves. His gesture is closer to suspicious than perplexed. "Because I think I've seen her before. Her face, her tits." He shrugs. "Those things I think I could forget. Even her ass. But not those legs. I am almost positive I've seen those legs before. I recognize them even in this light. I don't think anybody could forget those legs."

Lucas Giraut and Aníbal Manta follow Mr. Bocanegra's gaze past the bar of the Eclipse Room at The Dark Side of the Moon. Beyond the groups of customers drinking at the bar and toward the vicinity of the darts area. Where Iris Gonzalvo is playing darts in the company of half a dozen men. And leading the game in points, judging by the scores written on the chalkboard beside the dartboard. Winning the game in progress by a spectacular margin. A margin that any experienced dart player would undoubtedly deem humiliating. Although none of Iris Gonzalvo's rivals seem particularly humiliated. Most of them surround Iris Gonzalvo with sycophantic expressions and are lighting her cigarettes or bringing her glass after glass of Finlandia and tonic and clapping and cheering each one of her throws. The way Iris Gonzalvo throws the darts isn't that vaguely comical way that many women throw darts: she doesn't stick the tip of her tongue between her lips or let out nervous giggles or roll her eyes in self-parody every time one of her throws misses the board. The way she throws darts is self-assured and elegant. Bending her arm at the precise angle and with no more motion in her body than a slight swaying of the hips that reveals a triangular section of very pale and slender thigh through the side slit in her skirt.

Mr. Bocanegra, Lucas Giraut and Aníbal Manta are watching Iris Gonzalvo with contemplative faces.

"Where did you say she came from?" Mr. Bocanegra exhales a mouthful of cigar smoke that rises up between the bar lights of the Eclipse Room. In the shape of incandescent spirals.

The Eclipse Room is the most popular and most crowded area of The Dark Side of the Moon. Seven thousand and five hundred square feet of carpeted floor and velvet sofas and mirror balls and quality wood panels and statues. The statues, according to Mr. Bocanegra, are the element that sets The Dark Side of the Moon apart from just any old place. That gives it a different atmosphere from other adult entertainment spots. Because the statues, according to Bocanegra, transport you to other worlds, fantastical worlds. Like those gardens filled with statues that you see in movies. Or like those psychedelic gardens on the covers of British rock records from the seventies. If you want to create a special place, says Mr. Bocanegra, put in all the statues you can.

"She's an old friend of mine," says Lucas Giraut. He takes a cigarette out of his embossed case and taps it against the palm of his hand softly before putting it between his lips. "She's an actress. Maybe you've seen her in a commercial on TV."

Aníbal Manta looks at Iris Gonzalvo with his brow furrowed. The bar stool he's sitting on is too small for him, just like the bar itself. Producing the strange sensation that he is the only adult seated at a child-sized replica of a bar in an amusement park for kids.

"She looks familiar to me, too," he says. "Almost like I know her *from here*. Like she'd been one of our girls."

"I vouch for her," says Lucas Giraut. He takes a drag on the cigarette with his soft and slightly namby-pamby face. "She's exactly what we need. We have an opening. The sale operation starts in a few days. Mr. Yanel isn't in any condition to run the operation, because of his depression. She can do it. Almost better than Yanel."

A silence filled with sips on their respective drinks, pensive drags on their cigars and cigarettes, and surreptitious glances at Iris Gonzalvo's legs once again hovers over the three men at the bar. The way Iris Gonzalvo is playing darts, in the center of a ring of men that applaud her movements and attend to all of her needs, seems to be altering the very nature of the game itself. It's something in the way she throws the darts. Taking a couple of sips of Finlandia with tonic between dart and dart. Or perhaps licking a pinch of salt from the back of her hand just before downing a shot of tequila in one swig and biting a lemon wedge. There is something unyielding in the way she plays. As if the board and the darts and the cycle of turns were no longer just a simple game. As if it were an oracle. An arcane code. An astral or solar system for figuring out the universe. And the men that are playing with her seem to sense that on a very profound level. They seem to be worshipping their high priestess. That barely visible swaying of her hips is discernible on a deeper level and seems to be transforming into the very center of the universe.

"Fuck." Mr. Bocanegra wipes off a few drops of sweat that have started to drip off his exceptionally shiny bald head. "I wish she did work here. That girl has talent. Damn." He loosens the knot in his tie a bit. "Bring her a drink." He gestures toward Aníbal Manta. "The most expensive drink we have. Send them downstairs for it if need be."

Aníbal Manta leaves his empty drink on the bar. The bar of the Eclipse Room at The Dark Side of the Moon is circular and has multicolored lights. And in the center of the bar there is an elevator.

A burst of laughter comes from the darts area. Pavel is trying to throw a dart with his right arm, which is in a sling. Exaggeratedly leaning his body forward to compensate for his lack of mobility. He finally makes his throw. Whistles and applause are heard. The dart traces a weak downward parabola and sticks between someone's feet. Now insults are heard among the whistles.

Lucas Giraut watches how Aníbal Manta approaches Iris Gonzalvo and whispers something in her ear. The other dart players clear their throats and look away and feign interest in other things. Iris Gonzalvo nods blankly at whatever it is that Manta is telling her. She takes the large glass of Finlandia that one of the other dart players offers her and takes one of those sips that look like just a slight wetting of the lips but which actually lower the level of the drink considerably. Finally she looks toward the spot at the bar where Giraut and Mr. Bocanegra are and nods again. She raises her glass toward the owner of the establishment. Although she has stopped playing, her gestures continue to have that same oracular quality. Giraut suspects that the sensation could be due to Iris Gonzalvo's sexual appeal. To that ineffable and almost otherworldly quality that very sexually attractive people have. That quality that always makes you think that no matter how much you look at them, you are always missing something essential about them. That almost magical resistance to your gaze.

The men move aside as Iris walks to the bar. They watch each of her movements with animal attention. With that mix of caution and aggressiveness with which animals pay attention. Iris Gonzalvo's sex appeal and her ineffable aura produce a certain sensation that she is in a film, walking in slow motion. With that otherworldly elegance that slow motion bestows.

Finally she arrives at the bar. She puts a hand on Lucas Giraut's shoulder. An intimate gesture. No one present perceives the almost imperceptible shiver Lucas Giraut makes under her hand.

"Lucas tells me your name is Iris," says Mr. Bocanegra. In a vaguely wary tone. As if for some reason that information didn't seem altogether convincing.

Iris Gonzalvo puts her empty glass in Aníbal Manta's enormous hand. Manta stares at the glass. Then he looks at her. With an incredulous expression.

"I guess Lucas has brought you up-to-date on the kind of business we're dealing with." Bocanegra doesn't wait for her to nod or give any sign of having registered his words. "We aren't the kind of company that advertises in the yellow pages. In fact, we don't advertise anywhere. Fuck, even calling us a company is a bit much. We are a gentlemen's club. In other words"—Bocanegra's face transforms into an expression of open cruelty—"people don't put the jobs they do for us on their résumés."

"I've already brought her up-to-date on those things." Lucas seems to have unconsciously moved away from Iris's hand. "She knows that we don't have time to waste and that she's going to have to start studying her role."

Mr. Bocanegra lets out a grunt.

"In our line of work we deal with strange people," he says. He makes a wide gesture with his glowing cigar. "People who also aren't interested in advertising themselves. Eccentric people. Sometimes even paranoid. You have to understand how this world works. Collectors are passionate people. I myself collect statues. They're people who are forced to break certain laws and take advantage of other gray areas that the law doesn't mention. That doesn't mean they hurt anybody, most of the time. But they are forced to tread carefully. To sleep with a pistol under their pillows, to use a metaphor. I hope you are following me attentively, kid." He points to Iris with the incandescent tip of his cigar. "Because I don't look kindly on you just pouting your lips and showing me a bit of leg every once in a while instead of really *thinking* about what I'm saying."

Iris Gonzalvo doesn't seem intimidated. In fact quite the opposite. Her smile widens a bit. Her body settles a bit more comfortably on the stool. Her crossed legs uncross and cross again in such a way that the pale section of leg that's visible grows before the men's eyes.

"Tell me about this Mr. Travers," she says. Taking the glass of champagne that Aníbal Manta offers her. "The buyer."

"If I knew everything there is to know about Travers," says Bocanegra, "I wouldn't be sitting here in front of you and selflessly offering you the most expensive bottle of Krug that I have in my wine cellar. More expensive than all the clothes any of us are wearing, including my friend Mr. Giraut. Because Travers isn't a guy who lets people know anything about him. That's how these guys protect themselves. That's how they become almost untouchable. There are people who have found out things about him, sure." He shrugs his shoulders. "But they've disappeared without a trace. And I don't think they went anywhere very pleasant."

"We know that Mr. Travers has a house in Paris," says Giraut. "A palace in the center of the city. He does most of his business from there. The security system is almost as expensive as the house itself, or that's what I'm told. The truth is we don't have enough information yet."

"Travers is a rich fuck." Mr. Bocanegra waits for the waitress to serve him a cup from the bottle of Krug opened especially for this executive meeting. The waitress's expression as she serves the champagne is one of reverential fear. Like the face of someone handling something equipped with detonators and colored wires and a plutonium core. "Not rich like those guys in *Fortune* magazine or *Forbes*. Rich like the people that *aren't* in those magazines. You know what I mean. Let's just say there are two kinds of rich people." He pauses. He picks up the glass and takes a sip.

"We've been lucky enough to find out some things about Travers from my father's diaries," says Lucas Giraut. By this point he has moved far enough away from Iris that she's taken her hand off his shoulder. Now he is sitting in his familiarly rigid style on the bar stool. "He's an eccentric. We don't really know what kind of pieces he collects. My father's diaries say that they're extremely rare pieces. We can guess what some of them could be. Things that disappeared from the market, for example. But in general his collection is a mystery. Completely undocumented. And of course, we don't know where it is held. They say that Mr. Travers owns dozens of properties. And there's something else." He clears his throat. "Mr. Travers is supposedly a well-known occultist. Of course, that adds to his legend."

Iris Gonzalvo nods. Seated on either side of her, Lucas Giraut and Mr. Bocanegra exchange a glance. A glance too brief to be considered communication by anyone. Anyone but them. Somehow, Giraut understands what Bocanegra is thinking. Based on that single fleeting glance. They both seem to have perceived that certain something Iris Gonzalvo has that makes her strange. Beyond the questions associated with her sex appeal. And Giraut has also noticed the way Bocanegra is now looking at Iris. He isn't perplexed, that's for sure. Mr. Bocanegra's facial and gestural peculiarities don't allow him to express anything even close to perplexity. His features are too anchored in a strong, firm base of cruelty and power. His jaw seems made to destroy things. His mustache only bends into voracious expressions. His bald head is too wide and too shiny not to provoke associations with tyrannical leaders of the ancient world.

No, thinks Lucas Giraut, as the silence and the throat clearing seem to indicate that the conversation is drawing to a close. Bocanegra is not perplexed as he looks at Iris. Or suspicious. He's looking at her with something similar to genuine curiosity. Which is something Giraut has never seen on Bocanegra's face before.

"He's a man." Iris Gonzalvo shrugs her shoulders. "Men don't scare me. I know how to deal with them. There are some differences, sure. But in general they're all more or less the same. Men are almost never a problem." Her thin pale fingers hold up the glass of Krug very delicately. Her lips barely brush the edge when she takes a sip. "Women can be a problem, sometimes. It depends."

Stripped of Iris Gonzalvo, the group playing darts has regained their truly profane nature. Men involved in a competitive activity with no purpose beyond itself. One of the most truly profane rituals of humanity. Without any more peculiar elements than the contrast between Pavel's exaggeratedly tall and pale figure and his Jamaican-inspired hair and clothing.

"I still keep thinking I've seen you somewhere," growls Mr. Bocanegra. With a slight shaking of the head. With a slight furrowing of the brow. With a small, suspicious system of gestures. "I could almost swear I've seen you dance here. I don't like to be lied to."

The clientele of The Dark Side of the Moon is the type of clientele that have made the place what it is over the past thirty years. Local politicians. International businessmen. With their ties festively loosened. Industry magnates with loosened ties and shoes kicked under the table. Sitting on velvet sofas with their arms around two young women dressed in G-strings and high heels. Entire armies of women with their corporate uniforms of G-strings and high heels.

"I do very nasty things to people who lie to me," says Bocanegra. "Even when they're girls like you."

Iris Gonzalvo smiles. The elevator in the middle of the circular bar opens its doors and a couple of waitresses in G-strings and high heels emerge, each holding high trays filled with drinks.

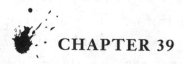

CHAPTER 39

Saudade's Finger Pistol

Koldo Cruz finishes spreading shaving cream on his face, his only eye looking alternately at the mirror and at the portable television on a shelf of the bathroom. In the upper floor of his house. The fact that he only has one eye forces him to make lateral head movements in order to shave and not miss anything on TV. The patch that usually covers his eyeless socket is on the bathroom shelf, next to the television and other personal hygiene objects. The images on television have supposedly been recorded by an amateur videographer on vacation in Indonesia. There are people running in terror. In what could be a coastal tourist complex. Then a gigantic wave appears and drags off all the people that were running in terror.

Cruz picks up his razor and turns on the faucet to wet the blades. Since surviving the bombing he has learned to feel his way through shaving so he doesn't have to look at his face without the eye, or at the steel plate that replaces his right temple. That was before he started lifting up the patch and showing his eyeless socket to satisfy the requests of his friends' nieces and nephews. Beside the television and the patch there are a couple of bongs and a bag with thirty grams of marijuana brought specially from Mexico. On the television, the guy filming the gigantic Indonesian wave realizes that the wave is coming at him faster than he can run and drops his camera. Cruz proceeds to shave his face according to his daily strategy: first the cheeks, then the neck and finally the mustache and chin.

He leaves the bathroom, shaved and with his patch back in place, dressed in a wifebeater and long johns, with his towel over his right shoulder. He greets the two workers that are installing the new electrified steel bars into the upper-floor windows and he reminds them that there are practically limitless supplies of beer available to them in the refrigerator downstairs. A refrigerator that looks more like a cold store. Koldo Cruz likes to show signs of largesse with people who lack his personal fortune. And the genius needed to amass a personal fortune like his. He passes in front of his young Russian fiancée's private bathroom where, like every morning, she's locked inside for at least an hour. Koldo Cruz likes to pretend, to her, that he doesn't know she shoots up heroin in the bathroom each morning. At the same time, he calls her dealer every other day to check up on her consumption levels. Standing in front of his bedroom's full-length mirror, he dresses and ties his tie as the workers sporadically walk around lugging steel structures at the back of the mirror's surface. Koldo Cruz would never admit that he's bored. In his opinion, it's a question of balance. Everything in life is about balance. And it simply happens that sometimes his inner demand for emotional balance leads him to do things that other people would find atrocious. Now he checks his Cartier watch with inlaid diamonds. Three minutes until his daily meeting at the Caipirinha café-bar, located exactly one and a half blocks from the electrified perimeter of his house.

The morning is sunny in a lackluster way. A lazy, lackluster sky floats over Pedralbes. Koldo Cruz buys *La Vanguardia* from a newspaper stand on the way to the café and folds it meticulously three times along its transversal axis. Forty seconds later, he pushes open the glass door of the Caipirinha café-bar and waits a moment in the doorway for the entire morning staff to greet him. Cruz started buying his own copy of *La Vanguardia* at the newspaper stand instead of reading the copy the café has available for customers after one morning a customer, who was not a regular, insisted on holding on to it for more than thirty-five minutes. Forcing a heated discussion that ended with threats of physical violence. Since that day, the entire morning staff of the Caipirinha café-bar has treated Cruz with awkward friendliness.

Cruz crosses the café with jovial strides and takes his regular spot at the bar. The waiter puts a Macallan with ice in front of him, meticulously prepared the way Mr. Cruz likes it, with a lot of Macallan and a little ice. Beside the whiskey a small plate of olives appears.

The pages of today's *La Vanguardia* are filled with photographs of gigantic waves in the Pacific. Koldo Cruz pays particular attention to the Business and Sports sections, which usually occupy the final pages in most of the world's newspapers. Every once in a while he looks up to inspect the people that come in and out. Due to the nature of his line of work, Koldo Cruz is always on the alert for the presence of strangers in his immediate personal surroundings. Especially since the bombing. And since that guy snuck into his house less than a month ago. There is a young guy with a basketball cap and sunglasses that he's never seen in the café before. Reading a book at an out-of-the-way table. Cruz is reading the Sports and Business sections and looking up once in a while to check him out above the upper edge of the newspaper. Something about the young man is familiar. Familiar in a strange way. As if his face were a face that came floating back from Koldo Cruz's youth. A mostly hairless face, from what Cruz can see from his bar stool. A soft face with big cheeks and blond, somewhat long hair sticking out from beneath his basketball cap. And who the hell wears a basketball cap with a ten-thousand-euro Lino Rossi suit?

Ten minutes later, Koldo Cruz eats his last olive, takes a last sip of his Macallan and makes his daily call to the foreman of his group of Russian employees. On his way to the door of the Caipirinha café-bar, he twists his head a bit to get a better look at the young man with the cap and sunglasses. Now that he's closer he can see that the novel the young man is reading is a Stephen King novel. And that he's reading it with an expression of intense concentration behind his sunglasses.

Lucas Giraut lets five minutes pass before closing his copy of *Wonderful World* and leaving it on the table. Koldo Cruz's daily activities are so firmly dictated by tradition that he barely had to look up to be sure he had him in front of him. Ensconced as always on his bar stool as if he owned the bar, exercising his authority over the stool and over the rest of the place. Then Lucas leans over to rummage through his bag located beneath the table and takes out the Highly Secret Accounting Ledger he found in Apartment 13. He pages through it distractedly and tears out a page completely filled with his father's small, neat handwriting. Then he takes out a blank sheet of paper and writes down the note he has been mentally preparing for a couple of days. The note is succinct and has no exact instructions. Both the vocabulary and the tone have been conscientiously chosen to not sound too threatening, yet at the same time transmit an air of absolute confidence. Lastly he sticks the note and the page from the Highly Secret Ledger into an envelope and seals it after peeling off the paper covering the self-adhesive strip. On the front of the envelope he simply writes Koldo Cruz's name.

A minute later he leaves the Caipirinha café-bar and crosses the street. He passes in front of the newspaper stand, where a woman with many dogs on leashes is chatting with the bored-looking guy who runs the stand. He walks up to the house with the electrified perimeter at the end of the street and stops in front of the wrought-iron gate. The scrupulously polished gold plaque on the gate reads "UMMAGUMMA 2." A bit farther up he can see the remains of a security camera that someone seems to have beaten with a blunt object.

Giraut lifts up the top of Koldo Cruz's personal mailbox and sticks the envelope inside. Without noticing the black Volvo parked on the same block where someone is watching his movements with binoculars. Within Koldo Cruz's electrically delineated yard there are half a dozen workers installing bars on the windows of the first floor. Giraut looks through the bars of the door and sees a very pale young woman with dark glasses who seems to be supervising their work. Then he readjusts his cap on his head and heads off down the street. Once again passing the black Volvo, which has a slight rhythmic vibration coming from inside it, like the vibrations you feel near the dance floor in a disco.

Inside the black Volvo, moving his head rhythmically to the beat of the strictly percussive dance music that comes out of his compact disc player, Juan de la Cruz Saudade watches Giraut with a satisfied expression. With one of those smiles that you only see on the faces of people who think they were born under a lucky star. With the neck of a bottle of Finlandia sticking out of the glove compartment. Saudade folds the fingers of one hand and points it at Giraut's increasingly far-away back, imitating the barrel and hammer of a pistol.

"Bang," he says. And he moves his hand brusquely to indicate firing his finger pistol.

CHAPTER 40

Wonderful World

Strictly speaking, Barcelona is nothing like the idea that Pavel had of Barcelona before getting onto the airplane that took him there. In general, he finds it gray and filled with cars and ugly people. Not to mention those fat little ladies with their short hair dyed ridiculous colors that go around staring at everyone with hateful expressions. He's not crazy about the Paseo de Gracia either. The brochure in Russian he brought with him in his suitcase said that the Paseo de Gracia is "an art nouveau architectural gem." Pavel spent a morning sitting on a strange-looking bench on the Paseo de Gracia looking at people and buildings. The most interesting thing he saw were the butts of the female tourists that passed by, their necks twisted upward to admire the building façades. And whose idea was it to paint the taxis yellow and black? A very overrated city, is what Pavel would say if anyone ever asked him. Which hasn't happened yet.

Pavel leaves the Russian book he's reading on the bar of his favorite spot on the Rambla del Raval and looks out of the corner of his eye at the butt of a black woman who is standing beside him. A big soft butt. Ample in every direction. The type of urban landscape that Pavel likes is the kind you see in the postcards of Jamaica he has tacked up near his bed. Short, brightly painted wooden houses with people sitting in some kind of garden chairs in front of the open doors. Colors that make you think of parrots or other tropical bird species. Black women in minishorts strutting among the men with a certain high and mighty attitude. The fact that the Jamaican men in the postcards pay no special attention to the women that parade around in minishorts arouses the suspicion in Pavel's mind that black women in minishorts are a species sufficiently plentiful in Jamaica so as not to be a highly prized asset. So that it doesn't seem preposterous to imagine nocturnal scenes starring Pavel and a black woman with an abundant ass touching each other in front of a fireplace. That is, if there are fireplaces in Jamaica. Pavel's not sure. There's no indication in the postcards. He raises a hand to his increasingly satisfactory dreadlocks in a flirty gesture. He is sure about the palm trees. There are palm trees in practically every postcard of Jamaica that he has in his room. Palm trees are one of the main reasons that Pavel likes to come to the Rambla del Raval and the seaside at dusk. The palm trees and the black women. Another image of Jamaica that often comes into his head is one of him beneath a waterfall in a jungle setting. He's not sure exactly why. One of those small waterfalls that often appear in television ads for soap. In the image, he is beneath the cascading crystal-clear water with his eyes closed, drinking water from a vaguely spiral mollusk shell. It is impossible to know where the image comes from.

The black woman with the ample ass walks to the jukebox with the black man that accompanies her and they both start to flip through the record selection system. A large part of the clientele of the bar is black people. Pavel picks up the package, which is shaped like a box that holds a tie, from the bar and starts to unwrap the Christmas gift wrap. The same gift wrap that his sister's Christmas gifts come in every year. It doesn't seem his sister is very good at wrapping gifts. The paper is always wrinkled and dented and the pieces of Scotch tape are irregular and in the wrong places. The book that Pavel is reading is one of those Russian pornographic novels they sell in the neighborhood Russian bookstore. In paperback editions with unpleasant stains on the part of the pages that you turn. It's unclear how his sister manages to have the same gift wrap every year. With snowmen and candy canes and some sort of little Christmas goblins printed on it. This year's tie is deep red and blue and has some sort of heraldic crest on it. It takes Pavel a minute to realize that it's a tie with one of the local soccer teams' colors. The kind designed to show one's allegiance to said team. He sighs and sticks the tie in the pocket of his combat pants.

The black woman and her black companion have chosen a song on the jukebox and are now dancing in front of it. The scene causes Pavel a slight stab of emotional pain. Black people have a special attitude and a credibility and an *authenticity* just because they're black. It's unfair. Not to mention the subject of the black man's supposed sexual vitality and genital size. Pavel doesn't so much want to be black as he wants to find a way to develop that same credibility. To be accepted in a way that would make him feel like real Rastafaris must feel, for example. Instead, Pavel is excessively tall and very blond and gangly and, even though he's twenty-nine years old, still can't get rid of the pimples on his cheeks and the area of his neck where he shaves. When he lives in Jamaica, he's already decided, he is going to devote himself to the music business. He'll set up his own discothèque and he'll wear really long dreads and he'll throw parties on the beach that will give him the credibility he needs.

The first thing Pavel notices is the *smell*. Even before he realizes that the black faces around him are looking suspiciously at something located right behind him. Before he feels the big hairy hand land on his shoulder like a big hairy bird of bad omen. The smell of industrial grease and an abandoned garage where all that's left is the smell of grease. Leon's unmistakable smell of grease.

"Nice tie," says Leon's high-pitched voice in Russian. Pavel turns to find his compatriot's big, shiny head that's morphologically similar to a bullet. Leon points with his head at the local soccer club tie sticking out of Pavel's pocket. "Can't say it goes very well with the rest of your outfit. But what the hell. . . ." He shrugs his shoulders. "It's a start, I guess."

Pavel finishes his glass of whiskey with ice in one slug. He puts the empty glass back on the bar beside the pornographic novel and the Christmas wrapping. He makes a sign to the black waiter and points to the empty glass with his finger. Which in international sign language indicates a refill. Some of the black people seem to now be looking out of the corner of their eyes at the two white men at the bar. Pavel decides that the best way to tackle the problem of the bullet head who just appeared by his side is to pretend, as much as he can, that the problem doesn't exist. The black woman with the ample ass is dancing in that way a lot of black people dance: subtly swaying her pelvis and neck while talking to her male companion and introducing coins into the slot of the jukebox. A way of dancing that's not really dancing. Which more just seems to form part of her general disposition.

"Sometimes I think you think I'm a boring guy." Leon is also looking at the ample ass of the black woman, but with a different expression. With the same expression a passenger sitting in an airport looks at the poster he has had in front of him for two hours as a result of a two-hour delay. "Maybe because I have a family and my own business and we always see each other for work-related stuff. It's an understandable prejudice, I guess. But mistaken." Leon shows a large set of teeth, in a shade ranging from white to grayish. "The truth is I really like music and dancing and all that stuff. I used to be a pretty good dancer when I was young. In Russia. In my day, there were good jazz and rock and roll bands. With really good Russian musicians. I like movies, too. Especially the *Alien* series. You know the *Alien* movies? I guess everyone does. The ones with that dyke and the creature that crawls out of people's bellies. Which brings me to the question of why I came here to talk to you. In case you were thinking that I was just passing by here and we met up by chance. The truth is that this isn't my kind of atmosphere." He looks around him with that expression that makes you think of air travelers during an excessive flight delay. "And I came here to make it clear to you that I'm an outgoing kind of guy. A good friend. More than that. A person perfectly willing to make friends with people who aren't his friends yet. Or who aren't his friends *anymore*."

Pavel picks up his second glass of whiskey on the rocks from the bar and shakes it in a vaguely unconscious way. Making the ice tinkle against the glass. The black woman with the ample ass has taken a seat. Expanding the ampleness of her ass. Expanding her ass in a movement similar to an overflowing that threatens to make her tight red pants burst.

"Tell me what you want to know." Pavel gets up from his bar stool with a weary gesture. The deep red and blue tie hangs from his pocket in a way that doesn't quite suggest a tail. "And I'll tell you if I can tell it to you."

"They've talked to me about this new guy." Leon lifts his eyebrows. "Some kind of antiques dealer. Seems he's the son of someone who was important here many years ago. And they told me about those stupid little paintings that are worth so much money to some people. And I have some idea where they might be. And I also think that all this has something to do with the fact that you broke into my friend's house. So what I want to know is: everything. Where those little paintings are going and when. So I can be waiting there. With Donald Duck and the rest of the boys."

"I've only seen the antiques dealer a couple of times." Pavel walks up to the dirty glass screen of the jukebox and starts pushing buttons on the panel. "At Bocanegra's club. And I don't know anything about the paintings."

Leon plants an enormous hairy finger on the jukebox's dirty screen. The finger is pointing to the face of a black guy with his mouth open very wide in some sort of chemically induced expression of enthusiasm. With his eyes open unrealistically wide. With an overall expression of chemically induced enthusiasm whose effect is vaguely terrifying. An enthusiasm that surpasses all known limits of the healthy and normal.

"Louis Armstrong." Leon taps on the glass screen with his fingertip a few times. "A genius of modern music. It can take a little while to get used to his voice. It's not like Russian voices. Russian voices are strong. Masculine and all that," he says in his high-pitched voice. "You know what I'm talking about. But, hey, Armstrong came to Russia. As an American cultural ambassador. And he made a lot of people happy." He nods with a satisfied expression on his bullet-shaped head.

He puts a coin in the machine and punches a numerical code into the panel. A slight buzzing is heard, similar to a bicycle chain. The buzzing every jukebox in the world makes when changing from one song to another. Pavel keeps making the ice in his glass tinkle languidly. After a moment the opening bars of a Louis Armstrong song are heard.

"Of course, what people *say* Louis Armstrong's music means is stupid," says Leon. While he moves his head to the rhythm of the song. The rocking of his head and hand is that stereotypical rocking that people associate with classical music lovers listening to chamber music in the smoking salons of their homes. "All that crap about the joy of being alive and waking up to see a new day. Bullshit. It's not about birdies in the sky and the joy of living. You just have to go out on the street. I don't see much blue skies or birdies singing or happy people frolicking. The truth is *the weather sucks* and the birdies are dead. No, sweetheart. What Louis Armstrong is saying, like the genius he is"—he makes a pause obviously designed to create a certain sense of mystery or paradox about to be revealed—"is that the world is wonderful *because* the world is horrible. And therein lies his great wisdom. The crazies who get on a bus with a bomb and kill all the passengers. Or that gigantic wave that was on every TV news show. *Those* are the things that make the world wonderful." He nods and begins tracing arabesques of cutaneous grease with the tip of his hairy and vaguely phallic index finger on the dirty glass screen of the jukebox. "A world like us. *For us.*" He looks at Pavel's face. "Isn't it *wonderful*?"

The soft winter breeze that enters through the open windows of the bar on the Rambla del Raval carries a characteristic Barcelona port odor with it, a mix of the smell of overflowing sewers, rotten fish and urine. No one in the bar or its surroundings seems aware of the odor. Pavel has finished his second glass of whiskey on the rocks.

"I'm a *locksmith*," he says, looking at the bartender and pointing at his empty glass again. "Bocanegra only uses me to open doors. Or to get into places he can't get into. What makes you think he'd explain his plans *to me*?"

Leon stares at him for a long moment. His expression no longer reminds one of passengers put out by inconvenient flight delays.

"Maybe Bocanegra is very happy with his new little friend the antiques dealer," he says. "But that's *not* the way things work. You can't just put a new fish into the tank without the other fish getting nervous. Without making waves. This city is my fish tank. It belongs to me and the people I represent," he adds, and although he doesn't move or turn toward the exit or make any motion that suggests he is about to leave, something in his tone and his general attitude seems to indicate that somehow *he's no longer in* the bar with Pavel. "And we're going to have to explain that to him. With your help, of course."

Pavel drinks his third whiskey in one gulp and tries to imagine the implications of Leon showing up in his favorite bar of the Rambla del Raval. The implications of the fact that he knows where to find him and that he also knows about things like the paintings. Particularly the implications having to do with his own personal safety. As for Leon, he's no longer in the bar.

 **CHAPTER 41**

The Somnambulist in an Ambulance

The landscape at dusk is truly Parisian. A landscape of palaces and eighteenth-century mansions in a popular middle-class Jewish neighborhood in the city center. Barely a mile north of the river. The landscape is Parisian in the way that certain overflow channels of clogged sewers are. Certain dogs that do their business in the middle of the sidewalk. Certain women that shout from the door of a café. The sun is just setting over the rooftops that look like forests of eighteenth-century chimneys. Iris Gonzalvo shivers inside her Adeline André red leather coat and takes a drag on her British cigarette while looking through the forged-iron fence of Mr. Travers's palace. On the other side of the fence, a dog is doing his business in the middle of the sidewalk. With his gaze lost on the horizon. The dog is tied with a leash to the hand of a woman with two other leashed dogs who is having a shouting match with someone in front of a café door. Iris Gonzalvo doesn't like to hear shouting in French. It makes her think of Eric Yanel. She takes a drag on her cigarette and releases a thick white cloud where the steam from her breath mixes with the smoke from her cigarette. Through the cloud she can see the horribly French face of the guard at the door. Becoming more and more defined as the smoke dissipates.

"This is your pass." The guard with the horrible French face hands a magnetic card to Iris Gonzalvo through the window of the guard box. His horribly French face consists basically of a nose shaped like a pepper jammed into a pale sponge riddled with pockmarks. "But he'll have to wait here." He makes a signal with his head in Aníbal Manta's direction, who is waiting with his enormous arms crossed over his chest about six feet behind Iris. "Those are the rules. You have to show the pass to anyone who asks to see it."

Iris takes her pass and sticks it in her purse. Then she looks toward where the guard in the box is pointing. The guard box is at the entrance to the courtyard of Mr. Travers's Parisian palace, at the end of a porticoed entrance for cars separated from the street by a forged-iron railing. The palace's main entrance is at the other end of the courtyard, past an ornamental fountain. And beyond some arches under which someone is polishing the bodywork of a Rolls-Royce. A second guard is signaling to Iris Gonzalvo with his hand from the staircase of the main entrance. Although he is too far away for her to see him clearly, Iris has the impression that the second guard carries a submachine gun.

Iris looks at Aníbal Manta, whose face is covered in sweat in spite of the fact that he is only wearing a trench coat over his suit. The fact that Aníbal Manta sweats so much in weather situations that are not extreme could be due to his enormous body mass. Manta looks back at her with a grim expression. With a grim expression on his sweaty red face.

"He says you're going to have to wait here," she tells him, and takes a pensive drag on her cigarette from behind her dark glasses. On the other side of the fence, the woman with three dogs is still shouting with someone invisible at the door to the café. One of her dogs has started to bark furiously at another dog that is passing by. The sound of the barks is added to the other shouts, barks and car horns of that Parisian winter evening. "Call Barcelona on the satellite line. Tell them that I want Mr. Giraut ready by the phone. He might have to authorize bank movements and that kind of thing."

The second guard escorts Iris Gonzalvo through the main entrance to the palace's hallway. Her purse and red Adeline André coat are passed through one of those metal detectors with a conveyor belt like they have in airports. Then a woman with the same security company uniform runs a portable metal detector over the twists and turns of her body and pats down the parts where there could be something hidden. During this process, Iris is vaguely aware that her image is visible from different angles on the different monitors in the bank of monitors that one of the guards is watching attentively.

"Miss DeMink, I presume," says a voice behind Iris Gonzalvo as she is putting her coat back on and gathering her personal effects that have come out on the other side of the metal detector.

Iris Gonzalvo turns. There are two men standing by a spiral staircase. She isn't sure how long they've been there. They could have just arrived or they could have been there the whole time. The spiral staircase is marble and has a giant balustrade and is covered with a dark red carpet. Iris has no idea which of the two men spoke to her. They are both simply there. Looking at her. The strangest thing, however, is not the fact that they're just standing there doing nothing at the foot of the staircase, nor that perhaps they've been there the whole time watching her. The strangest thing about the two men is that, in spite of not being identical, they give off the exact same feeling. They are both blond and suffer varying degrees of alopecia. They both have freckles on their faces, one more than the other. Neither of them wears glasses. They both could be any age between thirty-five and forty-five. They both look like that guy in *C.S.I.* That redheaded guy that solves all the cases. It's not that they look so much like him. They just give you the same *feeling.*

"Mr. Travers?" she says. Looking at each of them alternately.

The two blond, freckled, balding men smile at the same time.

Something in their simultaneous smiles tells Iris that they are used to giving people the same puzzling effect. Almost as if their silent and vaguely theatrical appearance at the foot of the marble staircase had been meticulously staged to that effect. As if it were some sort of theater trick they were used to doing.

"We are Mr. Fleck and Mr. Downey," says one of them, without specifying which of the two is speaking. Somehow, it seems to Iris Gonzalvo that the fact that the two men aren't related makes the situation even stranger. "You can say that we're Mr. Travers's legs. Our boss has problems traveling. So we travel for him. Although tonight our job is to make you as comfortable as possible."

Iris Gonzalvo turns her back to one of the blond, balding men so he can help her take off her coat again.

"Mr. Travers can't walk?" she says, taking a cigarette from the gold case the other man is offering her. "Is he very old? Or in a wheelchair?"

One of the men lights her cigarette. She lifts her chin and releases a mouthful of smoke toward the ceiling of the vestibule. There is a scene painted on the ceiling featuring something that looks like Egyptian gods. Those Egyptian gods with weird staffs and animal heads.

"Mr. Travers's problems are more *spiritual*." The man who just spoke smiles again. "Mr. Travers is a very spiritual man. As you will soon see."

"It would be more precise to say that Mr. Travers has problems *leaving the house*," says the other. "His spiritual problems get worse when he leaves the house. Any of his houses."

"Please, follow us," says the first man. "Mr. Travers is very excited about the possibility of acquiring your wonderful pieces. We are all excited. The photographs you sent were wonderful."

Iris Gonzalvo rolls her eyes behind her sunglasses and follows the two men up the stairs. Even the way they go up the stairs seems strangely synchronized. Leaning their respective hands gently on the balustrade, one of them two or three steps ahead of the other. Both peeking back with a smile over their shoulders the way people do when they want to make their guests feel as comfortable as possible. On the last landing is the largest statue that Iris Gonzalvo has ever seen in her life. It depicts a life-size Roman chariot with a charioteer at the reins and a group of rearing horses. Both the charioteer and the horses are broken and missing pieces the way ancient statues do. One of the two men points to black double doors. With some sort of climbing plants carved into them.

"The doors are of Etruscan alabaster," explains Mr. Fleck, or maybe it is Mr. Downey. "First century BC. Mr. Travers will now receive you in his smoking salon. And, please"—he places a hand gently on Iris's arm—"remember what we said about his spiritual problems. Be careful in there. Mr. Travers's special condition makes him a very delicate person."

Iris Gonzalvo stubs out her cigarette in a standing ashtray. Finally she walks between the two men and pushes the doors open.

The first thing that draws her attention on the other side is the smell. A smell of something like incense that inundates the room and makes it hard to even breathe. Iris Gonzalvo brings a hand to her mouth and waits for her eyes to get used to the half-light. She seems to be in a room so big that the far end gets lost in the distance. The only light comes mostly from a small reading lamp covered with a cloth and the fireplace that burns in a remote corner of the room. Mr. Travers, if he's there, must be hiding in the dim light. Iris wonders if everyone in that place is fond of dramatic entrances. Of surprise appearances in scenes out of gothic novels. She stands beside the door for a moment, almost waiting for a section of the wall to turn and for the owner of the house to appear from the other side with a book open in his hands and a malicious smile. Then she shrugs her shoulders. If he wants to play hide-and-seek, she doesn't have a problem with that.

"Mr. Travers?" she asks the darkness. Trying not to give her voice that vaguely singsong tone that children use when playing hide-and-seek to call out to their hidden friends.

She walks past a table larger than any table she's seen before, and covered by what looks like a diorama of a World War II battle. She walks past bookcases jammed with old editions. Past taxidermied animals. Past wooden rocking horses and other antique toys. Past glass cases filled with old coins and nineteenth-century signs. Finally she gets to the fireplace. In that part of the room the objects' shadows dance nervously against the walls. Like nervous animals. The flames in the fireplace are high. Someone has stoked them very recently. Iris Gonzalvo stares at the rug in front of the fireplace and the three cats that sleep curled up on it, united in a strange furry ball without any visible heads or tails. Then her gaze moves toward the slippers beside the cats, goes up the legs that lead to the armchair in front of the fireplace, and finally rests on the man seated in the armchair who is looking at her with a calculating expression.

"My oh my," says the man in the armchair with a British accent. "You are quite a beauty. There were no women like you the last time I was in Spain. There were pretty women, sure." He purses his lips in a dubious expression. "But nothing like you, I can assure you."

Iris Gonzalvo makes a gesture similar to a smile. With her arms crossed over her chest. One of the cats has woken up and is looking at her with that face cats have when looking at someone who's just arrived. Without curiosity. Without fear. Without sympathy. Without anything that can be associated with any kind of feline emotion. The man in the armchair is fat and has long curly hair and a puffy face and a weary look.

"Please, have a seat." Mr. Travers points to an armchair in front of his. "Make yourself comfortable. I suppose those ruffians Fleck and Downey haven't even made you a drink." He gets up heavily from the armchair. A cascade of something like crumbs of food falls from the front of his frayed wool sweater. "They must have already told you that I don't go out much."

Iris Gonzalvo moves a pile of books and boxes that is in the armchair. The room's dim light, plus her sunglasses, makes her visual field some kind of abstract composition of faint splotches. Finally she sits and takes the drink Travers holds out to her. She takes a polite sip. Port. Whoever this nutcase is, he keeps acting like he just escaped from a vampire movie.

"It's been a very long time since I've heard anything from Arnold Layne." Travers collapses once again into the armchair in front of the fireplace. "Almost thirty years. Heavens, you weren't even born, I'm sure. Then everyone that was seriously into collecting rare pieces had heard of Arnold Layne Experts. And that society with the funny name. What was it called? *Down With The Sun?*" His puffy face twists into an expression that could indicate nostalgia. Something in his long, dirty curly hair makes him look somewhat like an over-the-hill transvestite. "Do you have any idea what I'm talking about, Miss DeMink? Do any of these names ring a bell?"

Iris Gonzalvo begins to feel a burning desire to light another cigarette. After all, one of those blond guys had said this was the smoking salon.

"I'm not authorized to reveal the names of the people I represent," she says finally. "You understand."

Mr. Travers nods. He leans forward a bit and starts searching in a pile of papers on top of the little table beside the armchair. The shadows of his body and arm dance nervously along with the rest of the shadows in the room. To the rhythm of the high flames. Finally Travers pulls a business card out of the pile. He stares at it with a frown.

"Penny," he reads. "What is your name short for, Miss DeMink?"

Iris Gonzalvo thinks for a moment.

"Penelope," she says finally.

"Penelope." Travers smiles affably. "How appropriate. I suppose you must feel stuck in some dark cold place. Wanting to get out into the light." Some sort of crowing escapes his lips, which Iris imagines is an affable laugh. "I know you must think I'm a nutjob with millions coming out of my ass while I rot slowly in this horrible place." He gestures to his surroundings. "Don't be too hard on me. My illness took me by surprise one day, in the middle of the street. You can't imagine how it was. And now that I can't go out anymore, I like to have all my things in reach. That's why everything is so full of stuff. And you should see some of the rooms upstairs." He points to the ceiling and crows. "But don't think that I asked to become a hermit. I used to love strolling through London. Sailing. Visiting all those wonderful cities around the world."

Iris Gonzalvo lets her gaze wander around the room. Or, better put, around the closer parts of the room. The only ones she can really make out through her sunglasses. Her gaze finally lands on a painting above the fireplace.

"I see that you're not just a beauty." Travers looks in the direction of her gaze. "You also have good taste. The truth is that that painting is one of the most important pieces in my collection. *The Somnambulist in the Ambulance.* I bet you are familiar with the artist's other works. This one is a copy, of course. Almost everything in this house is an extraordinary copy. I live in a palace of forgeries, isn't that funny?" He takes a sip on a glass identical to hers. He shrugs. "Of course, if they knew I had the original, I'd have Interpol coming in through the windows in ten minutes."

Iris Gonzalvo focuses on looking at the painting. But from what she can tell, *The Somnambulist in the Ambulance* is nothing more than an abstract composition of colorful splotches. Some of the splotches look slightly like strobe lights, as if they had some relationship to an ambulance's warning lights. There's also a splotch in the middle that could be anthropomorphic, like the figure of someone lying down, but there's no way to be sure with sunglasses on.

Iris Gonzalvo rummages through her purse. She takes out a telephone connected to a satellite communication line.

"I have a secure line ready," she says. "Impossible to trace. And encrypted, of course. It's new technology. I think it was first used in the war in Iraq. So we can get started whenever you want. My bosses are waiting on the other side of the line."

Travers stares at her with an amused expression. His face is swollen like people with serious liver problems. Alcoholics with liquid retention issues. His eyes are so swollen that it looks like someone had been punching them. For a moment Iris Gonzalvo has the vision of the two crazy balding blond guys punching their boss in the eyes. And sitting him in the armchair in front of the cats with a glass of port in his hand to make him look like a vampire from a movie.

"I'm afraid there will be no negotiations today." Travers's tone is affable and slightly paternalistic. "I'm sorry to disappoint you. But you have to be patient with me. Everything will go fine. But you have to put up with my idiosyncrasies. I suppose they've already told you that I'm fussy about details. Do you think I'm going to do business with you and just let you leave?" He stares at her and for a very brief moment there is a flash of sincerity in his gaze. "A woman like you? Remember that *I can't go out on the street.* My pleasures are very limited. Merely conversing with you fills me with a warmth I haven't felt in years. Besides"—he shrugs his shoulders—"I have a lot of things to explain to you. Don't you think?"

"To explain to me?" Iris Gonzalvo takes her pack of British cigarettes out of her purse with a distracted gesture. She puts one between her lips. "What do you have to explain to me?"

Travers looks at her with a shocked expression.

"What do I have to explain to you?" he says. "Well, *everything.* The meaning of everything. The reason that I am here and the reason why you are here, too. Or haven't you realized that you are now part of a story that you've become involved in purely by chance? And isn't it true that you've always felt distanced from who you really want to be? And don't you want to know how it all started?" He lifts his glass of port toward her, in a silent toast. "I have the answers. I am the person in this story who knows the answers."

Iris Gonzalvo stares at Travers pensively while he lights her cigarette. In front of them, before the fire, one of the cats stretches out its entire body and opens its mouth in an unrealistically large yawn.

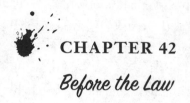

CHAPTER 42

Before the Law

The taxi stops in front of a cement esplanade surrounded by blocks of housing projects. The sky is pink. That icy pink tone of certain winter dawns. The blocks of apartments are morphologically similar to giant tombstones or alien monoliths from prophetic films. The classic housing projects in every working-class suburb in every city in the world. From a pictorial point of view, the scene's only special feature is the fact that the alien monoliths of housing projects have taken on a truly pink tone under the first light of day.

After a moment the back door of the taxi opens. The cement esplanade has basketball hoops and multicolored graffiti on all of its vertical cement surfaces. The air smells of burnt garbage. Of wild dogs. Of boiling urban subcultures. A leg covered in a powder blue and white Umbro sweat suit emerges from the taxi, followed by another identical one. Finally the upper half of a body comes out. It bears certain overall structural similarities with the person formerly known as Juan de la Cruz Saudade. His face has a clear greenish hue. His eyes are two red stains of broken capillaries. His greasy hair is stuck to his head where he was leaning against the upholstered backseat of the cab. A still-smoking cigarette butt between his yellow fingers. Saudade burps and closes the door with a sneaker that bears traces of an unidentified brown liquid. The cabdriver heads off shouting something unintelligible through the open driver's-side window. Saudade remains there for a moment, observing the alien skyline of his neighborhood on the outskirts of the city, his heart swollen with pride, until he notices the smell of his fingers burning, singed by the cigarette's cherry. He tosses the butt absentmindedly. It is in moments like this when Juan de la Cruz Saudade, twenty-six years old, feels most intensely the intrinsic beauty of life.

In addition to cement esplanades with basketball hoops and blocks of apartments, Saudade's neighborhood on the outskirts of Barcelona has a lot of staircases and abrupt cliffs, which at this time of the early morning are lit by blinking streetlights. Approximately two out of every three streetlights stopped working a long time ago. Saudade goes up half a dozen of the staircases. He dodges water balloons and other projectiles that insomniacs toss from their windows and he stands on some sort of elevated platform above the neighborhood that also serves as the main access to his own block of apartments. Saudade's block is a low, squat concrete box eaten away by the elements that houses more than five hundred souls. The way Saudade walks is powerfully reminiscent of those movies about corpses brought back to life by viruses from outer space. Though, unlike people who have suffered some kind of injury to their lower extremities and walk dragging a leg, somehow Saudade seems to be dragging *both* legs. Finally he turns around the final bend covered in tribal graffiti and arrives at the door of his house.

The feeling of well-being and general satisfaction with life that Juan de la Cruz Saudade is experiencing in those moments doesn't quite have to do with the chemical substances he's taken, which alter his perception of many things in general. Nor is it related to the proximity of his bed and the prospect of raiding the fridge beforehand. His feeling of well-being has more to do with the firm conviction that he is full of positive qualities and endowed with an enormous talent for getting the most out of life and enjoying himself enormously in the process.

Saudade pees on some cardboard boxes that someone has piled up beside a row of city garbage Dumpsters. Peeing intensifies his pleasure. Then he takes the elevator up, using the seconds in front of the mirror covered with graffiti to readjust his Umbro sweat suit and run a hand distractedly through his hair. Ready to rejoin his family unit.

A minute later, Saudade has tried every one of his keys in the lock to his apartment and he is now alternately studying his set of keys, the door to his apartment and the signs that indicate the floor and apartment number. His puzzlement has clear Homeric connotations. He tries all the keys again, one after the other, and runs a fingertip over a lock that seems newer and shinier than the lock he remembers his apartment having. Of course, he is absolutely unaware of the Homeric connotations of his situation. A faint, throbbing headache stirs in his right temple. A good portion of his feelings of satisfaction about life and his overall optimism begin to dissipate as he alternates pushing on the bell with kicking the door with his right sneaker.

"I must have picked up the wrong keys," says Saudade to the questioning faces of the neighbors who've opened doors on his landing. "My wife wakes up late. Ha ha."

In the elevator down to the street, Saudade examines a sock on the elevator floor with a pensive expression. The sock is vaguely familiar to him. Or at least enough for him to know that at some point it was white. The chain of implications of the episode he seems to be experiencing is too terrible to even consider. He exits the apartment building and looks up toward the balcony of his house. The plastic Christmas tree remains in the same place on the balcony where he left it two years ago. Then he turns to look at the boxes sprinkled with urine beside the Dumpsters. A powder blue and white sleeve with Umbro's rhomboid logotype sticks out of one of the boxes. Certain suspicions arise in Saudade's mind. Dogs barking and the screech of commercial gates opening are heard in the distance. Saudade kneels and picks up a piece of broken paving tile from the paved ground. He takes a few steps back and throws it toward his own balcony. The piece of tile breaks the glass of his balcony's glass doors with a sound that creates echoes in the early-morning air.

"Where's the other sock?" shouts Saudade to his wife's face when she appears on the balcony. Holding up the once white sock that he picked up in the elevator. "What did you do with my things?"

"Your son is calling the police," answers Matilde Saudade from the balcony. With her face transformed into a whirlwind of surprised eyebrow gestures. "Now I'm going to lower the blinds."

Saudade examines the sock in his hand with a pensive face. He uses it to wipe the sweat from his forehead and looks up again at the balcony. The sound of commercial gates screeching open seems excessive compared to the number of businesses in the neighborhood.

"I spent the night working in the warehouse," says Saudade with his hands placed at either side of his mouth, the way people do when they are trying to project their voice. Forgetting perhaps that he has a dirty sock in his hand. "If you don't believe me, call whoever you want. Remember your overactive imagination problems."

"I sold my wedding ring," says Matilde Saudade's face, suspended above the railing of the balcony. With her hair hanging from both sides of her face. The perspective that Saudade has of his wife's face from the street is both familiar and strangely unfamiliar. "To pay for the new lock. Go sleep somewhere else, please."

Saudade puts the sock in the pocket of his sweat suit and sits on a step at the building's entrance. His feeling of well-being seems to have almost completely vanished. If there's one thing that Saudade hates intensely in this world, it's problems. Up until that moment he was fairly convinced that he had managed to establish a pretty satisfactory strategy in his life for making problems abruptly swerve as they approached him and go piss off somebody else. Saudade doesn't have anything against other people's problems. Now he sighs. He hugs his knees and drums his fingers against one of his legs. In the distance, beyond and below the elevated concrete platform that dominates most of the neighborhood filled with apartment buildings, a new noise is heard. It isn't the screech of commercial gates or the barking of wild dogs. The sky has turned from pink to soft purple and then to an intense blue that you only see in deep winter skies. The noise heard in the distance is the sound of sirens from police patrol cars. Saudade is definitely beginning to suspect that a problem has just shown up in his life.

"I want you to go, too," says the voice of Cristian Saudade from some point located above his father's head. "You never talk to me. And *I hate* your soccer team."

Saudade approaches the boxes sprinkled with urine next to the Dumpsters and opens the first one. He takes out several pieces of clothing. Many of them look as if they haven't been washed in a long time. A pair of dark glasses from his days as a cop. Souvenir T-shirts from day trips to coastal towns overwhelmingly devoted to the leisure industry. Fruit-flavored condoms. He opens another box. Clothes. DVD movies. The seminal works of his pornography collection in DVD. *One Up Front and One Up Back 3. Barely Legal: Volumes 1 and 2. Anal Rapist 6. Anal Virgins 2.* Two regional police officers appear at the top of the stairs of the elevated platform. Saudade sticks several DVDs in the pockets of his sweat suit. Inside the pant legs. Inside the jacket of his sweat suit. The DVD movies he sticks inside the jacket of his sweat suit accumulate around his waist and give him a strangely marsupial look.

"Sir," says the voice of a police officer behind him. With that friendly and at the same time peremptory tone that police officers use in situations of potential conflict. "Sir, stand up and put your hands where we can see them, please."

Saudade opens another box. More DVD movies. Colored condoms. Condoms with latex rings. Saudade's thoughts include several rhetorical questions regarding what went wrong in his life to cause such an unfair turn of events. He takes a traditional Japanese *nunchaku* out of the box and holds it up with a vaguely melancholy expression.

"Sir," says the policeman's voice from behind his back, "it would be best if you left that on the ground, sir. Without any strange movements."

Saudade puts the *nunchaku* on the ground and stands up and turns slowly with his arms in the air. Out of the corner of his eye he can see his family and his neighbors looking out from their respective balconies. Obeying a gesture from the policeman in front of him who is aiming at him with his standard-issue firearm, he unzips the upper part of the sweat suit of his favorite sports team. A dozen DVD movies fall at his feet.

CHAPTER 43

Human Torso with Octopus Tentacles

The gym of the Giraut family house in the Ampurdan region is a structure of glass and steel beams attached to the main building of the art nouveau–style house with forged-steel balconies. Half a dozen pieces of gym equipment line the large front window with views of the breakwater. There are men squatting and men crouching. All dressed in business suits. There is a man in a suit, standing up on a stool, feeling the inside of a ceiling lamp with a hand sheathed in a latex glove. Another man is taking towels out of the closets. All the men in the room wear latex gloves. Except Fonseca. Fonseca isn't wearing gloves. Fonseca is standing in front of the large window watching Fanny Giraut's figure approach along the path from the breakwater. With the enormous system of treelike veins throbbing in his temples. Smoking a cigarette. There is a man in a suit squatting to examine the lower part of an exercise machine that's similar to one of those motorcycles without wheels in movies set in the future. With his butt pointed toward the Ampurdan sky.

The paved path meticulously lined with pebbles that leads from the breakwater to the Giraut family house is known as the Beach Trail.

Fonseca frowns. Fanny Giraut's figure has stopped in the middle of the path from the beach and is now watching the scene in the gym through the large window. With the inexpressive mask that is her surgically modified face. She is wearing a turban and the upper part of a two-piece bathing suit and a paisley sarong that reveals her legs below the knee. The number of operations to remove varicose veins that Fanny Giraut has undergone to date is eight.

"Sir," says one of the men in business suits and latex gloves behind

Fonseca's back, "we might have to move some of these machines, sir. To see what's underneath them."

To anyone who knows Fonseca either in his private life or in his public legal practice it is obvious that the system of treelike throbbing veins in his temples reveals a much higher degree of nervousness than the normal amount derived from situations of professional stress. The man who has just addressed him has both gloved hands held high the way surgeons hold their hands when they are about to perform an operation.

Fanny Giraut stops in front of the large gym window and waits for Fonseca to open the door for her. Neither of them says anything for a moment.

"Who are these people?" Fanny says finally. Without anything that's going through her head appearing in her features. "Fonseca, tell them to leave. And what are you doing smoking in here? Get rid of that right now."

Several of the men dressed in business suits and latex gloves are moving an exercise machine similar to a canoe's skeleton with oars so they can examine the tiles underneath it. There is something vaguely alarming in the uniformity of the general appearance and suits of the men that come and go through the gym. Fanny Giraut is standing with her arms crossed at one end of the gym of her house, without looking directly at Fonseca or any of the men in suits.

"I'm afraid that isn't going to be easy." Fonseca puts out his cigarette with saliva-moistened fingertips and puts the butt into a pocket of his pants. "It seems that something has happened. There are court orders. The forensics came. We have to go to the office to talk, just you and I." You can almost follow with your eyes the ebb and flow of blood through the inflamed branches of blood vessels in his temples. "*Now*."

A man in shirtsleeves with a lollipop stick coming from his lips and a generally satisfied and happy facial expression appears on the staircase that attaches the gym to the main house. Besides the gym, the other additions to the house include a solarium with pool on the former terrace, a game room in the basement and the Fishing Trophy Room on the second floor of the house's main building. With views of the breakwater. The Giraut family house in the Ampurdan is located in the middle of a horseshoe-shaped bay, with an enormous breakwater occupying the center of the bay and cliffs on either side. The guy in shirtsleeves takes the lollipop out of his mouth. A rolled-up automotive magazine sticks enigmatically out of one of his pants pockets.

"We really don't want to disturb you," says the guy in shirtsleeves. Smiling. He points to the group made up of Fonseca and Fanny Giraut with his lollipop. "You go on with your work and we'll go on with ours. I'm Commissioner Farina, by the way. We've never met, but you could say I've been following your career. I'm a fan." He makes a wide gesture around him. Toward the dozen men in suits with latex gloves that are going from one side of the gym to the other, emptying closets and moving furniture. "And I love your house, of course. Don't mind us. We'll be done soon, maybe."

Fonseca takes another cigarette out of the pack he carries in his pocket and puts it between his lips and leaves it there. Without lighting it. Several of the men in suits seem to be sucking on candy or chewing gum. It isn't clear if this coincidence is the result of some sort of coordination.

"Listen, clown." Fanny Giraut moves her head toward Commissioner Farina. Not the way people normally turn their faces, first moving their gaze and features and then adapting their posture. The way she moves her head is more like the rigid rotation of submarine periscopes or tanks' rotating turrets. "You're putting your job on the line. You *might* still manage to get sent to a desk job or wherever if you take all these lunatics and get out of here. You don't know who you're dealing with. All I have to do is this." She snaps her fingers. "Fonseca, call Aguirre. Tell him what's going on here."

There is a moment of silence. Commissioner Farina's expression of intense pleasure and satisfaction with life in general grows by the minute. His lollipop creates a vaguely spherical lump inside his cheek. From the other side of the staircase that connects the gym with the main building of the house comes the unmistakable sound of furniture being dragged. From the spot in the gym where Fonseca and Fanny Giraut are standing, looking away from the breakwater, over the heads and bodies of the men with latex gloves, the house's car entrance can be seen. With half a dozen patrol cars parked and another few unmarked cars that don't belong to any family member. Near the opposite corner of the gym, a guy in a suit with a spiral cable coming out of his ear is eating sunflower seeds and throwing the shells into the bougainvilleas.

"This is more complicated than it looks." Fonseca lowers his voice, perhaps unconsciously. But not enough that Commissioner Farina can't hear him. "It seems that Judge Aguirre is the one *who signed* the search warrant. The search warrants. They've also sent officers to the apartment in Barcelona and to my law firm. We have to talk," he adds in a pressing tone. "Now."

Fonseca and Fanny Giraut go up the stairs that connect the gym to the main building of the house. The contingent of Philippine cooks and domestic servants is gathered in the entryway with collectively contrite expressions. With those contrite expressions often seen on the faces of people who live on the poverty line. Fonseca and Fanny Giraut go into Fanny's office on the first floor, and they find that it is also being searched by a group of men in suits with latex gloves. The desk and file cabinet drawers are laid out in neatly organized piles on top of the Persian rug. Each pile with a numbered label. The lamps dismantled on the rug. The vases emptied. One of the officers is emptying the shelves of books and placing the books in piles on the floor. After flipping through them with his latex gloves. With jaw movements that indicate he's chewing gum.

"Who the hell was it?" Fanny Giraut goes up the stairs to the second floor with vigorous strides. Followed closely by Fonseca. "Chicote? Have we talked to Chicote yet?"

Fanny Giraut opens the door to the second-floor study. A member of the forensic police with latex gloves and a fingerprint kit is dusting a fine white substance over the study's wooden surfaces. With a spherical lump in his cheek. Another man in a suit with latex gloves is putting the contents of the paper shredder's wastebasket into several Ziploc bags for evidence. Fanny Giraut and Fonseca go through the door that connects the study to the Fishing Trophy Room. Fanny Giraut's face doesn't look exactly like a skull, or like a mask. It's more like the faces of second- or third-degree burn victims who, after getting a series of skin grafts, are left with a face covered mostly by unnaturally smooth and shiny tissue that bears little in common with normal facial skin tissue. Fanny Giraut and Fonseca go across the Fishing Trophy Room, dodging officers in suits who are rolling up the rugs and examining the wooden floorboards. They take the hallway that leads to the bathrooms.

"Chicote's clean," says Fonseca. "We've already talked to him. This comes from some other direction."

Fanny opens the door to her private bathroom. She holds it open so Fonseca can enter and bolts it closed when they are both inside. She sits on the closed toilet and gestures for Fonseca to give her one of his cigarettes. Fanny Giraut's private bathroom is larger than a lot of apartments in Barcelona and has three different kinds of Chinese porcelain. A television with a plasma screen hangs on the wall in front of the bathtub.

"What the hell do you mean by *some other direction*?" she asks.

And suddenly it happens. Even before she can finish formulating the question. The perpetually frozen and surgically constructed expression on her face breaks down for the briefest fraction of a second before recomposing itself automatically. And what he sees instead of the mask for that fraction of a second doesn't make Fonseca instinctively back up a few paces, but it does make his entire body replicate the configuration of a scared body about to instinctively back up a few paces. Fanny Giraut's voice drops an octave. The hand with which she lights her cigarette becomes a tense claw.

"That *bastard*," she says, exhaling a mouthful of smoke between two rows of gnashing teeth. "That little *monster*. I should have drowned him at birth. How the hell did he do it? What does he think he's trying to do?"

"He's got something." Fonseca sits on the edge of the bathtub. "Something he thinks he can use against us. And he sent a *blackmail* note. Along with a page from a certain accounting ledger. It seems to be a ledger that belonged to your husband. And the note is signed by *you*." He pauses, perhaps to verify the lack of expression on his main client's burn-victim face. "The note in and of itself can't hurt us. The forgery is good, but not good enough. The accounting ledger is more distressing. I can't figure out where Lucas could have found it. And that's not the worst of it."

Fanny Giraut's private bathroom is not only much larger than many apartments in Barcelona and has three kinds of Chinese porcelain and more lines of cosmetics than many specialized stores. There are also three original prints by Mario Testino on the main wall that show models in their late teens dressed in almost invisible underwear. Fanny Giraut inhales an anxious mouthful of smoke. The way that her rage arouses a certain degree of fear isn't the way that classical goddesses aroused fear with their majestically haughty attitudes. It's closer to the way certain hybrid mythological creatures aroused fear. Women with snakes for hair. Men with a single eye. Beings with human torsos and octopus tentacles. Things with a lot of heads.

"The worst part is where he put the blackmail note." Fonseca grabs the edge of the bathtub with both hands and shakes his head. "He put it in Koldo Cruz's mailbox. I never imagined he'd get this far."

Fanny Giraut makes a gesture with her hand that manages to be belittling in spite of its lack of concrete elements that are belittling in and of themselves or even together. The toilet she is sitting on is one of those toilets that have some sort of soft velvety cushioning on the seat.

"The note threatened to take the ledger to the police," says Fonseca. Seated on the edge of the bathtub. "The note that Lucas wrote pretending to be you. The ledger supposedly incriminates Cruz in some business dealings with your husband, thirty years ago. Except Cruz is in the clear, of course. The statute of limitations ran out long ago. So Cruz took it to the police." He makes a throbbing expression of concern. "Luckily for us. He must be getting old. Or they would've just found me and you floating in the sea."

Fanny Giraut takes a long drag on her cigarette.

"My son is ridiculous," she says finally. "As ridiculous and idiotic as his father. Makes me want to vomit." Her lips retract and reveal the two strips of frightfully pale and enamel-like flesh of her gums. "Just like the mental midget his father was. Like a stupid puppy showing his teeth. But he's wrong if he thinks that this is the end of this." She is interrupted by a noise coming from the bathroom door. The click of the door handle turning fruitlessly because of the bolt on the door.

Fonseca gets up from the edge of the bathtub and smooths his clothes with the palms of his hands before approaching the door and unbolting it. On the other side of the door there's a policeman in a suit. He is wearing rubber gloves up to his elbows and is carrying some sort of toilet plunger topped with a black rubber suction cup.

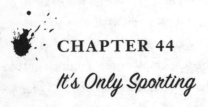

CHAPTER 44

It's Only Sporting

As executive director and principal shareholder of LORENZO GIRAUT, LTD., there is no reason why Lucas Giraut shouldn't go to work each day in the private company car. Yet, because of his fondness for private moments in public spaces, Giraut prefers to walk every day to the Plaza Catalunya and take the train from there to Reina Elisenda. Every morning. The 9:16 train to Reina Elisenda. Giraut always takes a lateral seat in the first car. With one of the many professional magazines he subscribes to. *Antique Trader* and *Art and Antiques*, the local versions of *Galeria Antiquaria* and *Arte y Coleccionismo* and, of course, *Antiques*. The world's magazine of reference in the field. With his reading glasses and once in a while barely looking up from his magazine to scrutinize the people that come in and out of the car. Giraut likes that feeling of isolation in a crowd. One of those feelings that for some reason he finds genuinely Barcelonian.

Today Lucas Giraut leaves the former ducal palace in the Gothic Quarter at five minutes to nine and slams the metal door shut. With his attaché case with its combination lock in his right hand. It's Monday. Lucas Giraut's favorite day. The day that marks the end of the vaguely comatose desolation of Barcelona Sundays; the day when the city comes back to life. Lucas Giraut stops in the middle of the street and frowns. The black Volvo in the plaza at the end of the street isn't so much parked as it is just left in the middle of the plaza with the motor turned off. Diagonally. With its nose pointing to the church and its tail illegally pushing aside a group of Dumpsters. A muscular arm covered in powder blue and white fabric is sticking out of the driver's-side window. Loud, rhythmic music is also heard. A couple of old women observe the car from the balconies of their houses, their brows furrowed. They talk to themselves the way old people do when they are watching other people from their balconies. Like people on a muted television. The hand that is sticking out of the window drums on the car door to the beat of the music.

Lucas Giraut walks up to the car in the middle of the plaza and leans down to talk to the face that is looking at him from the driver's-side window.

"This is the third day I've seen you around here." Giraut inspects the inside of the car as he speaks. There are remains of food and bottles on the backseat. Mixed with clothes. "I guess that means you have something you want to tell me. Your name is Saudade, right?" His gaze takes in the baseball bat with "I KILL BARÇA FANS" written on it in the passenger seat. "Does Mr. Bocanegra know that you're following me?"

Juan de la Cruz Saudade shows Lucas Giraut a wide smile filled with pieces of food in varying states of decomposition. Giraut can see that his powder blue and white Umbro sweat suit is very dirty and has various stains on the front and sleeves, as if Saudade has been wearing it for several weeks without a single trip to the Laundromat. His breath smells of carrion sprinkled with high-proof liquor.

"Mr. Bocanegra," says Saudade, in a mocking tone that imitates both Giraut's intonations and inflections, "doesn't know everything, little rich Mr. Snotnose Booger Eater. There's a lot of stuff he doesn't know. For example, he doesn't know that you've been putting things in Mr. Pirate Patch's mailbox. I also don't think he knows that the cops have been searching your offices. And I'm not the only one following you. At this point, Farina must know everything about your little painting scam. Just imagine what would happen if Bocanegra found out. You're lucky he doesn't know. But *I* do know." He pauses. He takes an open can of beer out of some invisible spot between his legs and brings it to his lips.

Giraut looks around him. The plaza at the end of his street is empty at that hour of the early morning, except for the occasional neighbor walking hastily to work. Shortly the groups of tourists with their guides will start to arrive. The patrolling police. The business owners. The unemployed bohemians. The roof of the Volvo is covered with pigeon droppings and pigeons, who are either drowsy or move in circles to the rhythm of their mating rituals.

"What do you want?" Giraut switches his attaché case from one hand to the other.

Saudade tosses the empty beer can and wipes his mouth with the sleeve of his Umbro sweat suit. The part of the sleeve that he uses to wipe his mouth already has a long beer-colored stain between the wrist and the middle of the forearm.

"I want *respect*," says Saudade. "That's the first thing. Then we'll talk about money. I want you to show me some respect, rich little Mr. Booger Eater, thinks his boogers taste better than other people's." His mouth opens in an expression that smells of carrion sprinkled with high-proof liquor, and which somehow gives the impression that he's appreciating the wittiness of what he has just said. "Now, get in the car." He grabs the baseball bat with its threatening inscription and throws it onto the backseat.

Giraut gets into the passenger seat. He places his attaché case with the combination lock on his knees.

"Good boy." Saudade burps and turns the ignition key. "Now leave your wallet and cell phone in the glove compartment. We're going to the beach. What better place. The people in this city don't appreciate their beaches."

Five minutes later, Saudade's black Volvo heads out of downtown along the Coastal Road toward the beaches near the mouth of the Besós River. Beyond the fish-shaped sculptures of the Olympic Port. Beyond the not-quite-identical towers of the Hotel Arts and the Mapfre insurance company. Like those puzzles in puzzle magazines where the reader has to mark in pencil the differences between two drawings. Saudade handles the steering wheel with his right hand and brings a can of beer to his lips with the left. Between his feet is a box of twelve cans of beer with at least four missing. There is a smashed empty can beside the gas pedal. It crashes into the side of Saudade's sneaker at regular intervals. Seen from close up, Saudade's powder blue and white Umbro sweat suit is much dirtier than it looked from outside the car. On his right wrist, partially visible under the sleeve, Saudade has a tattoo that reads "BB ☠ BB." In the green ink of discolored tattoos.

"You like my tattoo, huh?" Saudade finishes the beer and tosses it out the open window. The black dashboard is filled with traces of white powder that makes you think of a cement surface with traces of snow once the snow has almost completely melted. "I did it back when there were still people in this city with balls. Oh, yeah." The way he

nods his head is that clichéd way people nod to transmit nostalgia
for the good old days. "We made everyone respect us back then. Ten
years ago. That was our best period. Especially when the team traveled. Fear traveled with us. And not one fuckin' Barça fan dared to
come near our stadium. In the good old days when we had a stadium."
He spits through the open window. It is not clear whether the spitting
is related to the story he's telling or not. "Milan, Bratislava. When we
were runners-up for the UEFA. But in those days people had balls."

Saudade inhales and puffs up his chest. Giraut watches as he raises
his eyebrows high and adopts a pose somewhat like an opera singer
getting ready to sing. A pose that is vaguely reminiscent of Russian
choirs. Of boatmen on the Volga.

Real ees.
¡Tu nobleza justifica el adjetiii-vo!
Eres cluuub
A pesar de tu grandeza solo un cluuuub
Deportiii-vo.
¡El deporte es tu único objetiii-vo!

A coughing fit interrupts Saudade's vaguely Russian song. He
turns the wheel and exits the Coastal Road at Bogatell. Some sort of
no-man's-land of lots filled with garbage and remnants of construction
separates the neighborhood from the beachfront bars and restaurants.
There is not one single open place in sight on this Monday morning
in February. Some of the places have sculptures made up of outdoor
chairs piled up into complex shapes and chained together. Others have
graffiti and varyingly threatening messages that probably haven't been
cleaned off since the beginning of the summer season. Saudade parks
the Volvo in a lot located right behind the row of beach restaurants and
puts the keys in his pocket. Then he takes out several fifty-euro notes
from Giraut's wallet and sticks them into the pocket of his sweatpants
along with his cell phone. Giraut takes his empty wallet and watches

as Saudade hides the baseball bat inside his sweatshirt and signals for him to get out of the car.

"Out," he says. As if the sign he had made toward the outside of the car had left any room for doubt.

They both walk a few minutes along the sand with no apparent destination. The wind lifts papers and litter and every once in a while tosses a gust of sand onto the men. In spite of his being cold with his wool coat and Lino Rossi suit, Giraut doesn't notice any sign of cold from Saudade, who is only wearing his extremely dirty powder blue and white sweat suit.

"Everything I told you about was before I became a cop." Saudade shrugs his shoulders. "Really I was still chasing the same scumbags. What do you think of that, little Mr. Fancy Pants? Three years on the force. You think you coulda done all I did in my life?" he asks rhetorically. With his eyes almost closed to keep the sand out. "People like you make me wanna puke. You think I don't know what you think about us? With your fancy houses and your fancy women and wherever it is you go on those trips." His hands pat the long bulge of the baseball bat through the dirty powder blue and white fabric. He looks Giraut in the eye. "It's about time you started showing a little respect."

Lucas Giraut studies the beach, searching for some tranquil element. Some of those proverbially tranquil elements that people go to the beach to find. In the distance, on the wind-rippled water, some sort of merchant ship with an entirely rust-colored hull seems to be simply floating immobile near the docks. The mountain of Montjuïc in the background is like one of those cliffs covered in mist that you find in old gothic novels set on the coast of Cornwall. The sea is the color of lead. The sky is the color of lead. The sand on the beach is a pale, dirty shade of gray that's not quite the color of lead. Juan de la Cruz Saudade seems to have switched gears, fondling the bat through the fabric of his sweatshirt and muttering under his breath while staring at his feet. Seagulls fly threateningly in circles over the only two people on the beach and the more aggressive ones are already landing near them, with their beaks open and their wings extended. Giraut walks over to where the waves reach the sand and sits down on the ground, at least three feet from the stripe of sand darkened by the strongest waves. A zigzagging line of dried seaweed and sundry litter marks the farthest limits of the waves' reach. Like a scientific diagram. Like the zigzagging lines of a seismic diagram or an electrocardiogram.

Lucas Giraut sighs. He takes off his shoes and places them beside his attaché case, in which he carries a couple of magazines about antiques, as well as a book-restoring kit and a copy of the book *Learn to Restore Books in Just 100 Days*, from the "Learn in Just 100 Days" series. Saudade watches Giraut and kneels down to take off his shoes, too. He pulls a can of beer out of his sweatshirt and opens it, spilling some sort of giant foam phlegm ball onto his front.

"You think you know what you're playing at but you don't," he says to Giraut. "This isn't a game for faggy little rich kids like you. You could get hurt. You think you know Bocanegra because he was your daddy's little friend and all that, but the truth is you don't know shit." He takes a sip of beer. Foam now also slips down his chin. "You don't have a fucking clue as to what Bocanegra would do to you if he found out you're fucking with Mr. Pirate Patch. He'd chop you up so small you'd fit through a tennis racket. And about what you asked me before." He kneels to pick up a long, smooth stone from the zigzagging line of seaweed and litter that marks the reach of the waves and tosses it into the sea at that horizontal angle people use to make stones bounce along the water's surface. The stone just sinks among the waves. "I want fifty grand now and fifty grand at the end of the month. Then we'll talk some more. That old crap you got in your store must be worth a lot of money. I bet you don't even notice when you sell a coupla pieces."

Lucas Giraut runs a hand through his long straight hair, still damp from his morning shower. Deep down he is aware that his pale eyebrows and round, mostly hairless face and his slightly droopy eyes give him a namby-pamby look that makes a lot of people not give him the due respect conferred by his age and position. Or at least the conventional respect between adults in society. One of the reasons why he can't find any conventionally tranquil elements on the beach is that Giraut has no conventional experience of beaches. He never went to the beach as a child, except maybe to the breakwater by the house in the Ampurdan. There was no one to take him. Giraut imagines that the conventionally tranquil aspects of beaches are one more of the elements that distinguish him from the rest of the population. Now, sitting in front of an irregular line of shells and dried seaweed and litter, he realizes that he doesn't need to turn around or look over his shoulder to know that Saudade is no longer with him.

CHAPTER 45

The Third Golden Rule

Pavel thoughtfully observes his reflection in the glass display case of the jewelry store he's about to rob. In violation of most of the basic rules on how to rob a jewelry store. For example, every occasional jewelry store robber knows that the first golden rule of said activity is that more than one person is needed. Not just because there always has to be someone watching outside or at the door. There is also the danger of being outnumbered by the store staff, or even the difficulty of gauging the relative value of the pieces stolen and therefore the paradoxical danger of being *ripped off* by the victims. Of course, Pavel knows all of this *in theory*. But Pavel has a dream. A pressing dream, which has to do with palm trees and ubiquitous black women with ample asses. In normal circumstances, he himself would laugh at the idiot looking at himself in the display case. But Pavel doesn't even remember the last time he was in normal circumstances.

Standing in front of the jewelry shop's reflective display case,

Pavel adjusts his starter pistol inside his sweatpants and checks his dreadlocks. The way he is looking at himself is the way people look at themselves in reflecting surfaces when checking their hair. Sucking in their cheeks or maybe even biting the inside of their cheeks and lifting their eyebrows high and moving their head slightly from one side to the other. His dreads are fine. According to all the relevant parameters. Their length is approaching the desired length. The reason why he's carrying a starter pistol is because it's much cheaper than a real one. Besides the less catastrophic repercussions in the case of a trial for illegal possession of weapons.

The time for his scheduled entrance into the jewelry store is about to appear on the screen of his cell phone. Pavel isn't carrying his usual khaki canvas backpack from the army surplus store. He's carrying one of those black bags with very long handles that doctors used to carry back in the olden days. When they made house calls in the middle of the night. Those bags that make you think of shiny instruments with serrated blades and syringes the size of travel-size deodorant sprays. The wide section of the inside of the jewelry store that can be seen through the display window is dimly lit compared to the street. Pavel rummages around in his bag more appropriate to a doctor from the olden days and takes out a series of objects that include sunglasses and a gray wool hat. There seems to be someone inside the store. Behind the counter. Sitting in a chair behind the counter under a large horizontal painting. A girl who seems to be fingering something small with both hands. The way Pavel puts on the gray wool hat is: carefully making sure all of his dreadlocks are inside. On the door there's a sign that says "OPEN" and a sticker on the upper part with a schematic drawing of a camera that warns that the store is connected to the police station through closed-circuit television. Pavel puts on his sunglasses and pushes the door open.

The inside of the jewelry store is much darker than the street. Pavel blinks. His sunglass-covered eyes try to adjust to the level of light. On the door there are other stickers that depict the different credit cards one can use in the jewelry store and its membership in various professional business associations. Pavel turns the "OPEN" sign so that the side that says "OPEN" now faces inside the store.

The door closing activates an automatic sound similar to a bell ringing. Pavel scrutinizes the area where the wall meets the ceiling, looking for security cameras. The sunglasses aren't exactly helping him to make out the details inside the jewelry store. The salesgirl looks up from the small object in her hands that, judging from the high-pitched electronic noises it's making, seems to be some sort of portable game device. Pavel is standing in the middle of the jewelry store with his sunglasses and gray wool hat and his black leather bag hung over his shoulder. Staring at the large horizontal painting on the wall behind the counter. Right above the salesgirl. The painting depicts a fortified rectangular structure with defensive turrets and some sort of taller inner building. Pavel points to the painting.

"That the Temple of Jerusalem?" he asks. He takes off his sunglasses to get a better look. "The Temple of Solomon? The original?"

The salesgirl pushes a couple of buttons that interrupt the flow of electronic noises coming from her portable device. Then she turns her neck to look over her shoulder.

"I don't know," she says finally. "But I guess so. If that's what it says, then that's what it is."

Pavel approaches the counter. He rests his palms on it and extends his neck to look more closely at the pictorial representation of the Temple of Jerusalem, his eyes squinted. He can't say he knows much about the Temple of Jerusalem or its history, but he knows enough about the Rastafarian movement and Bob Marley's music to understand that the temple occupies a central place in his philosophy and is prominently featured in many of his song lyrics. What is most disconcerting to Pavel about the painting is how underwhelming the temple is, in every sense. Considering the whole people of Zion and the history of Babylonia and the lion that breaks his chains and all that stuff.

"How can be possible?" Pavel speaks without taking his eyes off of the painting. "I mean, it was someone what was there that painted it? Or they made the painting later, from memories of their mind?"

The salesgirl looks at the painting again. There is something incongruous about her appearance. Something probably having to do with the formality of her jacket versus the winding tattoo that peeks out from the collar of her blouse and runs up one side of her neck. As if for some reason the two things couldn't possibly belong to the same person.

"I don't know," says the salesgirl. "You'd have to ask my uncle. I can tell you the prices of the stuff on sale. I can even sell them to you."

Pavel thinks for a moment. Then he takes the pistol out of his sweatpants.

"Get on floor," he says to the salesgirl. "Flat on floor. Like this." Pavel puts his hands behind his head as a demonstration.

The salesgirl with the suit jacket and the tattoo lies facedown on the floor, with her hands behind her head. With the self-confidence of someone who has seen enough movies to know perfectly how the victim of a robbery in a jewelry store should lie down. Then she looks at Pavel with a vaguely expectant expression. Like a low-level employee waiting for instructions from a supervisor. Pavel thinks he can see the salesgirl chewing gum.

"Are you here alone? No?" Pavel waits for the salesgirl to shake her head. "Your uncle here? Your uncle the boss?" He waits for the salesgirl to nod her head. "Call this uncle now. Call him."

The salesgirl turns her head in the opposite direction, her hands still behind her head. The second golden rule of people whose profession requires the occasional jewelry store robbery is: whatever you do inside a jewelry store, don't do it yourself. You have to order the other people around to get them to do it. Pavel isn't sure of the origin of this second golden rule. If he wasn't in the middle of a robbery, Pavel would think that the salesgirl was deliberately careless in her posture on the floor, revealing a large section of thigh.

"Uncle!" shouts the salesgirl. "Come quick!"

Pavel remains standing beside the salesgirl, aiming at her with his starter pistol.

"Ring the bell," says the salesgirl. "Sometimes he doesn't hear so well. Ring that bell over there."

She takes one hand from behind her head and points to a bell located behind the counter. Next to the open door of what must be the storeroom. The bell doesn't look like an antitheft alarm or a device connected to the police station.

Pavel catches himself looking at the painting of the Temple of Jerusalem again. He finds it hard to believe that it's the same temple that took centuries and entire armies to destroy. In Pavel's opinion, any idiot with a ladder and a bomb could blow it to bits with no problem. Although he isn't sure that they had bombs in Ancient Times. He's trying to remember examples of ancient stories that involved the use of bombs when a middle-aged man appears behind the counter and looks at the salesgirl with a frown. He is wearing one of those argyle V-neck sweaters that a lot of little kids and middle-aged men wear for some reason. With the collar of a sport shirt sticking out through the V-neck.

"What are you doing on the floor?" asks the middle-aged man. Then he looks up at the man next to the counter with the hat and sunglasses and a pistol in his hand. Finally he nods with an expression that shows he has a general understanding of what's going on. "Uh," he says, "we have a security camera with a line to the police."

There is something inexplicably sexual in the way the salesgirl is lying facedown on the floor, with the skirt of her suit slightly raised, revealing a good chunk of her thighs. In Pavel's opinion. In spite of the fact that it's absurd to have sexual thoughts in a situation like the one taking place in the jewelry store. Pavel is vaguely aware that these completely inappropriate thoughts come to one's mind in moments of professional stress or high pressure. The salesgirl remains facedown, watching out of the corner of her eye. Pavel tosses the black leather bag to the middle-aged man.

"Put that in bag," he says. "And that. And that over there. All that." Pavel points to various display cases filled with items. "And faster. Fast as you can or you be out one niece. Come on."

The middle-aged man opens the glass cases with a key and is emptying them into the vaguely medical black leather bag. Another characteristic of the clothing of many little kids and middle-aged men is that their V-neck sweaters almost never match the colors of the shirts that stick out from underneath them. As if the chromatic rules of dressing didn't apply to certain phases of life. Pavel looks at the clock on the screen of his cell phone. The third golden rule of robbing jewelry stores is that the whole process, including the entrance, theft and getaway, can't take longer than three minutes. In order to avoid getting caught by the cops. Three minutes seems to be the international professional standard. In the case at hand, the deadline is fast approaching. The middle-aged uncle gives him back the black leather bag with handles. Pavel puts it over his shoulder, still aiming the starter pistol in the general direction of the salesgirl. She has two almost identical runs in the stockings of each leg. Pavel looks at the clock on his phone again.

"Wait," says Pavel to the overtly expectant faces of the salesgirl and the man who seems to be her uncle. Even though he says it to them, his expression and body language seem to indicate that he's really talking to himself. Like in those situations when people say "wait" when they are trying to give themselves time to think. He points with the starter pistol toward the painting. "The painting. Give me that painting. I'll take it."

The salesgirl looks at Pavel as if she didn't understand and then looks at the painting. Exactly three and a half minutes have passed since Pavel entered the jewelry store and took a look around. Now both he and the salesgirl watch as the middle-aged man gets up on a chair, takes the pictorial representation of the Temple of Jerusalem off the wall and offers it to Pavel. Although the idea is completely incongruous with the context and the situation, Pavel could swear there was a certain component of curiosity and amused interest in the face of the salesgirl who is now looking at him. Who is no longer lying facedown with her hands behind her head but rather lying on her side in a more comfortable position with her head resting on one arm. In a comfortable way that accentuates her sexual self-confidence. Pavel extends his hand to take the painting but stops and looks out of the corner of his eye at the camera filming him.

"Stick it in there," he says to the salesgirl's uncle. "Keep safe." He waves around the pistol the way people sometimes wave whatever's in their hand when they can't find the word they're looking for. "Wrap it up. That's it. Wrap it up."

The salesgirl and her uncle exchange a fleeting glance. Twenty-five seconds later, Pavel exits the jewelry store onto a street flooded with the sound of police sirens. He takes off his wool hat and throws it into a trash can. He quickly shakes out his newly unconstrained dreads.

Two blocks from the scene of the robbery, a police car passes by him and one of the officers inside takes a quick look at him as he walks down the street with his dreads out and the wrapped painting beneath his arm. The police car keeps going. Pavel looks at the clock on his cell phone again: now he has to hurry. If he wants to catch the flight tomorrow morning, he has to sell the contents of the bag in the next few hours.

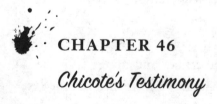

CHAPTER 46

Chicote's Testimony

Toward the second half of the preliminary hearing of his trial for mental incompetence, Lucas Giraut thinks he can see something in the last rows of the public that interferes with his ability to concentrate on what's going on in the courtroom. At first it's just a flash. A flash that seems to come from a metal plate located on the head of one of the people observing the hearing. Although it is impossible to be sure from where he's sitting. The flash is in a hidden area at the back of the room. A blind spot. Blocked by various columns and architectural elements. Giraut is sitting on some sort of platform to one side of the room. With his lawyer that's either Arab or from the Asian subcontinent. The area for the public looks in many ways like the seating area in a movie theater, with its lateral aisles and wider central aisle and its double doors at the very back. And yet, the district courtroom where the hearing is going on doesn't remind him of any movie theater. It's more like the pews in a church. Probably for not entirely conscious reasons.

Lucas Giraut leans over the railing of his platform to try to see the back of the room. From where he is sitting he can see the whole room except for some parts at the back obscured by architectural elements. Marcia Parini is among the witnesses. Iris Gonzalvo is in the audience. Seated beside a guy with the biggest ass that Giraut remembers having ever seen on a man who wasn't morbidly obese. There is someone in the audience with white earbuds coming out of their ears. Giraut rests both hands on the platform's railing and twists his head as much as he can and even leans over the railing again to try to make out the flash that he thinks he's seen a couple of times now at the back of the room.

"This is an *outrageous* scandal," the plaintiff's lawyer is saying. The same sickly-looking redheaded lawyer. "We already warned the court that this could happen. We already offered evidence that the defendant is involved with organized crime. And things have been allowed to go this far." He points to Carlos Chicote, head of the International Division of LORENZO GIRAUT, LTD., who is sitting in the witness area. Chicote's terrified, overwrought face is an attempt to smile sycophantically. "The witness is shaking like a leaf. I wouldn't be surprised if he was being threatened by someone in *this very room.*

And basically trying to sabotage this trial. When we have sworn declarations implicating the accused. Your Honor, this hearing must be suspended. Investigations must be made into this." The plaintiff's red-headed lawyer makes a gesture as if loosening his tie without actually loosening it. "I'm talking about an in-depth investigation of the defense's methods."

It appears that Giraut's lawyer is carrying out a series of ambiguous movements with his hand in his crotch area. Giraut doesn't see any female near the platform that could hypothetically be associated with those movements. The rings that the lawyer's wearing on his dark hairy hands somehow accentuate the overall lasciviousness of his appearance. Thick heavy gold rings. His little neat beard, like Peter Gabriel's in the eighties, also accentuates his lascivious air. Marcia Parini smiles nervously at Giraut and waves. From the witness bench. Most of the audience seems to be only partly paying attention to what is going on at the front of the courtroom.

"Let's see." The judge of the District Court now addresses Carlos Chicote. With a frown. The judge seems to be all brow and forehead with no chin. Creating a marked imbalance in his features. "Mr. Chicote, I will remind you that there are written statements. I will remind you that you have signed documents. And that this is a court of law. You say that you don't remember anything. But it is all very clear in here." He lifts up a couple of files from his judge's table. "Your written declarations are key evidence in this hearing and in the entire process. It is clear that we wouldn't have gotten to this point in the proceedings without them. I quote you a few examples. To refresh your memory," he says, opening one of the files. His thick glasses don't exactly help to mitigate his top-heavy features. "You state in your declaration: 'Mr. Giraut systematically blocks all the company's international operations. His behavior is erratic and inexplicable. He suffers fits of rage and flaunts his personal reckless spending. He goes through company offices with fewer clothes on than basic professional decorum dictates and often behaves obscenely in front of the female employees.

Sometimes he locks himself in his office the whole day and comes out dressed in period clothing.' I am quoting. On page seven of your statement there is a conversation quoted in extenso with the defendant. I'll remind you of just one small part: 'Mr. Giraut called me to his office one day and showed me a series of photographs of his friend V.P. and other underage girls between six and thirteen years old. He made sexual insinuations about the girls and told me that a child's beauty was the most exquisite kind. He said it was a shame that society only accepted one kind of love and that if some of the things he had done came to light he would be sent to jail.' "

The judge with the top-heavy face lifts his brow and forehead from the paper he is reading and looks at Chicote with his eyes slightly squinted behind his thick glasses.

"It sounds like a story that would be hard to forget, Mr. Chicote," he says. "It's very strange that your memory has deteriorated so much. Do you still state for the record that you don't remember anything?"

Lucas Giraut now not only has both hands on the railing of the platform but also his head and the upper part of his torso over it. Looking toward the back of the room. Several members of the public have noticed and turned their heads to try to see what Giraut is looking at. Seeing a flash at the back of the room doesn't necessarily mean that the flash comes from a metal plate on anyone's head. Mistaken associations, after all, are normal in situations of emotional stress. The ethnically ambiguous lawyer could also be from some part of the South Pacific or even North Africa. In his repeated hand movements over his general groin area there are no indications that he is looking at Iris Gonzalvo out of the corner of his eye. Somehow, even though the temperature outside is as cold as a Barcelona winter gets, the atmosphere inside the courtroom is such that everyone has taken off all their outer garments. Many men raise one hand instinctively to the knot in their ties. Marcia Parini fans herself with a magazine she's taken out of her purse. There is no trace of Estefanía Giraut or her lawyer Fonseca in the room. Iris

Gonzalvo is wearing a picture hat and dark glasses and a short dress with red tights. The man with the exceptionally large ass sitting next to her is leaning forward, taking notes or writing something in a notebook that rests on his thighs.

"I don't remember anything," Chicote answers with the same terrified expression. For some reason, the way he answered seems to suggest that he isn't responding to the judge presiding over the District Court, but rather to the smiling face of Aníbal Manta, who is sitting in the first row of the audience. "I'm not saying all those things never happened." He looks out of the corner of his eye at Aníbal Manta's face. "Of course, I'm not saying that they did either."

The sweat that drips onto Carlos Chicote's eyelids, forcing him to wipe his eyes every once in a while with the back of his hand, could merely be a product of the heat in the courtroom. Although there is nothing in his appearance that indicates he is in any kind of pain, certain nuances of his expression are reminiscent of the face people make when they've just hurt themselves. The judge is now extending his neck to see something in the back of the room. Many of the audience members have turned to look in the same direction. If Lucas Giraut's butt had any less contact with the chair he would be standing.

"The session must be suspended," says the plaintiff's lawyer. He makes the gesture again, of loosening his tie without really doing anything to it. He bites the end of his Montblanc fountain pen. "It's the only thing fitting in this situation. To avoid a scandal of unimaginable dimensions. One of those cases that cast shadows on the entire judicial system." He gestures widely around him with the bitten end of his Montblanc. "This requires an in-depth investigation. It's obvious that witnesses have been pressured. There was also a certain incident a week ago having to do with an extortion note that needs to be looked into. We have to bring to light all of the defendant's schemes and connections to the crime world."

Except for when he's addressing someone or somehow moving around the complex pile of files that he has on his table, the facially top-heavy judge remains stock-still. Looking at the person or persons who are speaking. Without blinking. Without any visible alterations to his facial musculature. The man with the unbelievably big ass keeps taking notes in his notebook and nodding his head and smiling enigmatically. Like those people that attend a conference or performance and nod and smile to show that they know exactly what is happening and even what is about to happen. The person in the audience with the small white earbuds coming out of his ears isn't the only person in the room wearing earphones. Giraut doesn't see any stenographer transcribing what is going on. Nor does he see magistrates with wigs, nor that stand, which looks vaguely like a cage, that they use for people accused of violent crimes. Maybe there's a special room in the building for violent criminals, with those cagelike stands. Lucas Giraut has never before been the accused party in any judicial proceedings. Before now. Beside him, the non-European lawyer has stood up and is clearing his throat with a brown, ring-filled fist in front of his mouth.

"With the permission of the court, Your Honor," he says. There are no foreign inflections in his voice. "I believe there are enough indications to suspect that the witness's written statements were signed under duress."

The facially top-heavy judge stares at the witness from behind his glasses and asks him if he signed any statement under any sort of duress. He reminds him that he is under oath. Part of the public's attention, which was diverted toward the back of the room, now returns to the front. The witness rubs his eyes with the back of his hand and smiles sycophantically and looks at Aníbal Manta. Who is sitting in the front row of the audience. With a T-shirt of the classic formation of the X-Men under his suit jacket. The witness shrugs his shoulders.

CHAPTER 47

The Crooked Lady Cops' Party

There is a crooked lady cop's uniform strewn on the floor of the Private Room of the upper level of The Dark Side of the Moon, the kind that is used every year for the Crooked Lady Cops' Party. About six feet from where Aníbal Manta is having sex with the young owner of the uniform, who is currently naked. The uniform is made up of six pieces of clothing: a police hat, a short-sleeve button-down shirt, a leather miniskirt, a pair of stiletto heels and a white cotton G-string. The way Manta and the owner of the uniform are having sex on one of the sofas is as follows: Manta seated with his pants at his ankles and his arms extended along the back of the sofa, and the young woman sitting on top of him with her legs on either side of his body and her arms resting on his shoulders. The muffled but constant beat of dance music comes from the floor downstairs.

"Mr. Manta?" says a woman's voice from the other side of the locked door of the Private Room of The Dark Side of the Moon. There is a hint in her voice that could convey some sort of fear or perhaps general awkwardness. "Sorry to bother you. But we may have a problem downstairs."

The signs of physical fatigue in the young woman having sex with Aníbal Manta are starting to show. Manta doesn't understand why it is practically impossible for him to get good erections even when his sexual partners are attractive young women from Eastern Europe like the dancers at The Dark Side of the Moon. Even when he doesn't have other men in front of him whose sexual vigor and genital size give him that familiar sensation of emotional stress. Manta turns his head to one side and checks his watch. It's obvious that what he's feeling during sex isn't what he should be feeling. The mere fact that the young dancer is trying with all her might to make him climax annoys him and makes him feel uncomfortable. Even though she's an exceptionally attractive nineteen-year-old. Even though he can't deny she's skilled and has considerable sexual stamina. In that sense, Mr. Bocanegra has always been in favor of paying more money for better dancers. It's as if the dancer's stamina and effort give Manta a feeling of psychological pressure and emotional tension that paradoxically keep him from achieving that level of satisfaction that his sexual partner expects of him.

"Mr. Manta?" repeats the voice from the other side of the locked door. "We have a guard down. I think his nose is broken. It's hard to tell with so much blood."

The dancer's movements on top of Aníbal Manta have become slower and less frequent throughout the almost forty minutes they have been having intercourse. Now Manta slaps her on the ass and grabs her with his enormous hands and picks her up off his lap like a little child. The dancer collapses onto the sofa with trembling legs. Manta lights a cigarette and expels a mouthful of smoke with his gaze fixed on the door. It is true that acts of violence are much more satisfying to him, in every sense, than sex. Which is something that his psychologist seems to not only find interesting in and of itself, but also indicative of many other things that Manta doesn't like to think about. In general, Manta finds it tedious and a bit annoying when his psychologist starts going on at length about the issue. The person on the other side of the locked door knocks hesitantly on it.

"Here you go, sweetheart." He tosses a wad of rolled bills at the trembling dancer. "Remind me to buy you a drink later downstairs. Or two."

The dancer drags herself over to one of the small glass tables and sniffs a line of coke. She lifts her nose and inhales sharply and stretches her neck in every direction like people do when they have a stiff neck. Manta keeps smoking with his pants at his ankles. All signs of any kind of erection he may have had in the last forty minutes are now gone. The dancer picks up her G-string from the carpet and puts it on one leg at a time and goes to open the door. Manta walks to the door of the Private Room with those short strides people take when they have their pants down at their ankles. Those penguin steps. In general, he doesn't understand why the hell people knock on the door and bug him when he has made it very clear that no one should come knocking on the goddamn door.

"I hope you have a good explanation," says Manta to the waitress on the other side of the door to the Private Room. The waitress isn't wearing a corrupt policewoman uniform. The waitress is wearing white minishorts and is chewing gum and has her hands on her hips. "I'm waiting."

The waitress makes a gesture with her hands that could convey something like impotence.

"It's Saudade. He climbed up one of the towers," says the waitress. "With a bat. We don't know how to get him down. One of the guards is down for the count. The other took a few hits, but looks like he'll recover. The girls are putting ice on him. And I think one of the male dancers has a broken arm. I think we have a problem. There are a couple of tables broken, and some chairs and the glass on the bar," she says. She stops to watch as the dancer finishes picking up her uniform from the floor and leaves. "Our problem showed up pretty wasted about an hour ago and kept drinking. Then he grabbed one of the girls by the hair and dragged her and tried to stick the . . ." She shrugs her shoulders. "Well, it doesn't matter. That's when the male dancer tried to stop him and got his arm broken." She furrows her brow. "No, wait. That was later, when he threw the chair over the bar."

Manta continues smoking in silence. With his shrunken, slightly bruised penis visible between his enormous hairy legs. Somehow, he thinks, fate could be offering him a wonderful opportunity. Something that he's been trying to do for years and which has probably turned into what his psychologist would probably consider some sort of repressed inner torment. Brought on by something he should have done a long time ago and never did. In the end, you shouldn't under-estimate the healing power of certain acts of violence. The waitress still hasn't mentioned the fact that Mr. Bocanegra is about to arrive any minute now to preside over the Crooked Lady Cops' Party. One of the most popular parties at The Dark Side of the Moon. Visitors from all over the country are expected, and others that made reservations from France and Italy. A large group of passengers from a cruise ship docked in Barcelona is expected. They set up a backdrop with a prison theme and two elevated platforms with searchlights on top, imitating the shape of prison observation towers. So the girls can dance on top of them. Bocanegra came up with the idea after seeing a performance in Amsterdam where the girls danced holding spotlights in their hands.

"Mr. Bocanegra could arrive at any minute," says the waitress. She blows a bubble with her gum and pops it almost immediately. "If we didn't have enough problems already."

Aníbal Manta sighs and pulls up his pants. Two minutes later and two floors below, the private elevator for staff and management of The Dark Side of the Moon drops Manta off inside the circular bar of the Eclipse Room. A dozen girls dressed in crooked cop uniforms are taking cover behind the bar with the waitresses and the inert body of one of the club's security guards. At hip height, the crooked lady cops wear a belt with a loop designed to carry their billy clubs. In the billy club loops, the crooked lady cops carry long latex double-sided dildos. The security guard who's down for the count has a face full of blood and a gap where his upper incisors should be. Manta picks a piece of chair up off the carpet and looks at it thoughtfully.

"He says he's gonna burn the place down," says the waitress to Manta. With her arms once again on her hips. The waitress seems to think that hands on hips is an appropriate stance for moments of emotional tension and conflict at work. "And he stinks to high heaven. Some of the girls are thinking that maybe we should call the police."

Manta stares at the dancers dressed as policewomen who are considering the option of calling the police. The dancers lower their eyes. Obviously ashamed. One of them is wringing out a wet rag above the unconscious security guard's head. Manta walks up to the stage platform overshadowed by a large banner that reads "THE CROOKED LADY COPS' PARTY" and looks up.

On top of one of the two towers with searchlights in the prison set, dressed in his Umbro sweat suit that it's hard to believe was once just powder blue and white, Juan de la Cruz Saudade waves at him with the hand that holds his baseball bat. In his other hand he has a can of gasoline.

"Manta." Saudade raises his voice from his position high up on the tower. "I know I wasn't invited to the party, but I decided to come anyway. I used *to be* a cop. Anyway, who wants to come to this hole?" He makes a wide gesture around the club with the baseball bat that says "I KILL BARÇA FANS" written on it in permanent marker. "I only had a little bit of gas left in the tank, so I decided to make good use of it."

Manta calculates the possibilities of climbing up the scaffolding that makes up the body of the tower and taking out Saudade without getting a potentially lethal blow to the head with the bat. The situation is definitely a picture-perfect occasion. The ideal occasion to give Saudade that thrashing that would be so positive for Manta's psychological evolution. A thrashing with broken bones and permanently altered facial features. Perhaps with spinal injuries that would leave the son of a bitch in a wheelchair for the rest of his life. This incident, after all, is worthy of such a thrashing. And leaving Saudade as a pile of broken bones on the floor would undoubtedly mean months of therapeutic progress in one fell swoop. But the question is how to go about it.

"Shoot 'im," shouts someone from inside the circular bar. "Aim at his leg."

Manta rubs his chin with a thoughtful face. Aníbal Manta's chin is much larger and wider and harder than the usual human chin. Shooting Saudade is definitely a viable option. And he'd probably break a bone or two in the fall. But it's not really the same as being able to grab him with his hands and feel his bones and facial features crack under the weight of his fists. He wonders if maybe there's some way he could get some kind of helmet and climb up the tower safe from Saudade's bat. But he can't quite see it. The dance music continues rhythmically hammering on the club's deafening sound system. Standing in front of the tower scaffolding, Manta feels like a not very diligent student faced with a complex logic problem.

"Hey, Manta." Saudade's voice sounds slightly singsong from the tower. "Did you tell 'em that your wife screws all your neighbors? The whole building. Except Manta, of course. I'm not surprised." There is a pause mixed with the sound of a cough coming from the top of the tower. Or maybe heaving. A few drops of something viscous fall on Manta from above. Then he hears Saudade's rich, mellow voice again. "Oh yeah. Smart girl, your wife."

Manta grabs the scaffolding with his giant hands. His face a grimace of emotional stress. The way he grabs the steel bars of the scaffolding is powerfully reminiscent of the way certain very furious large apes grab the bars of their cages at the zoo. Looking through the bars with a murderous expression. And that's when Manta notices something strange behind his back. Not exactly silence, because the music continues blaring. But the screams and threats of the waitresses and the dancers taking cover behind the bar have suddenly stopped. Indicating that something has just happened in the Eclipse Room. Manta turns slowly to look over his shoulder. Without letting go of the bars of the tower.

Mr. Bocanegra, Showbiz Impresario and owner of The Dark Side of the Moon, is standing at the door of the Eclipse Room. Flanked by statues. Imposing in his clearly feminine mink or sable coat. Planted in the doorway with his hands on his hips and a frown on his enormous, shiny head.

"What the hell is going on here?" Bocanegra looks at the remains of chairs, tables, bottles, trays and other objects that are strewn over the dark carpet. "What is all this stuff doing on the floor?"

The music plays at full blast for a long moment of no one answering. Someone makes a sign with his hand above the bar filled with broken glass. Bocanegra walks over to the bar of The Dark Side of the Moon and looks over it to the other side. He looks first at the group of kneeling dancers and waitresses and then at the still unconscious security guard who has bloody water running down his forehead and cheeks.

"You have *three seconds* to explain what is going on." Bocanegra slugs down the contents of one of the few intact glasses still on the bar. "Or heads are gonna roll."

Several dancers come out from behind their barricade and take refuge behind Bocanegra's back. At the foot of the tower, Aníbal Manta clears his throat and shuffles his feet nervously like a six-foot-two kid caught somewhere he shouldn't be. Bocanegra looks up toward where the fingers of the barricaded girls are pointing behind him. He is still wearing the obviously woman's coat and is rubbing his hands to warm them up.

"Ooooh, I'm so scared," says Saudade sarcastically from up on the tower. "Mr. Bocanegra. Ooooh, he's a real gangster! He could have our kneecaps broken!" He brings his fingertips to his cheeks like the actresses of the twenties did to convey fear. "Well, you don't scare me, you two-bit gangster." He holds up his can of gas proudly. "It's time to take it down a notch or two, you bald bastard. You've been laughing at me for years. But you're not laughing now, are you? Looks like it's time to start *negotiating*." He kisses the can of gas and almost loses his balance. "Unless, of course, you want me to just burn the place down."

No one says anything for a long moment. In the Eclipse Room at The Dark Side of the Moon there are not only velvet sofas and wooden platforms and statues. There are also tapestries on the walls and framed engravings that mostly depict female nudes and classical scenes with fauns and nymphs and women with pale chubby bodies fleeing from hefty men in forest settings. The set onstage represents some sort of back alley adjacent to a prison wall. With a garbage can and an old-fashioned streetlight.

"Aníbal," says Bocanegra. Without taking his eyes off the dance platform transformed for the occasion into a prison observation tower. "Bring me the ax. And you," he says to Saudade, "of all the cretins I've had working for me over the years, you are the biggest, stupidest cretin of them all. You take the *prize*. Congratulations. And now, we're going to *negotiate*." Bocanegra takes off his woman's coat. He gives it to one of the dancers and then removes his suit coat and rolls up his shirtsleeves. "The only difference is that my ax is going to do my negotiating for me. You can think of it as my agent."

Bocanegra grabs the ax that Manta has just brought out from the other side of the door near the bar that says "PRIVATE—STAFF ONLY" and wistfully taps the handle into the palm of his hand a few times. His forearms are so hairy that in some places his skin seems covered with some kind of closely-knit black cloth. His mouth is pursed under his mustache in a way that could convey rage but also has an element of cruelty that's hard to miss. His way of gathering momentum for the first blow makes you think of a golfer before a long shot. With a rotating motion of his entire upper torso accompanied by a swinging of the arms.

The first blow to the structure of the tower makes the entire thing tremble and sends back a sound of metal against metal that sets your teeth on edge. Someone lets out a whistle of admiration. Someone comments that after all, in the end, the Crooked Cops' Party only really needs one observation tower. Saudade grabs on to the scaffolding-like structure with one hand and starts frantically patting down his pockets with the other.

"One minute," he shouts from up on high. "Anyone got a match?"

The second ax blow sends pieces of the tower's base flying.

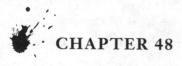

CHAPTER 48

German for Dummies

Barcelona's El Prat Airport first thing in the morning is a whirlwind of businessmen and women in suits that come out of taxis with cell phones stuck to their ears and pick up their boarding passes in the machines at the air shuttle terminal. There are pairs of national police officers that scrutinize the terminals with sleepy faces, looking for terrorists. There are invariably rosy-cheeked and healthy female exchange students dragging mountains of luggage behind them in carts with wheels. Their faces tired. In the midst of the executive whirlwind first thing in the morning at the airport, Pavel opens up his fake passport to the page with his photograph and contemplates his new identity. He trusts that the language exercises he's been doing the last two nights will solve any difficulties that might arise.

Pavel is in the check-in line for British Airways Flight 733 to London, where he'll change planes for Kingston, Jamaica. With a foam cup of coffee in his hand. Pushing his suitcase with his feet as the line moves forward at a torturous pace. Most of the other passengers bound for his flight are young Englishmen with hangovers. A guy with a shaved head and a Chelsea jersey is throwing up into a bag. Not one of those paper bags the airlines give you to throw up into. It is a regular plastic bag from a souvenir shop. There are also a couple of very serious Hindustani men who look like international terrorists, but Pavel doesn't see anyone who looks Jamaican, or like they're headed to Jamaica. There is someone in the line wearing a full-body bunny costume, the kind that have become popular in Barcelona this winter. Pavel takes a sip from his foam cup filled with coffee. The suit he's wearing is rented. He only had to pay the deposit and now it's his for the rest of his life. In Jamaica. Since Pavel is very tall and thin and only really looks good in custom-tailored suits, the light gray wool suit he's wearing is a little baggy in the butt and legs. A British Airways employee is examining the line for flight 733 and asking for identification from the passengers that look suspicious. When she passes Pavel she smiles and points to his suitcase with her head.

"Going to Jamaica?" says the British Airways employee.

"Yes."

"Very appropriate," she says. Pointing to Pavel's head. "The hairdo."

Fifteen minutes and one British vomiting emergency later, Pavel arrives at the front of the line, pushing his suitcase along with his feet. In the nearby police frisking zone, the giant bunny is taking off his full-body bunny suit so they can search him. Pavel puts his documents on the counter. The stewardess in charge of check-in picks up his fake passport and his plane ticket and does that classic visual operation they do in airports, looking alternately at the passport photograph and at its holder. Her eyes show no sign of suspicion.

"*Guten Morgen, herr Schumpfpeter. Sie reist nach Jamaica?*"

Pavel nods cautiously.

"Mathias," he says.

"Excuse me?" The stewardess at check-in looks up.

"I say you call me Mathias, please."

Pavel tries to speak in a tone that conveys self-confidence. That's how he imagines Germans speak. Always conveying self-confidence.

The stewardess picks his plane ticket up off the counter and starts typing into her computer terminal. While staring at the screen. Pavel places his suitcase on the conveyor belt for suitcases, which is immobile. Checking his ticket seems to be taking more time than necessary, thinks Pavel, but really it's the kind of process that always seems to take longer than it should. Pavel smiles and tries to duplicate the expression in the photo in the fake passport. Behind him, some of the passengers on British Airways Flight 733 start to show signs of impatience. In some part of the line a couple of heaves are heard and then the vaguely liquid sound of someone vomiting.

"Mr. Schumpfpeter," says the stewardess after a lapse of time that seems much longer than necessary for a routine reservation check. "There is a problem with your reservation."

Pavel looks around him out of the corner of his eye. There don't seem to be police officers or private security guards approaching with handcuffs in their hands or beating their billy clubs into their palms. Although his smile doesn't fade, Pavel's entire body seems to have suddenly acquired that elastic tension that athletes have on their marks, ready to run as soon as the starting shot is fired.

"Mr. Schumpfpeter," says the reservations stewardess. "It seems we have an overbooking problem. Your seat on the London-Kingston flight has been reserved for another passenger." The stewardess speaks without looking up from the monitor or pausing in her typing. Pavel notices some sort of stiffening in his neck region. "I'm sorry for the inconvenience, Mr. Schumpfpeter. Luckily, the plane isn't full. We can offer you a seat in first class. If you don't mind, that is." The stewardess looks up for a second and waits for Pavel to shake his head. "Okay. In that case, wait a moment and we will issue another ticket so you can pick up your boarding pass in London."

Pavel turns his head and gives an apologetic smile to the sour-faced Englishwoman behind him in line who is now looking at him with contempt. It's one of those apologetic smiles given to the people behind you in line during situations of involuntary conflict. To make it clear that you aren't the one creating the inconvenience. Or to try to create a situation of general solidarity among the members of the line. The sour-faced woman looks away. The stewardess is waving the ticket over the counter to get Pavel's attention back.

"Mr. Schumpfpeter," she says. She hands him several papers inside one of those paper sheaths airlines use. "Here is your boarding pass. Now follow that stewardess over there and we'll give you your new ticket."

Pavel looks over at where the check-in stewardess's arm is pointing. The second British Airways stewardess that approaches the check-in counter with a smile is identical to the first except for the fact that she is plumper and carries a very large walkie-talkie in her hand.

"Mr. Schumpfpeter?" says the new stewardess. "Come with me to the ticketing area, where we'll issue your new ticket."

Pavel crosses the terminal behind the second stewardess, letting his gaze wander over the groups of businessmen with cell phones and the sleepy policemen and the healthy exchange students dragging their mountains of suitcases. Every once in a while, some man offers to help one of the exchange students and they haul the crammed cart between the two of them, laughing and making internationally kind and understanding comments. Almost all the Arab and Hindustani men look like international terrorists. All the employees of the airport cleaning service have earphones in their ears. Pavel watches it all with the expression halfway between arrogant and disconcerted of someone convinced he will never set foot in that place again and if all goes well will spend the rest of his life in a much better place. With a lot more palm trees. With colorful houses that remind you of the colors of parrots and other tropical birds. With unpaved city streets where people set up their stalls to sell fruit and their hammocks to have a nap in or just chat with the neighbor. With that constant sound of crickets lulling you to sleep. And with the best music in the world. The music was what started it all. All of Pavel's current plans for a new life.

The stewardess stops in front of the British Airways ticketing offices. Which are still closed. A sign says that the ticket service opens at nine thirty, Monday through Friday. The stewardess opens a side door to the offices with a magnetic key shaped like a credit card and asks him into some sort of waiting room. The seats are covered in the British Airways corporate color scheme. There are no ashtrays.

There is no piped-in Muzak. There are piles of magazines on the small glass tables. And a man sitting in one of the seats reading a magazine. Pavel sits across from the other waiting passenger and takes a copy of *German for Dummies* out of his back pocket. The stewardess leaves through the other door. The face of the man sitting across from Pavel is covered by the magazine he's reading. Pavel is practicing pronunciation in his head, moving his lips to silently articulate the phrases *Ich bin ein Ausländer* and *Wo ist die Diskothek*, when he thinks to look up. The magazine the man sitting in front of him is reading is a magazine about cars. Pavel's teach yourself German book falls to the floor.

"Don't get mad." Commissioner Farina lowers the magazine he's reading and puts it in his jacket pocket. With a sleepy, happy expression. "We thought about nabbing you when you got home yesterday, but it turns out that the French had put out an arrest warrant on the idiot that bought the jewelry from you. You gotta make nice with the neighbors." He shrugs his shoulders. "Anyway, we didn't want to rob you of all these hours of anticipation. The wonderful night you just had. These hours of happiness courtesy of the Barcelona Police Force." He mimes putting a medal on the front of his shirt. Commissioner Farina's shirt, just like the rest of his clothing, looks like it was bought out of a catalogue on one of his coffee breaks. "We love you, Bob Marley. By the way." He takes a quick look at Pavel's attire. "Someone should have told you that Germans don't wear shoes like that."

Pavel looks down at his rented Italian shoes with the tips slightly pointed outward and the teach yourself German book between them. The carpet in front of the seat is full of round black cigarette burns that look a bit like coffee beans. Or maybe coffee beans *in negative*. Pavel rubs his temples with his index finger and thumb. The thoughts that come to his mind are once again alarmingly out of sync with any type of Rastafarian teaching.

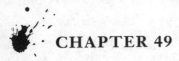

CHAPTER 49

The Years of Physical Impossibility

Iris Gonzalvo lights a postcoital cigarette with her eyes squinted and her mouth a bit twisted. The way people light cigarettes when they are lying horizontally on sweaty, messy beds. Especially postcoital cigarettes. She blows out the first mouthful of smoke and turns her head to look at Lucas Giraut, who is lying beside her. Naked except for his socks.

"That was horrible," she says. "Probably the worst I've ever had. I didn't feel a thing. Not to mention how boring and quick it was. I was about to grab a magazine. Didn't anyone tell you no one fucks in that position anymore? Drops of sweat were falling *on my face.*"

Iris Gonzalvo brings the cigarette to her lips again. In spite of everything she's saying, Giraut can't see any element of irritation or resentment in her face. He also doesn't see that amused expression people have when telling funny sexual anecdotes to a unisex group of their peers.

"I've never seen anyone so inflexible," she says. "Or who seemed so close to having a heart attack."

From the bed, lying faceup, Giraut can see the wooden beams and the high, slightly vaulted ceiling of what was, in its day, a room in a duke's palace. Maybe a duke's bedroom, or a duke's library. Or a duke's bathroom. Or a duke's fishing trophy room. Giraut imagines the bedroom he's in with the walls covered in fishing trophies and photographs of fishing expeditions. With taxidermied fish mounted on plaques. With six-and-a-half-foot-long swordfish. With the largest red tuna ever fished from the Mediterranean. With black-and-white photographs showing people with many-pocketed vests. A shiver runs down his back.

"I'm really sorry." Lucas Giraut takes the cigarette Iris Gonzalvo offers him between two fingers. "I guess you're used to doing it with another kind of man."

Iris Gonzalvo stares at Lucas Giraut as if she doesn't understand. Giraut shrugs. In his opinion, sex requires an intensity of physical effort and vigor practically incomprehensible in relation to the ephemeral and ineffable nature of its gratification. Not to mention the foreplay. Not to mention how hard it is to do it all well and give your sexual partner the satisfaction that guarantees her desire to retain you as a sexual partner. It's a mystery to Lucas Giraut how people manage to resolve sexual situations and keep their partners. None of that diminishes Iris Gonzalvo's sexual appeal. Which is undeniable.

"Did you screw that girl?" Iris Gonzalvo lifts up one leg in a right angle over her body and is running a fingernail over the tiny imperfections on her legs left by the waxing. "If you did, you can tell me. I've seen it all. You wouldn't be the first guy I know who did something like that. I mean fucking twelve-year-old girls."

Giraut takes a pensive drag on the cigarette and hands it back to his sexual partner. He isn't entirely sure why Iris Gonzalvo has a perfectly smoothly shaved pubis. In a way that doesn't at all suggest childlike associations. Nor does he really understand how she ended up with all those tattoos on her most private parts. It doesn't seem very likely that she just went into a tattoo parlor and took off all her clothes and pointed to her private parts and then lay down to wait for them to do them. Although he admits to himself that he could be wrong about that.

"Everyone thinks I did." Giraut blows out a mouthful of smoke. "Except Marcia, I guess. The girl's mother. Valentina says that her mother wants to marry me. Nothing sexual has ever happened between us. I mean with the daughter. Well, or with the mother either. We like to sit and talk in the courtyard. Sometimes in the winter we put out one of those portable heaters. We make up stories. Like for example that we're very powerful and can kill people. People that annoy us or people we hate. People like my mother and her lawyer. Valentina is a very special girl. She wants to be a writer. She's very smart. She could get the best grades in her school, but she wants to get bad grades. That's the kind of person she is. Special. Sometimes she gets really angry. I mean she has nervous fits. Now the doctors say that she has schizophrenia, but I don't believe it. I think she's angry. And growing up. Growing up isn't easy. It wasn't for me." He pauses and looks at Iris Gonzalvo's leg, lifted in a right angle. Iris is flexible and slender and one would have to have a screw loose to say that she wasn't exceptionally sexually attractive. "One time at school she said she saw a man throw himself into the garbage incinerator in the basement. The police came and they emptied out the incinerator and examined the remains and they even said they had found a piece of the man's bone. Later they realized it was a chicken bone. That was when they put her into therapy. And she's been in therapy since she was eight years old. It's hard to explain why she does those things."

Iris Gonzalvo lowers her leg to the bed. She turns on her side and leans on one elbow. Looking at Lucas Giraut.

"I don't know why I like you," she says. The position in which she is lying and leaning on one elbow doesn't allow her to shrug, but she moves her neck in a way that looks like a shrug or at least gives the same feeling. "You're weird and not very handsome and terrible in bed. I've never seen anything like it. But I think I like you. I'm not sure if I remember the last time this happened. I've gone out with so many maniacs and so many losers that I don't even care that you're weird. And I don't mean that we're going out or anything like that. In case you thought that's what I said."

"We're not going out," says Lucas Giraut.

"That's what I said."

Iris Gonzalvo sits on the bed and leans forward to pick up her underwear. Lucas Giraut's bedroom doesn't look like any bedroom Iris has ever seen. It's very big and has old windows with mullions and even one of those big trunks with rivets like you see in the movies.

If it weren't for the television and the walk-in closet separated from the bedroom by a curtain, she would feel like she was in one of those movies, like *The Lord of the Rings*, where people live in castles and fly on the backs of dragons. There is also a painting depicting a half-naked guy tied to a post with a ton of arrows sticking out all over his body. The guy with the arrows is looking up toward the heavens and looks like he's crying and his long upturned face somehow makes you think of Britney Spears's face. In Iris's opinion. The light from the streetlights of the Old City that enters the windows is halogen yellow colored and a little like a scary movie. Iris puts on a very small pair of panties and walks up to some sort of enormous antique throne made of painted wood that has a circular hole in the middle of the seat. A bag of golf clubs sticks out of the hole. She takes the golf clubs out and sits down. She puts her slender arms on the arms of the throne and looks at Giraut.

"Is this what I think it is? Must be worth a lot of money."

"It comes from Croatia." Giraut takes a drag on the cigarette with his gaze fixed on the floating beams of the ducal ceiling. "It's worth about five thousand euros. Depending on who you sell it to. It's from the seventeenth century. A unique piece. Only members of the high aristocracy could have one of those, of course." He pauses. "I've been thinking." He wipes off a bit of ash that has fallen onto his pale, almost completely hairless chest. "About Valentina. I want to get her out of that clinic. Although I don't know how to do it yet. I've been sending her chapters of her favorite novel. Sewn into other books. They won't let her read Stephen King. They don't let her read anything she likes. I've been talking to her doctors. I think they think that the things she likes are what's hurting her."

Lucas Giraut's wardrobe extends along an entire wall and has many dozen Lino Rossi suits hanging in it. Of different colors. All from the most recent season. There are also those kinds of hanging canvas drawers that people use to store shoes. Iris Gonzalvo takes one of the golf clubs out of the bag and pretends she is making a swing with both arms. Still sitting on the seventeenth-century toilet. Her body is slender and her pubis smooth and soft and Lucas Giraut doesn't remember ever seeing a more sexually attractive woman in his life.

"I've never much liked old things," she says. "I don't understand why they're interesting. At home the oldest thing we had was the television listings from the week before. Anyway it was impossible to keep anything for more than a week because Eric used to sell it all. He sold almost all my things. They just disappeared. That's something drug addicts do. It's a miracle he never sold our TV." She puts her feet up on the seat of the Croatian toilet made of antique polychrome wood and hugs her knees. "Not even Eric would dare sell the TV. In the end all we had was a mattress and the lamps and the TV. Although it's more than I have now. I don't know where I'm going to live. I've been staying at my friend's house for ten days and I haven't got any money."

Lucas Giraut keeps focusing on the architectural details of the second-floor ceiling of the ducal palace. The truth is he has no memories of his parents' separation. The only thing he seems to remember from his early childhood is blurry impressions of golden flashes from cocktail cabinets and the violent throwing of objects. Glimmers of his father's terrified face at the window of the Fishing Trophy Room. Seen through binoculars from a window of the North Wing. The guests seated among the taxidermied fish and black-and-white photographs of people wearing vests with many pockets. The already tree-like face of Fonseca seen from that child's perspective. More or less waist height. Neglected material in the abandoned corners of his mind. One of the possible reasons why Lucas Giraut doesn't remember his parents' separation is that it took place during the Years of Physical Impossibility, in which his parents were never in the same room at the same time. In some unclear period that Giraut situates near the deaths of Rock Hudson and the Ayatollah Khomeini.

"You can come live here." Giraut sits up and feels around for a pack of cigarettes on the bedside table. It has gotten dark very quickly and now the bedroom is lit only by the halogen yellow and vaguely scary light of the Gothic Neighborhood's streetlights, which comes in through the windows with mullions. "I don't mean living with me like we were boyfriend and girlfriend or living together as a couple. But there's a lot of room in this apartment. You can stay in one of the bedrooms. It could even be good for our mission." He turns to look at Iris, who is still sitting hugging her knees on the seventeenth-century toilet. "We can prepare your visits to Mr. Travers together. I can give you some private classes in the history of art. To perfect your role and all that. At least until he decides to buy the paintings."

Iris Gonzalvo looks at Lucas Giraut with a face not entirely devoid of sympathy. Her body has tattoos and piercings in places where Giraut had no idea you could get tattoos and piercings. In places that don't show even when you're wearing summer clothes.

"There's something that doesn't fit in this whole story." Iris extends her arm as far as she can to take the lit cigarette Giraut is offering her from the bed. "I don't understand what a guy like you is doing working with a guy like Bocanegra. It's really weird. And I think it has something to do with your father. With what happened to your father. And with you wanting to get revenge on whoever sent him to jail." She releases a mouthful of smoke and gives the cigarette back to Giraut through the space between the bed and the antique toilet. "I think you're hiding something. That you have plans you're not telling anyone. I don't know exactly what kind of plans. But I think you're planning to do something incredibly stupid. Like stabbing Bocanegra in the back. Stealing his money, or the paintings." She shrugs her shoulders. "Or both."

Lucas Giraut doesn't say anything. Through the floorboards you can hear the vibration of the music Marcia Parini is listening to in the apartment downstairs.

"Do you have *any idea* what someone like Bocanegra would do to you if he found out what you're planning?" Iris looks at Giraut with a frown. "Why do you think Bocanegra knows people like Travers, or that guy that forged the paintings? Because he's *powerful*. And I don't just mean rich. I mean that you can't steal anything from these people and then hide. Excuse me, but you don't know anything about criminals. I know a few things."

"A few months ago I found one of my father's accounting ledgers." Giraut gives the cigarette back to Iris again. "My father had it hidden in a secret place. In Apartment Thirteen. I still can't believe that no one found it before I did. It was his secret accounting. That didn't even show up in the company's private ledgers. You can't even imagine the amount of money my father was dealing with. I'm not surprised that the ledger was so well hidden. When I read it, I discovered something. I found the answer I was looking for." He sits up to lean his head on one arm so he can look at Iris while he talks. "My father had stopped doing business with Bocanegra three or four months before he was betrayed. All his dealings were with a guy named Koldo Cruz. They had shut Bocanegra out. They may have been doing business behind his back. And then my father was handed over to the police and sent to jail. And guess what else. A year later someone put a bomb in Koldo Cruz's house. And very nearly killed him. You understand?"

She stares at him blankly.

"It's obvious," continues Giraut. "It was Bocanegra. He betrayed my father. And then he tried to kill Koldo Cruz. I guess to protect himself. It all fits."

"And now you are going to betray him," she says. In a slightly lower voice.

"The money will go through my hands," he says. "And the paintings as well. Bocanegra has got it in his head that I'm like a son to him. So he trusts me completely." He pauses. "After what he did to my father."

"And you weren't planning on telling me any of this?" she says. In a hurt tone. "Imagine Bocanegra thinks that I'm mixed up in all this. Imagine what he could do to *a girl*."

There is a moment of silence. In spite of her words, Iris Gonzalvo's tone isn't the irritated tone of someone who has just realized that they are at the short end of a secret plan. In fact, it is more like the pitiful tone of someone that has just been set aside by someone they have special feelings for.

"I thought of something else I should tell you," says Lucas Giraut finally. Looking at the ceiling beams again, through a pale cloud of cigarette smoke. "I was thinking of taking you with me when I steal the money and the paintings. You and Valentina."

In the Years of Physical Impossibility, the terms in which said impossibility manifested itself were rigorously strict. Lucas's parents were never, ever seen together, not even in the Giraut family house in the Ampurdan. On the rare occasions that the entire family went to the house in the Ampurdan also known as Villa Estefanía, Lorenzo Giraut went there in his personal patriarchal car two days before the rest of the family. So when his wife and son arrived in the company car, he was already installed in his study with the windows covered by opaque curtains and it was impossible to see him beyond his occasional strolls at dusk along the breakwater or driving his car toward town. Watched by a boy with binoculars from one of the windows of the North Wing, also known as the Boy's Wing.

After a moment, Iris smiles. She points her head toward Giraut's crotch.

"I think your dick is small, too," she says. "I'm not sure."

CHAPTER 50

The Story's Ultimate Meaning

As the weeks pass and Iris Gonzalvo makes more visits to Travers's palace in the heart of bourgeois Jewish Paris, she has gotten used to her host's eccentricities. The strange place where Travers seems to spend all his time. Even his conversation topics. Now Iris flies to Paris a couple of times a week and a car takes her straight from the airport to the palace's porticoed patio. The sequence of events is always the same. When they are both sitting in front of the smoking salon's fireplace, they almost never mention the business that they supposedly should be doing, or the St. Kieran Panels. Most of the time Travers seems happy to have her keeping him company. He talks and she half listens, sometimes flipping through one of the magazines or catalogues that are strewn around the room. The lack of progress in the negotiation doesn't seem to upset anyone that she works for. Neither Giraut nor Bocanegra seems nervous. No news, Bocanegra said proudly to her one day, is good news. This afternoon, however, an absurdly cold afternoon in late February, Iris Gonzalvo is sitting as always in the armchair in front of the fireplace when Travers stands up. He goes to look for a book on one of the room's bookshelves and he opens it on the small table in front of Iris.

"You are an intelligent woman," says Travers. Today he seems to be wearing the tattered remains of a silk dressing gown over his frayed wool sweater. All his clothing seems to have been rescued from some sort of natural disaster. "In addition to being very pretty. Tell me, please, from your *heart*, what do you think this painting means?"

Iris Gonzalvo leans forward a bit to better see the reproduction in the book that Travers is showing her. Beneath the inadequate light from a table lamp covered with a cloth. The title of the painting, according to the caption below the reproduction, is: *And They All Hid in the Caves and Among the Mountain Crags*. The painting shows some sort of hellish landscape. The sky is black and in the middle of it a black sun shines, surrounded by a crown of pale flames. There are fires on the horizon. The rocky landscape is filled with skeletons and dead people in pools of blood. The survivors crowd together inside caves and holes in the ground. They all look up at the sky in terror. They are all very pale. They embrace each other. Others are on their knees with their hands at their chests, praying. In general, it is clear that they are hiding from something, but the painting doesn't give enough information to understand what it is they're hiding from. Iris Gonzalvo recognizes the reproduction. It is one of the four paintings whose sale she is supposed to have been negotiating for weeks now. But she has no idea what it means. No one's explained that to her. They explained how much it's worth in the international market and how much the price will go up when it comes to light that the copies in the Hannah Linus Gallery are fakes. But nobody thought to give her an interpretation of the painting's meaning. Personally it reminds her of the covers of the heavy metal records her brothers listened to when she was a kid.

Travers is staring at her. Iris Gonzalvo decides to make up a response. It can't be worse than sitting there like an idiot and not saying anything, she thinks. She looks at the book. She points to the people hiding in the caves and the holes in the ground.

"All these people think that they're safe," she says. She shrugs her shoulders. "But they don't have a chance. I don't think even one of them is going to make it. I've known people like that. My ex-boyfriend was like that."

Travers nods, with a satisfied expression. Now he seems to be scratching a shred of his silk dressing gown, in a nervous gesture a doctor would probably find worrisome. He picks up the book with both hands and closes it. With the book under his arm, he nears a monogrammed lighter to Iris Gonzalvo, who uses it to light a cigarette. If there is some trace of relief in her face, luckily there isn't enough light for her host to see it.

"The story of the St. Kieran Panels is fascinating." Travers nods to himself. In spite of his sloppy appearance, which could be taken for the eccentricity of the extremely rich, Iris Gonzalvo doesn't see anything about him that makes him look like a rich eccentric. "As fascinating as the story of their creator, Brother Samhael Finnegan. Although there is little information on his life, they say he painted locked up in his cell by the light of a single candle. They also say he spent thirty years without leaving his cell in the St. Kieran monastery. It seems he was agoraphobic and photophobic. Two illnesses that are much more common than people realize." He heads to his cocktail cabinet filled with delicate-looking cut crystal bottles. He serves a couple of glasses of port and takes a cup in each hand. "In his day, of course, there was also the fear of the Apocalypse. Which they thought would arrive at some point near the millennium. All these things are in the paintings, of course. After his death, his legend grew throughout Ireland. They started calling him the Mad Monk of Limerick. His paintings were much rawer and much more terrifying than what people were used to seeing at the time. And there was the question of his last painting. The fourth in the series." He puts one of the glasses into Iris Gonzalvo's hand. "Have you heard about the fourth painting, Miss DeMink?"

Iris Gonzalvo takes a sip from her glass of port.

"The one they covered with a sheet," she says, remembering something Giraut had told her a couple of weeks earlier. "The one they didn't let people see."

Mr. Travers collapses into the armchair again. In front of the fire, one of his cats is licking his paws with a sleepy face. Iris Gonzalvo hasn't asked about the painting over the fireplace again. *The Somnambulist in the Ambulance.* After a month of coming to this room twice a week, she's made her own interpretation of the painting's composition of colored splotches. Although maybe it's merely a matter of suggestion. Her seeing the man lying inside an ambulance. A man that for some reason she now sees with a beard and dressed in women's clothing.

"Exactly," says Travers. "It seems that the last painting in the series took centuries to see the light of day. They had it hidden or well covered. In any case, they didn't think it was appropriate to have it in the church. From the very beginning, Brother Samhael's paintings were seen as dangerous. Something more than a series of religious paintings. They say that just seeing them caused changes to your spirit. In time, they became considered pagan objects." He leans forward to pet his cats with a strangely wrinkled hand. His hands seem to belong to an older person than the rest of his body. "When you think about it, it's a miracle that they've survived. Don't you agree?"

Iris puts down the magazine she is flipping through. She takes a drag on her cigarette with half-closed eyes.

"Someone told me you believe in magic," she says. "That maybe you want to use those paintings in some sort of ritual. Do you really think that the paintings, you know"—she shrugs—"have *powers*?"

"Doesn't their power to terrify people impress you? To make everyone afraid to look at them? To make someone voluntarily lock themselves up in a cell and throw away the key? Or to make people *rob and kill* for them? Perhaps you need to re-pose the question, Miss DeMink." Travers lifts up a cat. A Persian cat with yellow eyes. He takes it in his arms as if it were a child and the two, Travers and the cat, stare at her with slightly mocking expressions. "Perhaps we should ask ourselves if what we do with things like those paintings is important. If fate is something we can bend to our wills. That would be true magic. Or if we are just simply characters in a story. And therefore it doesn't matter where we hide. Because fear will always find us. Like that boyfriend you mentioned. I come from an important family of wizards, miss. Starting with my great-grandfather, Mr. Arthur Travers. Perhaps you've read something about him. But now." He makes a gesture that seems to indicate impotence, or at least a certain mysteriousness. "Does it matter if we use those paintings to invoke an angel, or a demon? Using them as talismans? Or if we melt down the canvas and paint and breathe in the vapors to fill ourselves with their power? That, young lady," says Travers, and Iris feels the weight of both the man's and the cat's gazes upon her, "is something that we'll only know if we try. Don't you think?"

Iris Gonzalvo stands up. She starts to walk through the smoking salon of Mr. Travers's palace in central Paris. During the weeks she's been coming there, she has grown used to finding ways to pass the time in that room. Reading magazines while Travers talks, or even doing the crossword puzzles in the newspaper and nodding once in

a while or saying "mmm" in that way people say "mmm" to indicate
that in some part of their mind they're still listening. Most of the
time, however, she walks around the room. To the point that she is
already familiar with most of its elements. With the World War II
battle reconstructions and with the artworks and antiques piled up everywhere. With the antique toys that always make her think of horror
films. With the giant glass display cases filled with curios. Taxidermied things and things in bottles of alcohol. And yet, she thinks now,
she's never *really* understood what kind of place she's in. She has never
managed to assimilate *on a deeper level* the idea of the place and the man
locked up inside it. Surrounded by strange things and fake things. She
hasn't really considered what that man's mind must be like. Except for
the fact that she suspects that the smoking salon and the man's mind
must be very similar. If not one and the same.

Now she stops in one of the corners of the room. She stands there
looking at something hanging from the wall. It appears to be a fishing
trophy. A commemorative plaque with engraved nautical motifs and
the framed photograph of the winner proudly holding up the first-
prize winning piece. Grabbing it by the tail with an arm sheathed in a
glove up to the elbow. Iris furrows her brow. The photograph has suddenly made her think of Lucas Giraut. Wasn't Giraut talking to her a
few days ago about something having to do with his family and fishing
trophies? She can't remember, and yet she has the feeling that the photograph is important. Important in a way she doesn't understand. Like
the room itself. Like the man seated in front of the fire.

"The first day I came here," she says finally. Without looking at
Travers. "You told me that you could explain the meaning of everything to me. I mean, the meaning of what we're doing. Why we're here
and all that. You told me that you were the character in this story that
had the answers." She runs a finger along the fishing trophy plaque
and looks at her fingertip. It's black from the layer of dust covering the
plaque. "What exactly did you mean by that?"

"I mean that I'm the only one that knows the *whole* story." Travers's tone isn't mysterious. It is simple and natural. As if he were saying something perfectly obvious. "From the beginning. From Camber Sands. From the Down With The Sun Society. After all, I'm old enough to remember everything. You can't know a story's ultimate meaning until you know the whole story."

Iris Gonzalvo runs her fingers over the plaque on the trophy to remove the dust covering it. Until she can read the inscription. The plaque says that the winner of this first prize for deep-sea fishing is Estefanía Giraut. The trophy seems to be more than thirty years old.

"Do you also know what's going to happen?" says Iris finally. After thinking for a moment. "Do you know what's going to happen with the paintings? Will there be a deal? Are you going to keep them?"

Travers lets out one of his affable, crowing laughs.

"Is that a trick question?" he says. "Are you trying to worm an answer out of me?" He pauses, during which Iris can imagine him perfectly, stroking his cat's head. In that way that certain characters in vampire stories stroke cats' heads. "Don't worry. I'll make a deal with you. I'm interested in buying the paintings. You can tell your bosses. Everything is moving forward. As much as it pains me to lose you. But by my age, I've learned to get over farewells."

Iris Gonzalvo approaches the sofa where Travers is seated. With her arms crossed.

"And that's it?" she says. "That's all? That's the only thing I had to do? Sit here two afternoons a week for a month and wait?"

The way her arms are crossed is that way some people cross their arms when asking for an explanation. Especially some mothers or wives or teachers.

"Waiting is undervalued these days," says Travers, completely calm. "Imagine, in centuries past, people used to wait entire decades for the stars to align in a particular way. In your case, you just waited for certain things to happen."

Iris Gonzalvo takes her red leather Adeline André coat and her purse from one of the room's coatracks. She puts on her coat herself and takes out the satellite phone to see what time it is. Then she turns for the last time.

"One more question," she says, looking toward the flames in the fireplace.

"Yes?"

"What does the painting mean?" she says. "The one with the people hiding in the caves."

Travers gets up from the armchair and stares at her.

"Oh," he says in an amused tone, "that. It just means that something terrible is going to happen. It's the third sign that something terrible is going to happen."

Iris thinks about it for a moment and then nods. Mr. Travers has already become a mere black silhouette with the gleam of the flames in the background. A ragged, swollen silhouette, with a tangle of long curls that fall. Iris puts her purse over her shoulder. She waves goodbye and closes the door behind her.

CHAPTER 51

People Are the Ones That Leave

Lucas Giraut walks down the stairs that lead from his apartment on the upper floor of the former ducal palace to the door to the street, where someone has been ringing the doorbell for a minute already. The insistence of the ringer's ringing is the insistence of a lunatic. Although the door to the street is two large wooden doors with iron rivets, the door that opens is a smaller door inside one of them. The bell for the upstairs apartment where Giraut lives has a high-pitched sound that reverberates throughout the building. Unlike the much softer electronic buzzing sounds you hear when you ring most modern doorbells.

At the foot of the stairs, Giraut adjusts the lapels of his suit in an oblivious gesture, runs a hand through his hair and opens the small wooden door inside the larger ones. Eric Yanel smiles at him from the other side. He lifts a hand in greeting and gives Giraut a kick in the groin that makes him double over and leaves him on the ground, at the foot of the stairs.

"That's how I like it." Yanel goes in and closes the door behind him. "Now we're starting to understand each other. No, really. I think that from now on we can begin to have a more satisfying relationship. More equal. You've got her upstairs, right? I wouldn't want to have come over to this shithole and find she had just gone out shopping. Or that's she's out fucking someone. Just when I come to take her back *home*," he says. In spite of his impeccably clean and pressed white Paul Smith polo sweater and tweed trousers, certain physical changes that Yanel has undergone in the last few weeks are hard not to notice. His face is pale and soft and his eyes glassier than usual, and beneath his white Paul Smith sweater you can see the incipient but firm curve of a flabby belly that was never there before. Not to mention his hair. One could go on and on about the changes in his hair. "Well, what?" he says. With his hands on his hips. Watching as Giraut twists on the ground. "Are you going to just lie there? Because it doesn't seem very hospitable to me."

Lucas Giraut's face is very red and his eyes are tightly shut and he's chewing on his lip. His style of twisting on the ground consists basically in rolling on his back with his body shriveled, and bringing his knees to his chest. Yanel grabs him by the collar of his cobalt blue Lino Rossi suit, pulls him up until he manages to get him somewhat vertical and pushes him upstairs. The staircase that goes up to Giraut's apartment is one of those marble staircases with a carved marble balustrade. The kind that make you think of women from days gone by with complicated evening gowns elegantly descending the stairs. Under the attentive gaze of a multitude of suitors with tuxedos and expectant faces. Yanel half escorts, half pushes and half drags his host

up the stairs and into the living room of his apartment. Giraut, meanwhile, seems to be having trouble breathing.

Sitting on one of the living room's leather sofas, Iris Gonzalvo and
Marcia Parini look up from the photo album that Marcia is showing
Iris and stare at the two men who have just come in. The photos show
Valentina Parini in various stages of her life. Lucas Giraut collapses
into an armchair. Covering his crotch with his hands.

"Eric?" Iris Gonzalvo looks at Eric with a mix of surprise and
commiseration. "What happened to your hair? You look horrible."
She raises a hand to her immaculate neck. "I think that's the most
horrible hair I've ever seen in my life."

Eric Yanel looks at himself in a silver-framed mirror on the wall
in front of him. His hair is no longer long, blond and meticulously
coiffed in some sort of French side wave. Like Johnny Hallyday's. Like
Alain Delon's. Now it looks a little like a doll's fake hair, teased up with
grime after months in a closet. It also looks like those old brooms that
had very rigid fibers, made of something like straw. In the armchair,
Lucas Giraut seems to be regaining a more or less normal breathing
rate. It also looks like at some point in the last few weeks Yanel has
picked up the habit of moving his lips when he's thinking or talking to
himself. Without any sound coming out.

"No one understands how hard it is to be me." Eric walks from
one side of the living room to the other. He takes a cigarette out of a
pack, but instead of lighting it he just puts it between his lips and puts
the pack back in his pocket. His exceptionally glassy eyes are also filled
with small inflamed capillaries. "Because of all the prejudices. The . . .
what are they called? . . . the preconceived notions. The clichés about
the acting profession. People think I spend my life in luxury hotels.
Drinking expensive cocktails and *sunbathing*. That I have money for
my every whim. That I go around in a private jet. I don't know what
else. People think that women just throw themselves at me and that
I'm *incredibly happy*."

His cigarette is still not lit. Yanel is grabbing it with his fingers and bringing it to his mouth and sucking his cheeks in as if he were smoking. Even though it's not lit. The spatial pattern of his steps around the living room is like that mathematical symbol that can either be the number eight or infinity.

"People think I'm like Brad Pitt," he continues. "Or like George Clooney. Maybe more like Brad Pitt. That my life is like some young handsome single actor's life who has no problems and luck smiling on him all the fucking time. Maybe more like Orlando Bloom. People think I'm on Capri. Or on the Côte d'Azur. People call me up and say, 'Shit, Yanel. How are you? Are you on the Côte d'Azur? I wish I was as lucky as you.' People," he says in a vaguely melancholy tone. For a moment he seems to have lost his train of thought. He takes a drag on his unlit cigarette. "Well, that's *not* how it is. I may be handsome and well dressed, but my life *sucks*. I'm *broke*. I'm not on the Côte d'Azur. I'm in an idiot's apartment in a shithole of a neighborhood. But people don't like to hear that. People *hate* losers like me."

"I don't find you that handsome," says Marcia Parini with a calculating expression. "At most, kind of interesting." Marcia inspects Yanel with one of those vertical looks that travel over someone's entire body and make you think vaguely of a scanner's sweep. One of those looks that are traditionally associated with sexual predation. "The clothes are fine. Maybe if you fixed yourself up a bit more."

"I *hate* people," continues Yanel. Looking at Giraut. Looking him up and down with something similar to scientific interest. Giraut is still in the same armchair. He no longer has his hands at his crotch. He no longer has difficulty breathing. The dark red color in his face is now limited to his cheeks and where he would have cheekbones if his face weren't so round and soft. "If you don't fulfill their expectations of you, people shit all over you. They leave you by the side of the road *and* shit all over you. Acquaintances. Friends. Agents. Girlfriends. Especially girlfriends. They leave home when you're taking a little nap and forget to mention that they're going. That is what people are like basically. Always ready to leave when you don't have a yacht docked on the Côte d'Azur. When you are having problems and your agent only calls you for ridiculous commercials. When the only part of you that people recognize is your armpit. When your debts are as big as the foreign debt of a small third-world country." The pattern of his steps around the living room is still essentially identifiable with the number eight or the infinity symbol. Sporadically alternating with circular and spiral patterns. The general effect is vaguely hypnotic. "That's how people are. *People are the ones who leave.* They're equivalent terms. Everyone leaves. Girlfriends leave. The people that don't answer your calls are the ones who leave. People that don't call. People that don't want to lend you more money. People that don't offer you contracts." He pauses again and for a moment it seems he is out of breath. He takes a long, deep drag on the unlit cigarette as if the cigarette could give him some oxygen. "People that don't say good morning in the stairway."

There is a moment of silence. Marcia Parini is turning the pages of the photo album she has in her hands with a pensive face and once in a while looks up furtively at the guy walking around the living room with an unlit cigarette in his hand, blowing out invisible puffs of smoke. The way people look furtively when they feel they're in a situation they shouldn't be in and seeing things that are none of their business. Lucas Giraut remains seated in his armchair. In that posture of his, with his back very rigid and his arms horizontally rigid on the arms of the chair. Like some kind of replica of those pharaonic images sculpted in stone. Without looking at Yanel. Looking at a point that apparently doesn't correspond with the location of any of the people in the room.

"He doesn't even have nice armpits," says Iris Gonzalvo. Shrugging her shoulders. With an expression that says she's just stating a fact, not making any sort of judgment. "They let him be in the deodorant commercial because he gave the director a bag of coke this big." She makes a gesture with her hands to represent the size of the bag in question. "Which, by the way, he never paid for. The coke. And you aren't smoking a cigarette," she adds, now addressing Yanel and pointing to his unlit cigarette. "What the hell do you think you're smoking?"

Eric Yanel stares at Iris for a long moment. As if he wanted to make an angry comeback but he still hadn't thought up what to say exactly. With his mouth half open. As if he were about to reply. Then he looks down. He stares at the cigarette in his hand. His expression isn't exactly one of surprise. The moment is embarrassing. The only sound in the room is the sound of Marcia slowly turning the plastic-covered pages of her photo album. Finally Yanel sits down on the floor. On the rug. He sits on the rug and he hugs his knees and he buries his face between his knees and breaks out in tears. His sobs are too high-pitched and not very masculine.

"Typical," says Iris Gonzalvo. "I swear I was expecting this."

From the sofa comes the dull, somewhat leaden sound of Marcia Parini snapping the photo album shut. Iris and Giraut turn their respective heads to look. Marcia sighs. She gives the closed album to Iris, gets up from the sofa and goes over to where Yanel is sitting and crying noisily. She kneels down next to him and runs a hand over his shoulders.

"We all feel like that once in a while," she says. "Feeling alone is just that. A feeling. That's why you feel bad. I understand you. Look at me." Her tone of voice is not maternal. It lacks those soft, enveloping features that maternal voices have when comforting someone. "I'm thirty-four years old. My husband left me. My daughter is in a mental hospital and she hates me. And I can't find a husband. No matter how hard I try. And I really am trying. That might be the problem in and of itself."

Yanel stops sobbing for a moment, but doesn't lift his head up from between his knees. The only part of his head that is visible to the other people in the room is the back. Where the messy matted hair that looks like dusty, dirty doll hair is sticking up, like he hadn't washed it after sleeping on it.

"He can't stay here," says Iris Gonzalvo. "No one can invite him to spend the night."

Lucas Giraut passes a tissue to Marcia Parini. She tries to put it into Eric Yanel's hand.

"If anyone invites him to spend the night here I'm taking my things and leaving," says Iris Gonzalvo.

Out of the corner of his eye, still seated very rigidly on the sofa in a posture few would hesitate in calling pharaonic, Lucas Giraut can see that Marcia Parini is stroking Eric Yanel's dirty, messy hair.

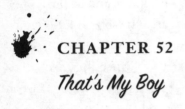

CHAPTER 52

That's My Boy

"That's my boy." Commissioner Farina jumps to his feet in the stands of the amateur racetrack. He pats Pavel on the shoulder and points to the amateur car of reduced dimensions that now makes its way along the start of the track piloted by Commissioner Farina's son. Pavel remains seated beside him with his handcuffed hands covered by a jacket. The car piloted by Commissioner Farina's son is now in second place and has the number two painted on the front. Farina applauds and puts the index and middle fingers of both hands into his mouth and lets out a long, powerful whistle. Then he sits back down in the stands to Pavel's right. "Do you want to know what I said to my boy when he got up this morning and we all had breakfast together at home? It's very important for us to have breakfast together. All at the same table. Even though my kids have to get up earlier than the rest of the kids in their class. We're one of those families, you know? What's the point of having kids if you can't show them the things that will guide them through life? And I'm very good at that. Because I'm a man with experience." He nods with satisfaction. "Nobody knows the things I've seen. Did I ever tell you my father was a policeman, too?"

Pavel moves his handcuffed hands forward and down, carefully so that the handcuffs don't show beneath his jacket, and picks up the cup of soda with a straw that he has in front of his feet. He brings the straw up to his mouth and takes a sip of soda. The cars in the race this morning are not professional ones, and were probably designed for children. They are not only reduced in size but they also don't seem to have any kind of bodywork beside the panel with the number painted on it. They look like unfinished prototypes, or chassis on wheels. Miniature car skeletons. Pavel is struck by the strange feeling that the machines are still growing and that in a few years they'll become normal race cars.

"I'm not saying that I want to do with my son *exactly* what my father did with me." Commissioner Farina applauds and whistles as the cars take the curve and make their way across the straight stretch on the other side of the circuit. The amateur circuit has an oval or elliptical shape, or actually more like if someone took a circumference and stretched its two diametrically opposed points. There are a lot of tires piled up around the track and in the island in the middle. Pavel isn't sure why there are so many tires everywhere. "I know times have changed and all that. What I told my son this morning while we were having breakfast is this. Son, I said. Sometimes I call him son and sometimes I call him David. David is his name. Son, this morning you are gonna make the whole family proud. You're gonna drive as if your father was chasing you with his standard-issue gun and you're going to beat all those other kids. But *above all*, most importantly, you can't come in second. Son, I told him, your father knows about life because it's his lot to see the things no one sees. Things that aren't pretty. And what I learned is this: in life only the people who win first place count. There's no prize for second place. You're the winner or you're the loser. That's what I told him. And he knows what he has to do if he doesn't want to spend the summer working in my father-in-law's garage."

Pavel puts the foam cup with a straw down on the ground in front of his feet and picks up the bag of salted peanuts next to it. He opens it with his teeth and spits out a piece of plastic. At the end of the first lap, Commissioner Farina's son's car, with the number two painted in white on green, is in fourth place. The car in the lead, very far ahead of the others, is the one with the number six. The number six is painted in red on white. You can't see any part of the kids piloting the cars except for their helmets and the gloves that grab the steering wheel. The gloves and helmets make their hands and heads look disproportionately large.

The official explanation for why Pavel finds himself this morning at an amateur racetrack instead of in a police custody cell is that Commissioner Farina didn't want to miss his son's first serious competition. Pavel looks around him. The stands are filled with adults and kids eating sandwiches that mostly come from the sausage stand at the entrance. Most of the adults seem to be fathers of drivers competing in the race. There are some mothers, too. They all shout and clap and whistle every time the cars pass. In a way that *also* seems like some sort of competition. A whistling and clapping competition. The various family groups look at each other suspiciously out of the corners of their eyes and seem susceptible to succumbing, at any moment, to an eruption of competitive tension.

Pavel looks around him with a frown. It doesn't seem to him that either the place or the situation are appropriate for any type of interrogation or official police conversation. Taking into account the risk that he now runs outside of his cell, given the circumstances. An hour ago, after they took him out of the police station and had him handcuffed on the sidewalk waiting for the car that would take him to the racetrack, a motorcycle pizza delivery guy had stopped in front of him and opened the pizza compartment on his motorcycle and Pavel had thrown himself to the ground and rolled about ten feet away to cover.

"Why have you bring me here?" Pavel talks with his cheek full of half-chewed peanuts. He swallows them and brings another handful to his mouth. "You can't fool me. I know you have scheme. I don't like it." He shakes his head, making his dreadlocks shake. "I want to go back in jail."

Commissioner Farina stands up again as the drivers make their way around the start of the third lap. Car number two has gotten ahead of one of its opponents and is now in third place. Commissioner Farina has lit a cigarette and is now alternating nervous drags with sporadic chewing on the cuticles of the hand that holds the cigarette. In the audience there are a good number of fathers on their feet and shouting to cheer their sons on or to protest the unsporting tactics of other people's sons. Farina pats down the inner pocket of the suit jacket he wears over a sport shirt and jeans. His jeans don't have the aerodynamic, second-skin cut of jeans popular with teens. And the hems have obviously been taken up. As is the case with the jeans of many married men over forty-five. Farina takes a wrinkled envelope out of the pocket of his jacket, gives it to Pavel and then returns to his paternal combination of cheers and cuticle biting and whistles of protest.

Pavel opens the envelope with his handcuffed hands still partially covered by the jacket. He pulls out the document inside and reads it. It is a ticket to Kingston with a layover in London for the plane leaving the next morning. In about twenty hours.

"You're basically a free man." Farina speaks without looking at Pavel. Standing up and ignoring the petitions of the spectators behind him who ask him to sit down. Smoking nervously and bringing his hand to his forehead in some sort of imprecise military salute meant to protect his eyes from the sun that falls directly onto the track. "Thank the Spanish police system. We're like that here. We have a long tradition of letting criminals go free. Almost everyone in business or politics is a criminal. And I personally don't see anyone bothering them." He pauses and whistles at the track again. The cars in second and third place seem to have closed in on the first, turning the race into what is technically referred to as *hotly contested*. "As for you." He shrugs his shoulders. "You're free, too. You're free to decide who orphans your sister of a brother. That's how you say it, right? You're free to decide if you want your friend Bocanegra to take you out or if you want it to be your Russian friends. In the end, it's an admirable situation. I mean it's admirable that you've managed to get everyone gunning for you. You must feel important. I can almost hear them sharpening their knives." He puts a hand near his ear as if he were listening carefully. "That's why I've brought you here, Bob Marley. So you can tell me some amusing story to brighten my day and make me a happy commissioner. Tell me a story or I'll set you free. And if you make it to the mailbox on the corner, I'll climb Montserrat in bare feet."

The sun falls directly on the unprotected stands of the amateur racetrack for cars built for, or adapted to, children. Cars that are like larvae of cars. Like arthropod cars. Pavel doesn't understand why the hell there are tons of tires everywhere. Pavel, by the way, doesn't give a shit about this race or any other kind of car race. He couldn't care less about a ton of people going around and around a cement island filled with tons of tires. In fact, he thinks, as he finishes the peanuts and throws the empty plastic bag to the ground and considers the possibility of bumming a cigarette from that idiot Farina, during the last few weeks he has gradually been discovering that most of the things that used to matter to him now mean nothing to him. Not his books of Rastafarian philosophy and his collection of music magazines with colored Post-its on the most relevant pages. Not his dresser filled with combat pants and T-shirts with the sleeves cut off. Not the pornographic novels that he buys at a bookstore in the Raval. Not his wonderful dreadlocks that have finally reached the approximate length of Marley's dreads on the cover of *Legend*. Not the extra money that he earns by ripping off Bocanegra and Leon and playing both sides. During the last few weeks Pavel has been thinking about going to live in the jungle. With the snakes and the bears. He's been thinking about building a house up in a tree so the Jamaican bears can't attack him at night, and building his own weapons out of wood and learning to hunt and fish. With a woman. With a black woman. Both of them naked all day long. Fucking all day long in his house up in a tree. And once in a while going down to Kingston, Jamaica. On weekends, maybe. To sell the fish and the game and exchange them for condoms and some bear traps, or something like that.

"Do you need a pen and paper?" Commissioner Farina hands him a notebook that doesn't look very official and a pen. "Let the ink flow, son. And the pen is just a loaner."

Pavel opens up the notebook to a blank page and pushes the button that makes the pen point appear. All kinds of pre-urban and pre-civilized images are running through his head. Pavel naked and up to his knees in a jungle river. Throwing a homemade spear with that same twist of his body that the Soviet javelin tossers used. With a twist that makes his waist-length dreads ripple in slow motion. And Pavel walking through the streets of Kingston on one of his highly awaited visits. With a string of bananas and fish over his shoulder. Wearing a loincloth and an old T-shirt where Bob Marley's face is now nothing more than a faded splotch. A souvenir from a much more confused period in his life. And all his Rastafarian brothers and sisters waving to him from the hammocks in front of their multicolored houses. Coming over to shake his hand in complicated ways reserved only for spiritual brothers. Offering him spliffs and hugging him. And the women's lascivious gazes running over his body, and him turning toward his ample-assed jungle concubine and shrugging his shoulders. With a resigned smile on his face. Tired but always high-spirited. Suddenly shouts are heard. Openly insulting shouts. Pavel looks up from his notebook. Now everyone is standing and Commissioner Farina and all the other fathers are shouting and waving their fists in the air. The amateur cars are rounding the final stretch. Behind him, two fathers appear to be fistfighting amidst the screams of their family members. Car number six comes in at first place followed closely by Commissioner Farina's son's car, number two. Pavel takes a sip of his soda through the straw as Farina shouts at his son, threatening to break open his stupid fat spoiled head. The rest of the cars cross the finish line in rapid succession under the glaring sun. Frowning, Pavel starts to write in the notebook in hesitant Latin letters.

CHAPTER 53

Smiling Dogs Chasing Butterflies

"She's obviously gotten worse," says the medical intern at the renowned children's psychiatric center where Valentina Parini is hospitalized. With serious professional consternation. "And all in the last two weeks. Paranoid attacks. Delusions. We've noticed an increase in the aggression that began before she came here. It seems there are security problems here at the center. We think she's been reading that book again. The Stephen King book. Which is where most of her delusions stem from. And yet"—he looks out of the corner of his eye at the table where Valentina is drawing with a box of colored pencils— "we don't understand how she could have gotten a copy. We strictly control everything that comes in or out of the center. We regularly search their rooms. Our committee reads all the books that come in. It's quite a mystery."

Lucas Giraut and Iris Gonzalvo nod their heads more or less simultaneously. They are both sitting with their legs tightly together and their hands on their laps at the foot of the child-size bed in Valentina Parini's room at the clinic. The colors and objects in the room seem to have been chosen based on their therapeutic qualities. The walls are painted in a sedative tone of light green. The television in front of the bed plays something that looks like a loop of calming images of deserted natural landscapes and animals in the wild. Around the bed, half a dozen members of the center's cleaning crew wearing very thin latex gloves are searching the room in search of Stephen King's New Novel. A female member of the crew is taking all of Valentina's clothes out of a drawer, unfolding them carefully and then refolding them into a cardboard box. Another one is standing on a bench and taking the curtains down. Another is kneeling on the ground checking to see if any of the floor tiles are loose. Giraut is wearing an ink blue Lino Rossi suit. Iris is wearing a sky blue Lilly Pulitzer dress with a low back but not a plunging neckline, and she decided not to wear much makeup. Considering that she's supposedly the stepmother of a poor girl locked up in a mental ward.

"How can you be so sure . . . ?" Iris reads the name on the ID tag that the medical intern has clipped to the front of his white coat and looks into his eyes. ". . . Victor? I mean, it doesn't seem possible that she's read that book. With such strict observation and so much staff here at the center. I imagine that you are investigating other possible causes of her deterioration. That's what *I* would do."

In one of the corners of the ceiling there is a security camera, which emits a buzz that's barely audible beneath the sedative music coming from the television. Iris Gonzalvo stares at the intern as she talks to him. With a convincingly maternal blend of frankness and worry. The intern whose name tag identifies him as Victor frowns.

"I *read* that book." He is turning the pages of his plastic-covered file as he speaks. Without looking at them. His expression of professional consternation sets itself apart from nonprofessional expressions of consternation by the slightly deeper tone of his voice and a hint of distracted calmness in the way he addresses them. "It's a good book. Entertaining, that's for sure. I'm not saying it's not interesting. Everybody likes that kind of entertaining book once in a while. But that's not the point. We have heard descriptions of certain creatures from Valentina. We have seen her make certain gestures with her hands when she's alone, on the security camera tapes. We've identified certain drawings on the inside of the bathroom stall doors." It seems that his way of turning pages in the file is just a nervous gesture, just like the chewing on a pen or playing with a little ball that other nervous people do when they talk. "It's obvious that she is identifying with what happens in the book." He shrugs his shoulders. "For example, she's convinced that I'm a slave to the aliens."

On the table where Valentina Parini is sitting, drawing with colored pencils on a pile of white drawing paper, there is a copy of *The Lost Rivers of London* by Álex Jardí. With the classic signs of wear on the spine that indicate it has been opened too wide. The book is on top of a tidy pile of books in large octavo format. All with the same dimensions. Valentina Parini doesn't seem to be trying to eavesdrop on what is happening on the other side of the room. Although her appearance hasn't changed noticeably since the last visit, somehow she isn't the same person. There is absolutely nothing childlike or prepubescent in her face or her expression. Her expression is determined and at the same time empty. They have cut her hair in a way that accentuates the verticality of her face and the wideness of her forehead and she is wearing a patch over her eye, held on by strips of translucent white hospital tape. What she's drawing on every sheet of paper are almost identical variations of the same drawing. A white dog with black spots chasing a butterfly.

"I understand perfectly how you must feel at times like this." The doctor crosses his arms in such a way that the plastic-covered file hangs from one of his hands beside his hip. "Considering that you have just flown in from Uruguay on the first flight after hearing the news and all that. But you have to understand that it is a very slow process. It could take weeks to get any response from her. We should be prepared."

One of the members of the cleaning crew clears his throat and indicates to Lucas Giraut and Iris Gonzalvo with a latex-glove-covered gesture that he needs to inspect the space under the bed they're sitting on. Giraut stands up and wipes the lower part of his back with both hands in an instinctive gesture that he does every time he gets up from a seat that isn't one of his own personal chairs. Next to him, Iris

Gonzalvo also stands. She picks up her handbag with the tag from the Montevideo airport still stuck to the handles and takes Giraut by the arm in a classic marital gesture. She kisses his hairless cheek, leaving an almost perfect red lipstick print. The intern looks at both of them with an intensified version of his slightly distracted expression of professional consternation.

"I'm going to leave you alone with the girl for a few minutes," he says. "It's the least we can do, I guess. Considering you haven't seen her in so many years. There's a button for emergencies by the door." The medical intern named Victor points to the corner of the ceiling where the security camera buzzes in a barely audible way. "And remember that we are watching the whole time."

Giraut waits for the members of the cleaning crew to leave, followed by the medical intern. The television is showing supposedly calming images of a group of male penguins chasing a terrified group of female penguins. In the Antarctic. Giraut approaches the tables, takes a chair and sits down. No one says anything. Iris remains standing by the bed.

"Valentina?" Giraut examines the drawings on the table with a frown. The dog chasing the butterfly has one of those anthropomorphic smiles typical of representations of animals in children's storybooks. The dog is smiling happily and chasing the butterfly with cheerful bounds through a field filled with flowers. The same drawing is repeated on each and every one of the sheets of drawing paper. "This is a highly secret meeting. We know what your situation is here."

Valentina rolls her only visible eye. Giraut thinks he can also see some sort of pursing of her lips that could be a mocking expression. The way she draws dogs chasing butterflies is: with the tip of her tongue sticking out through her lips, in that universal gesture associated with artistic concentration. She holds the colored pencils by grabbing them with almost her entire hand. Like little kids do. Giraut sighs and intertwines his fingers on top of the plastic surface of the table.

"You have lipstick on your face." Valentina speaks without looking up from the paper. "You don't have to explain anything. Thanks for the books." She shrugs. "I can't talk," she adds, and makes a subtle gesture with her only visible eye toward the only window in the visiting area.

Giraut looks at the window with a frown and then looks at Valentina. He gets up from his chair. He goes over to Iris and whispers something in her ear. Iris takes a pen out of her handbag with the airport tag and draws an X on the upper part of his neck. Then she turns so Giraut can draw an X on her neck, too.

"We bear the Mark of the Resistance," Giraut says to Valentina. Approaching the table again. "You can check it if you want."

Valentina stops halfway through drawing a canine smile with her tongue out and looks up. She puts the pencil down on the table. Her only visible eye looks at Giraut with interest. Giraut leans over the table and Valentina lowers the neck of his shirt a bit with her hand to examine the pen mark carefully.

"Is it grafted under your skin?" asks Valentina. The way she asks suggests that it isn't exactly a question. It doesn't exactly sound like a statement either. She runs her fingers over the recently drawn X and looks at her slightly ink-stained fingertips. "It's the mark of the rebels of the Resistance," she adds with a pensive face. "They must have a hidden laboratory. I've seen the Captors." Now she stares at Giraut. "They aren't hiding anymore. They don't care if we see them now. You can see them if you look through a window for a while and concentrate on the clouds. They don't look like angels. They look like those dinosaurs that had wings."

Giraut sits back down at the table and signals for Iris to come over. Behind and above their heads, the security camera buzzes and rotates very slightly on its base, which is drilled into the wall. Iris picks up one of the drawings on the table and looks at it blankly. Valentina brings her fingers to her face and tries to rip off the tape holding down her white patch.

"This is Penny." Giraut leans over the table to speak softly near Valentina's face. "She works with me now. We're going to get you out of here. Very soon. We have a plan. But you have to pretend that I'm your father. It is very important for you to remember that. You have to tell everyone who asks that your father came to visit you today. Your father and his second wife who came from Uruguay."

He stops when he sees that Valentina has managed to tear off half of the tape strips. A good part of her eyebrow is now missing from her face and stuck to the tape.

"We are in a very powerful control center." Valentina continues pulling on the tape. The skin on her face tenses and pulls away from her eye socket. There is no pain in her facial expression. Only the same mix of vacuity and determination. "The control centers are the only places they can communicate from. With their planet, I guess. Or with each other. You can see it's a control center because there are a few of them floating up above. Sometimes a lot more. Sometimes there are so many that if you see them from far away they look like a black cloud. And they can read our minds very easily here. It's like a transmission center." She pulls brusquely a few times and gets the patch completely off. The skin underneath is red and has traces of the tape's adhesive substance. You can't really call what's left an eyebrow. "This is a transmitter." She holds up the patch so Giraut and Iris can see it. "They can make them easily with their alien technology. Look at these strands here."

Lucas Giraut looks at Valentina's eye with a frown. The girl's left eye no longer looks in the same direction as the right one. Now it seems like her left eye is always looking at some place outside her visual field. At some point perpetually located to one side of wherever she's looking. The movement of Valentina's recently uncovered eye gives Giraut a strange feeling. It's hard for him not to look at it, or for him to concentrate on other things. Valentina throws the patch on the floor and steps on it with her institutional slipper.

"You can see your things again." Iris Gonzalvo picks up another drawing and looks at it thoughtfully. "When we get you out of here. We can go on a trip. Or you can go back to school if you want, or see your real father. Lucas told me you've never been on a trip. Since you were a little girl."

Iris Gonzalvo sits one butt cheek onto the plastic table. The way she's sitting doesn't convey informality, nor any neglect of the details of her public image. It's more like the way certain singers from other decades would sit one butt cheek on their musical accompanist's piano. With that old-fashioned feline elegance.

"This is very boring," says Valentina. "I have to spend all day drawing these stupid dogs. I look like a moron. But I have no choice. I have to keep my mind busy. Otherwise they can read my thoughts. If I draw what I'm really thinking about, they can learn more about me. So I draw these stupid dogs and try not to think about anything." She picks up one of the drawings and stares at it with a calculating expression. "I copied them from a kid's book."

Giraut stands up and walks to the window. The way he is standing in front of the window is: with his hands together behind his back. Looking at something that could be very close to the window, or very far away. In the novel *Wonderful World*, the characters that aren't mentally enslaved by the alien race known as the Captors carry out all sorts of repetitive mental activities to keep their minds empty and trick the alien mind readers. A group of boys from Portland, Maine, play video games during the hours they're on watch. While one of them stands guard at the window of the basement where they're hiding with a helmet protected by the Mark of the Resistance. Chuck Kimball, the main character, ends up perfecting the art of constructing models of historical buildings. A couple of old ladies in Augusta, Maine, play bridge all day and try to remain calm until they are found. A lot of the characters create games or mental routines during their workdays or when they have to venture out into the street, all the while hoping that someone from the Resistance will come to rescue them. Giraut doesn't remember there being anything in the novel about transmitters hidden in eye patches or threads of clothing.

"We only have one way out." Valentina balls up a fistful of drawings of smiling dogs, tosses them into a wastepaper basket and picks up a new pile of white drawing paper. "Getting to a place out of the transmitters' reach. Like a deserted island. And starting the world over. Having kids and all that."

Then she leans over the table and starts drawing again, with her brow furrowed and the tip of her tongue sticking out between her lips. With her left eye looking at some place located to the left of her visual field.

CHAPTER 54

A Vision of Smoke and Flowers

Iris Gonzalvo takes advantage of the privacy of her private compartment in the Talgo train to stretch out a slender leg, pull up her stocking and then do the same with the other leg. The first-class compartments of the Barcelona-Paris Talgo don't look like the private compartments of modern long-distance trains. They look like train compartments from the 1920s. The ones where sophisticated old ladies with fur stoles solved intricate murder cases before the disconcerted faces of police detectives. Iris finishes adjusting her stockings and is checking herself in the reflective surface on the inside of the compartment's glass door when the door opens with a heavy horizontal slide. Aníbal Manta stares at her with a frown as he holds the sliding door open with his enormous arms. His eyes still on her. Although his expression seems to be that of someone who has to go to the bathroom after holding it in for a long time, it is actually Manta's expression of intellectual effort that he usually uses to express some sort of suspicion. With his features drawn together and his brow awkwardly furrowed.

"Are you sure you have everything?" he says. "It's time to move."

The way he looks at Iris is that way people look at someone that has some sort of hospital gown sticking out from under their street clothes. Or someone that walks into a jewelry store with a guitar case. "Do you need us to go over it one more time?"

Iris takes a pack of cigarettes out of her purse and brings one to her lips. Then she leans forward and moves her butt along the seat until the tip of the cigarette is in reach of the lighter Aníbal Manta is holding out. This whole series of movements makes her breasts compress and project outward through the neckline of her blouse and makes her skirt retract to reveal most of her thighs. Manta lights her cigarette. Beneath his suspicious expression something else, something involuntary, appears. Some sort of spontaneous involuntary flicker of admiration. It isn't exactly an expression of sexual desire. It's more like that blend of admiration and confusion you can see in the faces of obese, introverted teenage boys when they look at explosively blooming teenage girls.

Iris stands up, her eyes squinted to keep the cigarette smoke out, and she pulls her skirt down with a pensive face. Looking at the snowy landscape on the other side of the window. The rural tableaux of livestock stables with snow-covered roofs. Cows completely still under the mist. Cows that look like statues of cows. They sometimes watch the train advance and sometimes don't. There is no trace of French shepherds or any other kind of French people. The train advances at full speed along some point on the route between Limoges and Orléans.

"Are you sure I don't know you from somewhere?" Aníbal Manta doesn't stop to speak as they walk in single file through the aisle between the different compartments of the Talgo. "There's something that doesn't fit."

Iris leads with her purse over her shoulder. Manta follows her closely with a black briefcase in his hand. The handle of the briefcase has the logo of Arnold Layne Experts. Personally designed by Mr. Bocanegra. Iris contemplates the snowy landscape of the countryside on some point of the route between Limoges and Orléans. While still walking. Through the partially steamed-up window of the aisle between the Talgo's first-class private compartments. Manta seems to have recovered part of his composure and continues his probing.

"What did you say your name was?" he asks. "Penny? I don't buy it. I'm convinced I know you from somewhere."

Iris keeps walking. In some of the fields the train passes there are fences made out of tree trunks that have doors for animals and openings too small for an animal to get through but big enough for a person to climb through, using a system of steps made out of trunks. During the first period of her romantic relationship with Eric Yanel, they spent three days at a horse farm in the part of France the Yanel family hails from. During one of those rare trips that Yanel took her on. Iris doesn't really have any bucolic memories of her visit to the horse farm. Not even close. Probably the most outstanding detail of said visit was the moment when she found Yanel having sex with the riding instructor. The same instructor that had given them a class that morning. The countryside was also snowy on that trip. In the guestrooms at the farm there were blankets that looked like untanned animal hides. With hair and everything. When Iris found them, the instructor was wearing her complete riding instructor uniform with the white pants around her ankles. The way Yanel was having sex with the instructor was: penetrating her from behind. In the position known as doggy style.

"You never worked at The Dark Side of the Moon?" says Aníbal Manta's voice from behind Iris Gonzalvo's back. With suspicious inflections that make you think of people with hospital robes sticking out from under their street clothes. Or dilettante grannies investigating complex criminal cases on board rural trains. "As a dancer? As a waitress? Or maybe working the private parties? This is ours."

Iris stops in front of a private compartment that's far from hers. She releases a mouthful of smoke and tosses her cigarette butt through a window. The tinted glass of the compartment only shows two anthropomorphic outlines sitting in facing seats. Iris knocks on the sliding glass door of the compartment and waits for one of the two occupants to open it. The door slides open and Iris is greeted by the identical smiles of Mr. Fleck and Mr. Downey. With their blond, freckled and partially bald heads. The one that has just opened the door looks first to one side of the aisle and then the other and finally makes a gesture indicating that Iris can enter.

"Miss DeMink," says Mr. Fleck, or maybe Mr. Downey, as he shakes her hand and moves aside so she can come into the compartment. "You can't imagine what a *pleasure* it is for us to see you again." He points with his head toward Aníbal Manta, who is standing on the other side of the door. "The bodyguard stays outside, as always."

Iris Gonzalvo sits down and waits for the two men to fill the seat in front of her. The Talgo compartment has opaque, reddish brown curtains. The seats are upholstered with a pattern that imitates tweed. The wall lamps have lampshades shaped like truncated cones. It all makes you think of dilettante old ladies and police detectives with waxed mustaches and an irrepressible fondness for a good meal. Of railway crimes involving numerous suspects and labyrinthine plots of personal betrayals.

"We want to convey our sadness at seeing you in these circumstances," says one of Mr. Travers's two employees.

"Talking about money is always unpleasant," says the other.

"If only we could skip this hassle." The first one makes some sort of helpless gesture with his hands. "But what can we do. It's the nature of business."

Iris Gonzalvo nods with a half smile and opens her purse. She pushes her hair off of her forehead and pulls out the envelope with the Arnold Layne Experts logo whose contents detail the amount of the financial request. Mr. Downey or Mr. Fleck takes the envelope and starts to tear the edge of it with a concentrated expression. Iris's gaze wanders to a building on the other side of the window that looks like a windmill without those giant blades that windmills have in puzzles and on posters at travel agencies. Something partially red moves through the fog near the windmill and Iris imagines that it is a riding instructor with her little red jacket and her white pants down at her ankles. Then she imagines more horseback-riding instructors with their butts in the air. Hiding from the train behind stables covered with snow and leaping through the fields with difficulty due to the fact that they have their pants down at their ankles. Dozens of riding instructors covering their butts with their hands. Chased by groups of teenagers with desire on their faces. Chased by men with their penises in their hands. Trying to jump over the fences made of tree trunks and falling into the snow because of the pants around their ankles.

A throat clearing brings her back to the reality of the compartment. Mr. Fleck or Mr. Downey takes the document out of the envelope and his gaze slides vertically down it until it reaches the money figure. He makes an expression of theatrical perplexity and passes it to his colleague. The second man reads the figure and looks at the first with an identical perplexed expression. Now that she has them in front of her, Iris Gonzalvo discovers that the similarity to the main character in *CSI* is less striking than she had previously thought. The freckled redhead that solves all the CSI cases, while not very expressive in general, gives off a powerful virility and self-confidence that these two guys don't at all. In fact, now that she can see them better under the natural light that comes in through the train windows, their skin has a texture that reminds her vaguely of plastic. Finally Mr. Fleck, or maybe Mr. Downey, folds the document again and puts it back in the envelope. Now both men have those stereotypical expressions of shock and perplexity and somewhat amused incredulousness that are part of the universal body language of financial negotiations. One of them lets out a giggle.

"The answer is *no*, of course," says the other. He takes a lighter out of his pocket and lights one of the corners of the envelope on fire. While holding it up by the opposite corner. "That, and that we are deeply disappointed. We aren't merchants, Miss DeMink. We don't

bargain. We don't talk about money like hawkers on a public street."
He pauses to watch how the envelope burns with a flame that's barely
visible under the light coming from the windows. Almost giving the
impression that the envelope is spontaneously turning black and being
consumed. "Mr. Travers is a very special person, we thought you understood that. A spiritually superior man. In many senses, more than
just a man."

Iris Gonzalvo watches as the building that could be a windmill
without giant blades becomes smaller and smaller in the distance.
Through the mist. The image of someone mounting a half-naked
riding instructor as if the instructor were a horse filters into her mind.
Smacking her on the ass with a riding crop. She blinks to make the
image disappear. She sighs and pulls a pack of cigarettes from her
purse. She stands up. Before the questioning gazes of the two balding
men with freckled, vaguely plastic skin.

"My bosses are very busy men." She brings another cigarette to her
lips and carries out the same gesture of asking for a light that makes her
breasts compress and project forward while at the same time making
her skirt retract toward her waist. Mr. Fleck and Mr. Downey simultaneously raise their hands to the inner pockets of their suit jackets in
search of their lighters. There is a moment of silence as she lights the
cigarette. Then she releases a mouthful of smoke and looks at first one
and then the other. "And even though you don't believe it, they aren't
interested in hearing stupid stories about spiritual leaders and dark
ceremonies. Because we *are* in business. So go home and explain to
Travers why you didn't get his beloved little paintings."

Mr. Fleck and Mr. Downey look at each other with worried faces.
Iris Gonzalvo reaches out her hand that isn't holding the cigarette
toward the handle of the compartment's tinted glass sliding door. On
the other side of which you can see the silhouette of Manta's back. A
silhouette larger than many clothes closets. One of the blond men
puts his palm against the door. Effectively blocking it from opening.
Iris stares at the freckled back of the hand. With her purse over her

shoulder. She takes a drag on her cigarette and releases a mouthful of smoke with her gaze fixed on the door and on the hand blocking her way.

"We all know what Arnold Layne *really* is," says the man whose hand is resting on the door. He gestures to Iris in the direction of the seat and waits for her to sit back down. Then he shakes his head. "And the kind of limitations it has when selling artistic material. Due to its very nature. That hasn't changed since the sixties."

"You guys are a band of two-bit thieves," says the other. "Basically, we're the only possible buyers for your paintings."

"Barcelona isn't even on the international map," adds the first.

Iris Gonzalvo takes the cigarette from her lips with a perfectly manicured hand. She feels none of the tension associated with danger that you supposedly feel when you get involved in the international crime world. What she feels has more to do with pieces finally falling into place in the enormous windmill puzzle of the cosmos. Through her mind float images of herself up on a giant stage. A stage much larger than the crappy stages at The Dark Side of the Moon. Filled with that horror movie smoke that looks like fog, the kind rock musicians used in the eighties. Standing on a stage filled with smoke, with an enormous bouquet of flowers in her arms, and offering her hand to a crowd driven wild with desire. A crowd made up of men that undress her with their eyes and clap wildly and throw both men and women's underwear onto the stage. Some seem to have their dicks in their hands. Behind the stage, a giant screen shows giant images of her. Sitting on a blue sofa. The sofa from the living room of Monica's apartment on *Friends*. Surrounded by the rest of the characters on the show. Discussing issues related to potential pregnancies and unexpected changes of sexual orientation.

"Your bosses don't have the kind of contacts in America or Japan that they'd need to move this kind of material," says one of Mr. Travers's employees. Sitting down again on the seat in front of Iris in the Talgo compartment. Wiping the sweat from his brow with a handkerchief. "Which means that you're bluffing. Which isn't very smart given the circumstances. I don't even think your bosses would agree with the way you're handling this negotiation."

Iris shrugs her shoulders. She takes a long drag on her cigarette with her brow furrowed and stands up again. She opens the heavy sliding door and steps out lightly before the questioning and vaguely alarmed face of Aníbal Manta.

Manta catches up with her at the end of the aisle. He grabs her by the arm.

"What's going on?" he says to her. The pressure he's putting on Iris's arm causes her to stare at him with an expression of hate and pain. "Where do you think you're going?"

A voice makes them both turn. Coming from the compartment's still-open sliding door. Through which sticks out a vaguely blond and partially bald face.

"Miss DeMink." The face traces a worried smile. "I think we can discuss your price. Although only as a provisional hypothesis. Without any firm commitment."

Iris looks at Manta with a defiant smile. Manta lets go of her arm.

CHAPTER 55

Fanny's Testimony

In the middle of the third hearing of his trial, sitting in the District Court's witness area, leaning slightly over the railing that separates his area from the rest of the room, Lucas Giraut confirms that something seems to have disappeared from the internal dynamics of his trial. Something almost impossible to identify. Something that has nothing to do with the trial's tension or any uncertainty about its outcome. Of course it has nothing to do with the sickly-looking lawyer's fervent attempts to change the course of that dynamic. On the other side of the railing, Carlos Chicote is sitting with his back curved. Rabidly chewing his nicotine-stained cuticles. Like some sort of accidental shipwreck survivor of the real questions that are being settled around him. Clinging to his scared smile. Which is like a facial floating plank of wood. The last stronghold of his businessman's identity.

"So then you are saying," says Giraut's lawyer of Hindustani or possibly Arab origin to Giraut. Talking into his microphone. Leaning indolently on the railing of the area reserved for the defense. With an indolence that somehow seems related to that indefinable something that Giraut's trial has been gradually losing over the three sessions. "You are saying that you met Mr. Chicote for the first time approximately a year and three months ago. At a birthday party for your mother. An event entirely unrelated to company business. That in fact you *never worked* with Mr. Chicote. That in fact Mr. Chicote *has never worked* in the building that houses LORENZO GIRAUT, LTD., in Barcelona. That you have never worked in the same workplace. What you are saying before this court, in other words," he says. With his tie indolently loose around the collar of his shirt. With his jacket indolently placed over the back of the institutional chair. "Is that you've only seen Mr. Chicote in person half a dozen times in your life. Before this trial began. That before this trial you had only seen Mr. Chicote on six occasions. And on none of those occasions did you deal with company matters. I want the bench to take good note"—he holds up a sheet of paper indolently for the bench members to see—"that Mr. Giraut was able to remember and precisely date every one of his encounters with Mr. Chicote. Including details regarding the date and place and motive for each encounter."

A court employee approaches the defense area to take the sheet of paper the non-Caucasian lawyer is holding up. The facially top-heavy judge is not leaning his head indolently on his hand. Nor has he taken off his shoes under his desk. Yet, there is something in his general attitude that seems to suggest the same indolent indifference of people who take off their shoes in public, or doodle on the paper in front of them, or rest their head wearily on the palm of one hand. The judge takes the paper that the court employee brings him and passes it to the court clerk, seated to his right on the bench. The clerk nods and passes it to a lower-ranking member of the judge's bench.

"Now I would like to ask you to remember," says the non-Caucasian lawyer. The way he privately plays with his pen as he talks consists in rhythmically pushing the button that makes the point appear against his chin. Creating a sound similar to a cricket's song. Which the microphone amplifies throughout the entire courtroom. "Can you remember other occasions in which your mother *made up stories*? I mean stories deliberately made up to damage your professional career or simply to cause you personal problems. Are you aware that your mother has been negatively manipulating the image others have of you? For example, when you were a child. For example, at school. Or perhaps in front of the other kids." He pauses as he reviews his copy of the interrogation script. The other copy is beside him. On the place at the defense table that Giraut has left empty to sit in the witness area. "I'm sure you can remember concrete examples. Moments in which your mother falsified documents to make you look ridiculous. In which she published false information about you. Or spread rumors."

"I object, Your Honor," says a voice from the area of the courtroom that is diametrically opposed to the defense area. A tense voice. That somehow *sounds* redheaded. If that's possible. "These type of considerations are not only irrelevant to the question at hand. They are *ridiculous*. These childhood incidents are not on trial here. Mrs. Giraut is not on trial here. And above all, we are not conducting a trial based on personal childhood recollections."

"Your Honor," says the non-Caucasian lawyer. With what appears to be complete calm bordering on indolence. "The question is relevant to my defense. And is based on proving the falseness of accusations against my client. Precedents of falsehoods are the argument on which my defense rests, Your Honor."

From the witness area, Giraut can clearly see Carlos Chicote's scared smile. On the other side of the railing. His curved back. His smiling mouth that is devouring his yellowed cuticles. His smile seems to have fossilized onto his face. His face seems to have entered a terrified vegetative trance state. Giraut realizes that he'd never noticed that Chicote must be more or less his same age. He's that kind of a person. The kind of person that can't be reduced to any sort of chronology outside of the business sphere. The audience in the first few rows also reflects the loss of something unidentifiable during the course of the judicial process. It isn't a mere question of entropic loss of energy. It's not a question of the usual inefficiency of district courts. It isn't a question of dramatic unexpected twists. Marcia Parini is in the audience. Passionately kissing Eric Yanel. Giraut can't see what's going on in the middle rows very well from the witness stand, but he has the impression that Yanel has a hand in Marcia's underwear. Fonseca and Estefanía "Fanny" Giraut's faces are, respectively, a treelike tangle of pulsating blood vessels and a mask partially hidden by sunglasses and a picture hat.

The judge sighs. He scratches his enormous forehead with a finger bent into a hook and finally signals with his vertically asymmetrical head for Lucas Giraut to answer his lawyer's question.

"My mother forged my grades in high school." Giraut answers with his hands on the railing of the witness area. With his back straight and a namby-pamby look on his hairless round face that doesn't seem to match his tall thin body. "For two trimesters of my secondary schooling. I still don't know exactly how she did it, but I suspect she must have hired someone to break into the school at night. It did no good, of course. I was one of the best students. The principal called me to his office and showed me the forgery. Which was a first-class forgery. He interviewed me with a psychologist present and asked me if I had enemies at school or if I could think of who could be behind what was happening with my grades. Then they gave me back my real grades. My mother had given me five Fs. I don't think I would have been able to go to college. Another time she threw a party for my birthday and showed a video in front of all the guests. Later I found out that she had paid the kids to come." He squints. His position within the courtroom is a distinct obstacle to his seeing exactly where Eric Yanel's hands are relative to Marcia Parini's underwear and nether regions. "Shall I explain more about the video and the birthday party?"

"Your Honor." The lawyer of Arab or more likely Hindustani origins makes a gesture indicating to Giraut that he doesn't need to continue. "I have no more questions. I will now give the members of the bench copies of the remaining pieces of evidence that have been mentioned in the hearing. The faxes and internal communication between Mr. Giraut and Mr. Chicote. The full transcription of Valentina Parini's clinical interview carried out by social services. And a selection of videos and written documents relating to the Giraut family in decisive phases of my client's personal growth."

The lawyer hands the evidence dossiers to a low-ranking subordinate of the court clerk. With his tie indolently loosened. With his sleeves indolently rolled up. With his gold pen indolently held between his teeth. There is a moment of transition during which the audience fills with whispering. Finally the judge bangs his gavel a few times to silence the room. The redheaded lawyer for the plaintiff stands up inside his prosecuting area delineated by a wooden railing. There are doors built into the railings of the specially delineated areas of the courtroom, which are indistinguishable from the rest of the railing when closed. The redheaded lawyer stands up and rests his knuckles on his desk and brings his mouth close to the microphone to speak.

"Mr. Giraut," he says. In *that* tone of contained moral indignation. That tone that's perfectly familiar to anyone who has watched a legal hearing or session of Congress on television. "Mr. Giraut," he repeats. "Please confirm the results of our investigations. If you would be so kind. So that this court can hear them," he says. His ears are of a color close to purple. Several wide sections of the skin on his face are now of a color close to purple. As opposed to his usual sickly paleness. "On the twelfth of January of this year you appeared at Mr. Koldo Cruz's residence. Who you knew to be a former professional partner and personal friend of your father. Instead of entering his building, you merely deposited an envelope in his private mailbox. The envelope contained a page from an accounting ledger and a letter that you forged. Written by you in the forged handwriting of your mother, with her forged signature. The ledger page confirms business contacts between the late Mr. Giraut and Mr. Cruz in the years between 1971 and 1977." He pauses. He clears his throat. "I'll remind you that all of the contents of the envelope are in this court's possession, Mr. Giraut. You found your father's accounting ledgers. His *second* set of ledgers. Which bring to light certain illegal operations carried out by your father. Certain connections with Russian criminal groups. And then you pretended to be your mother in order to extort Mr. Cruz. Because you were trying to incriminate your mother in a case of collusion with fraud and attempt at extortion. I don't need to note the seriousness of such facts." He stares at the judge's vertically disproportionate face. "I don't need to mention the importance of this *evidence* in my clients' lawsuit."

Lucas Giraut senses the expectant gazes of those watching the hearing. Like a single massive gaze focused on the witness stand. Like a small tingling at the back of his neck. He leans slightly forward with his body rigid and his hands resting on the railing and brings his face to the microphone.

"I don't know anyone named Koldo Cruz," says Giraut. "As I stated in my previous declarations. I never even heard that name before this trial. I have no knowledge of my father's business operations. Beyond the accounting ledgers and records I received from Mr. Fonseca. My father and I weren't very close." His voice starts to show nuances of perplexity and some degree of filial confusion. "Although I would have liked to know him better, of course."

"There is *no* proof." The definitely non-Caucasian lawyer speaks indolently in front of his microphone. With his pen between his teeth. With his shirtsleeves rolled up or, maybe, with one of those shirts that *come* rolled up. With one of those hems sewn into the sleeves. "There are no serious facts because there are no facts. There are no facts to refute. There are no fingerprints of any kind on that letter. The security camera at Mr. Cruz's home did not record any image of my client. The prosecution is basing his argument on mere conjecture. Not legal evidence, in short."

When the Hindustani or Semitic lawyer finishes his intervention there is none of the indistinct whispering the audience always does in courtrooms on television shows and in the movies. That whispering that always seems to suggest a mix of shock and malicious conjecturing. The only sounds coming from the audience are sporadic coughs and the clearing of throats and the occasional rustle produced by someone changing position on the benches.

"The witness Lucas Giraut may return to his seat," says the clerk's voice amplified by the speaker system. "The defense calls Estefanía Giraut to the stand."

A rustling of papers and pages turning spreads through the courtroom. Lucas Giraut enters the defendant's area through the section of the railing that functions as a door and closes it behind him. The new witness silently walks up the two steps to the witness stand. With her dark glasses. With her picture hat. With a stole over her shoulders. With the horrible, static mask that is her face sticking out under the glasses and the hat. Sections of unnaturally taut and shiny skin. As if instead of skin she had some kind of plastic substance that imitates skin in some old horror movie. One of those old horror movies from when special effects were in their infancy.

Fanny Giraut sits in the witness chair of the district courtroom. Giraut thinks that his mother has just placed her butt on the surface of the chair that is still warm from his own butt. For some reason the idea gives him some sort of small involuntary shiver down his back.

Estefanía "Fanny" Giraut looks out at the audience area. She does not clear her throat. She does not cross her legs. She doesn't do any of the semiconscious gestures or nervous noises associated with someone who has just taken the witness stand. Her face resides in a kingdom beyond all expressiveness.

"The defense may begin its questioning," say the speakers in a synthetic version of the clerk's voice. "The witness is reminded that she is under oath."

In the middle rows of the public, without the shield of any note-worthy architectural element, Eric Yanel and Marcia Parini are inter-twined in a position that suggests Elizabethan metaphors about beasts with two backs. With Yanel's hands exploring remote labyrinths of lace and silk. Technically speaking, Eric Yanel and Marcia Parini have been living together in Marcia's apartment in the Palau de la Mar Fosca for a week. Now, when he gets into his bed next to Iris Gonzalvo, Giraut usually can feel a certain vibrating in the beams and supporting walls of the ducal palace. Accompanied by stereotypically passionate shrieks from the apartment downstairs. Like those stereotypical shrieks and vibrations heard through the walls in sex comedies. Now it is Giraut's lawyer who opens the section of the railing with hinges that leads to the defendant's area and closes it behind him. With a bundle of papers in his hand. With his tie indolently loosened around his collar. With no piece of clothing specifically appropriate to a lawyer over his shirt with the rolled-up sleeves.

"Your Honor." The lawyer is rolling the bundle of papers in his hand. Creating a cylinder. "To continue I would like to demonstrate that Estefanía Giraut conspired and used illegal methods to prevent her late husband's last wishes from being carried out. In the sense that he designated his son as the primary shareholder in his corporation. I propose to demonstrate that Mrs. Giraut"—he points at Fanny Giraut with the paper cylinder—"met with her lawyer the day after her hus-band died to locate all existing copies of his will. And that, faced with the impossibility of replacing one of the copies, decided to begin a series of international operations designed to raise capital for an aggressive buyout of her son. None of these operations were authorized by the primary shareholder. Instead my client's signature was systematically forged. We attach a copy of these forgeries, Your Honor. My client was relegated to a position devoid of decision-making power while operations were carried out *behind his back* and without his consent."

The non-Caucasian lawyer points alternately at Fanny Giraut and at Fonseca with his rolled-up bundle. Using it in a way that makes you think of a scepter or a ceremonial staff. Giraut extends his neck from his area of the room in order to see the place where Fonseca is sitting. Fonseca's face is very pale and his jaw is tense in such a way that on his cheek a tense muscle trembles. The movements of the veins on his temples can't be made out clearly because of the distance.

"We will show," continues the lawyer, "that she tried to bribe and blackmail Mr. Lucas Giraut into giving up his stock. That she never gave him a chance. That there are documents supposedly written by my client that authorize illegal transactions to civil servants in the Bavarian government. Documents designed to implicate my client in cases of international corruption. That it was Mrs. Estefanía Giraut and her lawyer who deposited money into the Swiss bank accounts of various Bavarian politicians in order to obtain the concession for the restoration of an important public building. The Speyer Cathedral. And that, in the end, LORENZO GIRAUT, LTD., isn't qualified to take on that concession. That after a summary inspection, it's not licensed to operate in most of the countries that it operates in. That it is no more than a series of empty offices in various European capitals. With all their calls forwarded. We've looked into it, Your Honor. Empty warehouses. Without any consultants on the payroll. Without any international experts. Without any other executive positions than the one held by Mr. Chicote. Whose job seems to be contacting the payees of the deposits to the Swiss bank accounts." He unrolls the bundle of papers in his hand. He smooths it out with a few smacks of his palm. Then he holds it up so everyone in the courtroom can see it. Even though they're mostly smoothed out, the pages maintain a certain curl caused by the inertia of the materials. "And now we will present this evidence to the Court."

A court clerk takes the bundle from the lawyer's hand and distributes the different copies among the members at the table. The copy that he places on the desk of the fragile-skinned and copiously freckled lawyer for the plaintiff has a business card attached that reads: "BOCANEGRA GROUP, LTD., LEADERS IN THE ENTERTAINMENT SECTOR." With a cordial handwritten message on the back. The judge flips through his copy of the evidence dossier with his glasses almost at the tip of his nose and a complex system of wrinkles on his disproportionate forehead that look like isobars on a meteorological map. Then he takes off his glasses and looks at Fanny Giraut with an expression bordering on annoyance.

"Please respond to the accusations we have just heard, Mrs. Giraut." The isobars on the judge's forehead shake like low-pressure lines in the middle of a storm. The kind of forehead shaking usually associated with the elderly. "Since it seems the defense has just changed the course of these proceedings."

Estefanía "Fanny" Giraut doesn't say anything. Although her eyes remain invisible behind her sunglasses, somehow her face conveys the impression that her eyes are simply looking straight ahead. Straight ahead and into the distance. As opposed to eyes that look at some concrete element in the public or in the court. A long moment passes. Audience members clear their throats, and cough and shift in their seats. Fanny Giraut's face doesn't show any alteration that could be associated with emotional reactions or any other kind of reactions. Her mouth is perfectly visible. Her mouth injected with collagen and silicone and painted dark red. In the middle of her sunken cheeks and unnaturally taut skin. The frequency of the throat clearings seems to increase.

"This court will remind the witness," says the synthesized voice of the clerk, "that she is under an oath which also requires her to answer the questions she is asked."

Silence. There is something essentially nonvisual in the way Fanny Giraut appears to be simply looking straight ahead. Without her gaze focusing on any specific visual element. Lucas Giraut changes position, uncomfortable, and tries to get the idea of his mother sitting in a chair warmed by his own body heat out of his head.

"Mrs. Giraut?" says the top-heavy judge. Staring at the witness. With a hint of confusion or incomprehension in his tone.

And then something happens to Fanny Giraut's face. Something that can't be identified with any type of visible emotional reaction. Something that is still quite nonvisual. Not quite an answer. Some sort of facial expression. Which makes very clear that Fanny Giraut's face lacks the internal structure necessary for making an expression. Some sort of facial expression with her wide-open mouth and her intensely white, pointy teeth. An expression that bares her teeth. And which doesn't create any wrinkles around her mouth. A clenching of the tendons in her neck. An expression that bares her teeth and clenches her tendons, producing a not-very-human effect. A slight trembling of her picture hat.

"I should have strangled him at birth," says Estefanía Giraut through her teeth. Spraying little drops of saliva. With something that Lucas can't make out, but which seems to be a stream of white saliva slipping down her chin. With her voice strangely hoarse and a couple of octaves deeper than her usual tone. "I should have strangled him with the umbilical cord. I should have dropped him and stepped on his head. As soon as he was born." The trembling of her picture hat intensifies. "I should have thrown him against the wall. 'Til he had no head left."

The silence that follows Fanny Giraut's testimony is not sporadically interrupted by throat clearing or shuffling in the audience. It is a silence deeper than any Lucas can ever remember hearing.

WONDERFUL WORLD

By Stephen King

CHAPTER 59

The attack by the different factions of the Resistance on Capitol Hill had already been going on for twelve hours, according to Chuck Kimball's calculations. Without any kind of clocks, which would have immediately betrayed his location, Chuck had no way of knowing for sure. The mysterious electrical storm without any rain that had been battering the hill and its immediate surroundings since it got dark had kept him from telling the time by the sun or stars. The swirling mass of intensely black clouds already covered the entire sky. The Captors went in and out of the clouds, regrouping and plummeting down onto vehicles and the columns of the Resistance. It was an incredibly arduous battle, and the attackers had to fight bitterly for every inch of territory. Now Chuck had no doubt that the storm was Their work. It was one of their electromagnetic tricks.

Chuck crawled through the trees, followed by his group, to the mouth of the sewer that the Resistance had marked with a red cross. He used the crowbar he carried in his backpack to lift the round lid and looked around inside with his flashlight. The metal ladder that connected the entrance to the main tunnel disappeared into the dark depths. Chuck turned to look at Paul Clark and the rest of his command. There wasn't one of his men whose features didn't painfully show the effects of hunger and sleepless nights, and yet each of their faces showed a determination and courage that filled Chuck with pride.

Paul seemed to be able to see that in Chuck's look.

"We're ready when you are, Mr. Kimball," he said. Cocking his gun.

They all carried at least a couple of weapons, plus flashlights and the plastic explosives divided up among their four backpacks.

Chuck nodded and wiped the sweat from his forehead with his sleeve. He squatted beside the open sewer mouth, stuck one leg into the dark well, then the other, and finally began his descent. The descent that had to be the final episode in the war that began just two months earlier. The incursion that would decide the results of the conflict, one way or the other. The assault on Capitol Hill, with the hundreds of lives that would be lost before the sun came up, was nothing more than a distraction tactic to allow that small commando group to infiltrate the White House and find Doctor Angeli. The success of Chuck's mission would determine if that sacrifice was in vain.

Underground, in the main tunnel that, according to Chuck's map, connected the Hill's sewer system to the tunnel that led to the White House, Chuck moved forward in the middle of the group for what he calculated had to be four hundred yards. They all walked in silence along the elevated platforms that flanked the canal of wastewater. Paul and another young man in the local cell formed the scouting party, carrying flashlights taped to the barrels of their semiautomatic weapons. The beams of light swept the deserted tunnel as they advanced. There didn't seem to be any explosives or booby traps. If the Captors had foreseen an attack on the heart of their command center, their defense mechanisms were invisible to Chuck's group. For the moment.

Half an hour must have passed before Chuck found the tunnel fork. The walls and ceiling shook and resounded with each explosion on the surface, causing sand and rubble to rain down on the attack commando. Chuck pointed on his map to the steep uphill tunnel that split off to the right of the main tunnel.

"Here it is," he said. "This tunnel has channeled the piss and shit of every president of our nation for two centuries."

"Should I take off my hat?" Paul raised a hand to the bill of his cap jokily.

Stopped there at the entrance to the uphill tunnel, Chuck felt a knot in his stomach. There was no turning back. And yet, it was as if up until that moment he hadn't really considered the true magnitude and the very idea of what they had set out to do. Six people—five men and one woman—had set out to bring down an entire alien race who, by this point, had control over practically the entire planet Earth.

Paul must have sensed what was going through Chuck's head, because he put a hand on his shoulder and gave his collarbone a friendly pinch.

"We don't have much time," said Paul. "Our people are dying up there."

Chuck nodded and swallowed hard. They walked several hundred yards before the tunnel divided again. Now the commando members were splashing through a stream of cloudy water that flowed down with a babbling sound from somewhere high up on the hill. The sounds of the battle were constant and deafening.

After a moment, Chuck came up against Paul's back in the dark of the tunnel and realized that the scouting party had stopped. Paul and the other advance member of the commando were aiming their weapons upward. Pointing with their flashlights at the metal ladder that was the end of their underground expedition.

Chuck checked the map one more time and looked at his men. It was inevitable that he saw fear in their faces. None of the six had the least idea of what exactly they were going to find up there.

"Think of your loved ones," said Chuck, folding the map and putting it away in the pocket of his camouflage army jacket. The same American army that was now his enemy, and which was decimating them on Capitol Hill. "Of your families and your friends. We still have a chance to save them. I refuse to accept that the process is irreversible."

Five minutes later, the commandos had gone up the ladder and were in defense formation in some sort of underground room that Chuck identified as the lower section of one of those underground bunkers for the president. Part of the room had collapsed. The Resistance's rockets must have reached the White House.

"Let's go," he said, and undid the safety on his AK-47 automatic assault rifle—the same rifle that in the last fifty years had become a symbol of political resistance throughout the world.

The systems of bunkers below the White House seemed to be deserted. The elevators were run by magnetic cards, so they were forced to blow out a few doors and go up the emergency stairs. They went up four flights before arriving at the collapsed wall, saving them the problem of having to use explosives that could damage the building's structure even further. But where was everyone?

It didn't take them long to find out.

"Take cover!"

It was the youngest member of the commando team who had shouted. A boy that couldn't have been much more than eighteen years old.

The six team members took cover under the ruins. In that part of the building, the dim light was interrupted by flashes from the explosions outside that came in through the windows.

Chuck extended his neck to look in the direction the boy was pointing. There were half a dozen National Guardsmen, armed and wearing helmets, blocking the hallway right in front of them, beyond the rubble. It was the guardsmen's position that was strange. They seemed to be in a defensive formation, standing in the middle of the hallway, and yet their arms fell motionless at their sides, making the barrels of their guns drag along the floor. They also had their heads bowed, so their chins touched their chests. In that position of deactivated automaton that was beginning to be familiar to Chuck.

Chuck left his hiding spot.

"What the hell are you doing?" said Paul through his teeth from behind Chuck's back.

Chuck raised the palm of one hand to reassure him.

"Trust me," he said.

He walked up to the National Guardsmen and took off one of their helmets. He waved a hand in front of his face. The guardsman's pupils didn't respond to the stimulation.

"They're not here," said Chuck. "They're out there. In the battle."

The members of the Resistance commando unit slowly left their safe positions, but without lowering their guns and looking at their captain warily.

"The collective mind is busy with the battle," ventured Paul, stopping six feet in front of the National Guardsmen.

"Which means," said Chuck, "that the entire world is tuned into this battle. Probably the entire colonized world is filled with people like this." He nudged the chest of the National Guardsman in front of him with the tip of his AK-47. "Which means that we have a chance to get to him. To Doctor Angeli."

The six members of the commando unit resumed their path, following the signs on the walls that marked the way to the Oval Office. All the White House staff seemed to be at their posts. Sitting in front of their computers. The guides behind their counters. Office workers standing in front of photocopy machines, with their fallen arms still holding pages. There were National Guardsmen everywhere, some of them collapsed on the ground. Chuck and his men moved through them, stepping lightly and avoiding looking directly at their faces. At some point all those abandoned marionettes had been human beings like them. Maybe they still were in some corner of their minds.

They got to the Oval Office without any surprises. Paul blew out the retinal scanners and card readers with controlled explosions. The blasts from the plastic explosives could barely be heard through the thundering of the blasts outside. None of the commando members dared to peek out of any of the windows to see what was going on out there, to see how the battle was progressing.

And there it was, no doubt about it. The president's office. A place Chuck Kimball never dreamed he would visit and which he never would have had reason to visit if it weren't for all the horrible events of the last two months.

"Mr. Kimball," called out Paul from behind his back.

But Chuck was already making his way down the wide hallway filled with portraits. Walking slowly, with his gun lowered. His face showed uncertainty but also something new, something similar to curiosity or intense expectation. He wasn't sure if his men were following him or if they had remained in the doorway. He felt the carpet of the Oval Office, extremely soft and springy under his feet. The large office windows showed a panoramic view that was very similar to Chuck's idea of hell.

A large part of Capitol Hill was in flames. There were movements of troops around the Lincoln Memorial and—Chuck couldn't help seeing out of the corner of his eye—a black void where the obelisk of the Washington Monument should be.

Chuck walked along the springy carpet. There was someone, or something, in the middle of the office. Sitting in a chair. It was larger than a human being. Chuck stopped and stared at the office's occupant, fascinated. His entire body seemed to be in bandages, with bloodstains on several parts. On the wrists and on the sides and on the forehead. There was no visible head, although the bone configuration of its skull was undeniably similar to the skulls of the

Captors, which were structurally similar to snakes'.
Where the eyes should be there were two weak yellow
lights that could be seen through the bandages.

The office's occupant wasn't looking at Chuck. It
didn't seem that it was looking through the large
windows either. It seemed to just be concentrating
on something going on inside its head.

Chuck approached it cautiously. Now that he was
only about twelve feet from it, he could see a bit
more of its anatomy. That thing—whatever it was—was
one of them, or had been at some point. The bloodstains on its forehead matched the spot where the
Captors had those horns that moved like antennae.
The bloodstains on its sides could be easily linked
to the place where its wings had been, while the
stains on the wrists coincided with the spurs the
Captors had on the inner part of their reptilian
front limbs. So the rumors were true: that this
being related to the Captors—or probably the leader
or father of them all—had undergone several operations to remove body parts. And the result, thought
Chuck, was obscene: Doctor Angeli, if that was what
was sitting there imitating the posture of a human
being in the Oval Office, had been operated on so he
would look more human.

And that was when it happened: while Chuck was
thinking about all that, Doctor Angeli's head moved.
Just a little, just enough for the yellow lights of
his eyes to look in Chuck's direction.

Under that monster's gaze, which observed him as
it directed the battle, Chuck experienced an intense
feeling of guilt and shame. His hand was tightly
closed around his weapon, but he couldn't do anything
with it. What Chuck was feeling in that moment, as inexplicable as it was, was very similar to the feeling
of a child caught doing something he shouldn't. But
that creature wasn't his father or his mother. It
couldn't be, Chuck was telling himself. And yet, that
was exactly what he felt: an intensely filial remorse
and shame. That filled his mind completely. It didn't
matter that the conscious and still lucid part of

his mind knew perfectly well that that hellish being from another world was taking control of his emotions and his deepest feelings.

"Mr. Kimball?" said Paul's voice from the part of the office closest to the door. "What the hell are you doing?"

Chuck dropped his weapon on the desk of the Oval Office. Like some sort of offering to his parent. On the other side of the office windows, the battle seemed to be at its most bitter moment. It was almost impossible to hear over the booming explosions.

"Mr. Kimball!" said Paul's now openly alarmed voice. "Get away from it!"

But it was too late. Chuck had already given himself over completely to that yellow gaze. His entire being devoted to it. He fell to his knees and hugged that monster's leg and rested his head on its lap. Happily.

PART IV

*"Hide Us from the Face of He
Who Sits on the Throne"*

CHAPTER 56

Lucas Giraut

The lights come on over the dunes. Somewhere someone puts on a record. The lights that come on over the dunes are the kind that often illuminate dreams: like spotlights on a stage, although they don't seem to be hanging from any ceiling or supporting structure. And this *is* a dream. The Filial Dream of Camber Sands. As can be inferred by the partially destroyed, seaweed-covered sign that Lorenzo Giraut and his son Lucas are now looking at. "WELCOME TO CAMBER SANDS." Sitting on the dunes. At night. That's another of the main characteristics of the Filial Dream of Camber Sands. It's always at night.

"This doesn't make much sense." Lucas Giraut looks in the general direction of the beach's cafés and restaurants and a parking lot filled with cars. At its highest point, the sea is a half mile from the first buildings on the coastline. "I've never been to Camber Sands. You're the one who was here. This is where it happened. Where someone sold you out. I don't even like the beach." He shrugs. "Though I don't suppose you'd know that."

The relative ages of Lucas Giraut and his father are clearly off. As often happens in dreams. Lucas must be around thirty. His father is that indeterminate age fathers have when their sons are little kids.

"You have been here." Lorenzo Giraut smiles distractedly. "But you couldn't possibly remember. Because you haven't been here *yet*. But you will have by the time you have this dream."

Lucas Giraut furrows his brow. He searches in the pocket of his suit pants. He takes out a glossy brochure. With seaside views and full-color landscape photographs. The first page says: "THE FILIAL DREAM OF CAMBER SANDS: GENERAL OPERATING PRINCIPLES."

"If you've gotten this far," reads the brochure, "you must already have a pretty good idea of how this works. It's not like the signs are very *subtle*. Right, Lucas?"

Lorenzo Giraut shakes his head. Smiling.

"You never were very smart," he says. His tone isn't exactly mocking. It's that vaguely unintelligible something that Lucas has always associated with his father. That refusal to say things outright or to speak in any other way besides in enigmas. As if every conversation between father and son was some sort of unofficial test of his deductive reasoning skills. As if every one of his father's sentences was a reaffirmation of his father's essential unintelligibility.

"Wait," says Lorenzo. Looking into the distance. Toward something bright that approaches, floating over the beach restaurants. "One's coming. Hit the ground."

Lucas throws himself to the sand and lies facedown with his hands behind his head, just as he had seen somewhere that people do in potentially dangerous situations. Something moves a couple of inches from his sand-coated face. Maybe a crab. After a moment he can see a green glow reflected in the sand. Like the glow of radiation you see in some movies. He lifts his head slightly. Surreptitiously. The thing approaches, floating through the air. Over the restaurant roofs. Slowly. Bathing the coast of Camber Sands in its green glow. With its feet about four yards off the ground. The truth is it doesn't look like an angel. Its face is green. Green and very long, and it looks like the face of a corpse, except for the fact that its eyes are like very powerful flashlights or maybe like car headlights. It's missing a piece of its face, although it's hard to see because of the hood of its raincoat. Because the figure that floats over the rooftops giving off a green glow is wearing a raincoat. One of those long yellow raincoats fishermen wear. With seaweed and mollusk shells stuck to it and green fluorescent slime everywhere. With a starfish on its shoulder the way some storybook pirates have parrots.

"Is it one of them?" Lucas rests his face back on the sand. "One of the Captors?"

"I've never heard them called that," says his father. "Do you really think these things come from another planet?"

They both remain facedown on the sand for a minute. The floating green being approaches them and passes over them without making any sign of having seen them, and then finally heads off. Toward the north-northwest. During the seconds when the thing is right above their heads, Lucas can hear the sound it makes. An electric sound. A sound similar to an electric generator or the hum of an appliance. Like that sound refrigerators make at night, thinks Lucas Giraut.

Lucas waits for his father to get up before getting up himself and shaking the sand off of his suit and out of his hair. Over the roofs of the town, at least two hundred yards from where they are on the beach, there are more than half a dozen of those floating things. Floating. With their yellow slickers. With their arms extended out in front of their bodies. Some of them carry fishing rods in their hands. One of them has fishing nets tangled around its arms and head. The figures float and look down with their headlight eyes and Lucas understands what they're doing. They are searching. They are searching for survivors.

"Wait!" shouts Lucas to his father, who is already running with his bowed body toward the town. "I figured out who did it to you! Who *betrayed* you!"

A moment later he regrets having shouted. He covers his mouth with his hand. For a moment he had the impression that one of the floating figures turned its head and looked in his direction. With a pipe in its corpselike mouth. With the slime and the putrefaction eating away at its face. Then he starts running after his father.

The town of Camber consists of little more than a dozen tiny streets around the Lydd highway. That leads either to Rye or to Lydd-on-Sea. With the redbrick mass of the Hotel in the Sands at one side. The streets are small and have paving stones instead of asphalt and in general retain the placid picturesque atmosphere of the sixteenth century, which is when they were built. A placid, picturesque atmosphere that's quintessentially English. Now bathed in a radioactive green glow.

"Avoid open spaces," says Lorenzo Giraut to his son when they get to the first house in the town. Sitting on the ground and leaning on the back wall of the house. He picks up a stick and draws a sketch of the town on the sandy ground. "We have to get to the Map Store." He draws an X on the ground. "It's here, in the middle of town."

Father and son begin to walk, staying glued to the walls. At one point a space appears between the houses to his left and Lucas can see the far-off roofs of the village of Rye, bathed in green light. At a nearby corner they bump into a sign put up by the Local Tourism Office.

OLD LYDD ROAD ↑
FISHING TROPHIES AND AWARDS ↑
MERCHANTS DRIVE →
SEA ROAD →
OUTER DREAM & RYE ←
OTHER DREAMS ←

Following the sign's indications, they arrive at the enormous building that houses the Fishing Trophy Room. Lorenzo Giraut enters and makes a sign for Lucas to leave the light turned off. Lucas nods. Lorenzo flicks on his lighter and looks around. The walls are covered with display cases filled with fishing trophies and framed photographs of people wearing yellow slickers with fish in their hands. The decoration consists of fishing nets filled with mollusk shells and starfish and taxidermied fish. Lorenzo points to the other end of the room.

"We have to get there," he says. "You see that light?"

Lucas squints. At the other side of the room there is a window and at the other side of the window a light blinks on and off. Like those lights in spy movies that blink out Morse code. Giraut doesn't understand Morse code. Suddenly a deep, booming sound makes the walls and floor tremble. Several trophies fall inside their display cases and some of the framed photographs crash onto the floor. The sound continues. Becoming clearer and clearer. With the cadence of footsteps. Giant footsteps coming closer. Lucas looks at his father with a worried face.

"Don't blame me," says Lorenzo Giraut. In a mocking tone. "No one would have wanted to spend much time at home. With *your* mother." He shrugs his shoulders. "Blame that trip we made to London together. Before you were born. If we hadn't gone, later things wouldn't have gone so wrong. But none of that matters now. In fact, none of it ever mattered to me. You go on alone," he says. He gestures toward the window where the Morse lights blink. "Before she gets here."

Lucas Giraut starts to walk hurriedly along the trembling floor. Around him the trophy display cases are collapsing. Cracks appear on the walls. Rubble falls from the ceiling. Forcing Lucas to walk staying glued to the walls. Covering his head with his hands. Many of the framed photographs still on the walls are familiar to Lucas. They all seem to show the same person. Dressed in a yellow slicker. But in the photographs the person's face is always covered by a black square. On the black square it says "CENSORED BY THE DREAM AUTHORITY®." Lucas stumbles into the middle of the room, where there is a framed image larger than all the others. The frame is antique and gold and seems like it should frame a painting, not a fishing award. The black square, however, covers the entire image. Leaving a simple black square with a gold antique frame. "HIDE US FROM THE FACE OF HE WHO SITS ON THE THRONE," reads the label.

Lucas runs away from the censored picture across the last stretch of the room and arrives at the window, from which he can see the light. Whatever it is that is approaching with giant steps must already be upon them, because the thundering of footsteps is everywhere and several panes of glass are starting to shatter. Lucas looks back. His father is naked and old in a bed. Sweating. Waving good-bye. Then he opens the window and looks out at the place the lights are coming from.

It is an old store in an old building. The sign on the store says: "YE OLDE MAPPE SHOPPE." From the window of the Map Store, Valentina Parini is signaling to him with a flashlight. A patch covers one of the lenses of her small eyeglasses. When she sees that he is watching, Valentina starts to signal to him with her hand. She turns and points her flashlight at an X written in ballpoint on the back of her neck. The Protective Sign. The Fishing Trophy Room seems to be sinking around Lucas. Plaster dust rains down on his hair. The wall is crumbling. The sound of footsteps abruptly stops. Everything stops shaking.

The unexpected silence makes Lucas's ears ring. Suddenly, someone taps him on the shoulder.

CHAPTER 57

Mirror Ball

The events that take place in The Dark Side of the Moon at this point in this story unfold just like the images on the surface of a mirror ball. With the same flashing combination of simultaneity and succession. Warped into a mosaic of distorted fragments that appear and disappear with a blink and reappear every time the ball completes one of its rotations. Without any one of the images taking center stage for more than the infinitesimal instant it takes for it to be absorbed in your consciousness.

Mr. Bocanegra, Showbiz Impresario, is sitting on a bar stool in the Eclipse Room, flanked by two dancers dressed in G-strings and high heels. Holding a cocktail with a tiny umbrella in his right hand and a lit cigar in his left. Smiling broadly beneath his impeccably trimmed mustache.

Mr. Bocanegra is a bar, just as he often likes to say. Not exactly a catalyst or the glue that binds other elements together, like those people that everyone seems to know and around whom most of the leisure activities of a given city revolve. Not exactly like those people who always seem to be at the center of everything and whose function in life seems to be putting people who would otherwise act independently in touch with each other. Achieving groups that are more than the sum of their parts. Mr. Bocanegra is all that, but also something more. Something perhaps similar to what a bar is *literally*. Like a place. Like a comfy place where people can sit down and gather and talk and relax and order their favorite drink. Like a place designed for the enjoyment of life. Or at least that's how Mr. Bocanegra sees himself.

At the other side of the bar in the Eclipse Room, half a dozen waitresses under twenty years old and dressed in the official uniform of G-strings and stiletto heels serve drinks to groups of men in suits who unabashedly flirt with them and make the joke of trying to stick bills under the elastic strap of their G-strings. The joke is always the same. Night after night. The same boozed-up smile and the same arm reaching out over the bar trying to stick a folded fifty-euro bill under a G-string strap. The girls laugh at the joke and serve their drinks with professionally seductive smiles.

The Dark Side of the Moon's admission policy hasn't changed a bit in the last twenty-five years. Formal attire is still considered a requirement. Suits make Mr. Bocanegra feel good and comfortable and willing to show his Good Side. Suits are like the carpeted floor and the velvet sofas and the mirror balls and the quality wood paneling. They are like the thighs of The Dark Side of the Moon's girls when they brush against the velvet sofas. They are one of those things in life that make you feel good. They are, without a doubt, like statues. And there is nothing that makes Bocanegra feel as good as statues do.

On the stage of the Eclipse Room there are several dancers having sex with each other. On one of the tables closest to the stage, a member of the city government has gotten up on the table and is doing a supposedly erotic dance that consists mainly of rhythmic hip motions. With one of the table napkins tied around his head. A dozen of his sycophantic underlings laugh a little too hard at his attempts to be funny and clap to the beat of his pelvic movements.

Mr. Bocanegra has never been against the right kind of fun. In fact, he considers himself a *mastermind* of the right kind of fun.

Several customers at the tables closest to the door of the Eclipse Room have stopped paying attention to what's happening onstage and are now turned, with various degrees of concern on their faces, toward the door. Whatever's going on near the door, it still hasn't attracted the attention of the customers close to where Bocanegra is sitting. It still isn't visible to the waitresses serving drinks or to the drunken customers trying to stick wrinkled fifty-euro notes into their G-strings.

At the exact center of the room a gigantic mirror ball turns. Over the tables. The dancers having sex onstage and the clients reaching their arms over the bar and the statues are reflected in each one of its facets, as is the city government official dancing on the table. Whatever it is that's going on near the exit door is reflected there, too. And whatever it is, it is attracting more and more attention at more and more tables and some people are even standing up with alarmed faces. But for someone sitting near the bar to see what's going on at the door, the mirror ball would still have to make another full turn on its axis. The gigantic mirror ball that turns in the middle of the room turns slowly, and its rotations project hundreds and hundreds of brightly colored shapes onto the walls and the statues and the faces of the people. A statue near the bathrooms' entrance, representing the god Pan chasing a nymph, is dyed completely red, and then gold, and finally an amalgam of every color.

One of the dancers having sex onstage with two other dancers looks up, removes her hand from one of her sexual partners and stares at the door. Momentarily abandoning the sexual task she was in the middle of. She's just frozen, on her knees up onstage, looking at the door. With her brow furrowed. Other dancers onstage begin to stop as well. After a second, the politician dancing on the table with a napkin tied around his head, who has now also dropped his pants to thigh height and is festively shaking his rump, abruptly stops his dancing. He stares at the people coming in through the door for just a fraction of a second, and then pulls his pants up hurriedly.

The commotion spreads to the waitresses at the bar. To the customers farthest from the door. One of the waitresses at the bar, who has her back turned to the door, continues shaking a cocktail shaker with brio while all the others have stopped what they are doing and are now just looking at the door. Her shaking makes her bare breasts move awkwardly.

And finally the commotion reaches Bocanegra. As some of the customers have already gotten up from their tables and are literally running. Running between the tables. Jumping over toppled chairs and customers that have fallen to the floor in the midst of the confusion. Bocanegra turns his stool toward the place everyone suddenly seems to be fleeing from and looks. With his drink garnished with a tiny umbrella in one hand and his cigar in the other.

Commissioner Farina is walking toward the bar. With his hands in the pockets of his coat. Around him, about fifty uniformed policemen are intercepting customers trying to flee and in some cases taking them out of action with their official billy clubs. Some customers have climbed up onto the stage and are now trying to escape through the door to the dressing rooms behind the heavy velvet curtains. As usually happens in this kind of situation, the dancers that just a moment ago were practicing various modalities of sexual relations are now modestly covering their genitals and breasts with their hands. A couple of uniformed cops try to separate a middle-aged customer from a voluptuous statue of kneeling Aphrodite that he refuses to stop embracing.

Meanwhile, the mirror ball keeps turning in the middle of the room. Projecting its myriad shapes and colors on the walls and tables and terrified faces of the customers and the arms of the policemen, raised high as they bring down the more stubborn customers.

Commissioner Farina sits on the stool next to Bocanegra's. Bocanegra stares at him as he takes a pensive drag on his cigar.

"I'm guessing this is a joke," he says. Releasing a mouthful of cigar smoke in the general direction of Farina's face.

"Of course." Farina nods. Watching his lackeys work with something similar to paternal pride. Or perhaps with something similar to the amused pride of someone who has just made an effectively impressive entrance. "This is fun. I won't deny it. I'm having fun. Can we talk here?" He shrugs his shoulders. "Or are you going to invite me up to that famous private club upstairs?"

Onstage, the naked dancers watch the uniformed cops giving chase to the customers, from the same place where they were having sex. Bewildered and modestly covering their breasts and genitals. Some of them use the velvet curtains to cover themselves. There are customers in business suits lying facedown between the tables with their hands handcuffed behind their backs. There are customers with their heads bowed, talking to uniformed cops that are jotting down everything they say in their notebooks. The music is still playing. Somehow, the fact that the music is still playing is the most disconcerting element in the entire scene. The politician is on all fours, trying to escape behind the bar without being seen.

"Give the commissioner a drink." Bocanegra signals to a terrified waitress.

Farina looks around him. Clapping. Some of the uniformed cops make theatrical curtsies.

"I don't understand how you can stand to be around all these girls all day." He scratches his chin in a calculating gesture. "I would have arrested myself by now. I want the same thing you're having," he adds. "It looks good, with that umbrella. Elegant. Kind of like this place. It's got the Bocanegra style, I'd say."

One of the cops is posing with two of The Dark Side of the Moon's naked dancers while another takes a photograph with his cell phone. The posing cop takes the cap of his uniform off for a moment to run a hand through his hair and then smiles.

The terrified waitress gives Farina his drink, and he looks at it for a moment with an expression that blends sarcasm with genuine admiration.

"This is the message." Farina grabs the tiny umbrella in his drink with his fingertips and uses it to stir the contents of the glass in an absent gesture. The cocktail is a yellow color with hints of green that makes you think of nuclear waste and those spectrographic images they make of stars and heavenly bodies. "Before you get impatient. We've been talking to your friend Bob Marley. I'm not saying that it wasn't a bit of work to get him talking. But in the end we solve these things with psychology." He shrugs his shoulders. He looks around him. The Dark Side of the Moon customers that were putting up a fight are now lined up against a wall covered in fine wood paneling and erotic Indian engravings from the Mughal period. "The truth is that at first I had trouble putting things together. Your friend Bob Marley isn't very smart. A nice guy, sure. But I wouldn't give him any prizes for cleverness."

The multicolored reflection of the stage's spotlights on the rotating facets of the mirror ball illuminates, for a fraction of a second, the terrified face of a middle-aged man in a business suit that has just been discovered by the cops. Hidden behind a statue of Jupiter erotically chasing the mortal Alcmene. The multicolored light projects for a second onto his tense face and wide-open mouth and then continues its rotation. Bocanegra takes a drag on his cigar. A longer drag than any Farina has ever seen taken on any cigar ever.

"In general terms, you could say I know everything." Farina uses the toothpick stem of the umbrella to fish for a maraschino cherry in his radioactive cocktail. He spears the cherry and brings it to his mouth. He chews on it with an expression of someone chewing on something that wasn't really meant to be eaten. "I know the whole story. About the paintings you switched in the gallery that you're gonna sell to that

English guy next week." He smiles happily. "Actually I've made some appearances throughout the story. But discreetly. I suppose you already know that I picked up Bob Marley at your friend Cruz's house. Ex-friend. I'll admit that intrigued me. It was like I was seeing the details of something big, but I was missing the link between them. And then that name came up. Giraut. But Giraut was pushing up daisies. Then it hit me." He punches the palm of his hand the way some people do to show they've discovered something they hadn't been able to see up until that moment, due to paradoxical questions of proximity. "It was his *son*. When his father died you adopted the son. Not literally, of course. Is *that* who I think it is?" Farina points with his cocktail toward something crawling on the floor, followed by several uniformed cops.

Bocanegra looks toward where Farina is pointing. Things in The Dark Side of the Moon take place in a way very similar to the way things appear reflected in a mirror ball. Occupying the center of the scene both simultaneously and *at the same time* successively. In a way that makes it hard to concentrate on them. Bocanegra squints. To see better under the strobe lights that ricochet off the facets of the mirror ball. The city government official crawls between tables at the back of the room. Chased by several uniformed cops. Swerving to avoid people's legs. With a napkin still tied around his head. One of the cops throws himself to the ground and manages to grab him by a leg. A struggle ensues. The city official pulls the tablecloth off a nearby table and covers his face with it. Bocanegra looks away. The simultaneous and successive way that things are happening in The Dark Side of the Moon makes it hard to pay attention to them for more than a second.

"But of course." Farina points to Bocanegra with the tiny cocktail umbrella. It doesn't look like he's taken a sip of his drink yet. "If you wanted to adopt Giraut's little tyke there's something you'd have to do first. Because you and Giraut and Cruz make *three*. So you'd have to get rid of Cruz. Before the kid heard about him and decided to go with him. Like his pop did. When you guys were like brothers. Not literally, of course." He gestures with his glass toward the last traces of resistance among the clientele, entrenched on the stage and using chairs as weapons. As if said traces could offer some sort of support to what he's saying. "That's why you sent Bob Marley to his house. To take him out of circulation. I mean Cruz. Because you knew that sooner or later he'd find the little tyke or the little tyke would find him. And, anyway, I *don't* think this was the first time you tried it." He makes a theatrically intrigued look. As if he couldn't quite remember. "Wasn't there some story about a *bomb* or something like that? In the seventies?"

The last traces of resistance among The Dark Side of the Moon's clientele disappear. A couple of blows and a couple of groans are heard from the stage. Mr. Bocanegra, Showbiz Impresario, doesn't seem to be paying particular attention to what's going on around him. Apart from the fact that the drags he's taking on his cigar are much larger and deeper than any drag Farina has seen anyone take on any cigar ever, the only sign of worry that crops up on Bocanegra's face is a focused expression that's hard to decipher. It's not exactly that expression of furrowed brow and clenched jaw of someone trying to hide a mind racing with worry. Nor one of those impassive expressions betrayed only by an occasional, slightly awkward, swallowing of saliva. It's closer to that overly impassive and almost paradoxically distracted expression of large predators waiting crouched behind a thicket for the moment to leap onto their prey.

Farina signals with his hand to the uniformed cop that seems to be in charge of the operation.

"This is a courtesy visit," he says, leaving his untouched drink on the bar. "You can tell that to all these gentlemen. Purely routine. We're looking out for their safety, in a manner of speaking. One of those visits to make sure that everything is still going fine. I'm glad to see that everything's going fine." He stands up and absently smooths down his suit with his hands. "Although I'm afraid I'm gonna have to shut the place down. The mayor doesn't like this whole illegally bringing in underage girls stuff. Anyway, who's going to come after what happened tonight? This is the end, and you know it." He pauses thoughtfully. "That doesn't mean that I want to send you to jail. I can keep you out of jail. If you scratch my back, of course. You can give me the paintings now. Or better yet, give me the paintings and Giraut." He smiles. "Or even better still, next week you can give me the paintings, Giraut and the buyer."

Bocanegra watches Farina's back as Farina walks toward the door. The mirror ball projects a series of infinitesimally minute multicolored shapes on the back of his jacket.

At the back of the room, several Dark Side of the Moon employees in G-strings and various city government minions are helping the city official. Who is lying on the floor. Partially covered by a tablecloth. Having what seems to be a momentary fit of hyperventilation.

CHAPTER 58

Suitology

The beams of morning sunlight fall between the balconies of the Gothic Quarter like rubble from the ceiling falls onto fleeing characters in the dramatic climax of an action movie. Juan de la Cruz Saudade's grimy head appears among the shadows surrounded by bags of garbage in one of the doorways. Partially wrapped in cigarette smoke. With his eyes half closed and a beard obscuring the lower half of his grimy face. His resolutely threatening expression is one that doesn't necessarily mean he has a gun hidden in his pants, but which is often found on the faces of people with guns hidden in their pants. He tosses his cigarette butt onto the paving stones. He steps on it with a circular movement at the tip of his foot and finally spits on what's left of the butt. A dog that's rummaging around in the bags of garbage stares at him with a vaguely interested gesture. The way Saudade usually spits on the sidewalk and throws his butts down and releases the contents of his nasal passages onto the ground by pressing one wing of his nose with his finger suggests some sort of primitive territory marking. The dog wrinkles his muzzle and stretches out his back in a movement analogous to shrugging his shoulders and heads off down the street.

Now Saudade sticks his head and one shoulder out of the shadows of the doorway. With that smooth turn of the body you associate with people hiding in doorways in spy movies. He makes a pistol with his fingers and shoots an invisible bullet while making a shooting sound with his lips. He is aiming at the door of the former ducal palace where Lucas Giraut lives, which, in that precise moment, opens. Saudade hides in the shadows of the door and, a second later, peeks out again cautiously. A woman has just come out of Giraut's doorway. One of those women devoid of noteworthy sexual features that make Saudade feel somewhat depressed. He watches the woman's butt as she walks away. With his lips pursed disapprovingly. Saudade's clothes could be classified as decidedly filthy. His face looks like the result of taking an unwashed face that hasn't slept for four days and running it over with a ten-ton truck.

Five minutes later, Saudade closes the door to Giraut's apartment behind his back and stows his professional case filled with picklocks in the back pocket of his implausibly grimy sweatpants. He looks around. Giraut's apartment doesn't have an entryway with beaded curtains or one of those frosted mirrors. Or one of those buckets for people to leave wet umbrellas in. The front door opens directly into a living room where you could easily play a game of soccer. Everything displays that lack of common sense that Saudade associates with people who don't have to worry about money. In his experience, you can always tell a rich person's house because there's too much space between things. It's like they don't know how to make good use of the space, or like they want to brag about how much space they have in their houses, so much that they don't know how to fill it up. He'd sure know how to take full advantage of a big room like that. He'd get rid of all those fancy-pants little rugs and weird sofas and he'd put in a gym on one side, and a wood bar on the other, the good kind of wood. And one of those giant TVs with a good three-seater sofa in front of it. And he'd still have plenty of room.

After a first look in the closets, Saudade makes himself comfortable on the sofa with a glass, a bottle of Macallan, a bottle of Finlandia, two cans of Diet Coke and the remote. For some reason, ever since he became homeless a week ago, and jobless, and ran out of gas for his car, he feels overwhelmed by an intense feeling of vulnerability. Of imminent doom. As if he were walking in his team's colors through the stands of the city's *other* team, watching as the rival fans approach with iron bars and brass knuckles. Somewhere deep in his mind he trusts that this sensation of lost omnipotence has nothing to do with being about to turn thirty. He shakes his head sadly. He takes a long sip on his glass of Macallan and Diet Coke, leaving it half empty, and changes the television channels several times until he finds something that looks like a lingerie runway show. Except for the fact that it's on a television set and the entire audience is elderly women who watch the models with obvious disapproval. What is happening to him? he asks himself bitterly. With all his comings and goings from the world of crime to the police force and back again, there was always one constant in his life. A certain feeling that the world was, in some way, designed to display his excellence in the art of life. And now people move away from him on public transportation, with disgusted expressions and holding their noses. He frowns at the empty bottle of Macallan and throws it against the wall in front of him. The stain that remains on the white wall is shaped like a starfish that's been stepped on.

He goes up the unvarnished wood staircase with the bottle of Finlandia in one hand and the remote in the other. He stops for a moment to look at the wall of the landing with his flashlight's beam. It would be a really nice place if someone with half a brain had decorated it. Who's the asshole who decided to leave the bricks showing along the whole staircase? He shrugs and tosses the remote into the landing's ornamental fish tank. On the upper floor he amuses himself for a few minutes tipping over bookshelves and emptying out the contents of closets onto the floor and attacking the paintings with the foot of a steel lamp. He lights a bedspread on fire with his lighter and after a minute changes his mind and takes the smoking, balled-up bedspread off the bed and puts it under the faucets of the bathtub. Somehow all that destruction makes him feel good, but at the same time makes him feel intensely bad. His small individual acts of vandalism against Giraut's furnishings give him overwhelmingly ephemeral doses of satisfaction, followed by waves of despondency. Nothing seems to give him the well-being he needs. He pisses on the pillows and manages to rip the sink out of the wall. In a closet on the stairway he finds a toolbox. He starts a general remodeling of the apartment with a mallet and five minutes later he's crying inconsolably on the sofa, covering his face with his forearm.

What's the point of so much effort? What's the point of living in a world that doesn't reward work and personal merit? Like take this asshole Giraut, thinks Saudade as he vomits on Giraut's sofa. What the hell did he do to have this apartment and that collection of fancy suits upstairs and a bathroom so lovely it makes you want to move in there? And what's the point of destroying it all? As much as he destroys the apartment now, even if he destroyed it ten times over, Mr. Filthy Rich Shit for Brains can just come in with his credit cards and his bank accounts and put it back the way it was. The truth is, he now thinks, dropping from the sofa to the rug and crawling toward the cocktail cabinet, is that he'd give anything never to have met that dickwad Giraut. Maybe Giraut hadn't caused all of his current problems, but there was no doubt that he symbolized them. A hair-salon-going, fancy-suit-wearing, odiously unflappable symbol. With that stupid chubby-cheeked poker face. As if the world wasn't worth stopping to think about. Saudade twists on the rug. With his teeth gnashing. He stretches out an arm, as if with his last dying breath, toward the cocktail cabinet. He manages to open its door. He grabs

422   Javier Calvo

a second bottle of Finlandia and takes the top off with his teeth. If only he had never laid eyes on that fucking filthy rich moron's stupid face. In Saudade's opinion, the class war is something that mostly takes place between the individual class made up of Juan de la Cruz Saudade and the class made up of all the fucking filthy rich morons in the world. The modus operandi of said war, in general terms, is analogous to the way someone parts a crowd, moving through it with an ax. It's not about any intentional self-centeredness in Saudade's general attitude toward life. It's not about any basic aggressiveness either. His attitude is closer to the way certain animals eat very quickly and keep glancing suspiciously over their shoulders.

When he wakes up in his tightie whities inside the bathtub, peacefully hugging an empty bottle of Finlandia, he doesn't have the slightest idea how long he's been there. The inside of his head seems to have turned into a handful of swollen nerves that someone is rhythmically beating on with a guitar. He throws up on himself twice before managing to stand up in the bathtub and he takes a freezing cold shower, watching the remains of vomit swirl around the drain clockwise. He looks at himself, for the first time in several weeks, in the mirror over where the sink used to be and discovers he has a cut through his eyebrow and a series of strange liver spots under his eyes. Then he goes to Giraut's walk-in closet and chooses a charcoal gray suit. From his collection of the latest season of Lino Rossi suits. In the office next to the bedroom he finds a new checkbook in Giraut's name and half a dozen Cartier, Rolex and TAG Heuer watches in a drawer. For a moment he contemplates the Louis XV cartonnier that dominates the room. He uses the mallet to make several holes in the polychrome rosewood and finally, somewhat satisfied, throws the hammer into the fish tank on the landing and goes down the stairs whistling, his haul distributed between the pocket of the suit jacket and his two wrists.

Judging by the growling in his stomach, it must be past lunchtime. Saudade is thinking about checks that can buy hot meals in expensive restaurants as he goes out onto the street and someone brusquely pulls him by the arm and pushes him into a car. It all happens very quickly and through the opaque, sticky screen of his headache. The inside of the car he's just been pushed into seems to spin on various axes at the same time. Finally he manages to look up and he sees that he's lying on his side in the backseat. Next to him, a guy with a repugnant smile is pointing a gun at his face. For a moment he considers the advantages of telling him that he has three luxury watches on each wrist.

"Delighted to meet you, Mr. Giraut," says Leon, pointing the gun. With a Russian accent that, given the circumstances, makes all of Saudade's body hair stand on end. With an absurdly high-pitched voice, considering his giant shoulders and his enormous bullet-shaped head. Still smiling, Leon indicates that he should sit in the middle of the backseat. Between the guy with the gun and the other enormous guy, who also looks Russian, that pushed him into the car. Saudade obeys. "I've heard a lot about you, Mr. Giraut. An important guy, huh? Lately it seems everyone wants to be your friend, huh?" Leon says, and pauses as if what he just said was a joke and he was leaving time for people to laugh. One of the main reasons why Leon is repugnant is the contrast between his enormous hairy body and his absurdly high-pitched voice. Another reason is the smell of industrial grease that seems to emanate from his body. And which none of the people in the car, except for Saudade, seems to notice. "I personally know someone who wants to meet you, too. To really get to know you. Because he's convinced you'll understand each other perfectly. And I agree, of course. This person's name probably won't be familiar to you." He arches his eyebrows in a vaguely afflicted gesture. "But you can call him *Donald Duck*. That's what we all call him around here."

Saudade follows Leon's gaze to a tiny little man sitting in the passenger seat. The little man turns and says something that *does* sound quite a bit like something Donald Duck would say. His voice comes out of one of those surgical collars people who've had their vocal cords operated on wear. With a transistor in the front. Saudade looks up and considers the barrel of the gun that is pointed at his face. The car is turning onto one of Vía Laietana's packed lanes. Something tells him he'd better think fast. Find a way out of the predicament he's gotten himself into. That *they* got him into. It's obvious that that asshole Bob Marley sold Giraut out to the Russians. But it's also clear that trying to convince these Russian assholes that he isn't Giraut is gonna sound like the typical thing Giraut would say to save his ass if he were the one sitting in that car. In Saudade's aching mind the dilemma starts to look grimly like a vicious circle.

"Listen," says Saudade, in that overly obsequious tone you use when you want to be extremely careful not to piss off the person you're talking to. "*I know* this is the typical thing I would say if I really was Giraut and wanted to convince you that I'm not," he starts to say, with a nervous smile. Wiping the sweat from his temples. And he stops. Staring at Leon's bullet-shaped face, which is staring at him while aiming at his face.

And he realizes he's made a mistake. As the signs of anger start to furiously bubble up in the frowning, elephantine and suddenly red face of the guy pointing a gun at him.

CHAPTER 59

Biosphere Park

Iris Gonzalvo looks up through her Versace sunglasses and observes the upside-down heads of about thirty people, shouting as they rush along at a hundred and forty miles an hour, their heads and hands hanging over the backdrop of the cloudless Mediterranean sky. She takes a drag on her cigarette-shaped plastic mentholated inhaler with a thoughtful face. The tortoiseshell Versace glasses Iris is wearing have aquamarine and blue sapphire chips on the sides. She is also wearing a burgundy Versace dress and black gloves up to her elbows. Now she leans forward to look through one of the telescopes on the scenic lookout and moves it until she can focus on Aníbal Manta, who waves with an enormous hand from the other side of the Palace of Gravity fence. As he eats what looks like a reddish cloud of cotton candy. Iris straightens up and takes another drag on her plastic mentholated cigarette. With a design similar to a spool of wire bent erratically by some spectacular explosion, the Evolution roller coaster is silhouetted against the sky above the wide, low dome of the Palace of Gravity. The screams of its passengers during the upside-down stretches are heard every twenty seconds, exactly.

Iris rests her butt on the railing of the scenic lookout and watches as Mr. Fleck and Mr. Downey come through the crowd of families with digital video cameras and school groups. With their blond, partially bald heads. With their identically freckled faces that could be any age between thirty and forty-five. The scenic lookout at Biosphere Park is the place stipulated for the meeting with Mr. Travers's two employees. In front of the entrance to the Palace of Gravity. At the convergence of the paths that lead to the Amazon of the Past and the Amazon of the Future.

Mr. Fleck and Mr. Downey stop a few feet from Iris and rest their butts on the same railing where her butt is resting. Without looking directly at her. Without making any sign or addressing her in any way. The lookout's terrace at midday is packed with families with kids and school groups only partially controlled by desperate-looking teachers. Beside Iris, several schoolkids try to destroy one of the telescopes by both hanging off of one end and pulling down. Iris notices that Travers's two men are sucking on plastic mentholated inhalers just like hers.

"This *does not* look like a safe place to make the exchange, Miss DeMink," says Mr. Fleck in a smooth tone. Or maybe it's Mr. Downey. He takes a drag on his inhaler and looks at Iris Gonzalvo out of the corner of his eye.

Iris shrugs. The idea of meeting Travers's men at the Biosphere

Park scenic lookout on the Costa Dorada initially seems to be based on it being a busy, crowded place. Or at least that's what Iris figured when she got her instructions. The same reason she always figured the exchange of microfilm and hostages in the movies takes place at amusement parks. Now a woman holding a child with each hand stops in front of Iris with a furious face and gestures toward her plastic cigarette and then at a giant sign telling visitors that there is no smoking in the park. The sign shows a drawing of a koala with its eyes popping out of its head, choking in a cloud of smoke. The koala, according to what Iris read in a brochure, answers to the name of Kooky and represents the park's commitment to environmental and scientific education. Everywhere you looked, there was Kooky. On giant billboards where Kooky asks visitors to turn off their cell phones during the educational performances. With a napkin tied around its neck at the entrance to all the fast-food restaurants. There are people walking among the crowd in Kooky disguises handing out coupons for the McDonald's, Starbucks and Dunkin' Donuts franchises in the park. Iris puts her menthol inhaler in her pocket.

"Please," says Mr. Fleck, or maybe Mr. Downey. With that indirect, or more like *implicit* way of addressing Iris. "Meet us on the other side of the fence."

Mr. Travers's two employees, followed at a certain distance by Iris, join the river of people moving toward the fences of the Palace of Gravity. The path goes by a bridge that overlooks the grounds of the Amazon of the Past and the Amazon of the Future. To her right, Iris can see the Amazon of the Past's luxuriant forest with its dozens of animal and plant species meticulously locked up behind bars and labeled. To her left, the Amazon of the Future is a black, smoking plateau filled with animal corpses and mutant-looking bushes through which actors playing zombies graze. Next to the Amazon of the Future's exit there's a hut with a medical team to attend to the dozens of kids that have nervous fits from their visit.

Five minutes later, Iris gets to the doors of the Palace of Gravity.

Without a doubt, the park's Top Attraction. A postadolescent employee wearing a Biosphere Park uniform and intensely depressed expression reads the bar code on Iris's ticket with a device vaguely similar to a pistol and wishes her a good visit with the tone of voice people usually use to wish someone a horrible slow death. On the other side of the fences, Iris stops beneath the palace's entrance arch. The sign at the entrance says "PALACE OF GRAVITY" in enormous, very rounded letters beside which there's a drawing of Kooky the koala flying through the air, grasping a balloon in one of his front paws. Iris leans her head down to see over her Versace sunglasses and examines the place. A few feet from her is Aníbal Manta, finishing his cotton candy and looking furtively at her over his comic book. A bit farther on, in the line to get in, are Travers's men. Who aren't looking anywhere. Indistinguishable in their identical suits. Sucking on their menthol inhalers. Iris sighs and gets in line.

The inside of the Palace of Gravity is, for some reason, reminiscent of a covered ice-skating rink. Except for the fact that all of the people inside are floating. As the educational panels at the entrance explain, the main rink surrounded by stands replicates the gravitational conditions of space travel. Or of moon landings. The conditions universally known as Zero Gravity. For the price of a ticket plus a small supplement visitors can rent special harnesses tied down with a special nonabrasive cord to the monitoring and security area and float in zero gravity for thirty minutes. For the littlest ones and the less brave there is the option of floating holding on to one of the monitors' hands. Iris walks up to the security railing around the Zero Gravity rink and stares at the groups of people floating. Many of them do pirouettes and prance around in slow motion. Others are doing the zero gravity equivalent of the dead man's float. Some seem disconcerted and only a very few seem to be panicking. One of the floating visitors seems to be chasing his wallet through the air.

Mr. Fleck and Mr. Downey lean on the security railing next to Iris. One of them leaves an envelope on top of the railing. Halfway between where they are and where Iris is. Iris takes the envelope and puts it into her purse.

"Locker number fifty-two," says Mr. Fleck, or Mr. Downey. "At the coat check."

Iris pretends that she's watching the people floating in the Zero Gravity area while her gaze searches for Aníbal Manta. The public-address system warns visitors that entering the Zero Gravity area without the protective harness is strictly forbidden. Manta is sitting on one of the lower spectator stands. With his superhero comic rolled up in one of his coat pockets. Staring at Iris. Or what looks like Iris. It's hard to tell with all the people in the middle, floating around. Finally Iris looks around in her purse and takes out another envelope. One that looks very much like the first one. She leaves it on the railing. Near Travers's two men.

"Parking lot number three," she says. "Row twelve. Spot number eighty. It's a white van." She pauses and her gaze wanders toward the stands where Manta is sitting. The rolled-up comic book that sticks out of his coat pocket looks kind of like an antenna. Manta doesn't wave. Iris turns toward Travers's men. "Enjoy your visit," she says to them.

Mr. Fleck and Mr. Downey stare at her with blank faces. With their plastic menthol inhalers between their lips. Iris has the sudden sensation that there's something in the general structure of their faces that looks like it's about to disintegrate. As if that something had precariously withstood all the negotiations and meetings in safe spots and only had enough ontological resistance to hold out until the end of the exchange. As if Travers's two employees that she had met in his palace in Paris were nothing more than some sort of transitory identity limited to this sale. Iris stares at the two men's faces while one of them picks up her envelope and puts it in the pocket of his suit jacket. Their faces are definitely much more freckled than the first time she saw them. Their hair seems blonder and thinner. Their eyelids seem to be trembling due to some sort of malfunctioning in their nervous systems. Iris stares at them through her Versace sunglasses as they head off toward the exit. The public-address system requests that the parents of a boy who has exceeded his flotation time come by the security area to pick him up. Iris takes the menthol inhaler out of her purse and takes a thoughtful drag on it. Then she starts walking toward the exit.

When she is approaching the lines for the exit she feels the soft but firm pressure of an enormous hand on her arm. She looks up. Her gaze travels the long and mostly suit-covered path from the enormous hairy hand to the face of Aníbal Manta. Who is looking at her with a frown. With all of his features wrinkled into that expression of intense intellectual effort that he makes when he is at all suspicious of the person in front of him. As if he were watching real surgery on TV. Or as if he had to go to the bathroom and had been holding it in too long. For a fraction of a second they both just look into each other's eyes.

"Not so fast, pretty lady." Manta lets go of her arm. He clears his throat. He watches as Iris raises a hand instinctively to where he had been grabbing her arm. "What you've got in that purse is for me."

And that's when it happens. The kick Iris gives Aníbal's knee is enough to throw him off balance and a reflex makes him fold his leg. The push she then gives him with her entire body propels him backward and over the railing of the security strip. Into which he falls backward. Impelled by his own weight. And of course, without the chance to extend his arms to protect himself from the fall, since he is grabbing his leg with both hands. The sound that comes out of his mouth as his back hits the ground on the edge of the Zero Gravity area is somewhere between heavy breathing and a horse snorting. Something like the sound of an air chamber emptying abruptly.

Manta lies on the floor on his back for a moment, his face very red. And all of a sudden, before he can get up or even get his breath back, his butt is no longer touching the ground. His shoes are no longer touching the ground. Most of his back is no longer touching the ground at the edge of the Zero Gravity area. A Palace of Gravity monitor starts to blow his whistle to sound the alarm. Iris Gonzalvo watches wide-eyed for a moment as Aníbal Manta rises, floating slowly above her head. Looking at her with an expression that blends rage with horror. With the tails of his coat rising like two flaccid wings. His comic book comes out of his coat pocket and starts its own, completely independent, journey. Iris Gonzalvo runs away.

As she leaves the Palace of Gravity and runs through the crowd of park visitors, beneath the warm winter sun, Iris thinks of all the climactic movie scenes set in amusement parks that she's seen throughout her life. Those scenes of adrenaline-filled exchanges of hostages and briefcases full of cash. Where villains with evil grimaces put guns to the temples of innocent women and children. Somehow she no longer feels like herself. Somehow she has the feeling that it's someone else running through the crowd, bumping into people and knocking them down. It's not a feeling of inner transformation. Or of split personality, although it is true that one part of her brain is imagining her race through the park *from outside* of her own head. Like movie directors supposedly imagine things. In an epic panoramic shot. Or maybe an overhead view. Now she runs past the Sustainable Agriculture Pavilion, where several groups of kids are throwing stones and soda cans at actors playing traditional farmworkers. The silhouette of the shack that holds the coat check appears in her visual field. Still tiny but already magnificent. Shining in the distance like some kind of magnificent palace. Somehow, Iris feels that her strides through the crowd are taking her along the path she always wanted to travel, but could never find.

Inside the shack, with her hair sweaty and stuck to her forehead, Iris tears open the envelope and unlocks locker number fifty-two with the key she finds inside it. The briefcase inside isn't a briefcase. It's a bottle green Puma sports bag. She opens it and takes a look inside and then sticks her Prada high heels into it before turning and running off toward the parking lot. The camera inside her head follows her from a cinematographic point located somewhere above the roofs of the pavilions. Maybe from the peak of the Evolution roller coaster.

In the parking lot, Iris runs barefoot through the apparently infinite rows of parked cars. With the Puma bag hanging from her shoulder. Stopping every once in a while to wipe her hair out of her face and look around and check the maps printed on informative panels distributed throughout the parking lot at regular intervals. After many wrong turns and backtracking filmed in her imagination by cameras in helicopters, she finally sees her brick red Alfa Romeo wedged between several rows of family cars. She is already at its door, feeling around in her purse for her keys, when she realizes that the keys aren't in her purse. That the keys must still be in Manta's pants pocket, since Manta parked the car and then put them there. Desperate, she looks around. Her desperation is filmed in her imagination by a circular crane that revolves around her slender, desperate frame. And then she sees him. Limping in the distance. Enraged. Manta approaches limping through the rows of parked cars. Some of the park visitors have stopped to watch Aníbal Manta approaching, his face red with fury. Like a large mammal seething in its quest for revenge.

Iris takes a few steps back, scared. Everywhere you look, there are only hundreds and hundreds of parked cars. Cars as far as the eye can see. Epically filmed by cameras installed into small aircraft. Manta is already close enough for Iris to be able to see his tightly clenched fists with their white knuckles. His crew cut somehow messy. The slightly reddened whites of his eyes. And in that precise moment, one of the parked cars starts suddenly and hits Manta. Manta goes flying and lands on the hood of a family car parked in the row in front. Setting off the car's alarm.

The car that has just hit Manta turns abruptly. It makes a U-turn, hitting the fenders of several parked cars and stopping with a screech of its brakes beside Iris. Iris recognizes the maneuver as something she saw Eric Yanel do in a car commercial a year earlier. One of those commercials where Eric would do a spectacular maneuver and then emerge with a helmet under his arm, filmed by an aerial camera, into the company of a pair of models in bikinis. The car window opens. Eric Yanel sticks an arm through the open window.

"Lucas told me you might need a little help," he says. With a radiant smile, the kind you see in commercials.

Iris goes around and gets in on the passenger side. Beneath the vaguely alarmed stares of the families and school groups in the parking lot.

CHAPTER 60

Plasma Ball

Mr. Bocanegra pushes the bell of the former ducal palace the tourist guides refer to as the Palau de la Mar Fosca. With a hand behind his back. With a bouquet of flowers in that hand. Hiding a bouquet of flowers behind his back the way people hide something they're about to present as a surprise gift. He combs his scant hair with the fingers of a large, hairy hand and smiles. There is something intrinsically ferocious in his smile. A certain element related to the fact that his teeth are unrealistically large and too shiny to be a real person's teeth. Like teeth painted on with an airbrush. His stance is the one children usually employ when waiting in front of a door, with his legs slightly crossed and his hands behind his back.

A funny-looking municipal cleaning vehicle seems to have colonized most of the passable area of the street this early Monday morning. Equipped with an enormous hose that looks alive and is connected to something underground. The cleaning crew sweeps the paving stones. They move their heads rhythmically to the music on their headphones and, every once in a while, shout something at each other, the way people shout when they're wearing headphones. Except for one. One of the members of the cleaning crew doesn't seem to be listening to music or shouting at the others. He's not wearing headphones, either. The cleaner who is not like the others is sweeping a corner of the street from which he has a completely clear view of the doorway of the palace known as the Palau de la Mar Fosca. Without looking up. What he's wearing instead of headphones is one of those little ear devices halfway between a hearing aid and a microphone headset. Like those things nightclub bouncers wear. Bocanegra clears his throat with a fist in front of his mouth. The small door inside the two larger ones opens and Marcia Parini appears in the threshold. Wearing a pearly robe. With Bugs Bunny slippers. Although she doesn't have curlers in her hair or a cigarette hanging from her lips, her pale morning face with sheet marks still on it makes you think she should be wearing curlers in her hair and have a cigarette hanging lazily from her lips.

"You don't look like the furniture delivery man." Marcia looks at Bocanegra with a frown. The suit Bocanegra is wearing this Monday winter morning is cream colored and has the meticulously triangular point of a red handkerchief sticking out of the breast pocket. Under a fur coat that seems to have been designed to be worn exclusively by a woman. Marcia hugs herself in a gesture that suggests she's cold. Both her and her visitor's breath materialize in the shape of little clouds of steam. Marcia's little clouds of steam seem smaller and somehow less dynamic than the little clouds of steam coming from the corpulent, mustachioed man standing in front of her door. "Unless you've got my blackboard and man's dresser and all the rest behind your back."

Bocanegra stares at the bouquet of flowers in his hand with a theatrical expression of surprise. With that overly surprised expression for surprise gifts you've been hiding behind your back while waiting for the recipient to open the door. Like a clichéd joke. The bouquet is wrapped in some sort of shiny paper that crunches when you grab it. Marcia grabs the bouquet by the crunchy lower part and stares at it without any particular expression.

"How stupid of me, you must forgive me." Bocanegra combs his scant hair with his hairy hand again in a gesture that somehow manages to not be at all flirtatious. His strangely feminine coat is simply draped over his cream-colored shoulders. "I should have called. But the *truth* is

I didn't have your phone number. And I'm only in town for one day. You must be my nephew's girlfriend. Who, by the way, has very good taste. My nephew. As they say. I'm his uncle Oscar. Lucas's uncle. Although we haven't seen each other in many years. I'm kind of a wayward uncle. That's why we've never met. But I've been meaning to call for some time. And suddenly I said to myself: why don't you pay good old Lucas a visit? Since I'm passing through the city and all. For old times' sake." His eyes half close as he studies Marcia Parini's slightly swollen eyes. Marcia has the kind of brown eyes that are completely dull and devoid of any idiosyncratic elements. Like standard-issue eyes. As if there wasn't time or money to come up with some *real* eyes. "The truth is I'm not *exactly* his uncle," continues Bocanegra. "You could say that Lucas and I are more like distant cousins. Very distant. Uncle Oscar is what he calls me. Because of the age difference, I guess. It's a joke. You know. Like Uncle Oscar from the Oscar awards and all that. It's one of those family jokes people make. What can I say." He shrugs his shoulders. Both his smile and his half-closed eyes now contain clear hints of ferociousness. "Family is the most important thing there is."

Marcia Parini hugs herself in a gesture that suggests intense cold as well as unexpected conversations with strangers early in the morning in insufficient attire. From under the lower edge of her pearly robe the skin on her legs seems covered in a uniform eruption of little bumps brought on by the cold, which lends her a certain helpless charm. Helpless charm is probably Marcia's strong suit. Her robe is one of those thin silk robes that are no help at all against the cold. The street cleaner who isn't moving his head rhythmically or shouting keeps sweeping in a way that suggests he isn't really paying attention to what he's sweeping, nor is he really committed to cleaning the sidewalk. His head is leaning to one side at a pronounced angle. As if he were surreptitiously listening to something happening on the other side of a door.

Marcia moves her feet in a vaguely impatient gesture.

"I'm not Lucas's girlfriend," she says. The sheet marks are mostly on one side of her face. "My mother and his mother were best friends, before they each got married. He lives in the apartment upstairs. I live in the downstairs apartment. We visit each other a lot. Sometimes it's all a bit confusing. Or at least it was, until two weeks ago." Marcia Parini's pale little clouds of steam lend her a certain helpless charm. The way she hugs herself over her silk robe gives her a helpless charm. Her helpless charm now emanates in waves toward Bocanegra. "Right now Lucas isn't home. But I could invite you in for a cup of tea. We have a wide selection of teas."

Five minutes later Mr. Bocanegra is sitting on a leather sofa, with his fingertips resting on the surface of one of those plasma balls filled with gas whose capacitor emits colored electrical charges when you touch it. Like small, fantastically colored lightning bolts that come out from the middle of the ball toward the hands that touch it. On the glass coffee table in Marcia Parini's living room, besides the plasma ball, there are other objects like a lava lamp, a tranquility fountain and a Chinese checkers board. Without any marbles. Even though Marcia Parini's living room isn't small, the excess of objects makes it a bit claustrophobic. There are also sticks of incense in varying states of consumption on a nearby chest of drawers. Bocanegra moves his hands over the surface of the plasma ball. Changing the form produced by the electricity making the gas inside the ball glow. Without taking his eyes off the electric form. The temperature in the living room is also stifling. Like the house had been overheated all night.

"Did I mention *we* have a wide selection of teas?" Marcia's voice comes from some invisible place located on the other side of the rectangular horizontal opening that connects the tiny kitchen with the living room. The opening has a varnished wood ledge covered with more little bottles of spices and herbs than Bocanegra has ever seen in one place in his life. Even something that looks like very small logs of firewood. Marcia's voice is mixed with the vaguely metallic sound of a transistor radio or maybe a CD player in the attached kitchen. "I've been a big tea fan for a while now. You can have any kind you want. I think I have them all. I can also make blends. Sometimes I think I have *too* wide a selection of teas. If you know what I mean. I mean that if they gave me a euro for every euro I've spent on tea I'd probably be rich. This is all to say, ask for a cup. Don't be afraid. You won't catch me off guard."

Bocanegra keeps moving his hands over the plasma ball. Contemplating the different configurations that appear inside it. Like heavenly bodies. Each movement of his hands creates changes in the structure and color system. There are no two identical configurations. Not even when he puts his hands in the same place.

"Do you have a cup of tea?" he says distractedly. Without taking his gaze off the center of the ball.

"That's not how you do it," says the voice from the other side of the horizontal rectangular opening to the kitchen. Patiently. "You have to say something like: I want a spicy breakfast tea, one that's strong and fruity. That kind of thing. I could also make you a crêpe. To have with your tea. That's my favorite breakfast." Her face and upper torso appear in the opening. With her silk robe. With a large glass of Macallan in her hand. She brings the glass to her lips and takes a sip. "I can also give you a whiskey, if you want. I'm not saying it's the best thing for you at this time of the morning. But I don't think it's the worst either."

Bocanegra moves his hands over the glass ball with the circular and vaguely sweeping motions that crystal ball readers use. The kind that usually wear turbans. And have little pointy beards. On the surface of the ball, with a backdrop of colored lightning bolts and otherworldly fog, his own distorted face looks at him severely. In that convex, centripetal way faces are reflected onto round surfaces. The tinkling of ice and glasses is heard from the kitchen. Bocanegra looks at the ball with a frown and moves one hand in a kind of wave. The way you wave at your own reflection. As much as he goes over it in his mind, he can't seem to find any metaphorical implication in the nature or workings of the ball. The plasma ball appears to be an element devoid of any metaphoric possibilities. Not relatable to any other element in the universe. Like its own world. A relatively pretty, boring and meaningless world. There doesn't seem to be any lesson here, thinks Bocanegra with the mental equivalent of a sigh. He crosses his legs and smiles at Marcia, who has just appeared with two large glasses of Macallan and ice.

"I know this may seem strange," says Bocanegra. He leans the upper half of his body forward without uncrossing his legs to take the glass of Macallan Marcia offers him. Marcia sits in front of him. With a glass in her hand that's identical to her guest's glass except it's missing a couple of large sips of whiskey. Sections of pale, correctly moisturized skin peek out from under Marcia's silk robe. "Since I'm practically a stranger that just showed up without even calling first. I know it's a strange question and all. But tell me, dear. Have you noticed anything strange about Lucas lately? Any change in his behavior? Anything that struck you as strange? Like strange people coming over. Strange people that come at odd hours. People that look like policemen, for example. And forgive me for the strange question. But perhaps you've seen someone prowling around the street. In the little plaza over there. People that look like they're prowling. Pretending to do something else. Like someone reading a newspaper on a corner. Sometimes they wear those little gadgets in one ear. You know." He raises a large hairy hand to his ear. Bocanegra's ears are small. In marked contrast with the rest of his facial features. "Like those devices nightclub bouncers wear in their ears."

Marcia Parini looks over the edge of the glass of Macallan she's sipping. Then she places it among the objects cramming the glass table. The lava lamp and the plasma ball and the Chinese checkers board and a Ganesh elephant and something that looks like one of those fountains with a motor inside that generates a supposedly tranquilizing sound.

"I haven't seen anything strange," she says. "Lucas *isn't* strange. A lot of people think he is, but I don't. He's a good guy. Maybe he does have a few problems. His mother is a difficult woman. And it seems like his father was, too. I mean a difficult *man*. But I don't care what they say. I don't care if they say he did things with Valentina. I don't care that they want to fire him from his job. I know the real Lucas. Like do you know he saves all the notebooks he wrote when he was a kid? And he has a secret room at work. He never told me but I figured it out." She takes a sip of whiskey with her brow furrowed. Then she continues talking with the glass in her hand. "What I mean is that he's a *special* guy. An interesting person. I used to be in love with him."

Marcia's body language isn't exactly childlike, or exactly feminine, or even exactly adult. There is something about Marcia Parini that makes Bocanegra not exactly realize that she's almost naked in front of him. Something that seems to contradict the very idea of nakedness. Bocanegra runs a hand along the rocky texture of the upper part of the tranquility fountain on the glass table and gets up from the sofa. With unexpected agility considering his size. He walks with his hands behind his back to a coatrack near the wall and pensively touches a couple of men's coats hanging there. As if the coats reminded him of something he couldn't quite place.

"Those aren't Lucas's," says Marcia. "They're my boyfriend's. He moved in with me a couple of weeks ago. That's why I'm expecting a blackboard and a dresser and all that. We're planning to get married. Although he hasn't met my daughter yet. He's a good guy." She takes another sip on her glass of Macallan. This new sip distinguishes itself from the previous ones with a certain nostalgic glint in her gaze. A mere instant where her gaze stops looking at anything in the room. "He's not a good guy in the same way Lucas is a good guy. Let's just say my boyfriend has less clear ideas about what he wants to do with his life and that kind of thing. In spite of his age." She shrugs. "But I guess that's my fate. To be with men who haven't got it all figured out." She stops. She stares with a frown into the bottom of her half-full glass of whiskey. As if she had just seen something inside the glass that shouldn't be there. "Listen, you didn't come about some inheritance, did you? I mean, you're not one of those uncles that show up after twenty years in Australia to leave an inheritance, right?"

Bocanegra has stopped thoughtfully touching the coats on the coatrack and is now focused on studying the collection of framed photographs on top of a chest of drawers in Marcia Parini's living room. Photographs that are mostly of Valentina Parini. The way Bocanegra is looking at the photographs is: leaning forward. With the upper half of his body at a right angle to his legs and his palms resting on his knees. After a moment he picks up a photograph in which Valentina Parini appears with Lucas Giraut. Both of them very serious. Sitting in a courtyard. Valentina has a Stephen King novel in her hands. Bocanegra brings the photograph over to the window to see it better under the morning light.

"This is the girl they say Lucas is screwing?" he says. Examining the photograph with a calculating expression. "They seem to be quite close." Then he looks in Marcia's direction. "Where's the girl now? Wasn't she in some kind of hospital?"

Marcia doesn't answer. On the reflective surface of the framed photographs on the chest of drawers, Bocanegra can see that Marcia is looking into her glass of whiskey with an indecipherable expression.

On the other side of the window, holding the city's broom idly in one hand, the headphone-less member of the cleaning crew no longer pretends he's sweeping the sidewalk. Now he has his head slightly tilted to one side and a finger on his ear device and seems to be talking to himself while staring intently at the handle of his broom.

CHAPTER 61

Doctor Angeli

Valentina Parini isn't so much sitting in as *collapsed into* the wheelchair Lucas Giraut is now pushing along a hallway of the hospital that's lit by white fluorescent bulbs. With the upper half of her body fallen to one side of the chair and her head hanging on that same side. One of her alarmingly skinny prepubescent arms hangs in such a way that her knuckles drag on the floor. Picking up dust from the floor of the hospital hallway. Her mouth is slightly open and although a string of saliva isn't hanging from the corner, she does have a dried white stain that indicates she has been drooling at some point. Her state is not technically catatonia, according to the explanation given by the intern in charge of her case, but rather a semi-catatonic state induced by the medicines she's being given.

Lucas Giraut arrives at a bend in the hallway of the renowned children's psychiatric center that Valentina is about to be released from, and maneuvers the wheelchair to make a ninety-degree turn. He is wearing a gunmetal gray Lino Rossi suit and nonprescription glasses. Beside him walks a shockingly young and svelte nurse, compared to the idea of psychiatric nurses Giraut had been led to believe from every movie about such places he had ever seen. The group composed of Giraut, the nurse and the semi-catatonic girl in a wheelchair takes a new hallway and stops abruptly when a door opens in their path. As a result of the sudden braking, Valentina leans even farther to one side.

The door finishes opening and out of it comes the intern in charge of Valentina's case. Looking at something that's written on a sheet of paper attached to a plastic clipboard. Giraut looks at the intern through his nonprescription glasses. Glasses that he thinks give him a paternal air. The doctor looks up from the clipboard and looks at Giraut with his head slightly leaned down.

"Mr. Parini?" he asks in a tone that doesn't manage to be probing in the least. A tone that somehow manages to be imperious and perhaps convey certain suspicion. "Would you mind if we spoke in private for a moment? If you want I can ask that they call your wife."

Giraut readjusts his glasses on his nose with his middle finger the way he's seen people who usually wear glasses do so often. For a moment he considers the advantages of declaring that anything the intern has to say he can say in front of his daughter. As part of his interpretation of the character of Valentina's father. He's aware that the shockingly svelte nurse and the intern are looking at him with openly inquisitive faces. Finally he shrugs his shoulders.

"Is there some problem with the paperwork?" he says. Drumming his fingers on the anatomical handles of the wheelchair. One of Valentina Parini's hands is completely crumpled on the ground. "I assume that all the signatures are where they should be. I've already spoken with our legal counsel. I found his advice to be very rigorous."

Valentina Parini's face is blank except for a series of sporadic muscle spasms similar to tics that seem to give her features some sort of intermittent activity. In her face that is no longer at all childlike. Valentina's face is the face of someone that has experienced in some indirect, torturous way what is usually known as an initiation into postpubescent life. Including the addition of an aura of sexuality that's not related to the appearance of secondary sex characteristics. Valentina's alarmingly skinny and inert body isn't sexual in any concrete way, but at some point it has lost that absence of sexuality that children's bodies have. The patch held on with white tape that covers one eye is falling off. So that a couple of strips of white tape are hanging off one side of her face, like two oversized fake eyelashes.

"Technically speaking," the intern starts to say. Giraut can see that the doctor is avoiding looking him in the eye. "All the paperwork is correct. The transfer to the center in Uruguay seems to be in order. Although I've already mentioned what I think about the unclear communications we've received from that center. The reports from the doctors that will be taking care of her seem perfectly competent. Their opinions are pretty respectable. You have made it quite clear that they have qualified nurses available for her transportation. Valentina's mother was here yesterday to give her consent. And of course, it's natural that you would want to have your daughter in the center you see most fit." He pauses. That pause that always separates the apparently conclusive reasons in an argument from the counterargument that will disprove that conclusion. "And however . . ."

Another pause. Time seems to freeze for a few seconds under the white fluorescent lamps of the hospital hallway.

Lucas Giraut opens and closes his hands around the handles of the wheelchair. He changes the position of his feet on the linoleum hospital floor. The hallway walls are partially covered by those signs you find in medical centers with lists of recommendations and pro-scriptions. A muscle spasm runs across Valentina's face, followed by another that looks like a low-voltage electrical shock.

"And however," continues the medical intern. With his gaze fixed on the papers in his hand. His doctor's coat isn't long and white. It's more like some sort of man's blouse that's a blue color that makes you think of the blue color of certain medicines. Of surgical sheets covering sliced-open bodies. "And however, I want to insist on how ill timed a transfer is for Valentina's treatment right now. Maybe we could postpone it a few weeks. Maybe a few months. We're talking about the possibility of *losing your daughter* in many respects. On the other hand . . . ," he starts to say, and at this point he lifts his gaze for the first time from his clipboard and looks around him. With serious professional consternation. And certain cautiousness. As if he feared that someone might be listening from behind one of the hall doors. "On the other hand, we understand that you haven't had any contact with Valentina for more than six years. Not even a single phone call."

A new muscle spasm animates Valentina's features. A spasm that this time moves across the right side of her neck and through her shoulder to the arm touching the floor. A dry sound is heard when Valentina's knuckles hit the linoleum floor. Lucas Giraut readjusts his glasses with his middle finger again and runs a hand through his long straight hair. The sheet of paper the doctor has on his clipboard doesn't seem to be a medical document of any kind. It looks like a regular sheet of white paper with notes and doodles, like the kind people make when they're talking on the telephone.

"*He's not my father*," says a hoarse and alarmingly subdued version of Valentina Parini's voice. From the wheelchair. From the head fallen to one side of the wheelchair. Which now starts to slowly rise. "This man. He's not my father."

Everyone looks at Valentina. The silence in the hospital hallway seems to change. Into a silence that's different from the simple absence of sounds. Different from that metallic, reverberating silence typical of hospital hallways. Somehow, Valentina's words seem to have reconfigured the scene. They seem to have endowed it with something intensely surreal. Not as if her words had revealed that the man claiming to be her father isn't her father and that had reconfigured the network of relationships between the four people in the hallway. More like that Valentina's words had just revealed that none of the people in the hallway were who they claimed to be. Like those moments onstage when the characters in a scene turn into actors.

"Valentina?" asks the intern. His brow furrowed.

Valentina sits up with a crunching of bones and stiff joints. The various parts of her body move with a marionette's disjointed motions. Or like those dolls whose different parts are held together with string. Finally she lifts her neck and looks around.

"He's not my father," she says. And beneath her chemically induced hoarseness, her voice seems to take on the important tone characteristic of revelations. "He's Doctor Angeli. Don't be fooled by his appearance." She makes a series of facial and hand gestures that seem to be some sort of secret code. "Doctor Angeli has no *true* form."

The three adults standing in the hospital hallway are now looking at various different points of the hall, in a way that suggests they are each trying to avoid looking at each other. Valentina's wheelchair occupies a blind spot right at the center of their gazes. Or at the exact center of what their gazes seem to be avoiding.

"Don't trust the disguises," continues Valentina. "Doctor Angeli is Doctor Angeli *until proved otherwise*. I know him well. He came when I was very little. Saying he was my father. But I unmasked him. I gave him a special alarm clock to fix and he had to escape. That was the test. Fixing the alarm clock." Valentina's lower lip sticks out slightly as she speaks, the way some psychiatric patients' lower lips stick out slightly or are too wet. "Doctor Angeli often passes himself off as people's mothers or fathers. Really, *almost everyone* that claims to be a mother or a father is Doctor Angeli."

The intern is looking at the notes and doodles on the paper clipped to his clipboard. With a frown. Without bothering to hide said doodles. Someone clears their throat. The throat clearing breaks the essentially elusive nature of the scene. The nurse looks at the doctor. The doctor looks at Giraut. Giraut looks at Valentina and pushes her chair forward. As he heads down the hallway, flanked by the warnings on the hospital posters, he hears the intern's voice.

"You can still change your mind, Mr. Parini," says the doctor. "Think of the girl."

Five minutes later, in the parking lot of the pedestrian street that holds the children's clinic, Giraut pushes the chair up to the back of Iris Gonzalvo's brick red Alfa Romeo. He helps Valentina stand up and get into the back of the sports car. Valentina does all this without any sign of surprise. Iris Gonzalvo covers her alarmingly skinny body with a travel blanket. It all happens quickly.

"There are clothes in the backseat," Giraut says to Valentina after the car leaves the lot. In that way that drivers speak to the passengers in the backseat. Looking up and through the rearview mirror. "You can't wear hospital clothes. We are in a somewhat complicated situation. This city isn't safe for us anymore. We have to leave the country. We'll meet up with your mother and her boyfriend abroad. Your mother found a boyfriend. His name is Eric."

The car moves through upper Barcelona until it has left behind the last old stately homes on the outskirts and enters the tunnels that go through the hills. Sitting in the passenger seat, Iris Gonzalvo looks through the rearview mirror with concern. She is wearing a white Kenzo dress that reaches her knees and Yves Saint Laurent sunglasses and her hair is gelled back into a bun. The light inside the tunnels makes them orange. That color that reminds you of the glow of jack-o'-lanterns with candles inside. Giraut doesn't seem to have noticed what it is in the rearview mirror that is worrying Iris. In the backseat, Valentina is putting on the sweater and pants they brought for her.

"We are the people with no father and no mother," says Giraut. Looking at Valentina through the rearview mirror. With both hands on the steering wheel. "The world begins with us."

"The world begins with us," repeats Valentina from the backseat.

Lucas Giraut follows Iris's worried gaze to the mirror. There is a car closely following the Alfa Romeo. Giraut squints and can make out the face of the car's driver. A face distorted by rage. With something in his hand that Giraut trusts isn't what it looks like. Beneath the jack-o'-lantern glow of the tunnels, the distorted face of the driver of the car following them doesn't look human. It is a wet, shiny face. Wrinkled and bald. Giraut swallows hard. It is the face of Mr. Bocanegra. And what it looks like he has in his hand is a gun.

In the backseat, Valentina turns to look through the back window.

CHAPTER 62

One with the Universe

The hospital Juan de la Cruz Saudade is in is no prestigious private clinic on a pedestrian street uptown. It's one of those desolate public hospital landscapes. Without individual rooms. One of those hospital landscapes perpetually bathed in the smell of bleach and excrement. That make you think of hospitals in horror movies and hospitals in allegorical films where the main character seems to be in a hospital, but it turns out he's really in hell. The patients' whining and sobbing is heard everywhere. Just the way people supposedly whine and sob in hell. But not Juan de la Cruz Saudade. Saudade's not whining or sobbing or panting or making any other kind of sound to show his suffering. His state is too precarious and whining or crying would intensify the pain of his numerous injured parts.

"I know you're really messed up and all," says Hannah Linus, seated in a folding chair beside Saudade's hospital bed. "And that you're not supposed to give bad news to people when they're in the hospital. But I've been wanting to tell you this for a while. That's why I came when you called. Because I wouldn't have dared break up with you in any other moment. But here it's different. Let's just say you're not very seductive. You're so messed up that I don't find you impressive anymore. So that's it."

She makes a happy gesture, like the happy sigh of someone who's just had a heavy burden lifted. "I said it."

From his hospital bed, Juan de la Cruz Saudade tries to move his neck enough to be able to see Hannah Linus. He looks like a hospital patient in a comic strip or a cartoon. With both legs in casts and both arms in casts and his torso and head partially covered in bandages. He even has a leg lifted and held by a system of straps to the ceiling over his bed. A dry snap in the area of his cervical vertebra dissuades him from continuing to try to see the woman sitting next to his bed. Some of the parts of his body, the parts that aren't in bandages or casts, show burns covered with ointment and stitched-up wounds. Even still, Saudade is pretty satisfied with the results of his encounter with the Russians. He's alive, and that's definitely a consolation. In the end, he managed to convince them he wasn't Giraut. Well, actually it was that weird guy with the plate in his head that convinced them. The only problem was after confirming that he wasn't Giraut, everyone seemed to forget about him. Everyone except that little man who talked like Donald Duck. Saudade shivers slightly when he remembers the little man and his drill and the rest of his do-it-yourself tools.

"Well, I guess that's all I have to say." Hannah Linus picks up her purse. She takes a little mirror compact out of it and redoes her lipstick. "I'd better be going. So you can start getting used to never seeing me again and all that."

Hannah Linus closes the compact with a vaguely metallic click and puts it back in her purse. At the end of the hall a terrified scream is heard. One of those screams that echo through the halls of Spanish public hospitals and make you think of the screams of damned souls in hell. Not so much screams of pain as screams of *pure, unadulterated* suffering. Saudade's room is one of those shared rooms that have several beds separated by threadbare curtains. Saudade moves his head a bit and lets out some sort of soft, unintelligible croak.

"What's that?" Hannah Linus frowns.

"Gggggggrrrl," Saudade seems to be saying.

Hannah Linus leans over the bed a bit. With a hand beside her ear. In that universal gesture used to indicate someone needs to speak louder or more clearly.

"You're going to have to speak more clearly," she says. "I can't understand you."

Saudade lifts an arm in a cast to indicate to Hannah Linus to wait a minute. Then he clears his throat. Or something similar. His throat clearing is long and painful, and sounds like he's choking on his own phlegm. Finally he blinks.

"Thanks for coming," says Saudade. "If you ever need anything, you have my cell number."

Hannah Linus looks at him with a confused expression.

"That's all?" she says. Her tone seems slightly disappointed. "That's it? You're not going to threaten to kill me? You're not going to come to my house and stab me in the chest?"

Saudade seems to be considering the question. Although it seems difficult to believe, merely thinking hurts the injuries on his head. With the only finger he has out of the cast, he pushes the button that sends painkillers into his vein. He closes his eyes and searches inside himself. And to his surprise, everything he finds is good. The seed of unhappiness, wherever it came from, seems to have withered and died at some point. Probably while they were beating him up. All the asphyxiating feelings of vulnerability and imminent doom and loss of omnipotence have vanished into thin air. Along with the doubly asphyxiating and oppressive sensation of living in a universe marked by injustice and a lack of cosmic meaning. He feels fucking great. Finally he's back to his old self. The complete, fulfilled, vigorous person who Juan de la Cruz Saudade *really* is. The fact that he's alive fills him with a peaceful, and intensely mature, euphoria. You could almost say he feels affection for his fellow man. Of course, he knows that the very idea of feeling affection for others is an idea that could have only been unnaturally induced in his mind by the painkillers and medicines they're giving him. But he's not angry with Hannah Linus. In fact, Saudade doesn't really understand people who get mad at women. He's never really believed that women are real people. Sure, they talk and all that, but it never occurred to him to stop and listen to what they're saying.

"I'm fine." Saudade lifts his hand and makes some sort of thumbs-up sign with the only finger that's not in the cast. "Don't worry about me. Good luck with the gallery."

Hannah Linus stares at him without saying anything. Her face screws up into a disgusted grimace and bit by bit the disgust transforms into rage. An enraged grimace with her mouth screwed up and her forehead trembling.

"And *that's it*?" she says, raising her voice. "That's how you end *our relationship*? You're not even going to object?" Now Hannah Linus's screams echo through the room and probably through the rest of the rooms on that hall of the hospital. "That's all I *mean* to you? That's all I'm *worth*?"

Lying in his hospital bed with both arms and both legs in casts and a system of straps and harnesses holding up his multiply fractured leg, Saudade struggles to raise his neck to look at Hannah Linus. Suddenly there is a change in the room's lighting. For a minute Saudade thinks that there's been a power outage. Then he realizes that that's not it. It's just that something very large is blocking the overhead light and the lamp. Something the size of a prehistoric animal that would have to be hunted by several prehistoric hunters. The pupil of his eye with less broken blood vessels moves down until it locates the upper part of the mass that is Aníbal Manta. With his closely cropped hair and his hoop earring and his mammoth head and neck. And with his favorite X-Men T-shirt. The one with the original members.

"Aníbal?" says Saudade. In that vaguely tearful tone of someone getting choked up at seeing an old friend or family member that they thought they'd never see again.

Aníbal Manta looks at Hannah Linus. With a slightly uncomfortable expression.

"Oh, don't worry about me," says Hannah Linus. As she puts on her coat. "I was just leaving. Obviously I have nothing more to do here. It's obvious I shouldn't have come." She takes a last look at Saudade's hospital bed. "What for? This *son of a bitch* doesn't care if I'm dead or alive."

Aníbal Manta watches as Hannah Linus strides out of the hospital room. Then he looks back at Saudade. With his classic expression of intellectual effort. With a look of intellectual effort that could indicate he's planning something or that he's come with something on his mind.

"My old friend," says Saudade tearfully. He pauses to happily hawk a phlegm ball. "How're things going? How'd the whole painting thing go? I'm really glad to see you," he says, his eyes filling with tears, and he's surprised to discover that it's almost true.

Aníbal Manta doesn't say anything. He turns toward the threadbare curtain that separates Saudade's bed from the bed of the patient next to him. The patient next to him seems to be dead, or very close to it. Manta grabs one end of the threadbare curtain and pulls it all the way closed. De facto separating Saudade from the rest of the shared room. In addition to smelling like a mix of bleach and excrement, the hospital room has several buckets and bowls on the floor into which leaks from the ceiling fall. Juan de la Cruz Saudade watches carefully as Manta closes the curtain and comes back to the foot of the bed. You could say he would be furrowing his brow if he had any brow left to furrow.

"Aníbal?" repeats Saudade in a suspicious tone.

"Things went *bad*," says Manta. "The Dark Side of the Moon got shut down by the police. The money from the sale got stolen by Giraut and that bitch he brought in. And they kept the paintings, too. The van where they were supposed to be was empty. In other words, the buyer is gonna come after us. Bocanegra's disappeared. Giraut's disappeared. And I'm leaving the country tonight."

Saudade thinks about what Manta has just told him. It's strange, but none of it causes him any kind of pain or emotional stress. Nothing seems able to cloud his new mood. Bocanegra can go to hell. He doesn't even care about Giraut anymore. Let him choke on his millions. And yet, there is something that doesn't fit. He furrows what's left of his brow. Something about this situation he's in. It takes a moment for him to understand what it is. When he finally does, he opens his eyes very wide.

"Hold on," he says. "What are *you* doing here? *Why* did you come visit me?"

But before he can even finish formulating the question he knows the answer. He is struck by a clean, luminous moment of revelation. And in that moment he also understands how serious his situation is. Completely powerless in a hospital bed. He moves the only one of his eyes that he can see out of at all to look at Aníbal Manta's face. And there, in the eyes of his partner of many years, he sees it all. The endless years of humiliation and emotional stress and intense, deep pain. Pain and emotional stress that date back to elementary school and the constant mocking and hurtful nicknames. The internalized shame about his physical appearance. That dates back to school-yard games whose goal was always to torture that absurdly oversized kid. An emotional stress that survived intact the journey into adulthood. Provoking a chronic failure to adapt. Provoking sexual problems.

Provoking a chronic inability to achieve satisfactory erections and to successfully use his unsatisfactory ones. Causing his wife to start visiting the neighbors more and more regularly. Causing a life of fruitless therapy. Saudade could now see all of that, crystal clear, in Aníbal Manta's eyes. Who seems to have transformed right before his eyes. Who seems to have become *even bigger* than he usually is, if that's possible. Bigger and more formidable. More than ever like The Thing from the Fantastic Four. His arms are the arms of a superhero born of mutagenic overexposures to radiation. Of plutonium explosions. Of mad scientists' laser beams. And his face.

Aníbal Manta's face has changed, too. Saudade has never before seen the smile that is now on that face.

An enormous smile. A smile that speaks of retribution. Of sacred laws of retribution that affect every story and are stronger than the strongest character. Because they belong to the realm of Fate.

"Wait a minute!" shrieks Saudade. "Think! Shit, Aníbal! *Think!*"

Aníbal Manta takes an iron bar out of the leg of his pants. His expression conveys something more than fierce joy in the face of imminent retribution. Something that terrifies Saudade even more. Some sort of inner peace. Saudade realizes that Aníbal Manta has become one with the universe. And his terrified scream is heard throughout the entire floor of the public hospital.

CHAPTER 63

Fire Ball

Iris Gonzalvo's brick red Alfa Romeo moves at a speed close to the maximum allowed on a four-lane highway, heading away from Barcelona. Northward. Toward the rocky coasts of the Ampurdan. Followed closely by the convertible two-seater Jaguar that's been following them since they left the city. Probably since they left the children's psychiatric clinic. Now no one speaks inside the Alfa Romeo. Neither Lucas Giraut nor Iris Gonzalvo says anything. They don't look at each other, or do anything besides frown at the image of the Jaguar reflected in the car's mirrors. And in the middle of the image, there is a face shaken with rage. Kneeling on the backseat, Valentina Parini is carrying out a series of indecipherable, mystical-looking hand signals directed at the Jaguar's driver.

"This shouldn't be happening," says Iris Gonzalvo. Almost to herself. With a very subtle inflection in her despondent tone that could indicate something like sarcasm. She pulls on the hem of her tight white Kenzo dress until it covers her knees and seems to become even more wrapped up in her own thoughts. "We had it all planned. What are we supposed to do now? Do we have to kill him? I don't suppose you have a gun."

Lucas Giraut's expression as he drives north on the four-lane highway is his same vaguely namby-pamby expression reinforced by his hairless face and thin blond eyebrows. A lock of pale chestnut-colored hair that has detached from the overall wave in his hair and now falls obliquely over his forehead is the only discordant element in his appearance. The only thing that could indicate that Giraut is living through one of those dramatically conclusive situations that mark the end of a story. One of those situations that generally involve a chase that leads to a conclusive confrontation.

Outside the car, on the four-lane highway from which the rocky cliffs of the Ampurdan can now be made out on the horizon, it is that hour of the day when the sky isn't yet dark but the streetlamps have already begun to glow with a tenuous, blinking light. That hour of the day that doesn't exactly produce a transitory or provisional sensation, but rather the feeling that you're entering a new ontological state. A state bathed in the misty, melancholy light found at the end of stories. At the romantic apotheoses or the meetings with alien races. In the backseat, Valentina Parini has taken off her sweater and is wrapping it around her head like a turban. Or like one of those towels many women wrap around their wet hair when they come out of the shower.

Giraut observes the shaken, enraged face of Mr. Bocanegra, Showbiz Impresario and Lorenzo Giraut's Childhood Best Friend, with its wrinkled grimace shiny with sweat. In the middle of the rear-view mirror. Under the light that's almost dusk, but not dusky enough for the edges of things to start softening, it definitely looks like what Bocanegra has in his hand is a gun. A gun that he keeps shaking over his head. He is now furiously pounding the butt of the gun against the Jaguar's dashboard. With those inane gestures of pure rage. It's possible that the tiny spot Giraut sees in the mirror at the height of Bocanegra's mouth is foam. Just maybe.

"There's a really big black spot in the sky above us." Valentina has both hands resting on the back of the backseat and is looking out the back window of the Alfa Romeo. Looking at the sky above the car. The highway at dusk appears to be empty except for the Alfa Romeo and the Jaguar following it. "I think it's moving. That could mean several things. It could be a radiation area. They can *hear* better in those areas. Although they could also hear worse. It's hard to tell." She lifts up the edge of the sweater knotted around her head like a turban so she can see better and glues her face to the window. "Although it could also be *them*. Now they show themselves. Hundreds of them. Thousands. Flying together. So many thousands of them that from a distance they look like a black cloud."

Lucas Giraut and Iris Gonzalvo study the sky in search of black clouds. To the west, on the car's left, the sky at dusk begins to turn a dirty red color.

"We can't destroy them," continues Valentina, with her voice slightly distorted by the fact that her face is glued to the pane. "But we can't live with them, either. They don't want us to. They want us to be like them. But we're different, of course. Because we're immune to their control and all that." She turns for a moment to look at the two other people in the car. Not exactly as if she were seeking their approval. More like making sure no one was raising any objections. "The best thing to do is to find a shelter. That's what you usually do in situations like this. It could be a desert island. Or up on a very high mountaintop. Some place they can't get to. Where they can't hear us. We can wait until they leave or the germs in the air kill them. Anyway . . ." She pauses. The strips of white tape and the eye patch now both half hang off her face, revealing an eye that doesn't look in any direction even close to where the other eye is looking. "In either case, now we have to start the world over."

"Valentina!" shouts Iris Gonzalvo, looking over Valentina's head.

She extends her arm over the back of her seat and pushes Valentina's head down, forcing her to lie down on the backseat just as Bocanegra sticks an arm out of his car and shoots at the Alfa Romeo twice. The shots sound muffled from inside the car.

Giraut looks through the rearview mirror. Bocanegra is driving with one hand while the other aims at the back of the Alfa Romeo. The rage in his face seems to have transformed into cruelty. There is another shot and this time they can hear how the bullet buries itself into the bodywork of Iris's car.

"Son of a bitch!" Iris grapples with the back of her seat as she turns. "Now I *am* gonna kill him!" She makes her way through the front seats into the back, where Valentina is adjusting her sweater turban. Iris rests the palm of her hand on the back window and starts gesticulating to the Jaguar. "I'll teach you to shoot my car, you fucking son of a bitch!"

The atmosphere of the four-lane highway at dusk is quickly becoming the atmosphere typical of the conclusion of a story. With chase scenes and shoot-outs and expectations of imminent confrontations. With streetlamps that give off that tenuous blinking light under a sky that's getter redder every minute. With the asphalt of the highway taking on a rusty tinge. With barely any cars passing sporadically on the lanes of the four-lane highway. With Valentina Parini making strange, mystical-looking hand gestures in the backseat. Like those esoteric hand gestures you use to try to protect yourself from a mystical threat. Lucas Giraut looks alternately at the rust-colored highway in front of him and at the rearview mirror and steps on the gas as hard as he can, in an attempt to elude Bocanegra's Jaguar.

Iris continues gesturing furiously toward the Jaguar. Something appears on the horizon, to one side of the highway. A structure that is still too far away for the car's occupants to see it well under the dusky light.

"I think that now you have to hit your car against his," shouts Iris. "I mean *my* car. Let's see if you can knock him off the highway." She frowns and seems to be thinking. "But try not to total *my* car."

At that moment Bocanegra sticks his arm with the gun out of the car again. Iris and Valentina throw themselves onto the backseat.

A shot is heard, and a tire bursting. The Alfa Romeo skids to one side and it takes Giraut a second to regain control.

"There," says Valentina. Pointing to a spot outside of the car.

Lucas and Iris look toward where Valentina is pointing. It is the structure on one side of the highway, which now starts to be clearly visible under the dusky light. It seems to be an abandoned service area. Dark and apparently deserted. The reddish, rusted quality the sky has now is just perfect for the end of a story. Lucas Giraut drives the Alfa Romeo onto the exit ramp that leads to the structure. Followed closely by Bocanegra's Jaguar. Finally he charges at the barrier sealing off the abandoned service area and knocks it down. Shortly followed by the Jaguar.

Giraut goes a few yards into the service area's parking lot and steps on the brakes. Before Iris can stop her, Valentina opens the back door and runs out of the Alfa Romeo. The sweater tied around her head falls to the ground behind her. The Jaguar charges into the back of the Alfa Romeo. Provoking another furious scream from Iris.

A few seconds later the scene has decisively reconfigured. Giraut and Iris are now out of the Alfa Romeo with their hands in the air, Bocanegra's gun pointed at them. Several locks of Iris's hair have come loose from her meticulously gelled hairstyle and hang dramatically over the cantankerous expression on her face. Giraut holds up the bottle green Puma sports bag with the money from the sale of the St. Kieran Panels in one of his raised hands. Seen from up close, Bocanegra's face isn't so much a sweaty, wrinkled mask of rage as a more clearly wrinkled and sweaty version of Bocanegra's face. With a horrible cruel smile beneath his sweaty mustache. The suitological analysis that Giraut quickly does of Bocanegra's bone-colored suit indicates: comfort in situations of power; explicit sadism; awareness of the fact that the world will never evolve in a positive direction. Unless, of course, the person wearing the suit wants it to evolve in that direction.

"What a lovely family portrait," says Bocanegra with a growl that has something of the cruelly amused purr of a cat playing with its cornered prey. "And I'm a big fan of families. Don't worry about the girl." He makes a lateral gesture with the gun toward the direction Valentina Parini has headed off running. "I'm not going to do anything to her. Why bother? She's completely batshit anyway. You can tell that just by looking at her."

Valentina Parini has stopped running and is now watching the scene from a safe distance. She pulls her shirt up and covers her head with it, without taking it completely off. Revealing her alarmingly skinny belly and prepubescent breasts. Under the dusky light you can see she has a lot of mystical symbols drawn with a ballpoint pen onto the skin of her belly and chest.

The abandoned service area has a two-story building that at some point was a restaurant. There are also some shacks with sealed-off bathrooms and a playground and some picnic tables. The scene seems perfectly convenient as the setting for the final scene of a story. The colors are appropriate. The lighting works. The very fact that the place is abandoned seems to have been specifically devised for one of those confrontations that take place at the end of stories. And yet, something's not quite right. Something's missing, something that would make the story's ending truly conclusive. And in some way that's hard to put your finger on, the four protagonists' faces reflect that. That lack of conclusion.

Bocanegra growls with sadistic pleasure and addresses the two figures with their hands up under the categorically reddish sky.

"You," he says, slightly moving the barrel of his gun to point at Lucas Giraut. "Of all the backstabbing pieces of shit in the world, you are the worst. The King of the Backstabbing Pieces of Shit. You *knew* I don't have kids. Although I highly doubt that ever mattered to you. Seeing the circumstances. After all those conversations about what I felt for your father and how I felt for you, like the son I never had, and all the other things I told you about how hard it is to be me and have everything I have. Seeing my *pain*. My pain here, inside." He beats on his chest a couple of times with the gun. "The things I felt about what *you* represented for *me*. The things we never did and all that." The grimace of happy rage is gone from Bocanegra's expression. His face looks like the face of a man imprisoned by rage and cruelty. The face of those men whose rage and cruelty is about to make the world around them implode violently. "Sundays in the park. The *goddamn* Sundays in the park. All those things that I can't do with my greedy, repulsive nieces and nephews. Seeing how your face lights up when I give you a puppy. Taking you to soccer games with me. To the racetrack. To all those things kids like. Sitting with you on the beach and putting a hand on your shoulder and talking to you the way fathers talk to their sons. About serious things. In that serious tone, you know. Saying things like: 'Son, it's time you knew about such and such.' Teaching you what I know and watching you grow up. I know a lot of things. I'm a man who takes his work very seriously. Fuck, you could almost say I invented my line of work. And I have no one to teach it to. No one to talk to in that serious tone on the beach while we watch the fucking sun set. And all those things that make fathers proud. Seeing you be successful in life with that happy face parents have. You know that happy face? That *tired but happy* face."

The color of the sky could be called dramatic. The rocky hills of the Ampurdan that rise on the horizon aren't particularly majestic but they could be confused with majestic hills under a certain light. Iris Gonzalvo rolls her eyes. Without lowering her hands.

"*Bo-ring*," she says. "Can you just kill us already, please?"

Bocanegra raises the hand holding the gun to his forehead. His expression of rage and cruelty has started to decompose his features the way certain very extreme feelings can *decompose* features. They're still the exact same features but they've become completely unfamiliar. His forehead wrinkles like plastic right before it burns. His skin tenses over his tendons and his lips fold over his teeth in an infinitely cruel smile.

"How come no one *understands* the pain of a childless man?" he says. None of his features has moved and yet their arrangement has become fundamentally *different*. His mouth no longer looks exactly like a human mouth, or at least it doesn't give off the same feeling. "It's not like having knives stuck into your chest. I know that's what people say, but that's not it. It's not like getting stabbed in the back or anything like that. It's like burning here inside." He touches his belly and chest with the gun. "It's like a fire that grows and grows with each day and every year and in the end turns into a *ball of fire*. Into a fire ball that makes me want to break things and start *shooting people*." Now Giraut can literally hear Bocanegra's teeth gnashing. With a sound like two pieces of metal scraping together inside a mechanism. Like that little noise that makes drivers furrow their brows and listen carefully to the little noise coming from somewhere in their car. "And now I want to shoot someone, goddamn it." He stares at Giraut. Moving slowly toward him. With something in the gleam in his eyes and the trembling in his face that evokes the moment right before a violent implosion of the world around him. "You'd really rather go off with that bitch instead of staying with me? After all the things I promised you? After I promised you we'd have fun together and do thousands of things and be business partners just like your father was my partner and maybe someday you'd be the heir to everything I have? But you never have enough, right?" He raises the barrel of his weapon very slowly toward Giraut. "That's why I can't hold back this yearning I have, to shoot. Because you never have enough. No one ever has enough and that makes me *sad* and it pisses me off."

Iris Gonzalvo has stopped paying attention to Bocanegra and is looking at something that approaches along the highway beyond the abandoned restaurant and playground.

"You'd better hurry up and shoot us already," she says. And she brushes aside the locks of hair that fall over her pale forehead. "Because it looks like this place is getting popular."

The three main characters in the scene plus Valentina, who is off to one side, look at where Iris is pointing. At the three rental cars with tinted windows approaching along the highway that have now taken the exit that leads to the abandoned service area. None of the four seem surprised by the appearance of the three cars. As if somehow they were all waiting for them, in some part of their minds. As if somehow they had all been aware the whole time that some dramatic element was missing to make the scene satisfactorily conclusive as a final narrative piece. As if they had been postponing the dénouement and buying time with their speeches until this new dramatic element arrived on the scene. Which is arriving right now. Driving in single file to the parking lot of the abandoned service area. The first rental car in the line of three rental cars passes over the remains of the broken fence and crashes into the back of the Jaguar. Moving the Jaguar several yards and causing a small rain of glass to fall onto the ground.

Iris Gonzalvo crosses her arms. She snorts.

"*Since when* do you park cars by crashing into the car in front of them?" she says. "Because I swear, no one told me about the new rules."

Several individuals of above-average size and Slavic features come out of the cars. Some of them carry automatic weapons and one has a Soviet-made assault rifle. Finally the doors of the third car in the line of rental cars open and a bullet-shaped head leads the way for Leon's heavy figure. The last person to get out of the last car takes a moment getting out. The first thing that appears is one leg sheathed in black trousers with burgundy pinstripes, and then another. Finally the rest of the exquisitely dressed body appears, followed by a head with a patch covering one eye and a metal plate where there once was a right temple. Koldo Cruz stands up beside his car and pulls the lapels of his suit coat in an unconscious gesture of royal vanity. The suitological analysis that Giraut carries out on Koldo Cruz in their first official meeting yields the following results: an elegance too exquisite to be of this world and that melancholy that accompanies some emperors in history that have arrived at the peak of their imperial power and are now experiencing firsthand the loneliness of having it all.

"You." Bocanegra stares at Koldo Cruz. With his eyes open very wide. With that face reserved for the appearances of people who are supposedly dead in movies where supposedly dead people appear at the end. With that expression members of pre-civilized tribes had on their faces as they watched the arrival of explorers from technologically advanced civilizations. *"You. Here."*

The metallic sound of half a dozen automatic weapons and one assault rifle cocking in unison is heard. Bocanegra throws his gun to the ground and lifts his hands. Without blinking. Without taking his eyes off of Cruz.

CHAPTER 64

Kingston, Jamaica

This is a story about people that started the world. About people who have no father and no mother. This is not meant to be understood metaphorically. This is literally the story of the people who started the world.

Pavel leaves the arrival terminal at Norman Manley International

Airport in Kingston, Jamaica. He stands on the other side of the automatic doors for a moment. Just standing. Looking around. With his military knapsack over his shoulder and his dreadlocks rocking softly beneath the sea breeze. The sky is a *bigger* sky than any he's ever seen. The ocean he can see behind the roofs and the highways is much bigger than the sea in Barcelona. And the airport. Pavel has never seen such a big airport. Spreading in every direction as far as the eye can see. Bigger than a lot of towns he's been in. Nothing like his fantasies of little aerodromes with palm trees and people dressed in white with sweat stains under their arms fanning themselves with wicker fans. There are quite a few men in suits and most of the people's clothes fall into the category of what Pavel considers normal, non-Jamaican attire.

Pavel clears his throat and spits on the ground. The last traces of European fluid in his lungs. The spit is scattered at his feet. Pavel observes it with detached curiosity. It's a strange spit. Strangely dark. Like some sort of dark thick fluid that's not like anything he can remember ever coming out of his lungs before. He shrugs and decides that it's as good a moment as any to light a cigarette.

In the line for taxis to the center of the city, Pavel is at least seven inches taller and much whiter than the rest of the people waiting in line. The people that look at him lift their heads and scrutinize him for just a second before going back about their business. The sun is bigger and hotter than any sun Pavel has ever felt before. For some reason, it seems to be summer instead of winter. When he gets to the front of the line, Pavel gets into a taxi driven by someone with a scar on the back of his neck and tries to explain that he wants to go to the city center. He takes a map out of his pocket and points at a spot. The taxi driver nods and takes off. Jamaica's Norman Manley International Airport is on a small peninsula surrounded by an endless stretch of dark blue ocean just south of Kingston. The taxi goes along a dilapidated highway surrounded by slums for five minutes and stops in front of a piece of open ground where the sun seems to have completely burned up all the vegetation. Pavel waits. The taxi driver turns halfway around and points a nine-millimeter pistol at him. A strange model, much older than any Pavel has seen before.

Thirty minutes later, Pavel parks the taxi on a street in the center of Kingston and throws the ignition key on top of the unconscious body of the taxi driver in the backseat. He sticks the pistol into the waist of his pants and leaves the car with a cheerful slam of the door. The streets of downtown Kingston are also much bigger and more crowded than Pavel had imagined. Wide avenues surrounded by mostly dilapidated buildings. Pavel throws his knapsack over his shoulder and starts walking down the street.

After walking several blocks, Pavel sits on the sidewalk to count his dollars and have a look at the people. A pretty large group of kids have been following him for a while and now seem to be both asking him for coins and making fun of his appearance at the same time. One of the kids is doing what looks like an imitation of Pavel, walking on tiptoes and chewing the inside of his cheeks and rolling his eyes. Pavel looks his map over several times, trying to find the beach. After a little while he decides to throw a rock at the group of kids and they start shouting at him threateningly and shooting at him with finger pistols.

Getting to the beach takes him a while. When he gets tired of wandering he stops another taxi and this time he decides to put his pistol at the taxi driver's temple while he shows him the map. The driver takes him to a pretty wide, nice beach, with various sizes of palm trees and little shacks with very loud music where they serve colored drinks in plastic cups.

Pavel throws his knapsack onto the sand and sits down, hugging his knees. A few feet from the waves. The sun is high in spite of it being late afternoon, according to Pavel's calculations. Or maybe late morning. He's not really sure. The beach is mostly filled with groups of young people with bottles and boom boxes. Some of them are dancing in a strange style that Pavel doesn't recognize, and passing joints around. No one seems to be wearing anything more than a swimsuit and a hat.

After a few minutes he stretches and decides to take a dip. He takes off all his clothes except for his underwear and starts running toward the tall, luxuriously foamy waves.

The water is hot and Pavel plunges in, enjoying the feeling of having his entire body wrapped in the warm Caribbean waters. The feeling isn't exactly like being in a womb, but has certain elements of that. Then he comes back up to the surface. He floats for a minute on his back on the swaying surface and shakes his dreadlocks back the way you shake your hair back when you are enjoying a pleasant swimming experience. The water of the Caribbean also seems saltier than the seawater he's known before. Now he observes the beach from the top of a wave. A group of black kids runs off along the beach with his clothes and his knapsack. Pavel thinks about it. He doesn't feel especially upset.

He plunges into the water again. Being underwater fills him with a quite peculiar feeling of power. The power of powerful creatures that live under the sea. He decides that he's a shark. Gluing his hands to his sides and moving the way he imagines a shark would. It's definitely the most fun thing he's done in a long time.

"I'm a shark," he tries to say underwater.

But the only thing you can hear is an unintelligible gurgle.

CHAPTER 65

Fire Ball (2)

In the opinion of Mr. Bocanegra, Barcelonian Showbiz Impresario and the Main Non-Paternal Figure in this story, the Universe is an abandoned service station by the side of the highway. One of those run-down service stations at the mercy of the elements. Abandoned by the highway administration and the chains of roadside franchises.

With broken windows and cracked walls covered with water damage. With those faded signs that are missing letters, the kind photographers usually take pictures of to represent the relentless advance of time. Of course, none of these ideas *as such* has ever passed through Mr. Bocanegra's head. It's not that Bocanegra has ever consciously made those associations and decided that he could establish a satisfactory analogy between the Universe and a service station. It's that for him, deep down in his brain, the Universe *is* a service station.

The dramatic sunset reflects on the surrounding hills and the buildings in the service station just like certain Caribbean skies reflect on the crystalline waters of paradisiacal beaches. Strictly speaking, this *isn't* a moment in the story. The characters in the final scene are stock-still, the way characters in some action movies freeze in sculptural groups in the middle of an action scene. With the camera spinning dizzily around them along an impossible axis. Valentina Parini is paralyzed in the air, in the middle of an ecstatic leap. With her arms and legs splayed out.

And the universe is an abandoned hotel. A haunted house. One of those enormous buildings with the windows broken and boarded up. With the inside filled with garbage and rats and wild animals. With long halls filled with strange sounds with tattered curtains at the end, swaying to a ghostly gust of wind.

And Mr. Bocanegra, Showbiz Impresario, owner of the recently shut-down nightclub The Dark Side of the Moon, is in the middle of the group of people standing in the parking lot of the abandoned service station. With his arms still held high. With his mouth and eyes open very wide and the palms of his hands facing the general direction of a group of Slavic men that have just gotten out of the recently arrived cars.

"A week ago we put one of those things on your car." Koldo Cruz shrugs his shoulders and looks around. "Every time you get in your car to go buy a quart of milk, there's a satellite telling us where stupid Bocanegra is buying a quart of fucking milk."

In Bocanegra's opinion, *evil* nieces and nephews are unquestionably the main population of the Universe. Scampering through dark, dilapidated hallways the way evil kids scamper in movies. Lifting their knees high. Softly singing lullabies to themselves in evil tones. With short pants and lace dresses and other stereotypically childish clothes. With evil smiles and bloodstained chins. With messy hair and open mortal wounds in their skulls. But there's something more. Something that you can't see at first glance. Something that was once there, smiling in a much less evil way when the universe wasn't yet a haunted house. In the happy days when the cafeteria at the service station was filled with that thick cafeteria light, and between its walls the sound of programmed radio music was heard, and there were people lining up with trays filled with food in front of the cash registers. Something soft and warm and almost forgotten.

Valentina Parini brings both hands to her chest and makes a sound like "ughhh" and sticks out her tongue the way kids do when they are pretending they've been shot in the chest or are having a heart attack. The newcomers look curiously at the small, alarmingly skinny figure that seems to be looking at them with her T-shirt over her face and her torso covered with ballpoint pen drawings. Several feet from where the scene is taking place. Valentina tosses her head way back and extends her arms in a gesture of slow agony. And she falls onto her bare knees on the concrete ground and continues acting out her death in slow motion, with her tongue out and her eyes rolled back in her head.

What could have been forgotten between the cracked walls of the abandoned hotel? Like those things that are inexplicably forgotten in dreams: homework to do or tests to take or babies wrapped in baby blankets. Mr. Bocanegra's life isn't flashing before his eyes in a si-multaneous confluence of temporal events. Somehow, what's going through his head at that moment is the simultaneous confluence of spatial coordinates. The universe reduced to a place. Life reduced to a stage. And without his being conscious of any of this *as such*, nor as a mental image he can recognize, Mr. Bocanegra is *in that place*. In that haunted house. Which in turn is inside his mind. And magically transported to the foot of a concrete staircase covered with the crumbling remains of a carpet, Bocanegra touches the termite-eaten railing with his brow furrowed and looks at the fingertips of one hand. With an uncertain look of recognition. And he goes up the stairs covered in the remains of carpet and walks through a dark hallway, dodging the evil nieces and nephews that scamper by and finally arrives at a full-length standing mirror covered by a sheet that is in the place where the window with tattered curtains should be. And he moves the sheet aside.

"Blah, blah, blah," says Valentina, in some part of the hallway. With her face covered by her shirt. Bringing her fingertips together rhythmically the way kids do when they want to show that someone is talking a lot. "Blah, blah, *blah, blah.*"

And in some part of the house all those lost things should be found. The era of the lines with trays in the cafeteria and the cheap souvenir shops. The story of the three friends and the woman with the furious face and the promises made in crowded pubs on Tottenham Court Road. And all the rest too, of course. The fake business fronts and the meetings on board ships. The meetings on ship deck, with both parties dressed in wool coats and hats. The call from a British police station after Lorenzo Giraut was arrested in Camber Sands. The money accruing in Swiss bank accounts and the active capital of companies located on fiscally convenient archipelagos. And the hasty calls and the secret meetings. And the explosion in Koldo Cruz's house. The first house called Ummagumma. And "The Fletcher Memorial Home." The song that plays in the abandoned house is "The Fletcher Memorial Home" by Pink Floyd. With the flaming pieces of Koldo Cruz's house raining over the streets of Pedralbes. And everything deteriorating a bit more with each passing year. Everything cracking and sinking and getting covered with water stains. As the Swiss bank accounts were filling up with money.

"Blah, blah, blah," Valentina keeps saying. Faking her own death in slow motion. To one side of the group of Slavic men led by Koldo

Cruz and Leon that are aiming at the group composed of Bocanegra, Lucas and Iris.

This is what you can see if you look closely at Valentina Parini, with her shirt over her head and her no-longer-childish belly covered with mystical drawings: the beginning of an absence. The *shadow* of an absence. Something still too subtle to define itself but which clearly indicates the beginning of a process. The first sign that Valentina is already starting to pass *to the other side* of the story.

Bocanegra approaches Koldo Cruz. With his eyes still glued to him. In his face rage and cruelty are combined with a new element: some sort of fundamental ambiguity. His face is still trembling. The wrinkles on his forehead continue to redefine and reorganize themselves in a way that some could only define as *tectonic.* Tracing intricate fractal designs made of folded flesh. His mouth is still a horrible grimace. His hand lifts, trembling, to signal to Cruz. One of the Slavic thugs kneels to pick up the gun he has dropped.

"Very well," he says. "Lovely. A *triumphant* entrance. With your little Russian friends and everything." He makes a disgusted face. "With your impeccable suit and your eye patch and *all the rest.*" He grabs the bottom of his absurdly feminine fur coat and takes a couple of stiff, ridiculous little steps. Moving his butt a lot. Like an exaggerated parody of someone strutting with stiff, ridiculous little steps. Then he stops. He looks at Cruz, his eyes swollen with rage. "And I guess I'm supposed to get down *on my knees* and ask for forgiveness for all these years. And tremble, and beg you *not to kill me.* And I guess everyone else"—and he makes a wide gesture with his arm—"thinks it's all *very well* and fitting. Well *I.*" He beats his chest with one hand. Releasing a cascade of little drops of saliva whose trajectory is discernible depending on your relative position to the setting sun. "I'm *pleased as punch.* And why should I repent and beg if I'm happy and pleased."

No one says anything. The Slavic thugs of a size clearly larger than average just look forward in a way that doesn't allow you to see if they've understood Bocanegra's words or not. Valentina rolls her eyes and grabs her throat, a few feet to one side. Lucas Giraut and Iris Gonzalvo still have their arms in the air but they've dropped a bit, like people who've had their arms up but then realized no one was really paying attention to them. In a certain way, everything seems to be in place. The elements of the scene have reconfigured in such a way that you could practically say that they are now the essential elements to satisfactorily conclude the story. There are only a few details missing. Minor details. Those minor details that set apart a perfectly realized conclusion.

Koldo Cruz sticks his hands in the pockets of the pants of his suitologically impeccable pinstripe suit. Now that Lucas has him there in front of him, he notices that Cruz has an indefinable *gleam* to him. It doesn't just have to do with his impeccable suit, nor with his certain strange, mutilated beauty, nor with the majestic aura he definitely projects. It's a gleam similar to the flash Giraut caught sight of in the courtroom during his hearing: something that makes you turn your head and stare in his direction. Some sort of powerful flash that comes off the plate on his head. Like the beam from a lighthouse.

"You're Giraut's son." Koldo Cruz looks at Lucas Giraut out of the corner of his only eye. As he walks among his Slavic thugs of above-average size. With his hands comfortably in his pockets. His tone isn't questioning. Nor is it exactly curious. His words are slow, and seem measured. "I understand why you're here. I understand why you kept the money and ran. Although you got the wrong person." He shrugs his shoulders. "He wasn't the one who did it. He didn't sell out your father. Bocanegra wanted *to keep* your father. All to himself. That's why he put a bomb in my house." He pauses. "It was her, of course. In case you're interested. It was your mother. Your mother and the lawyer."

According to one of those ancient oral legends, childless men have no reflection in the mirror. The legend says that it's because they've already started to disappear, or because in a certain sense they're already dead. Like those people that in a certain sense have already started to disappear from a story. In a similar but inverse way, people who have no father and no mother observe the world as if they were on the other side of a mirror that *no one* is in front of. People without a father and without a mother, as the most basic logic dictates, are the exact opposite of childless men.

"We'd been expecting something like that from her for a while before it happened." The part of Koldo Cruz's face that isn't covered by the patch or the metal plate adopts a pensive expression. "She had started to do strange things. Change her face and things like that." He shrugs. His aura seems to flicker the way beautiful things or things once lost and now found flicker. "She was the one who organized the ambush and called the police. She was the one who pretended to be the buyer and sent your father to that fleabag hotel in Camber Sands. After paying off the lawyer, of course." He brings a fist to his mouth and clears his throat. "I suppose she offered him part of the business once your father was in jail."

Cruz stops pacing through the Slavic thugs with their weapons at the ready. He stops. With his hands in his pockets. He looks at Lucas Giraut.

"I guess this is sad news," he says. "Since she's your mother and all." He points with his partly metallic head at the bottle green Puma sports bag that Giraut is still holding up in his flagging raised hand. "As far as I'm concerned you can keep the money. The way I see it, that money belongs to your father. It's the money he would have gotten that night in Camber Sands."

Giraut looks at Iris. Iris looks at Giraut. They both look toward where Valentina was a moment before. The sun has already set on the horizon of rocky hills and Valentina Parini is now only a blurry silhouette in the distance. Scampering toward the hills. A bit like an evil niece. With her shirt over her head and lifting her knees high and leaping cheerfully in what looks like an evil parody of a happy child's leaps.

Bocanegra stares at her for a moment before she disappears on the horizon. Then he wipes his brow with a meticulously folded handkerchief and points with the trembling handkerchief at the thugs that are aiming their guns at him. With a defiant expression.

"I'm *extremely* proud of everything I've done," he says to them. Showing his big white teeth. In a final cruel grimace. "*That's* the key to my success in this world."

No one does or says anything that could be interpreted as an immediate response to Bocanegra's words. From where he is, on the edge of the group of people in the parking lot, Lucas Giraut has the impression that Iris is rolling her eyes or even muttering some malicious comment under her breath.

A long time ago, a young man closed all the curtains in his room for the first time. He closed all the shutters and enjoyed the *peace* he got from the lack of natural light. A long time ago, a woman took the bandages off of her face for the first time and discovered that her rage lines had disappeared.

Giraut and Iris are heading away from the service area's parking lot. Without looking back. Not walking particularly quickly or particularly slowly. The sky is no longer red. The sky has grown dark and night is falling fast around the service area. Like someone were turning off the lights on a stage. A dramatically conclusive fade to black, if you will. Giraut and Iris walk hand in hand toward the lights of the highway.

A long time ago, a boy threw a stone into the water of a bay in the Ampurdan. Then he covered his eyes so he wouldn't catch sight of the emerging sea monster.